FENTON'S WINTER

KEN McCLURE is an award-winning medical scientist as well as a global selling author. He was born and brought up in Edinburgh, Scotland, where he studied medical sciences and cultivated a career that has seen him become a prize-winning researcher in his field. Using this strong background to base his thrillers in the world of science and medicine, he is currently the author of twenty-four novels and his work is available across the globe in over twenty languages. He has visited and stayed in many countries in the course of his research but now lives in the county of East Lothian, just outside Edinburgh.

Other Titles by Ken McClure

The Steven Dunbar Series

THE SECRET
LOST CAUSES
DUST TO DUST
WHITE DEATH
THE LAZARUS STRAIN
EYE OF THE RAVEN
THE GULF CONSPIRACY
WILDCARD
DECEPTION
DONOR

Other Novels

HYPOCRITES'ISLE
PAST LIVES
TANGLED WEB
RESURRECTION
PANDORA'S HELIX
TRAUMA
CHAMELEON
CRISIS
REQUIEM
PESTILENCE
THE SCORPION'S ADVANCE
THE TROJAN BOY
THE ANVIL

FENTON'S WINTER

Ken McClure

Saltoun

A sad tale's best for winter

William Shakespeare
The Winter's Tale

PROLOGUE

Edinburgh1988

The power-driven door of the sterilizer swung slowly shut. Its side shields clamped it in an air-tight embrace and a vacuum pump began sucking out the air until, four minutes later, the automatic controller stopped the pump and opened up a valve. Scalding steam from the hospital's main supply line flooded in to raise the internal temperature to one hundred and twenty-six degrees centigrade. The pre-formed vacuum ensured that the steam found its way into every nook and cranny of the load, giving up its latent heat and, in doing so, destroying all vestige of microbial life. The smallest virus hiding in the remotest corner of a crease would be sought out and exterminated by the relentless steam. There would be no hiding place, no escape, no reprieve. An orange light flicked on as the temperature reached its target and triggered an electric timer. A relay clicked on and off as it held the temperature steady on 126 degrees.

Half way through the cycle Sister Moira Kincaid returned from lunch and furrowed her brow. She walked over to the unattended sterilizer and took down a clip-board from the side of the machine, checking through the one line entries with her fore finger and frowning even more. Last entry nine fifteen, eight packs of surgical dressings, fourteen instrument packs, gloves, gowns...Cycle Normal...Emptied eleven thirty...Signed J. MacLean. There was no further entry, no indication of what the present load might be or who had commissioned it. Two sins had been committed and Moira Kincaid was annoyed. As sister in charge of the Central Sterile Supply Department at the Princess Mary Hospital it was her job to know everything about everything in her own department. She was a stickler for order and routine. Someone had upset that routine and that someone, she decided, was going to have a very uncomfortable afternoon.

Sterilizer Orderly, John MacLean, was whistling as he returned from his lunch break but the off-key rendition died on his lips as he saw the vinegar stare that welcomed him.

"Is something wrong?" he asked tentatively.

Moira Kincaid tapped the edge of the clipboard against the side of the sterilizer and paused for effect. "This autoclave is running yet there is no entry on the board."

MacLean sighed slightly with relief. "Not me," he said, "It was empty when I went for my break, besides, there was no load for it."

Moira Kincaid looked puzzled. "That's what I thought," she said quietly.

"Might be MacDonald Sister."

"MacDonald?"

MacLean looked uncomfortable. "Harry sometimes sterilises his home brewing equipment in it," he said sheepishly.

"Ask him to come and see me when he gets back," said Moira Kincaid as she turned on her heel and walked across the tiled floor to her office.

Moira Kincaid closed the door behind her and leaned back on it for a moment before letting her breath out in a long sigh. She was glad to have these few moments before MacDonald arrived. It would give her time to calm down and get things into perspective. She would give MacDonald a dressing down but it would go no further than that for, facing facts, MacLean and MacDonald were the best orderlies she had had since taking over the department. She would be loath to lose either of them. Running the Sterile Supply Department was very different to ward work for there was no chain of command, simply because none was required. The work of preparing sterile dressings and instruments did not demand qualified nursing personnel, only the application of average intelligence. As a result her staff of seven, five women and two men were all of equally unqualified status. Keeping harmony among the seven was a prime consideration; petty niggles and jealousies had to be stamped out as soon as they occurred while the vital nature of the work had to be stressed constantly. An unsterile instrument pack in theatre would almost certainly mean infection and death for an innocent patient and should such an event occur there would be only one head on the chopping block...hers. A knock came to the door. "Come."

"You wanted to see me Sister?"

Moira Kincaid turned in her chair, "Come in MacDonald. Close the door." She held the man's gaze till he broke eye contact and looked briefly at the floor. "Now understand this," she began, "I personally have no objection to your sterilizing your brewery in the autoclaves but one thing I do insist on, as you should well know by now, is that every sterilizer run should be properly logged and signed for by the operator."

"I'm sorry...I don't understand," said the man.

Moira Kincaid was irritated. "Number three autoclave, your home brewing utensils man. You didn't log the run."

"But I'm not using the autoclave," protested the man

"Then who..." Moira Kincaid's voice trailed off and she got to her feet to follow MacDonald out in to the main sterilizing area. They joined MacLean in standing in front of number three sterilizer.

"How long to go?"

"Two or three minutes."They waited in silence while the machine's safety systems sent reports to its silicon brain about conditions inside the chamber. They saw the pressure recorder fall to one atmosphere and traced the painfully slow descent of the temperature gauge until a buzzer began to sound and the green OPEN-DOOR light flashed on.

"Right then, let's have a look, open it up.

MacLean pressed the door release and the steel shrouds slowly relaxed their grip on the seal. With a slight sigh the air-tight joint broke and the heavy door swung open allowing a residual cloud of steam to billow out.

"Well John, what is it?"

MacLean stayed silent. His eyes opened wider and wider until they stopped seeing and he collapsed on to the tiled floor in front of the sterilizer. There was a sickening crack as he hit his head on the corner of the door shield and blood welled up from a gash on his forehead to spill on to the tiles. Together, Moira Kincaid and John MacLean went to his aid but, as the steam cleared, all concern for their colleague evaporated for there, in the chamber of the sterilizer, sat the pressure-cooked body of a man.

MacDonald stumbled to the nearest sink and voided his lunch; Moira Kincaid's nails dug into her cheeks in a sub-conscious attempt to divert attention from the horror before her eyes but there was no denying the fact that she recognised the man. Despite flesh peeling off the cheek bones and the congealing of the eyes she knew that she was looking at the body of Dr Neil Munro from the Biochemistry Department.

CHAPTER ONE

Small groups of people were discussing the tragedy in nearly every room of the Biochemistry Department but Tom Fenton did not join any of them. He cleared his work bench, washed his hands and put on his waterproof gear. The big Honda started first time and, switching on the lights, he pulled out into the early evening traffic. As he neared the City centre a double deck bus drew out sharply in front of him causing him to brake hard and correct a slight wanderlust in the rear wheel but he remained impassive. He weaved purposefully in and out of the rush hour traffic in Princes Street, not even bothering to glance up at the castle, the first time he had failed to do so in the two years he had worked in Edinburgh.

The flat felt cold and empty when he got in. "Jenny!" he called out as he pulled off his gloves.

"Jenny!" he repeated, looking into the kitchen then he remembered that she was on late duty and cursed under his breath. Without pausing to take off the rest of his leathers he poured himself a large Bell's whisky and walked over to the window. He revolved the glass in his hand for a moment while looking at the hurrying figures below then threw the whisky down his throat in one swift, sudden movement taking pleasure in the burning sensation it provoked. He returned to watching the people below as they hurried homewards, heads bowed against wind and rain but he really didn't see them, his mind was too full of what had happened at the hospital.

On impulse Fenton turned and threw the glass he had been holding into the fireplace; he had to break the awful silence. But almost immediately he felt ashamed at what he had done and began picking up the pieces cursing softly as he did so. When he had finished he took off his leathers and poured more whisky into a fresh glass before sitting down in an arm chair and hoisting his feet on to the stool that lurked round the fireplace.Half way through the bottle he fell asleep.

Just after nine thirty Fenton was aroused to a groggy state of wakefulness by the sound of keys rattling at the lock and the front door opening. A blonde girl in her mid twenties with bits of nurses' uniform showing beneath her coat came into the room and stood in the doorway for a moment before saying, "God Tom, I've rushed all the way home and now I don't know what to say."

Fenton nodded.

"It's just so awful. I keep thinking it can't be true. How could anyone...Isn't there a chance it could have been some kind of freak accident?"

"None at all. It was murder. Someone pushed Neil into the autoclave and pushed the right buttons," said Fenton.

"But why? What possible reason could they have had?"

"None," said Fenton, "It had to be a lunatic, a head case." He swung his feet off the stool and sat upright in the chair.

"Have you had anything to eat?" asked Jenny.

"Not hungry."

"Me neither but we'll have coffee." Jenny leaned down and kissed Fenton on the top of his head. As she straightened up she removed the whisky bottle from the side of his chair and put it back in the cabinet before going to the kitchen. She returned a few minutes later with two mugs of steaming coffee. Fenton took one in both hands and sipped it slowly till the act of drinking coffee together had re-established social normality.

"Do the police have any ideas?" asked Jenny.

"If they did they didn't tell me," said Fenton.

"I suppose they spoke to everyone in the lab?"

"At least twice."

"What happens now?"

"We just go on as if nothing..." Fenton stopped in mid sentence and put his hand up to his forehead.

Jenny reached out and took it. She said softly, "I know. Neil was your best friend."

Tom Fenton was twenty-nine years old. After graduating from Glasgow University with a degree in biochemistry he had joined the staff of the Western Infirmary in the same city as a basic grade biochemist. One year later he had met the girl who was to become his wife, Louise. In almost traditional fashion, Louise's parents had disapproved of their daughter's choice, frowning on Fenton's humble origins, but had been unable to stop the marriage which was to give Fenton the happiest year he had ever known. Louise's gentleness and charm had woven a spell which had trapped him in a love that had known no bounds, a love which was to prove his undoing when both she and the baby she was carrying were killed in a road accident.

Fenton had been inconsolable. He had fallen into an endless night of despair which had taken him to the limits of his reason and had threatened to push him beyond. Time, tears and a great deal of Scotch whisky had returned him to society but as a changed man. Gone was the happy, carefree Tom Fenton. His place had been taken by a morose, withdrawn individual, devoid of all drive and ambition.

After a year of being haunted by the ghost of Louise Fenton had taken his first major decision. He had applied for a job abroad and, four months later, he had been on his way to a hospital in Zambia.

Africa had been good for him. Within a year he had recovered his self confidence and could think of Louise without despairing; he could even speak about her on the odd occasion. He had enjoyed the life and the climate and had renewed his contract on two occasions bringing his stay to three years in all before he suddenly decided it was time to return to Scotland and pick up the threads of his old life. The prevailing economic climate and the perilous state of the National Health Service had made it difficult for him to find a job quickly and he had spent a year at Edinburgh University in a grant aided research assistant's post before applying for, and getting, his current position at the Princess Mary Hospital.

The sudden return to the demands of a busy hospital laboratory after a year of academic calm had been a bit of a shock but he had weathered the storm and established himself as a reliable and conscientious member of the lab team. The fact that the Princess Mary was a children's hospital and the lab specialised in paediatric techniques pleased him. Working for the welfare of child patients seemed to compensate in some way for the child he had lost.

After a year he had scraped together the deposit for a flat of his own in the Comely Bank area of the city and, on a bright May morning, assisted by Neil Munro and two of the technicians from the lab, he had moved in. The flat was on the top floor of a respectable tenement building that had been built around the turn of the century and featured high ceilings with cornice work that had particularly attracted him to it in the first place. It had south facing windows which, on the odd occasion that the skies were clear in Edinburgh, allowed the sun to stream in from noon onwards. The undoubted reward he reaped from having to climb four flights of stairs up to the flat was the magnificent view. As Autumn had come around he had watched the smoke from the burning leaves hang heavy in the deep yellow sunshine and had come to understand fully what Keats, who had once lived in the same area of the city, had meant by 'mists and mellow fruitfulness.' In the last year Fenton had met Jenny, a nurse at the hospital. She was very different from Louise but he had been attracted to her from the moment they met. Their relationship was easy, undemanding and good. Marriage had not been mentioned but Jenny had moved in to the flat and they were letting things take their course.

Jenny Buchan was twenty-four. She had been born in the small fishing village of Findochty on the Moray Firth, the youngest of three children to her father, George Buchan, a fisherman all his life. He had died in a storm at sea when she was fourteen leaving her mother, Ellen, to fend for the family but luckily it had not been too long before her two older brothers, Ian and Grant, had reached working age and had followed their late father into the fleet fishing out of Buckie. They now had their own boat, the Margaret Ross, and, between them, they had provided Jenny with three nephews and two nieces. Jenny herself had travelled south to Aberdeen after leaving school and had trained as a nurse at the Royal Infirmary before moving further south to Edinburgh and the Princess Mary Hospital where she had settled in happily. She had spent her first year in the Nurses' Home before moving into a rented flat with two other nurses and living in traditional, but pleasant chaos.

She had met Tom Fenton at a hospital party and had been drawn to him in the first instance because he had seemed genuinely content to just sit and talk to her. His dark, sad eyes had intrigued her and she had resolved to find out what lay behind them until, after their third date, he had told her about Louise and alarm bells had rung in her head. If Tom Fenton had decided to dedicate his life to the memory of a dead woman then she, Jenny Buchan, had not wanted to know any more. She need not have worried for, after an idyllic picnic in the Border country, Fenton had taken her home and made love to her with such gentleness and consideration that she had fallen head over heels in love with him. Despite this she had still decided to make her position clear. One night as they lay together in the darkness she had turned to him and said, "I am Jenny, not Louise. Are you quite sure you understand that?" Fenton had assured her.

The rain assisted by a bitter February wind woke them before the alarm did. "What's the time?" asked Fenton.

"Ten past seven."

"What duty do you have?"

"Start at two."

"You mean I've got to get up alone?"

"Correct."

"Good God, listen to that rain."

"Jenny snuggled down under the covers.

Fenton swung himself slowly over the edge of the bed and sat for a moment holding his head in his hands. "I feel awful."

Jenny leaned over and kissed his bare back. "The whisky," she said.

"Coffee?"

"Please,"

Fenton returned to sit on the edge of the bed while they drank their coffee.

"Are you on call this week-end?"

"Tomorrow."

Jenny put down her cup on the bedside table and put her hand on Fenton's forearm. "You will be careful won't you?"

Fenton looked puzzled. "What do you mean?"

"You said yourself it must have been a lunatic who did what he did to Neil. Just take care that's all."

Fenton was taken aback. "You know," he said, "I didn't even think of that."

The rain drove into Fenton's visor as he wound the Honda up through the streets of Edinburgh's Georgian 'New Town', streets crammed with the offices of the city's professional classes. The road surface was wet and the bike threatened to part company with the cobbles at every flirtation with the brakes. The infatuation with two-wheeled machinery that most men experience in their late teens and early twenties had proved, in Fenton's case, to be the real thing. Apart from a brief period when he had succumbed to the promise of warmth and dryness from an ageing Volkswagen beetle his love for motor cycles had remained undiminished. There was just no car remotely within his price range that could provide the feeling he got when the Honda's rev counter edged into the red sector. Tales of being caught doing forty-five in the family Ford paled into insignificance when compared with Fenton's one conviction of entering the outskirts of Edinburgh from the Forth Road Bridge at one hundred and ten miles an hour. The traffic police had shown more than a trace of admiration when issuing the ticket but the magistrate had, however, failed to share their enthusiasmand had almost choked on hearing the charge of 'exceeding the speed limit by seventy miles per hour.' His admonition that a man of Fenton's age should have 'known better' had hurt almost as much as the fine.

Fenton reached the hospital at two minutes to nine and edged the bike up the narrow lane at the side of the lab to park it in a small courtyard under a canopy of corrugated iron. The Princess Mary Hospital, being near the centre of the city, had had no room to expand over the years through building extensions and had resorted, like the university, to buying up neighbouring property as a solution to the problem. The Biochemistry Department was actually one of a row of Victorian terraced villas that the hospital had acquired some twenty years previously. The inside, of course, had been extensively altered but the external facade remained the same, its stone blackened with the years of passing traffic.

Fenton pushed open the dark blue door and took off his leathers in the outer hall in front of a row of steel lockers. Susan Daniels, one of the technicians, saw him through the inner glass door and opened it. "Dr Tyson would like to see you," she said. Fenton buttoned his lab coat as he climbed the stairs to the upper flat then knocked on the door bearing the legend, 'Consultant Biochemist.'

"Come."

Fenton entered to see Charles Tyson look up from his desk and peer at him over his glasses. "What a day," he said.

Fenton agreed.

"We are going to have the police with us for most, if not all, of the day," said Tyson. "We'll just have to try and work round them."

"Of course," said Fenton.

"I've requested a locum as a matter of priority but until such times..."

"Of course," said Fenton again.

"I'd like you to speak to Neil's technician, find out what needs attending to and deal with it if you would. I'll have Ian Ferguson cover for you in the blood lab in the meantime."

Fenton nodded and turned to leave. As he got to the door Tyson said, "Oh, there is one more thing."

"Yes?"

"Neil's funeral, it will probably be at the end of next week, when the fiscal releases the body. We can't all go; the work of the lab has to go on. I thought maybe you, Alex Ross and myself could go?"

"Fine,' said Fenton without emotion.

He walked along the first floor landing to a room that had once been a small bedroom but had, in more recent times, been the lab that Neil Munro had worked in. He sat down at the desk and started to empty out the drawers, pausing as he came to a photograph of himself holding up a newly caught fish. He remembered the occasion. He and Munro had gone fishing on Loch Lomond in November. They had left Edinburgh at six in the morning to pick up their hired boat in Balmaha at eight. The fish, a small pike, had been caught off the Endrick bank on almost the first cast of the day and Munro had captured the moment on film.

There had been no more fish on that occasion and the weather had turned bad in early afternoon ensuring that they were soaked to the skin by the time they had returned to MacFarlane's boatyard. Munro had ribbed him about the smallness of the fish but, having caught nothing himself, had come off worst in the verbal exchange. Fenton put the photograph in his top pocket and continued sifting through the contents of the desk. He was working through the last drawer when Susan Daniels came in. "I understand you will be taking over Neil's work," she said. "Can we talk?"

"Give me five minutes will you," said Fenton.

A system involving three piles of paper had evolved. One for Munro's personal belongings, one for lab documents and one for 'anything else.' The personal pile was the by far the smallest, a Sharp's scientific calculator, a University of Edinburgh diary, a well thumbed copy of 'Biochemical Values in Clinical Medicine,' by R.D. Eastham, a few postcards and a handful of assorted pens and pencils. Fenton put them all in a large manila envelope and marked it 'Neil's' in black marker pen. The 'anything else' pile was consigned mainly to the waste-paper basket, consisting of typed circulars advising of seminars and meetings and up-dates to trade catalogues. Fenton started to work his way through the lab document pile while he waited for Susan Daniels to return. Much of it was concerned with a new automated blood analyser that the department had been appraising for the past three months. Neil had been acting as liaison officer with the company, Saxon Medical and the relevant licensing authorities and from what Fenton could see in copies of the reports there had been no problems. The preliminary and intermediate reports that Munro had submitted were unstinting in their praise.

Fenton turned his attention to Munro's personal lab book and tried to pick up the thread of the entries but found it difficult for there was no indication of where the listed data had come from or what they referred to. Munro, like the other senior members of staff, had been working on a research project of his own, something they were all encouraged to do although, in a busy hospital laboratory, this usually had to be something small and relatively unambitious. Fenton stopped trying to decipher the figures and went over to look out of the window. It was still raining although the sky was beginning to lighten. He turned round as Susan Daniels came in.

"Sorry I'm late. The police wanted to talk to me again."

Fenton nodded.

"It all seems a bit pointless really. Who would want to kill Neil?" said the girl.

Fenton looked out of the window again and said, "The point is, somebody did kill him."

"I'd better brief you on what Neil was doing," said Susan Daniels.

"Do you know what his own research project was on?" asked Fenton.

"No I don't. Is it important?"

"Maybe not, I just thought you might have known."

"He didn't speak about it although he seemed to be spending more and more time on it over the past few weeks."

"Really?"

"Actually he seemed so preoccupied over the last week or so that I asked him if anything was the matter."

"And?"

"He just shook his head and said it probably wasn't important."

Fenton nodded. That would have been typical of Munro. Although he had been a friend, Neil Munro had been a loner by nature, never keen to confide in anyone unless pressed hard. He himself had not seen much of him over the past few weeks, in fact, since Jenny had moved into the flat, they had seen very little of each other socially although that would have changed when the fishing season had opened in April.

"You've been running the tests on the Saxon Blood Sampler I see," said Fenton picking up the relevant papers.

"In conjunction with Nigel. He's been showing us how to use it."

'Nigel' was Nigel Saxon, the chief sales rep from Saxon Medical who had been attached to the department for the period of the trial. Like most reps, he had a pleasant, outgoing personality which, when combined with a generous nature and the fact that he had the financial clout of being the boss' son, had made him a popular figure in the lab.

"Neil seemed to like the machine," said Fenton, looking at Munro's intermediate report.

"We all do," said Susan.

"What's so special about it?"

Susan Daniels opened one of the wall cupboards and took out a handful of what appeared to be plastic spheres. "These," she said, "These are the samplers. They are made out of a special plastic. You just touch them against the patient's skin and they charge by capillary attraction. All you need is a pinprick, no need for venipuncture."

"But the volume?"

"That's all the machine needs to do the standard values."

"I'm impressed," said Fenton. "What stage are the tests at?"

"They are complete. It just requires the final report to be written up and signed by Dr Tyson," said Susan.

"Is all the information here?" asked Fenton.

"I've still got the data from the last set of tests in my note-book. I'll bring it up after lunch."

"I'll come down; I'd like to see the machine working. Anything else I should know?"

"Neil was running some special blood tests for Dr Michaelson in the Metabolic Unit; perhaps you could contact him and have a chat."

Fenton nodded and made a note on the desk pad. "Anything else?"

"There are a couple of by-pass operations scheduled for next week Neil was supposed to organise the lab cover."

Fenton made another note. He looked at his watch and said, "Why don't you go to lunch? If you think of anything else you can let me know." He got up as Susan left the room and returned to the window to check on the weather. It had stopped raining.

Fenton pulled up his collar as he felt the icy wind touch his cheek. He decided to give the hospital canteen a miss, knowing that it would still be buzzing with talk of Neil's death and a new day's crop of rumours. Instead, he walked off in the other direction, not at all sure of where he was going. He paused as he came to the entrance to a park and entered to find himself alone beneath the trees. The wide expanse of grass that would be crowded with lunch-time picnic makers in July was, on a cold day in February, utterly deserted.

A bird wrestled a worm from the wet, windswept grass and flew off with it in his beak. That's the awful thing about death, thought Fenton; life goes on as if you had never existed, the ultimate in searing loneliness.He reached the far end of the park and let the iron gate clang shut behind him as he returned to the street and paused to look for inspiration. He saw the beckoning sign of the 'Croft Tavern' and crossed the road.

A sudden calm engulfed him as he went in through the door and made him aware of the wind burn on his cheeks. He ran his fingers ineffectually through his hair as he approached the empty bar counter to pick up a grubby menu. The barmaid tapped her teeth with a biro pen in readiness.

"Sausage and chips, and a pint of lager."

"I'm only food; you get your drink separately,' said the sullen girl with an air that suggested she had said the same thing a million times before.

Fenton looked to the other barmaid. "Pint of lager please."

"Skol or Carlsberg?"

"Carlsberg."

A plume of froth emanated from the tap. "Barrel's off."

"All right, Skol."

Fenton looked behind the bar at a poster on the wall which proudly announced, 'This establishment has been nominated in the Daily News pub of the year competition.' By the landlord, thought Fenton.

"Hello there," said a voice behind him. He turned to find Steve Kelly from the Blood Transfusion service. "Didn't know you came here for lunch," said Kelly.

"First time," said Fenton.

"Me too," said Kelly. "I'm sitting over there by the fire. Join me when you get your food."

Fenton joined Kelly in sitting on plastic leather seats in front of a plastic stone fireplace. They watched imitation flames flicker up to plastic horse brasses.

"The breweries really do these places up well," said Kelly without a trace of a smile. Fenton choked over his beer. Kelly smiled.

Fenton's fork ricocheted off a sausage causing chips to run for cover in all directions; one landed in Kelly's lap; he popped it into his mouth.

"You can have the rest if you want," said Fenton putting down his knife and fork.

"No thanks, I've just tasted it."

"What brings you here?" asked Fenton.

"I was looking around for a nice quiet wee place to bring that nurse from ward seven to one lunch time."

"You mean somewhere where the wife wouldn't be liable to find you?"

"You've got it."

"Well this place seems quiet enough."

"Aye, but it wasn't exactly food poisoning I was planning on giving her."

"Point taken."

They sipped their beer in silence for a few minutes before Kelly said, "So who's the loony Tom?"

Fenton kept looking into the flames. "I wish to God I knew," he said.

"Munro was a friend of yours wasn't he?"

Fenton nodded.

"I'm sorry."

Fenton sipped his beer.

"Who will be taking over his projects?" asked Kelly.

"Me for the moment."

"Then you'll be wanting the blood?"

Fenton was puzzled. "What blood?"

"Munro phoned me on Monday; he wanted some blood from the service."

"Better hold on that till I find out what he needed it for."

"Will do."

"Another drink?"

"No."

They got up and moved towards the door. "Would you mind returning your glasses to the bar?" drawled the lounging barmaid.

"Aye, we would," said Kelly flatly. They left.

Fenton waited while Kelly finished buttoning his coat up to the collar. He hunched his shoulders against the wind. Kelly said, "So you'll let me know about the blood?" Fenton said that he would and they parted.

Fenton was grateful that the wind was now behind him, supporting him like a cushion, as he walked slowly back to the hospital. This time he avoided the park and opted instead for the streets of Victorian terraced housing, black stone houses that looked cool in summer but dark and forbidding in winter, the bare branches of the trees fronting them waved in the wind like witches in torment. As he reached the lab he had to pause to let a silver grey Ford turn into the lane beside the lab. One of its front wheels dipped into a pot hole splashing water over his feet. He raised his eyes to the heavens then saw that the driver was Nigel Saxon and that he had realised what had happened. Saxon stopped and wound down the window looking apologetic, "I say, I'm most frightfully sorry."

Fenton smiled for it was hard to get angry with Nigel Saxon. He waited while Saxon parked his car then watched him attempt to side-step the puddles as he hurried to join him. Saxon was everyone's idea of a rugby forward running to seed, which indeed he was. He had played the game religiously for his old public school till, at the age of twenty-five or so, he had discovered that it was possible to have the post-match drink and revels without actually having to go through the pain of playing. Now at the age of thirty-two he was beginning to look distinctly blowzy, a fact of which he seemed cheerfully aware. He had managed to scramble a poor degree in mechanical engineering before joining his father's company, Saxon Medical, where his engineering skills had been completely ignored in deference to his amiable personality and confidence that had made him invaluable in sales and customer liaison. Fenton thought it ironic that Saxon would never appreciate what his greatest talent was in that direction; he made the customers feel superior.

"You've got lipstick on your cheek," said Fenton

Saxon pulled a handkerchief from his pocket, scattering as he did so, some loose change over the pavement. Fenton helped pick it up and paused to look at something that turned out not to be a coin. It appeared to be some kind of silver medallion with a tree engraved on it. "Very nice," he said and handed it back to Saxon only to be surprised at the intense way Saxon was looking at him. It was as if Saxon had asked him a question and was waiting for an answer.

Saxon dabbed absent-mindedly at his cheek.

"Other one," said Fenton.

There were three policemen in the hallway when they entered the lab. "Mr Fenton?" said one. Fenton nodded. "Inspector Jamieson would like to see you again sir if that's convenient?

"Of course. I'll be in one-oh-four."

"You know I still can't believe it," said Saxon as he and Fenton climbed the stairs to the first floor, "I keep expecting to see Neil." Fenton nodded but managed to convey to Saxon that he did not want to speak about it.

"I was wondering if we might have a talk about the Blood Analyser," said Saxon.

Fenton said that he was about to suggest the same thing himself and told Saxon that he had arranged with Susan Daniels to see the machine in action that afternoon. Saxon said that he would join them and asked when. "As soon as I finish with the police," said Fenton

As Fenton closed the door he heard the rain begin to lash against the windows once more He glanced out at the sky and saw that it was leaden. Mouthing a single expletive he turned to Munro's personal research book and started through it again. He wanted to know why Munro had asked the Blood Transfusion Service for a supply of blood and what exactly he had planned to do with it. Kelly had not said how much blood Neil had asked for and he had neglected to ask. He picked up the internal phone and asked the lab secretary to check the official requisition.

As he waited for a reply a knock came to the door. It was Inspector Jamieson and his sergeant, whose last name Fenton could not remember. He motioned them to come in and said that he would be with them in a moment.

"What day did you say?" asked the secretary's voice on the phone.

"Monday."

"That's what I thought you said. There isn't one."

"Are you quite sure?"

"I've checked three times."

"Perhaps I misunderstood," said Fenton thoughtfully. He put down the phone. So Neil had made the request privately without going through channels. Curiouser and curiouser. He became aware of the policemen looking at him and put the thought out of his mind for the moment.

Fenton had taken a dislike to Jamieson after their first meeting but had been unable to rationalise it, thinking perhaps that he might have taken a dislike to anyone who had appeared to be asking such apparently pointless questions.

"I thought we might just go through a few of these points again sir?" said Jamieson.

"If you insist," said Fenton.

"I'm afraid I do sir," said Jamieson with an ingratiating smile.

So, thought Fenton, the dislike was mutual.

Jamieson at five feet ten was small for a policeman in the Edinburgh force but what he lacked in height he made up for in breadth and his shoulders filled his tweed jacket, providing a firm base for a thick neck and a head that appeared to be larger than it actually was because of a thick mop of grey hair. He sported a small clipped moustache and this, together with the twill trousers and checked shirt, gave him the appearance of an English country gentleman in week-end wear. The voice however belied the image. It was both Scottish and aggressive.

As the interview proceeded Fenton was convinced that he was answering the same questions over and over again. It irritated him but, not knowing anything of police procedure, he concluded that this might be a routine gambit on their part.Annoy the subject till he loses his temper then look for inconsistencies in what was being said.It annoyed him even more to think that he might be being treated as some kind of laboratory animal. His answers became more and more cursory while, silently, he became more and more impatient. Of course Neil had not had any enemies. He had no earthly idea why anyone would want to kill him. Wasn't it obvious that some kind of deranged psychopath had committed the crime? Why were they wasting time asking such damn fool questions? Did the police have no imagination at all?

"Miss Daniels tells us that Dr Munro seemed very preoccupied, to use her word, over the last week or so. Do you have any idea why sir?" asked Jamieson.

Fenton said that he did not.

"Miss Daniels thinks it may have had something to do with his personal research work." There was a pause while Jamieson waited for Fenton to say something. When he did not Jamieson asked, "Would you happen to know what that was sir?" Again Fenton said that he did not. "But you were a friend of the deceased were you not?" said Jamieson, turning on his smile which Fenton could see he was going to learn to dislike a great deal. "Yes I was, but I don't know what he was working on."

"I see sir," said Jamieson, smiling again. "I understand from Dr Tyson that you will be tidying up the loose ends in Dr Munro's work?"

Fenton said that was so.

"Perhaps if you come across anything that might indicate the reason for Dr Munro's state of mind you might let us know?"

Fenton was nearing the limit of his patience. What possible relevance could Neil's 'state of mind' have had to the lunatic who murdered him? Were the police seriously considering suicide? Did they imagine that Neil had climbed into the sterilizer and closed the door with a conjuring trick? Did they believe that he had operated the controls from inside the chamber by telepathy? A child of ten could have eliminated the suicide notion within seconds but he bit his tongue and refrained from pointing that out. Instead he said that he would pass on anything he came up with.

"Then I think that's all for the moment sir," said Jamieson getting to his feet. "But we may have to come back to you."

"Of course," said Fenton flatly.

Fenton came downstairs to join Susan Daniels in the main laboratory, a large bay-windowed room that had once been a Victorian parlour. He apologised for being late. Nigel Saxon was already there and was making an adjustment to the machine in response to something that Susan had mentioned. "Well, impress me," said Fenton.

Susan picked up one of the plastic sample spheres that Fenton had seen earlier and held it over a blood sample. "In normal times we would be doing this at the patient's bedside after a simple skin prick with a stylette, but for the moment we're using samples that have been sent in the conventional way." She touched the sphere to the surface of the blood and Fenton saw it charge. "That's all there is to it," she said, removing the sphere and introducing it into the machine. She pressed a button and the analyser began its process.

"Amazing," said Fenton, "But what happens when the temperature varies and the sampler takes up more or less blood. The readings will be all wrong."

"That's where you are wrong old boy," said Saxon with a smile. "The plastic is special. It's thermo-neutral; it doesn't go soft when it warms up and it doesn't go hard when it's cold. It's always the same. Well what do you think?"

Fenton admitted that he was impressed. Saxon beamed at his reaction.

"I suppose this stuff costs a fortune," said Fenton.

Saxon smiled again. "Actually it doesn't," he said, "It costs very little more than conventional plastics."

"But the potential for it must be enormous," said Fenton.

Saxon shook his head and said, "We thought so too at first but the truth is it's just not strong enough to be useful in the big money affairs like defence and space technology. But for medical uses, of course, it doesn't have to be. We've manufactured a range of test tubes, bottles, tubing etc from it which will cost only a fraction more than the stuff in use at present. We think the advantages will outweigh the extra cost and hospitals will start changing to Saxon equipment. "

"I take it you have a patent on the plastic?"

"Of course," smiled Saxon.

"It sounds like a winner," said Fenton.

"We think so too. We are so confident that we have gifted a three month supply of our disposables to the Princess Mary."

"That was generous," conceded Saxon.

"Well you were kind enough to put our Blood Analyser through its paces for the licensing board, it seemed the least we could do."

A printer started to chatter and Susan Daniels removed a strip of paper from the tractor feed. "All done," she said.

Fenton accepted the paper and looked at the figures. "Normal blood," he said.

"A control sample," said Susan Daniels.

"How do the figures compare with the ones given by our own analyser?"

"Almost identical and the Saxon performed the analysis on one fifth of the blood volume and in half the time."

"Maybe Saxon will gift us one of their machines as well as the Tupperware." said Fenton, tongue in cheek.

Nigel Saxon smiled and said, "There has to be a limit even to our generosity."

Susan Daniels handed Fenton a sheaf of papers. "These are the results of the final tests. You'll need them for the report."

Saxon said to Fenton, "I hate to press you at a time like this but have you any idea when the final report will be ready?"

"End of next week I should think."

Fenton left the room to return upstairs but paused at the foot of the stairs when he saw a small puddle of water lying in the stair well. He looked up and saw a raindrop fall from the cupola and splash into the puddle. "All we need," he muttered, going to fetch a bucket from glassware preparation room. He placed the bucket under the drip before calling in to the chief technician's room. "The roof's leaking Alex."

"Again?" said Alex Ross with a shake of the head. "It's only two months since they repaired it." He made a note on his desk pad and said he would inform the works department.

When he got back to his own lab Fenton found Ian Ferguson, one of the two basic grade biochemists on the staff, hard at work. He looked up as Fenton entered and said, "Dr Tyson asked me to cover for you."

"He told me. Thanks. How's business?"

"Brisk," smiled Ferguson. "But I think everything's under control. There are a couple of things I think you better look at but apart from that it's been largely routine."

Fenton picked up the two request forms that Ferguson had put to one side and nodded. "I'll deal with them," he said. "You can go back to your own work now if you like. I can manage now."

Ferguson got up and tidied the bench before leaving. As he turned to go Fenton said to him, "Did Neil mention anything to you about requesting blood from the Transfusion Service?"

Ferguson turned and shook his head. "No, nothing,"

Fenton made his third attempt at phoning Dr Ian Michaelson. This time he was successful. He asked about the special blood monitoring that had been requested and Michaelson explained what he had in mind. "We could postpone the tests for a week or two if you can't cope after what's happened," said Michaelson.

"But it would be better for the patient if they were done this week?" asked Fenton

"Yes."

Fenton did some calculations in his head, equating the required tests to man hours. "We'll manage," he said. Next he contacted the cardiac unit about the proposed by-pass operations and learned that there were now three on the schedules instead of two. "This is not good news," he said. Once again he was asked if the lab could cope. "Some of us won't be going home too much," he replied, "But we'll manage."

Despite the fact that Ferguson had cleared most of the morning blood tests Fenton found himself busy for most of the afternoon. He found it therapeutic for it was impossible for him to dwell on anything other than the work in hand but at four thirty he was disturbed by the sound of raised voices coming from downstairs. He looked out from his room and asked one of the junior technicians, what was wrong.

"It's Susan," the girl replied, "She's been taken ill."

CHAPTER TWO

Fenton ran downstairs to find Susan Daniels lying on the floor outside the ladies' lavatory. She was surrounded by people giving conflicting advice. Help her up! No, don't move her. Loosen her clothing! Keep her warm!

"What happened?" he asked.

"She fainted when she came out the toilet," said a voice.

"She's bleeding!" said another voice.

"I've sent for Dr Tyson," said Alex Ross. Tyson was the only member of the staff to be medically qualified, the others being purely scientists.

Fenton knelt down beside the prostrate girl and felt her forehead; it was cold and clammy. "Who said she was bleeding?" he asked.

Liz Scott, the lab secretary knelt down beside him and said quietly, "There's blood all over the floor in the toilet."

Fenton reached his hand under the unconscious girl's thighs and felt her skirt wet and sticky. "She's haemorrhaging!" he said, "Get some towels!" The crowd dispersed. "Was Susan pregnant?" Fenton asked Alex Ross.

"If she was she never said," replied the chief technician.

"She seems to be having a miscarriage," said Fenton.

"Poor lass."

Someone handed Fenton a bundle of clean linen towels. He folded one and pushed it up between Susan Daniels' legs then followed it with another. He was relieved when Charles Tyson arrived on the scene to take over. He stood up and noticed one of the juniors wince at the sight of his blood soaked hand.

"She's lost a lot," said Tyson, "We'll have to get her over to the main hospital."

Responsibility passed from Tyson to two nurses in casualty who wheeled Susan Daniels into a side room leaving Tyson and Fenton waiting in the long corridor outside where they sat on a wooden bench in silence. Fenton leaned his head back against the wall and turned to look along the length of the corridor. An orderly was buffing the linoleum with an electric polisher in a steady side to side motion some forty metres away at the other end. A nurse, dressed in the pink uniform of a first year student, flitted briefly across his field of view. Distant sounds of children's voices echoed along the high Victorian ceilings. He turned his attention to the posters of characters from Disney which had been stuck up at intervals along the walls to lighten the atmosphere. The sheer height of the walls swamped them making them pathetic rather than effective.

A figure hurried towards them, white coat billowing open. His eyes fell on Tyson, "Sorry sir, 'couldn't get here any sooner, we've got a mini-bus accident to contend with."

Tyson nodded. "She's in there," he said.

Fenton noticed Tyson visibly wonder whether or not to join the registrar in the treatment room and decide not to. It had been over twenty years since he had last been involved in direct patient care.

A heavy trolley, being pushed by two porters, swung erratically to the side as it passed them and made them draw in their feet. Each porter blamed the other. Tyson looked at his watch and displayed uncharacteristic irritation. "Come on...come on," he muttered. Another two minutes had passed before a nurse accompanied by an orderly appeared. They were carrying transfusion equipment, the orderly weighed down on one side by a green, plastic crate containing six blood packs. They almost collided with the registrar who chose that moment to emerge from the room. He ignored the new arrivals and came directly towards Tyson. Fenton thought he looked embarrassed and had a sense of foreboding.

"I'm sorry," said the registrar, as if unable to believe what he was about to say, "We've lost her."

Fenton felt pins and needles break out all over his skin. 'We've lost her.' That's what they had said on that awful night when Louise had died. The words echoed inside his head rekindling every second of that hellish moment. After the phone call he had run through the streets in the pouring rain desperately trying to wave down a taxi but the weather had made sure that they were all occupied. He had ended up running the entire three miles to the hospital to stand there, dripping wet under the daylight glare of the lights in casualty to be told that his wife and child were dead. He remembered every pore on the face of the house officer who had told him, the way he had touched the frame of his glasses, the way he had looked at his feet. Now he waited for the next line, 'We did all we could,' but it didn't come. Instead, Tyson's voice broke the spell. "What do you mean, 'lost her'?" he asked hoarsely.

The registrar had gone a little red in the face, "I'm sorry," he said, making a gesture with open palms. "We couldn't stop the bleeding in time. It's as simple and as awful as that."

"But why not?" insisted Tyson.

The registrar made another helpless gesture with his hands. "I'm afraid we really won't know the answer to that until after the post-mortem.

Tyson got slowly to his feet and walked past the registrar into the treatment room; Fenton followed. The nurses melted back from the table to reveal the body of Susan Daniels, very still and very white. Fenton thought that she looked more beautiful than he had ever realised, like a pale delicate flower that had been cut and left lying on its side. Soon it would wither and fade. He was filled with grief and looked for some mundane object to focus his eyes on while he regained control of his emotions. He settled his gaze on a steel instrument tray and kept it there.

On looking up he saw tears running down the face of one of the nurses. He squeezed the girl's shoulder gently and indicated to her that she should leave the room. He himself followed a few moments later. He pretended to look at one of the Disney posters while he waited for Tyson.

In the background Fenton could hear Tyson and the registrar discussing the post-mortem arrangements then he had the feeling that he was no longer alone. He looked down to see a little boy dressed in pyjamas staring up at him. His nose was running. The child did not say anything but had a questioning look on his face. Fenton said, "Now where did you come from?"

The child continued to stare at him then said, "I want my mummy."

Fenton gently asked the boy his name but before he could answer a distraught nurse appeared on the scene. "Timothy Watson! So there you are!" She swept the child up into her arms and said to Fenton, "You just can't turn your back on this one for a moment or he's off!" The boy put his thumb in his mouth and snuggled down on the nurse's shoulder."

"Good-bye Timothy," said Fenton as the nurse walked away. He decided to walk back to the lab on his own without waiting any longer for Tyson who was still deep in discussion with the Casualty registrar.

It was already dark outside and the sodium street lights glistened in the puddles of rain water as he walked back towards the old villa. As he drew nearer he saw three figures standing in the bay window of the main lab and knew that they were waiting for news of Susan. One of them, Ian Ferguson, came to the door to meet him. "How is she?" he asked. Fenton stepped inside the hallway and saw everyone standing there. "Susan's dead," he said softly, "She bled to death."

Ferguson and Alex Ross, the chief technician, followed Fenton into the 'front room', closing the door and leaving the others out in the hall. Fenton crossed the floor and put his hands on the radiator by the window. "God, it's cold."

"Did they say what it was?" Ross asked.

"No, I don't think they know. They are going to do a post-mortem on her." Fenton sensed that his answer had failed to satisfy Ross; he turned round to face him.

Ross said, "It was natural, wasn't it? I mean, she wasn't murdered like Neil?"

Fenton was shocked. "Christ, I hadn't even considered that. I assumed it was some gynaecological thing."

"Me too," said Ferguson.

"You're probably right," said Ross. "It was just a thought."

"What a thought," said Fenton turning back to look out at the rain that had just started again.

On Saturday the lab staff finished at one pm leaving Fenton as duty biochemist till Sunday morning. He picked up the internal phone and gave the hospital switchboard his name and 'bleep' number, adding that he was about to go to lunch. He hurried up to the main hospital leaning forward against a fiercely gusting wind and climbed the stairs to the staff restaurant; it was half empty. He looked around for a familiar face but failed to find one save for Moira Kincaid from the Sterile Supply Department who was just leaving. He nodded to her as she passed.

Fenton paid for a cellophane wrapped salad and took it to a table by a window where he could watch the trees bend in the wind. It seemed to be blowing more strongly than ever.

'Want some company?" asked a voice behind him.

Fenton turned to find Jenny and smiled.

Jenny laid down her tray and Fenton held the edge of it steady while she extracted her fingers. "What a morning," she complained, "The ward's going like a fair."

Fenton smiled, paying scant attention to what she was saying but thinking that Jenny Buchan was the best thing that had happened to him in a very long time. "I didn't hear you leave this morning," he said.

"You were asleep. It seemed a shame to wake you."

Jenny joined Fenton in looking out of the window at the rain as it lashed against the blackened stone in wind-swept frenzy. "Do you think you will manage home tonight?" she asked.

Fenton shrugged his shoulders without taking his eyes off the rain and was about to reply when the bleeper in his jacket pocket went off. He shrugged again and Jenny nodded as he got up to leave. Outside in the corridor he picked up the phone and called the switchboard. "Fenton here."

Although the biochemistry lab was primarily concerned with the patients of the Princess Mary Hospital, it also carried out paediatric work for other hospitals in the city. Fenton had been informed that a blood sample was on its way from the maternity unit at the Royal Infirmary, a sample from a jaundiced baby for bilirubin estimation. He sat in the front room until the clatter of a diesel engine outside told him that it had arrived. Taking the plastic bag from the driver he signed the man's book and took the sample upstairs for analysis.

With the blood sample in the first stages of assay Fenton turned on the radio and tuned it to Radio 3. The sombre music seemed appropriate to a grey Saturday afternoon in February. He changed the settings on the analyser for the next stage and, with a fifteen minute wait in prospect, went along the corridor to Neil Munro's lab to collect Munro's research notes. He settled down to read them as, yet again, the rain began to hammer on the windows. The sound made him appreciate of the warmth of the lab. He wondered for a moment if the house had ever been this comfortable when it had been home to a well-to-do Victorian family. No trace of a fireplace could now be seen along any wall, in fact, the only trace of the original fittings lay in the ceiling where a plaster repair had failed to conceal the rose from which a chandelier had once hung. Fluorescent fittings were now bolted to the ceiling, incongruous against the cornice.

The bilirubin result chattered out of the printer. Fenton looked at it and compared it with the standard graphs on the wall. "Well, young..." He checked the name on the request form, "John Taylor, aged three days, you won't be going home for a little while yet." He called the maternity unit with the result and asked the nurse who took the call to read it back to him. "Check."

Finding that he was making little or no progress with Munro's book Fenton decided to make some coffee and came downstairs to switch on the electric kettle in the common room. The front door rattled in the wind as he came down the spiral stairs and crossed the hallway. He paused in front of one of the lockers to look at a photograph stuck up on one of the doors. Summer '86, said the caption in Dymo tape. It had been taken on the lab staff picnic in July, one of the few occasions Fenton could remember when a planned outing in Scotland had coincided with a dry sunny day. The good weather had made all the difference to the occasion and the smiles on the faces in the photograph said it.

Fenton looked at Neil Munro, relaxed, smiling and now dead; Susan Daniels in Tee shirt and shorts, young, carefree and now dead. He thought about Susan's death and on what Alex Ross had said. Surely it couldn't have been murder. But the thought had been voiced; it would not go away. Two people in the lab murdered? Considering the notion, albeit briefly, spawned another thought that was even colder than the icy wind that sought entrance to the hall through the cracks round the door. If two people in the lab had been murdered did that not suggest that the killer was one of the lab staff? One of the people in the photograph? Impossible, he decided and went to the common room.

The phone rang as he drank his coffee; he swivelled in his chair to pick up the receiver. Four blood samples were on their way. The phone was to ring twice more that afternoon for the same reason keeping him busy till a little after seven when things seemed to quieten down. He began toying with the idea of going home, deciding finally to give it till seven thirty before committing himself. At twenty to eight he phoned Jenny to say that he was on his way and then called the switchboard to say where he would be should his bleep fail.

The smell of cooking greeted him as he opened the door of the flat making him think how nice it was to come home to a warm bright apartment instead of the cold, dark silence that he had been used to before Jenny.

"How was it?" Jenny asked.

"Busy," Fenton replied, grunting as he pulled off his motor-cycle boots. "You?"

"It quietened down a lot this afternoon but we had one admission for the by-pass op."

Fenton washed his hands and joined Jenny at the table.

"I've got some bad news Tom," said Jenny.

"What?" asked Fenton.

"I'm going on night duty soon."

Fenton made a face. "What does that involve?" he asked.

"Four nights on, three off."

"Well, at least the bed will never get cold," said Fenton, "There will always be one of us in it."

Jenny came towards him and put her arms round his neck. "And we'll still make sure that there are plenty of occasions when there are two."

They finished their meal and shared the washing up before sitting down in front of the fire to drink their coffee. "Did you manage to make anything of Neil's research notes?" Jenny asked.

Fenton replied that he had not but, on the other hand, he had not had that much time to look at them.

"Do you think that Neil was on to something important?"

Fenton shrugged and said, "There's no way of knowing until we decipher the notes but I wish I knew what he wanted the blood for."

"Blood?"

Fenton told her about the request Munro had submitted to the Blood Transfusion Service and how the requisition had not gone through normal channels.

"Why would he have done that?" asked Jenny.

"Another question without an answer," said Fenton.

"I suppose when you think about it that was quite like Neil. He kept things very much to himself didn't he?"

Fenton agreed and gave a big yawn. Jenny smiled and said, "Was that some kind of hint?"

Fenton kissed her lightly on the forehead. "Early night?"

"Nice idea."

Fenton was taking off his second sock when his bleeper sounded from the chair his jacket was stretched over. He put his head in his hands before looking at Jenny who was already in bed. "God, you'd think they knew."

Fenton fastened the strap of his crash helmet and looked out of the window, shielding his eyes from the glare of the room lights. The look on his face when he turned round told Jenny that it was still raining.

"Take care."

It was six in the morning when Fenton returned. Jenny was already out of bed and putting on her uniform; she stopped buttoning her dress when Fenton came in and walked over to him. "Bad night?" she asked putting her arms round his neck.

"One thing after another," said Fenton.

Despite his tiredness Fenton still felt aroused by Jenny's nearness. He kissed her hard on the lips and felt her respond after initial surprise.

When they parted Jenny said, "At six in the morning on a cold, damp winter's day?"

"Any time and any day," said Fenton drawing her close again.

Jenny giggled and Fenton slipped his hand inside the top of her uniform to feel the warm swell of her breast. Pushing her back on to the bed he felt the muscles of her face relax as he pressed his mouth down on hers. Her lips parted to let his tongue probe the soft warm inside. "I want you," he murmured.

"I believe you, I believe you," Jenny giggled, struggling with his trouser zip to free him. She raise her bottom slightly to let him pull her panties down half way then raised her knees as he knelt over her to pull them down the rest of the way. He let his erection rest between her calves as he looked down at her. "I love you Jenny Buchan...God knows how I love you." He ran his hands gently up the inside of her thighs.

Jenny looked at her watch. "Duty calls," she said. There was no reply from Fenton. She raised herself on her elbows and looked at him; he was fast asleep. She got up quietly from the bed and smoothed her uniform then, looking at Fenton again, she smiled and bent down to kiss him lightly on the forehead before leaving.

Tyson called a meeting of the lab staff on Wednesday afternoon in the common room. The wind and rain that had lashed Edinburgh for the past week had still not abated and the windows rattled as he looked around to see if everyone was present. Fenton was missing, delayed by an urgent blood test, but he arrived before anyone had been sent to fetch him. He entered to find Tyson and Inspector Jamieson looking grim.

"We are now in possession of the post-mortem report on Susan Daniels," said Tyson. "Inspector Jamieson obtained it from the fiscal's office this morning. Susan did not suffer a miscarriage as some of us had imagined. She wasn't pregnant. She died because the normal clotting mechanisms of her blood were no longer functional. She had received a massive dose of an anticoagulant drug so that when she started bleeding there was no way of stopping it. It seems unthinkable that she administered the drug to herself which leaves us with the unpleasant, but inevitable alternative, that she was murdered." Tyson paused to let the hubbub die down. Fenton looked at Ian Ferguson who returned his glance. The nightmare was coming true.

Jamieson rose to put everyone's fears into words. There had been two murders in the hospital and both victims had been members of the Biochemistry Department. As both killings were apparently without personal motive the possibility that there was a psychopathic killer at large in the hospital, and with a particular grudge against the lab, had to be faced. Jamieson concluded by saying, "I'm sure I don't have to tell you but, if you have the slightest suspicion, the vaguest notion, of anything not being quite right, tell the police. We will be here in the hospital. Nothing is too trivial.

The possibility that the killer might actually be one of the lab staff was not mentioned but it ran through everyone's mind. The staff of the lab was small, sixteen in all including the two women who washed the glassware. There were no convenient strangers to suspect. Everyone knew everyone else, or so they thought.

39

Another day passed and the work of the lab went on as usual, it had to, but the atmosphere had changed dramatically. The light, good humour which had made it such a pleasant place to work in disappeared overnight. Neil Munro and Susan Daniels had gone and in their place had come fear and suspicion. The constant comings and goings of the police only served to heighten the tension as they returned to ask the same questions time and time again.

Fenton's spirits hit a new low on Friday at Neil Munro's funeral. The unrelenting wind and rain swept through an unkempt cemetery as they lowered Munro's coffin into the ground with prayers that were carried away on the wind and a handful of earth that spattered irreverently on the lid and turned to mud almost immediately. Tyson, Ross and Fenton, the three representatives from the lab, went to a nearby pub afterwards and drank whisky without speaking as water still trickled down the back of their necks and wet grass from the graveside clung to their shoes.

Fenton got home at six to find Jenny already there. "It was that bad?" she asked, reading his face.

"That bad," Fenton agreed quietly

"Do you want to stay home and brood about it or shall we go out?"

Fenton thought for a moment then said, "We'll go out. Somewhere noisy."

They had no trouble finding a noisy pub in Edinburgh on a Friday evening. They picked one near the west end of Princes Street that proclaimed 'Live Music Tonight' and pushed their way through the throng to the bar. Jenny watched the changing expressions on Fenton's face as he tried unsuccessfully to attract the barmaid's attention. He had the most expressive of face of anyone she had ever known. His eyes could sparkle with good humour one moment and turn to dark pools of sadness the next. His mouth, wide and generous, always searched for a reason to break into the boyish grin she loved so much. As he turned away from the bar she smiled quickly to conceal the fact that she had been watching him. "Hey, look," said Fenton, pointing with his elbow, "They are just leaving."

Jenny saw the couple who were about to rise and led the way over to the table. Fenton followed, holding their drinks at shoulder level to avoid being bumped and saying, "Excuse me" at appropriate intervals. He laid the glasses on the table then took off his jacket and draped it over the back of his chair before sitting down to look around at the Friday night people. Groups of girls, groups of boys, all pretending to be engrossed in their own conversations but being betrayed by constant side-long glances, the occasional loner, more interested in the alcohol than the company, couples old, couples young.

Intermittent and discordant tuning noises suddenly coalesced into a solid wall of electric noise, wiping out conversation like a shell burst. "Release me!" demanded a spotty youth through his over amplified microphone as he gyrated inside black leather trousers. 'Satan's Sons,' proclaimed the gothic script on the bass drum. Fenton exchanged painful glances with Jenny, his head reeling against the sheer volume. He saw her mouth move but could not lip read the comment. The song ended leaving their ears ringing in the sudden quiet. "I feel a hundred years old," said Fenton.

"Let's go," said Jenny. They finished their drinks and got up to leave as the spotty youth prepared to launch his second front.

The wind had dropped and the air smelled fresh and sweet as they emerged from the smoke and noise on to the still wet street. "I think a trifle more sophistication is called for at your age," said Jenny with a smile.

They walked for a while before turning off along a wide, sweeping Georgian terrace where most of the houses had been turned into hotels, each engaged in a neon struggle with its neighbour to attract attention. They decided on the 'Emerald Hotel' and found the bar to be uncrowded and, more important, quiet. Green shaded table lamps and oak panelling on the walls suggested a country house library.

"How are things in the lab?" Jenny asked.

"Terrible," said Fenton, "Nothing is said but suspicion is rife. One of the juniors brought me a cup of coffee this morning and I actually toyed with the idea of pouring it down the sink when he had gone, just in case."

"But surely the killer could be an outsider?"

"I suppose so but it's obvious that the police are concentrating on the lab."

"What do you think?" asked Jenny.

Fenton shook his head. "I have no idea, no idea at all."

On Monday the secrecy contrived at by the police and hospital authorities came to a sudden dramatic end. 'Mystery Hospital Deaths' in The Scotsman became, 'Maniac Stalks Hospital Corridors' in the Daily News and ensured that the hospital switchboard was jammed all day with calls from anxious relatives seeking reassurance. Tyson called the lab staff together to warn against talking to reporters and making things worse. The official line was to be that two members of staff had died in suspicious circumstances and the police were investigating. No details were to be furnished. But too many people in the hospital knew the details. Tuesday morning brought, 'Sterilizer Horror,' and, 'Girl Dies in Pool of Blood.'

The idea of a psychopathic killer being at large in a city hospital fired the imagination of the front page of every newspaper in the country. Radio and television reporters interviewed anyone with even a remote connection with the Princess Mary and the Chief Constable of Edinburgh appeared on television, in full dress uniform, to assure a worried public that matters were well in hand and a speedy arrest could be confidently expected.

In private, Inspector Jamieson could not share his superior's optimism. With no obvious logic or motive behind the killings police routine was largely useless. Their best hope lay in the possibility that the killer might get over confident and reveal himself in the process. Of course there was always the chance that the murderer, like Jack the Ripper, might just stop but he would not be betting his pension on that. Special passes were hurriedly printed and issued to staff and relatives to allow them to cross the police picket at the gates which had been mounted to keep the morbidly curious at bay.

Fenton was speaking to Nigel Saxon about the enforced delay in completing the paperwork for the Saxon Blood Analyser when Ian Ferguson came into the room. Ferguson was obviously surprised to find Saxon there and said, "Sorry, I just wondered if I might have a word."

Saxon got to his feet, "No problem. I was just going anyway."

Ferguson stood to one side to allow Saxon to pass then closed the door. He seemed embarrassed.

"What can I do for you?" Fenton asked.

"'Fact is," faltered Ferguson, "Well...I've decided to apply for another job. Can I put you down as a referee?"

Fenton stared at him for a moment for it was the last thing he had expected to hear from Ian Ferguson. "What's the problem?" he asked.

Ferguson looked at his feet. He said, "There's a job going at the Western General. I quite fancy a change. More experience and all that..."

"And you are scared," said Fenton.

Ferguson looked as if he were about to argue but then he simply sighed and said, "Aren't you?"

"Yes," said Fenton.

An uneasy silence reigned for a moment before Ferguson said, "You must think I'm a right coward."

Fenton turned to face him. "I don't think that at all. I'll even give you a good reference but, what I won't give you is a round of applause. There are three hundred children in this hospital and if you leave we will be three under strength. We'll manage but it will be that much harder on those of us who stay."

"Well," sighed Ferguson, "I hadn't quite thought about it that way. You don't beat about the bush do you?"

The question was rhetorical but Fenton chose to reply anyway, "No, I don't."

Charles Tyson put his head round the door as Ferguson left. "What was all that about?" he asked, feeling the atmosphere in the room."

"Ian is thinking of applying for another job."

"That would be a pity," said Tyson. "He's one of the best we have."

"It would also leave us up shit creek without a paddle," added Fenton.

Tyson grimaced at Fenton's expression and said, "A fact I'm sure you managed to convey to him with admirable clarity."

Fenton grunted.

"Did Nigel Saxon see you about the report?" Tyson asked.

"Yes, but I'm still up to my eyes. It will have to wait."

"Fair enough," said Tyson. "The patients come first."

It was after seven when Fenton got home. He arrived to find Jenny in particularly attentive mood. "Do I have to guess what you are going to ask or are you going to tell me?" he asked.

"It's Mrs Doig's fan heater. I said that you would have a look at it. There's a smell of burning."

"Sure," said Fenton.

"I love you," said Jenny.

Mrs Doig was their next door neighbour, a woman in her seventies who lived alone with two cats and her memories. Jenny had adopted her as a personal responsibility with Fenton providing the technical back-up, changing tap washers, mending fuses and the like.

They finished their meal and went next door, Fenton carrying screwdriver and pliers. The old woman was clearly pleased to see them and bade them enter. "You'll have a cup of tea?" she asked. Fenton was about to decline when Jenny nudged him, knowing how much the old woman liked to feel she was doing something for them. Fenton removed the back of the fan heater as the women chatted but still found time to observe Jenny in action. Whereas he himself would adopt a cheerful air and make forced conversation about the weather Jenny was quite sincere in her care and concern for the old woman. She would joke with her, tease her, cajole her into laughter until her spirits rose visibly and she would begin to speak freely. Fenton felt a lump come to his throat. He knew that Jenny would like them to marry and have children. If only he could get over the awful mental block of associating marriage with the agony of losing Louise, the unreasonable yet undeniable feeling that he would be tempting fate.

He found the fault in the heater and repaired it. Like everything else in the flat, it was old, the black, coal fired grate, the dark, varnished wallpaper, the five amp wiring, all just waiting for the old woman to die before being stripped out at the end of an era. "All done," he said.

Fenton poured out a couple of drinks when they got back to their own flat and they sat in front of the fire nursing their glasses. He mentioned his conversation with Ian Ferguson.

"Ian Ferguson?" exclaimed Jenny. "You surprise me."

"Why so?"

He's a public school product. I thought that all that emphasis on character building would make him the last person to run away from an unpleasant situation.

"Maybe 'character' has to be innate after all," said Fenton dryly.

"You know what I meant," smiled Jenny soothing Fenton's socialist hackles.

"We have the same problem on the wards," said Jenny, "There's been a sudden outbreak of 'flu' so we're about a third under strength. In fact, I may have to go on nights sooner than I thought.' Flu' seems to have hit the night staff worst of all."

"People associate darkness with danger," said Fenton.

Jenny got up to switch the television on. "Anything in particular you want to see?" she asked.

Fenton said not. He was going to have another attempt at deciphering Neil Munro's notes.

"You're working too hard," said Jenny. "You'll make yourself ill and that will do the lab no good at all."

"Just an hour or so. I promise."

Fenton collected Munro's book, a notepad and some pencils and took them to another room where he would have quiet. His immediate problem was that the front room of the flat was so cold. He switched on the electric fire and crouched down in front of it till it made some impression on the still, icy air.

Just as on previous occasions the stumbling block in Munro's notes lay in the fact that he had given no indication of what units the figures, in neat columns, referred to. Temperature? Volume? Time? Without that information the notes comprised several meaningless columns of figures interspersed with occasional letters of the alphabet. Fenton tried fitting the figures to various biochemical parameters but without success. After an hour he kept his word to Jenny and put the book aside. He rejoined her to watch the News on television.

CHAPTER THREE

In Ward Four of the Princess Mary Hospital Timothy Watson was not having a good day. It had started badly when he had not been allowed any breakfast and had got worse when a man in a white coat had pricked his arm with a needle after personally assuring him that it was not going to hurt. Grown-ups were not to be trusted.Shortly afterwards the protests had died on his lips as the drowsiness of pre-medication had stolen over him and the world had suddenly become lighter, warmer, fluffier, fuzzier until suddenly it wasn't there any more. Now his bed lay empty, with the covers turned down and his Teddy Bear sitting on the pillow, limbs askew, patiently awaiting his return.

The plastic name tag on Timothy's wrist was his only introduction to many of the green clad figures who now hovered over him, intent on freeing him from the breathlessness that had plagued him from birth. The comforting blip of the heart monitor sounded regularly as synchronous spikes chased each other across the green face of an oscilloscope and the muted sound of classical music emanated from concealed speakers in Theatre number two.

James Rogan looked up at the theatre clock and gave a satisfied grunt. "Going to knock three minutes off my record eh Sister?"

"Yes sir," answered theatre sister Rose Glynn without moving her eyes. Dutiful laughter added to the already relaxed atmosphere round the table, an atmosphere not left to chance. The green smocks, the smooth pastel walls, the shadowless light, the perfect temperature and, of course, the surgeon's own choice of music conspired to produce perfect conditions for the surgical team.

"How is he doing?" Rogan asked the anaesthetist.

"Steady as a rock."

"Money for old rope eh Sister?"

"Yes sir."

"Spencer - Wells!"

Rose Glynn slapped the forceps into Rogan's gloved hand as he continued with a commentary for the benefit of his two assistants. Without pausing he asked for instruments in mid sentence and Rose Glynn slapped them into his hand; she never missed a request; she had worked with Rogan so often before.

"All Right Allan, sew him up," said Rogan to his chief assistant. He stepped back from the table and stripped his gloves off in dramatic fashion before saying, "Thank-you everybody," and turning on his heel to make an exit through both swing doors.

"Who was that masked man Mummy?" asked one of the assistants under his breath but loud enough for everyone in the theatre to hear. Eyes met above masks and twitching ears signalled smiles hidden behind gauze. A student nurse giggled and Rose Glynn froze her with a stare. "Can we start the count sir?" she asked.

"Yes Sister, thank-you."

Rose Glynn and her student nurse ran through the swab and instrument count ensuring that all were accounted for. The tally was agreed, the stitching completed and the patient wheeled out into the recovery room. Two hours later he was back in bed with his teddy bear and sleeping soundly. His parents who had spent an anxious day at the hospital were able to leave for home and their first good night's sleep for many weeks.

At eight fifteen Staff nurse Carol Mileham noticed Timothy Watson become restless in his sleep and went over to him. She smoothed the hair back from his forehead and found that he was very hot. Half turning to go and call the duty houseman she was stopped by a gurgling sound from the boy's throat; she bent down to listen and a cascade of bright red blood erupted from his mouth, drenching her apron and splashing silently on to the sheets.

The surgical team and Timothy Watson had their unscheduled reunion in theatre number four and the atmosphere was very different from the previous occasion. There were no smiles, no jokes and no music. The irregular blip of the heart monitor probed the team's nerves like a dentist's drill, the spikes constantly dodging anticipation. Rogan had come directly from home on getting his houseman's call. 'Massive internal bleed,' had been the message that had brought him racing to the hospital still in carpet slippers.

Timothy's chest was re-opened and the flesh held back by retractors. "Ye gods," murmured Rogan, "He's awash...Suck please!"

Rogan's assistant started clearing the blood with a vacuum suction tube while he himself dabbed with cotton swabs. A nurse changed the transfusion pack for the second time.

"Mop!" Rogan inclined his head for Rose Glynn to wipe away the sweat from his brow but only to see it reappear almost immediately. Rogan was losing the battle and the tension in his voice conveyed that fact to everyone. Tension like laughter was infectious.

"He's leaking like a sieve." Exasperation took over from anxiety as Rogan realised that there was nothing he could do. "There's something wrong with his blood damn it...I can't stop it."

Four minutes later the heart monitor lapsed into a long, continuous monotone. The tension evaporated leaving silence in its place. "Thank-you Sister," said Rogan quietly. He lowered his mask and took off his gloves, this time slowly and deliberately. "Get some blood to the haematology lab will you." His assistant nodded. Rose Glynn looked at her student nurse and saw that her eyes were moist. She had planned to have words with the girl about her earlier giggling episode. She resolved not to bother.

Malcolm Baird, consultant haematologist at the Princess Mary, phoned Rogan personally next morning but only to say, rather cryptically thought Rogan, that there was to be a meeting of all consultants at eleven thirty in the medical superintendent's office to discuss the Watson case. He should bring his case notes.

Charles Tyson was last to arrive at the meeting and got the least comfortable seat as his just desert. He apologised for his lateness but did not offer up any reason. Cyril Freeman, medical superintendent at the Princess Mary for the past seven years opened the meeting with a short history of Timothy Watson's illness leading up to his admission. Rogan was invited to follow and duly gave his account of the operation and the subsequently tragic, and ultimately fatal, internal haemorrhage. He sat down again and Baird got to his feet to make his report. "A thorough haematological examination of the blood sample taken from the boy Watson has shown conclusively that all coagulation potential had been lost, just like Daniels in fact. A massive dose of an anticoagulant drug is indicated."

Tyson leaned forward putting his elbows on the table to support his head. "So the bastard has started on the patients now," he said.

Anger vied with gloom and despondency around the table.

"What the hell are the police doing anyway?" demanded George Miles from Radiology.

"Running round in circles if you ask me," said Rogan.

"It's not easy in a case like this," said orthopaedic surgeon Gordon Clyde.

"I didn't say it was," snapped Rogan.

Freeman intervened to prevent further disharmony. "Gentlemen," he said, "We have one overriding and immediate problem to discuss." All eyes turned to him. "We have to stop the press from finding out about the Watson boy. If the papers get hold of this there will be blind panic amongst patients' relatives."

"And people would be right to panic," said Tyson.

"Would you mind explaining that remark?" asked Rogan.

Tyson said calmly, "Let's not pretend that we are taking steps to prevent unnecessary panic. The truth is we are quite powerless to prevent another killing. This hospital is entirely at the mercy of a lunatic."

The desire to argue was stillborn on the lips of Tyson's colleagues; it was left to Fenwick to break the silence. He said, "We have, of course, discussed the option of closing the hospital with the police and local authorities but we simply cannot do it. We are too big, there are too many patients to transfer and, as the police point out, the staff who went with our patients would almost certainly include the killer. We would just be transferring the problem."

"So we sit tight and do nothing?"

"Yes, and hope the police come up with something," said Fenwick. The frown on Rogan's face suggested a feeling shared by the others.

What about the Watson boy's parents?" asked Tyson. "They are bound to talk to the press."

Fenwick looked uneasy. He fidgeted with his pen before saying quietly, almost inaudibly, "They don't know."

"What?" exclaimed Tyson and Clyde together.

"They are not in possession of the full facts surrounding their son's death, just that the boy died after post-operative complications."

"But that is..." Rogan was interrupted by Fenwick.

"Don't lecture me on ethics Mr Rogan," he said firmly. The police suggested this course of action and I agreed. There is no way we could expect the parents to suppress their anger and keep this matter quiet. Just how much you tell your own staff I leave to your discretion."

"I suggest nothing," said Clyde.

"I think Tyson might disagree with you," said Fenwick.

Tyson looked over his glasses and nodded slowly. He said, "So far, my department has taken the brunt of the strain in this affair. We have lost two people and have had to live with the fear that this psychopath had a particular grudge against the lab and, worse, that he might actually be one of our number. This latest death makes both these things less likely. I think that at least some of my people should be told to lessen the tension. A murmur of agreement filled the room.

"Sorry Tyson," said Clyde, "I didn't think."

Tyson left the meeting and walked back along the main corridor past the room where Susan Daniels had died. Two nurses were standing talking outside it, laughing about some idiosyncrasy in one of their colleagues. Tyson excused himself and squeezed past. The voices dropped to a whisper as he did so making him reflect on how often this had happened in the past. It was part of being a hospital consultant; people tended to stop speaking when you came near.

By the time he had left the corridor and battled back to the lab against the wind and spitting rain he had decided to tell Alex Ross, Ian Ferguson and Tom Fenton about the Watson boy's death.

The relief that Fenton felt on hearing that the killer had struck somewhere else was followed almost immediately by a wave of guilt at having found a child's death any cause for relief. His guilt doubled when he remembered that Timothy Watson had been the name of the child who had spoken to him in the corridor when Susan had died.

Before Tyson left the room Fenton asked him a question about Neil Munro's personal research project. Did he know what it was? Tyson replied that he did not. Fenton opened Munro's notes and pointed to a page heading; it said, C.T. "It's just that I thought that this might stand for Charles Tyson?" he said.

There was a long silence while Tyson looked at the page. "Doesn't mean a thing," he said and left before Fenton had time to ask anything else.

Ian Ferguson came into the room and put some keys down on the desk, "These were Neil Munro's lab keys. Alex Ross asked me to give you them. He said something about a locked cupboard?"

Fenton thanked him and added that he had asked Ross about a locked cupboard in Munro's room that he had been unable to find a key for.

"If you find an electric timer in it let me know will you? Neil borrowed mine and I Haven't been able to find it since." said Ferguson.

"I'll check right now if you like," said Fenton and got up to lead the way to Munro's lab.

Ferguson looked on while Fenton tried the keys and found success at his third attempt. "There's no timer here," said Fenton.

"Damn."

Fenton sifted through the contents of the cupboard while Ferguson stood by. Test tube racks, plastic tubes and beakers and several brown glass bottles with chemicals in them. He examined the labels. Potassium oxalate, sodium citrate, heparin, EDTA, Warfarin. "What do you make of that?" he asked Ferguson.

"They're all anti-coagulants," said Ferguson quietly.

Fenton nodded. "Indeed they are," he said softly.

"I don't understand," said Ferguson.

Fenton did not reply for his mind was working overtime in trying to work out why Munro had been using anticoagulants at all and why they had been locked away out of sight. It must have had something to do with his research project, he concluded, but what? He needed time to think, time to ponder the frightening coincidence that Munro had apparently been working with the same sort of drugs and chemicals that had been used to murder two people in the hospital.He looked at Ferguson who was obviously thinking the same thing but was waiting for him to say something first. Fenton said, "I think it might be best if we didn't say anything about this for the moment."

"Of course," said Ferguson. "Whatever you think."

Fenton took out the one remaining bottle in the cupboard and looked at the label. Dimethyl-formamide.

"What's that?" asked Ferguson.

"A powerful solvent." said Fenton.

Jenny came to the lab at five thirty hoping for a lift home. Almost as soon as she entered the downstairs hallway she became aware of the absence of Susan Daniels who, in the past, had always come out of her lab to chat to her. A junior went to find Fenton leaving her looking at the notices on the general information board by the staff lockers. Ian Ferguson saw her standing there and stopped to say hello. They spoke about the weather until Fenton appeared at the head of the stairs to say that he would be another ten minutes.

"She can come and speak to me until you're ready," said Ferguson.

Jenny sat on a swivel stool in Ferguson's lab while he continued to add small volumes of a chemical to a long row of test tubes. She was about to ask what he was doing when Ferguson opened the conversation by asking how things were going on the wards. "We're busy," replied Jenny, "We're at least a third under strength. People are frightened." Jenny remembered what Fenton had told her about Ferguson applying for a new job and felt embarrassed at what she had said. As casually as possible she said, "I understand from Tom that you are applying for an exciting new job?

"I was," replied Ferguson. "But I've changed my mind. Tom made me realise just what it would mean to the department."

"But if it was a good opportunity..." said Jenny.

"There will be others," said Ferguson.

"I see," said Jenny, although she was not sure that she did.She hoped that Fenton had not been too hard on him, had not embarrassed him into changing his mind for in many ways Ferguson was very like Tom Fenton. He was tall and dark and very intelligent. She supposed that, in the classical sense, Ferguson was more handsome than Fenton for Fenton's face was too open, too frank, too honest to be considered handsome whereas Ian Ferguson had the dark broody quality so beloved of women's magazines. There was an air of introversion about him but it was certainly not bred of shyness and there was nothing in his eyes to suggest any lack of confidence.

The sound of Fenton's voice outside the door prompted Jenny to get up and wish Ferguson good-night adding that she hoped her presence had not distracted him too much. "Not at all," replied Ferguson. "It's always nice to see you."

They had missed the worst of the rush hour traffic and were home in under fifteen minutes, both agreeing that they had had a hard day.

"Let's eat out," said Fenton.

"Where?"

"Somewhere nice. We haven't been out for a meal in ages."

"Queensferry?"

"Why Queensferry?"

"I want to be near the sea," said Jenny. "There is one thing..." she added tentatively.

"I know. No bike. We'll get a taxi."

Fenton got out of the shower and towelled down. His body still bore signs of the tan that he had acquired during the summer and frequent exercise in the form of squash and running had kept the flab of sedentary occupation at bay. Wrapping the towel round his waist he padded through to the bedroom and opened the sliding wardrobe. He laid out his clothes on the bed, a plain blue shirt, navy socks, black shoes, dark blue tie, dark blue suit. He shrugged his shoulders as he put on the jacket and looked at himself in the mirror to straighten his tie. He flicked at his hair with his fingers but there was little he could do about it. It was curly and unruly and that was that. Dark curls licked along his forehead taking five years off his age. Fiddling with his cuff links, he walked through to join Jenny.

Jenny was sitting at an angle on the sofa, her stockinged legs crossed and her elbow resting on one knee with her hand supporting her chin. She was wearing a close fitting dress in royal blue, the very plainness of which accentuated her smooth skin and high cheek bones. Her silky blonde hair was swept back from her face and held tightly with a dark blue clasp. Round her neck she wore the gold pear drop locket that Fenton had given her for Christmas.

"You look good," said Fenton.

"You're no slouch yourself Mr Bond. Did you call the cab?"

A thick sea mist lay on the still water of the Firth of Forth as they got out of the taxi in the village of South Queensferry, some eight miles from the heart of Edinburgh. The lights of cars high above them on the Forth Road Bridge twinkled in and out of the fog while the huge, red painted spans of the famous old railway bridge towered silently up into the damp air. The regular drone of fog horns was the only thing to break the silence as they crossed the road to look over the sea wall.

"It's creepy when it's like this," said Jenny looking down at the unbroken surface of the water.

"But nice," said Fenton.

They entered the bar of the restaurant to find it practically deserted. "Thursday night," said the barman by way of explanation. "Nothing happens on Thursdays."

"Except elections," said Fenton as he and Jenny were drawn to a large coal fire like moths to a flame.

They finished looking at the menu and ordered before lapsing into silence for a few moments. Jenny held her drink between her palms. She said, "A child died in theatre yesterday did you hear?"

"I heard," said Fenton, feeling uncomfortable.

"Do you know anything about it?" asked Jenny.

Fenton stayed silent.

"Oh dear," said Jenny, I see that you do.

"Jenny I..."

"Don't say anything. Just listen. Today at lunch I heard Rose Glynn, mention 'excessive bleeding' then later I heard someone else say that the haematology report wasn't available. I put two and two together and came up with four."

"Three," said Fenton, "Timothy Watson was the third victim. I felt so awful just now when you asked and I couldn't tell you."

"Relax, you didn't. I worked it out for myself. So the killer is not someone with a grudge against the lab?"

"No, it's someone who murders five year olds."

Jenny noted the bitterness in Fenton's voice and was forced to ask. "You didn't know the boy did you?"

"Well enough to be able to put a face to the name. He was running around the main corridor the day Susan Daniels was murdered."

They left the restaurant just after ten thirty and crossed the road to take a last look at the water.Fenton picked up a handful of gravel and began to flick it idly into the water with his thumbnail. As they leaned on the railings Jenny said, "You know, when you think about it, it's a strange way to kill people isn't it? Anti-coagulants?"

"That's how they kill rats."

"Rats?"

Fenton flicked some more gravel into the water and watched the rings spread. "That's how rat poison works. It knocks out the clotting mechanism in their blood; one scratch in the sewers and they bleed to death."

A ship's siren sounded out in the Forth. They peered into the swirling mist but saw nothing. Jenny said, "I just don't see how the drug could have been administered, can you?"

"Rats have to eat it, so maybe it was mixed into the victims' food or drink. I can't see anyone having an injection without knowing it."

"Unless the victim was a patient who was having injections all the time, or a child who trusted anyone in uniform."

"Susan wasn't a patient or a child and she wasn't having injections," said Fenton.

"Are you sure?"

The question made Fenton think before saying, "No, I suppose I'm not, come to think of it. All of us in the lab get protective vaccines from time to time because we handle so much contaminated material."

Jenny said, "Just suppose Susan had been given a large dose of anti-coagulant instead of say, an anti-typhoid injection. She wouldn't have known would she?"

"That would make our killer a doctor or a nurse, someone with access to the wards and the staff."

"Can you find out if Susan did have any inoculations shortly before her death?" Jenny asked.

"It will be in the lab personnel files."

"I could try to find out who has been on duty in the staff treatment suite over the past few weeks."

"I've just had another thought," said Fenton, pausing for a moment to see if it made sense before committing himself. "The staff treatment suite is next to the Central Sterile Supply Department, where Neil was killed."

"And anti-coagulants are not on the restricted drugs list; they're not kept under lock and key..."

"So they would be readily available and the killer would not have to account for them..."

"Let's suppose some more," said Jenny, the adrenalin now flowing fast. "Suppose Neil went to the Sterile Supply Department to see Sister Kincaid and found that she wasn't there. We know she wasn't; she was at lunch. He went next door to look for her and stumbled on the killer messing with injection vials."

"So the killer murdered Neil to keep him quiet? Makes sense."

"It also makes it a man," said Jenny, "I can't see a woman overpowering Neil can you?"

"No, and there was no sign of a weapon having been used. You are right; it had to be a man, and a powerful man at that. Neil was no seven-stone weakling."

At seven fifteen next morning Jenny left for the hospital, leaving Fenton still in bed. They had arranged to meet at lunch time to discuss progress in what they had agreed to find out. Fenton rose at eight, washed, dressed and sat down at the kitchen table with orange juice and coffee to read 'The Scotsman' which had popped noisily through the letter box while he was shaving. He scanned the front page for mention of the hospital and was relieved to find only a few lines near the bottom to the effect that inquiries were still continuing into the sudden deaths of two members of the biochemistry department.

Finding the silence oppressive he turned on the radio. '1-9-4-Close to you...' droned the jingle as Fenton took his glass and cup to the sink. The sound of the 'current number four in the charts' filled the kitchen briefly before he changed the waveband and found Vivaldi instead. He tidied away the dishes and wiped the work surface where he had spilled orange juice.

The minute hand on the kitchen clock moved jerkily on to eight thirty as Fenton switched off the radio and checked that he had his keys in his pocket before leaving. He tried to keep the noise of his feet on the stone steps down to a minimum as he descended but they still echoed around the stair well; the noise reverberated off the high ceramic walls.

Fenton waited until ten o'clock, when he knew that Liz Scott, the lab secretary, would be at her busiest then went downstairs to the office. "Good morning Liz, I just want to check when my next T.A.B is due...Don't worry, I can find it myself."

"Thanks, I'm snowed under at the moment."

Fenton took the keys that were handed to him and approached the filing cabinet by the window. The sound of rain against the grimy, barred window all but obliterated the noise of the top drawer being pulled out. He flicked through the index cards till he found what he was looking for. Daniels, Susan...Age...Weight...Height...Blood Group...X-Ray Record...Inoculations! Last entry...T.A.B. vaccine given on...Fenton's heart missed a beat. February fifteenth! Two days before she died! He steeled himself to present a calm exterior when he turned round and handed the keys back to Liz Scott. "'Find what you wanted?" she asked without looking up. Fenton said that he had and returned upstairs. Instead of going to his own lab he went into Neil Munro's room and sat down for a moment. Should he tell someone what he had discovered? And, if so, who? Tyson? Jamieson? It was too soon to say anything he decided; he needed more to go on. He would wait until he had seen Jenny at lunch time.

Fenton took out the chemicals and equipment he had removed from Munro's locked cupboard and spread them out on the bench in front of him. He re-arranged a number of plastic test tubes into a symmetrical pattern on the desk top and idly balanced two small beakers in the centre while he considered what he knew. Munro had requested blood from the transfusion service and he had been working with anti-coagulants. These two factors made him feel very uneasy. But what else was there to go on? A meaningless series of figures in a notebook and the letters C.T. which Charles Tyson said were nothing to do with him...So what did they stand for?

Fenton was balancing a third beaker on top of the other two when the door opened and the pile collapsed. Nigel Saxon stood there. "Sorry, did I do that?" he asked.

Fenton reassured him and admitted that he had just been playing with the tubes.

"I see," said Nigel Saxon, but sounded as though he didn't really. "I hate to keep pressing you like this but..."

"I know, the report on the analyser." said Fenton.

"Have you managed to look at Susan's final figures?"

"I've been through them.They seemed fine apart from one failure, a patient named Moran. Susan wrote that no analysis was obtained. Were you with her when this test was performed?"

"Neil Munro and I were both there," said Saxon. "We decided that the ward must have sent the sample in the wrong kind of specimen container."

"It happens," agreed Fenton.

"Was that the only thing?"

"Everything else seems fine."

Saxon smiled broadly and said, "Good, then we'll still get our license by the end of the month."

"That soon?" exclaimed Fenton in amazement.

Fenton's surprise took Saxon aback and he flushed slightly in embarrassment. "Sometimes the wheels of bureaucracy can turn quite smoothly you know." he said.

"Saxon Medical must have a magic wand," said Fenton.

"A plastic one," said Saxon.

As Saxon made to leave Fenton said, "The Moran sample, it was run through the conventional analyser wasn't it? I mean as well as the new one?"

"I presume so".

"Same result?"

"As far as I know."

Fenton met Jenny at one o'clock. She was standing at the main gate as he walked up to the hospital from the lab. She smiled as she saw him but had to wait to allow an ambulance to pass before crossing the road to link her arm through his. "Where shall we go?" she asked.

"Let's walk for a bit," said Fenton. They didn't speak until they had left the noise and bustle of the main road and turned down a side street. "How did you get on?" Jenny asked.

"Susan Daniels had a TAB inoculation two days before she died." said Fenton. "It looks as if you could be right."

"I don't think I really want to be," said Jenny. Fenton asked her if she had managed to come up with anything.

"Sister Murphy has been in charge of the staff treatment room for the past three months."

"Old Mother Murphy? Florence's batman?"

"The very same."

"Doesn't sound too hopeful." said Fenton.

"There's more." Jenny had to pause for they had rejoined the main road and a bus roared past them making conversation momentarily impossible. When it had passed she said, "The doctor doing the staff inoculations is one of the new residents, Dr David Malcolm. He's been doing it for about a month and what's more...he is the resident on ward four, Timothy Watson's ward."

"Do you know him?"

"By sight. He's about six feet tall and broad with it."

Fenton halted in his stride to allow a woman pushing a pram to pass them, he caught up again. "Do you know any more about him?"

"Only that it's his first residency and that he hasn't asked any of the nurses out."

"Maybe he's married."

"No."

"Gay?"

"If he is he's not the effeminate type I'm told."

The sky darkened and Fenton felt the first spot of rain on his cheek as another brief respite from the weather came to an end. The man in front of them stopped walking in order to put on a plastic raincoat. An old woman threatened Jenny's eyesight as she struggled to put up her umbrella. Fenton pushed it gently out of the way as they passed getting a dirty look for his trouble. They took refuge in a small cafe where the air was already dank with the condensation from wet clothing. The coffee was lukewarm and instant. "What do we do now?" Jenny asked.

"Tell the police," replied Fenton.

"I'm glad you said that," said Jenny. "This business scares me to death."

When they returned to the hospital Fenton left word at the administration block that he would like to see Inspector Jamieson as soon as the policeman found it convenient. Jamieson duly turned up at the lab at half past two as Fenton was loading blood samples into a centrifuge. He watched what Fenton was doing for a few moments before moving across to the bookcase and peering through the glass doors in order to read the titles while he waited. He quickly tired of that and moved to the window.

Fenton closed the lid of the centrifuge and set the timer to run for ten minutes before pressing the start button and crossing the room to wash his hands in the sink. Jamieson still had his back to him; he was silhouetted against the cold grey light in the window.

"Sorry about that," said Fenton apologising for the delay. Jamieson turned round and smiled dutifully. "How can I help you?" he asked.

Fenton told Jamieson everything. He told him how he and Jenny had come to suspect that the killer was one of the medical staff and how they had gone about gathering evidence to support their contention. Everything, he said, seemed to point to Dr David Malcolm being implicated in the killings.

Jamieson listened without interruption, fiddling throughout with his moustache, brushing it upwards with his forefinger then smoothing it down again with both thumb and forefinger. "I see sir," he said when Fenton had finished. There was a long pause during which a distant clap of thunder heralded even more rain. Fenton was puzzled for, although he had not expected Jamieson to leap to his feet in excitement, he had anticipated a bit more than the catatonic trance that he appeared to have gone in to. At length the policeman got to his feet and said, "Thank you sir, you did the right thing in telling us."

"That's all?"

"What did you expect?" asked Jamieson pointedly dropping the 'sir'.

"Some comment I suppose. Some reaction?" replied Fenton.

"I'm a great believer in horses for courses sir," said Jamieson.

"What does that mean?"

"It means that I don't tell you how to run your lab and you don't tell me how to do my job."

Fenton saw the anger in Jamieson's eyes and was about to argue that he was only trying to help when Jamieson interrupted him.

"Give the police a little credit sir. We were perfectly well aware that Miss Daniels had had an inoculation shortly before her death; we also know that Sister Murphy administered it because Dr Malcolm was off duty that day. We also know that Dr Malcolm wasn't here on the day that Dr Munro was murdered because he was attending a one day seminar at Stirling Royal Infirmary; in fact, we were able to eliminate Dr Malcolm from our inquiries some time ago. We know all that sir because it is our job to know all that."

Fenton felt foolish. "I'm sorry, I've wasted your time," he said contritely.

"Not at all sir," said Jamieson. He left the room.

Fenton was left sitting astride a wooden lab stool watching the rain stream down through the grime on the windows. He had made a fool of himself and now suffered the humiliation in silence. The sound of the decelerating centrifuge said that his blood samples were ready for analysis.

Jenny was equally dejected when Fenton told her what had happened but, in characteristic fashion, she looked for something positive to take out of the experience and said, "At least it shows that police know what they are doing."

Ferguson ignored the comment and said, "I felt about two inches tall when Jamieson put me in my place. He enjoyed doing it too, I could tell."

"You're probably imagining it," said Jenny.

"No, I don't think so," said Fenton reliving the experience as he stared into the fire.

Jenny looked at him and smiled. "Well, we can't really blame him can we," she said. "We were trying to do his job for him."

Fenton returned to the present and shrugged. "I suppose you're right," he sighed.

"And if we are absolutely honest with ourselves," said Jenny getting to her feet and ruffling Fenton's hair, "Thomas Fenton was never one to like being proved wrong..."

"There's a letter for you on the hall table," said Fenton changing the subject.

The sound from the hall told Fenton that Jenny had not opened a bill. "Tom! It's from my brother Grant, he's coming to Edinburgh next week with Jamie. Do you remember? Jamie fell off his tricycle and injured his eye a while back. He's to see a specialist at the Eye Pavilion."

"What day?"

Jenny paused in the doorway, scanning down the letter for the answer. "Wednesday...next Wednesday. They've to be at the hospital on Friday morning."

"They can stay here if you like," said Fenton.

"Tom, could they?" asked Jenny, obviously pleased at the suggestion.

"Of course." said Fenton. He stretched his arms in the air and then put his hands behind his head.

"Why don't you have a nice warm bath before the film comes on?" said Jenny.

The sound of Fenton cursing from the bathroom brought Jenny out into the hall. "The main cistern is overflowing," he said looking at the stream of brownish water that was trickling into the bath from the overflow pipe.

"Can you fix it?"

"I think so, I'll need the ladders." Fenton fetched a pair of step ladders, propped them up outside the bathroom and climbed up to open the door leading to the cistern. Jenny handed him a torch then waited patiently at the foot of the steps. "Can you see what's wrong?"

"Well, missus," said Fenton, affecting a loud sniff, "Looks like your grommet sprocket's gone and that's no joke."

"Oh my goodness," said Jenny in a dizzy blonde voice, "My grommet sprocket! Whatever shall I do?"

"Well, yer gonna need a new one, and that's fifty nicker for a start. An' if yer globbin shaft's gone as well, that's another fifty, and then there's me time..."

"Good gracious I didn't realise it was so serious, however can I pay you? I'm only a poor little nurse..." Jenny rubbed her hand gently up and down Fenton's leg.

"Well missus...I think we can come to some arrangement. Steady! I'll fall off this ladder."

Jenny paid no attention. She slid her hand into Fenton's crotch. "Heavens, what's this?" crooned the dizzy blonde voice, "Could this be the globbin shaft? Seems to be in excellent condition." She started to pull down Fenton's zip.

"Jenny, for God's sake..."

CHAPTER FOUR

The following morning brought yet more wind and rain and Fenton, who had harboured a lifelong hatred of wind, found his patience strained to the limit. "Will it never let up!" he growled as he opened the curtains to look on wet roofs and whirling chimney pots. "Another wrestling match with the bike."

Jenny was about to point out the merits of four wheeled transport but then thought better of it for there was no need, she reasoned. She looked at the black sky. Another couple of weeks of this and it could be a nice little Ford by the Spring.

Fenton arrived at the lab with water running off the front of his leathers like a mountain stream. The letter box in the heavy front door of the lab rattled in the wind as he stood in the outer hall peeling them off with hands that had gone numb with cold. He hung them up as best he could and opened the inner glass door, blowing his fingers in an attempt to restore circulation.

"And Jack the shepherd blows his nail..." said Ian Ferguson.

"Pardon?"

"Shakespeare," said Ferguson.

"Oh," said Fenton, following him into the common room where he found Alex Ross speaking to Mary Tyler.

Mary Tyler had previously been employed on a part time basis in the department but had been coerced back into working full time by Charles Tyson since the demise of Neil Munro and Susan Daniels. "Good morning Mary, back to getting up early in the morning eh?" Mary Tyler replied that, with three young children, she was always up early. Fenton poured himself some coffee and warmed his fingers on the mug.

Charles Tyson arrived, brushing the rain from the shoulders of his overcoat as he put his head round the common room door. He asked that Fenton go up to see him when he was ready. Fenton allowed Tyson enough time to reach his office and take off his wet things before joining him. He waited patiently while the consultant organised his papers and settled into the seat behind his desk. "It's about the Saxon report," said Tyson still rearranging piles of paper.

"I left it on your desk," said Fenton.

"The sterilizing records are missing from it."

"What sterilizing records?" asked Fenton.

"We have to include details of how we sterilised the plastic samplers for the machine."

"I didn't find any records among Neil's things."

"Damn. He must have been aware of the fact."

"Perhaps they are still down at the Sterile Supply Department?" suggested Fenton.

"Would you check and let me know?"

Fenton said that he would, adding that he was just about to go up to the administration block anyway. He would call in to see Sister Kincaid on his way back. "Nigel Saxon told me that they were confident of getting a license for their machine by the end of the month," he said.

"I heard that too," said Tyson. "And from the number of phone calls I've been getting from the Scottish Office about this damned report I don't think he is being overly optimistic. All the stops have been pulled out for Saxon.

"Friends in high places?"

Tyson grunted.

"It's funny when you think about it," said Fenton.

"What is?"

"The Scottish Office with their trouser legs rolled up."

Tyson smiled but did not say anything.

Fenton saw from a ground floor window that the rain had slackened off and decided to sprint up to the main hospital without changing out of his lab coat. He ran up the drive and took the stone steps three at a time to reach the shelter of the main entrance. A domestic, dressed in green overalls, was polishing a brass plaque set in the wood panelling, placed there in remembrance of some long forgotten names. The woman looked down at his feet and the muddy prints he had just made on the mosaic floor. "Sorry," he said. The woman shook her head and returned to her polishing without comment. A nurse was having an argument over laundry baskets with a porter as he passed along the main corridor.

"I'm telling you! Ward ten gets..." The voices trailed off behind Fenton and merged with new sounds, clangs from ward kitchens, children's yells, hurrying feet. He reached Jenny's ward just as she was crossing the corridor with a steel tray in her hand.

"What brings you out of your ivory tower?" she asked.

Fenton told her that he was on his way to the administration block to sort out some misunderstanding over service contracts taken out on lab equipment.

"What's the problem?" asked Jenny.

"Archaic equipment and no money to replace it."

"So what's new? Do you have time for a cup of tea?"

"A quick one."

Fenton was sipping his tea in the ward side room when a student nurse came in looking ashen faced. Jenny put down her cup and got to her feet. "What's the matter?" she asked.

Another nurse came into the room. "It's Belle Wilson," she said, "She's dead. I think she killed herself."

"The ward maid," said Jenny in answer to Fenton's look. They followed the second nurse next door to the sluice room where a small, middle aged woman, dressed in green overalls, was lying slumped over one of the large white porcelain sinks. Her eyes were wide and lifeless, her right arm dangled limply in the sink in a pool of red.

"She cut her wrist," said the nurse.

Jenny felt for a pulse in the woman's neck but knew that it was useless. She was quite dead.

Fenton stared at the marble white face under the crop of recently dyed red hair and thought that she looked like a clown lying over a theatrical basket.

"I'll phone the front office," said Jenny quietly.

Fenton was left alone in the room. He looked more closely at the woman's wrist. There was something odd about it. He looked even closer. The cut was not in her wrist at all. It was in the palm of her hand! He went to find the nurse who had discovered her and asked, "What was Belle Wilson doing before she cut herself?"

The nurse was taken aback, "I'm not sure," she stammered.

"Think!" said Fenton.

"Eer...eer...cleaning vases. Yes, I remember now. Staff Nurse asked her to wash out the flower vases."

"Where?" asked Fenton looking about him. "In here?"

"Next door," said the nurse, "In the broom cupboard."

"Show me."

Fenton followed the nurse into a small, dark, wood panelled room that smelt strongly of Lysol. His foot hit noisily off a metal bucket before the nurse had had time to find the light switch behind a forest of brush and mop handles. They saw the broken glass on the floor. Fenton knelt down to gather the pieces.

"She must have dropped one," said the nurse, still puzzled at Fenton's behaviour.

"Any more bits?" asked Fenton.

"There by the sink."

Fenton picked up a jagged piece of glass from the draining board and saw the red stains on it. He swore under his breath.

"I don't understand," said the nurse.

Belle Wilson cut herself accidentally on the broken vase and bled to death from a cut on her palm. She didn't deliberately cut her own wrist. She was murdered. She's another victim of that bloody lunatic."

Fenton found Jenny in the sluice room and told her what he had discovered. She approached the body and bent over the sink to examine the dead woman's hand. She could now see that, as Fenton had said, the river of red emanated from a deep wound on her palm, not her wrist. "Look at the blood in the sink," said Fenton.

"What about it?"

"It's still liquid. It hasn't clotted."

The police were on the scene quickly, being already on hospital premises with a mobile incident room that had been parked behind the administration block since the death of Neil Munro. Fenton called Tyson at the lab to say that he was going to be delayed and why. He was still on the telephone when Inspector Jamieson came into the duty room and found him there. He waited till Fenton had put down the receiver then continued to look at him without saying anything. Fenton could almost hear his mind working.

"Well, well, Mr Fenton," growled Jamieson, "A bit out of our way aren't we?"

"I was just passing," said Fenton limply.

It was another forty minutes before Fenton was allowed to leave the ward and continue on up to the management offices, an errand that he now had little patience for, knowing how far behind with his work he was slipping.

Fenton was waiting for a clerk to return with the relevant file when Nigel Saxon appeared at his elbow and read the frustration in his face. "Trouble old boy?"

Fenton told him what the problem was. Saxon was less than sympathetic. "I love hearing about problems with our competitors. Now, if you were to buy a Saxon Analyser..."

"This is the National Health Service," said Fenton by way of an answer.

"What on earth is going on?" asked Saxon noticing people scurrying about. Fenton told him.

"Another one? Dear God."

Fenton asked Saxon what he was doing there.

"Lunch with the health board, their way of saying thank-you for the disposables." said Saxon.

"Bon appetit," said Fenton.

The clerk returned with the service contract file and Fenton flicked through the pages to find the relevant section with Saxon looking over his shoulder. "Damnation," he said softly, "The company are right; there's a clause excluding the main transformer board. We'll have to pay."

Two orderlies were loading a sterilizer with goods taken from a metal trolley as Fenton entered the Central Sterile Supply Department. They lined up the heavy cage with the rails on the floor of the chamber and slid it slowly inside, taking care that nothing tumbled off. On the other side of the room three women, wearing white overalls and hair nets, were sifting through a massive pile of forceps, wrapping each pair individually and placing them in an assembly tray. Fenton walked over to them. "Sister Kincaid?"

"In her office," said one of the women, pointing with the instruments she held in her hand.

Moira Kincaid looked up from her desk as Fenton's shadow crossed the glass panel on her door. She motioned him to enter and asked to what she owed the honour of a visit. Fenton told her what he was looking for and got a positive reaction. "They are here," said Moira Kincaid. She opened her desk drawer and withdrew a pink cardboard folder. "I didn't know what was to happen to them but they are all in here."Fenton flicked through the papers and said, "This seems to be what's required."

"They are just simple record sheets of the sterilizing cycles used for Dr Munro's samplers. They are all the same, just the standard run."

"Pieces of paper to you and I Sister," said Fenton, "But a career to some others not a million miles from here." He was still angry about a contract exclusion that he felt the administrators should have picked up on at the time of signing. Through the glass panel he saw a porter come into the sterilizing bay and speak to one of the orderlies. Shortly afterwards the orderly burst into the office. "Have you heard Sister? There's been another murder!"

Moira Kincaid looked at Fenton who nodded and said, "A maid in ward twelve."

As he left the office and closed the door behind him Fenton heard a warning buzzer sound and the ventilation fans turn on. He paused to watch the orderlies he had seen earlier lower their face visors and pull on heavy gauntlets. They manoeuvred a trolley into position and the door to one of the autoclaves swung open letting steam fill the white tiled area like a Turkish bath before the fans started to deal with it. They locked their trolley on to the guide rails and pulled out the load cage, grunting with the effort as one of the wheels refused to engage properly. Fenton saw the number above the autoclave and realised that this was the sterilizer that had been used in Neil Munro's murder. He shivered involuntarily at the thought. Even with its huge mouth open and its insides empty the shiny steel cavern seemed full of menace. Just a machine, he reasoned. It had no mind of its own. It was only obeying orders but whose orders? That was the question.

Fenton walked out through the swing doors and climbed the stairs to ground level wondering just what it was about the Sterile Supply Department that he disliked so intensely. As he reached the top of the stairs he realised what it was; it didn't have any windows. It was situated in a basement and lit entirely by artificial light, white fluorescent light that made everyone look sickly pale.

Charles Tyson was taking news of the latest death badly. Fenton thought that he had never seen him look so ill and was very much aware of the change that had come over Tyson since the start of the killings; the man had aged quite visibly. The pastel shirts that he favoured now seemed several collar sizes too large and a universal greyness had descended on him, making even the stubble shadow on his face seem grey against the winter pallor of his skin. Fenton had begun to wonder whether or not the strain was the only reason for the change or whether there might be some underlying clinical reason for it.

Fenton respected Tyson. He did not know if he liked him for the truth was that he hardly knew the man. He doubted whether anyone did for Tyson was a very private person. As head of department he was excellent but that was the only role anyone had ever seen him play. Neil Munro had told him once that Tyson had served in the army and had seen active service in Korea but that and the fact that he was not married was about the sum total of his knowledge of the man.

"Seems fine," said Tyson looking through the folder that Fenton had brought him. Fenton told him about the problem with the service contract. "How much is it going to cost?"

"Seven hundred pounds."

"All because somebody in the office didn't read the small print. This will practically wipe out all the benefit the hospital gained from the free supply of plastic disposables from Saxon Medical," said Tyson shaking his head.

"You could kick up hell at the next board meeting," said Fenton.

Tyson shook his head again and said, "No, they would only close ranks. Besides I don't want to antagonise the management at the moment. I was thinking of trying for one of these new analysers for the lab. Rumour has it that there's some charity money up for grabs."

"What are the chances?" asked Fenton.

"Who knows? Actually, I was thinking it might strengthen our case if we could reuse the plastic samplers. They work out quite expensive if we have to throw them away each time."

"I could run some tests," suggested Fenton.

"You have enough on your plate at the moment," said Tyson.

"It shouldn't take long," said Fenton I could get the lab staff to volunteer a few drops of blood, run the samples through the analyser, autoclave the samplers a few times then re-run the samples. Compare the values before and after sterilizing?"

"If you really think you could manage?" said Tyson thoughtfully.

"No problem," said Fenton.

It was late in the afternoon, as Fenton was trying to cajole Mary Tyler into providing a blood sample for the new tests, that Nigel Saxon came into the lab to collect a copy of the final report on the Blood Analyser. "Don't give into him Mary whatever he's after," joked Saxon. "Now, if you would care to have dinner with me this evening..."

"I'm a respectable married woman," protested Mary Tyler.

"They're always the worst," grinned Saxon.

"As you are here Nigel..." said Fenton in a tone of voice that put Saxon on the defensive."What are you after?" he asked suspiciously.

"Your blood," said Fenton. "Quite literally." He told Saxon that he was collecting blood samples from 'volunteers' to run some new tests on the Saxon Analyser. It could even lead to a sale, he confided. Saxon agreed as did Mary Tyler, Ian Ferguson, Alex Ross and four of the others.

"When?" asked Saxon.

"Before you leave if that's all right?" said Fenton. Saxon said that it was but seemed a bit dubious about the whole business. He came back after collecting the report from Charles Tyson and was led into a small side room by Fenton. "Slip off your jacket and roll up your sleeve." Saxon did as he was bid and sat down with his arms on the table in front of him. He looked nervous.

Fenton finished rummaging in a drawer and joined Saxon at the table holding a piece of rubber tubing in his hand. "I'll just wrap this around your upper arm," he said. "Perhaps you could hold it there?" Saxon reached across and held the tubing in place while Fenton slapped the inside of his arm to make the veins stand out. He slipped a sterile needle on to the end of a disposable ten ml. syringe, swabbed the exposed area of Saxon's arm with an alcohol impregnated swab and pushed the needle smoothly into the vein. Dark red blood flooded into the syringe until it had reached the ten ml. mark then Fenton withdrew it and pressed another alcohol impregnated swab over the site of entry. "Just hold that there for a moment," he said to Saxon.

With the sample safely in its container and the container in the fridge Fenton held Saxon's jacket for him while he put it back on. Saxon said, "I hope my father appreciates what I do for our company!"

He suffixed the remark with a loud laugh but Fenton noticed the beads of sweat along Saxon's forehead. He really had been afraid. It was nearly a quarter past seven when Fenton finally got through with his day's work. Thinking that he was the last one left in the lab he was surprised to see a light on under one of the doors when he came downstairs. It made him feel a little uneasy. He crossed the hall quietly and listened outside the door for a few seconds. There was no sound from inside. He opened the door cautiously and looked in startling Alex Ross who had been sitting writing. "Good God, you nearly gave me a heart attack," said Ross.

"Sorry. You're here late this evening."

"The monthly accounts," said Ross. "I didn't have time during the day."

"Fancy a drink?"

"Good idea," said Ross, putting down his pen and rubbing his eyes. "I've had quite enough for one day."

The two men walked the short distance to the Thistle Arms and joined the early evening drinkers. It was a grimy little pub that relied much more on the custom of regulars than passing trade. Little or no concession had been made to decor and it remained essentially a Scottish man's pub, a place where still the presence of a woman would be frowned upon. The solid Victorian bar counter was highly polished but bore the scars of countless generations of carelessly stubbed cigarettes while the floor was covered in linoleum that had once been green but was now an indeterminate dark shade under the dim, inadequate lighting.

Several solitary drinkers sat at tables along a wall, their faces bearing tell tale signs of a life that had been none too kind; escape lay in the amber fluid in front of them. A few small groups chatted at the bar, men on their way home, some still carrying the badges of their trade. A railway guard in his gendarme's cap, a security guard with his hat moulded to suggest that he was really Burt Lancaster in Submarine Alley, an insurance agent in grubby raincoat with battered briefcase. A noisy group of students sat in the corner, savouring the haunts of the working man but retaining their university scarves as an insurance of distance.

The two barmen were of the old school, spotless white aprons and hands that were never idle, constantly wiping imaginary spillages from the counter, eyeing the levels in the glasses along the bar, anticipating where the next order would come from. The smaller of the two, narrow shouldered and bespectacled, looked up as Ross and Fenton approached. "Still cold outside?" he asked.

"Freezing," said Ross. He ordered whisky for them both.

As they stood at the bar Fenton ran his eye along the gantry noting that nearly all the space was taken up by whisky, a good range of single malts and nearly every known blended variety. Other spirits were represented by solitary bottles. The contents of the glasses along the counter reflected the stock on the gantry, and probably constituted the reason for it, with the traditional 'half and a pint' clearly to the fore. He took comfort from the fact that some things never seemed to change. It might be a sociologist's nightmare but in certain places in Scotland drinking remained a man's game.

Ross threw back his head and drained his glass, declining Fenton's offer of a second drink and pleading 'hell from the wife' as a legitimate excuse. Fenton wished him good night and ordered another for himself. The barman handed him a copy of the evening paper to look at and said that Rangers had bought another English player.

"Really?" said Fenton, not having any interest in football but feeling obliged to display some reaction.

"Not that it will do them any good," said another man at the bar, taking the strain off Fenton and diverting the barman's attention.

Fenton drank up his beer and went to the lavatory. It was a dingy, brick-built cellar that had been painted so many times that the grouting between the bricks had all but disappeared. Rust clung to the pipe work and old iron cisterns fixed to the wall above the urinal. He stood there, head tilted to one side to read the graffiti and heard the door open behind him. But no one joined him at the wall.

Feeling more comfortable Fenton zipped his fly and turned round to find two men standing there, they were looking straight at him. The older of the two, a thickset man wearing leather jacket and jeans came towards him, the other remained leaning against the exit door. Without saying anything the first man swung his fist into Fenton's stomach with a power that suggested he might once have done it for a living. Fenton's eyes opened wide as he doubled over but only in time to meet the boot that was directed up into his face. His cheek bone shattered in a haze of pain.

The whole affair seemed to be being conducted in absolute silence, no jeers, no insults, no words, just the cold, professional application of pain. The boot swung in again, this time into Fenton's ribs, overloading his appreciation of agony; he felt consciousness slip away from him. The frustration of not even being able to protest vied with the pain for his receding attention as he slid slowly down the wall, feeling the porcelain of the urinal cold against his cheek before his face finally came to rest in the gutter at the bottom. The stench that filled his nostrils made him vomit weakly, adding to the cocktail of blood and urine. The boot thudded into him again but it was by now a long way from Fenton who had drifted off into oblivion.

Fenton emerged sporadically from the darkness to snatch an occasional sight or sound, a flashing blue light was reflected in glass somewhere, rain drops caressed his forehead, a hand touched him gently. There was a moustache...a cap...a siren that never faded into the distance, search light beams on a low ceiling, voices, but far away...very far away.

Fenton surfaced from the blackness and opened his eyes to find everything still and bright. He stared upwards till the object he had elected to focus his attention on resolved itself into a light fitting. There were dead flies in it. He took a deep breath and, in doing so, attracted the attention of a nurse who now saw that his eyes were open. Her voice was soft and gentle. "So you're back with us," she said

Fenton opened his mouth to ask where he was and a flight of burning arrows tore into his cheek. His gasp brought a gentle chide from the nurse; the soft voice said, "Lie still...rest...don't try to speak."

Three days had passed before Fenton could sit up and concern himself with the more humdrum matters of life like the itch that persisted inside the heavy strapping on his ribs, the whereabouts of his motor bike, his jacket, the unpaid electricity bill in the pocket. He attempted to smile when Jenny came to see him but immediately wished that he had not when his broken cheek bone did not see the funny side of things. He had been able to give the police good descriptions of his attackers but no clue as to motive. It had been just a mindless act of violence.

The novelty of grapes, Lucozade and get well soon cards began to wear thin after a couple of days; Fenton was now well enough to feel bored stiff and said so with increasing frequency to the nursing staff who, had heard it all before. But his persistent badgering paid off on Friday when he was allowed to go home by taxi after promising to take things easy. He was just in time to see Jenny's brother Grant who was on the point of leaving for home with his son Jamie who was wearing a patch over one eye. Fenton asked how the boy had got on at the hospital.

"The surgeons decided that they should delay operating until he's a little older, maybe next year." said Grant.

Fenton looked down at the little boy who was staring up at the plasters on Fenton's face. It was as if they both suddenly realised that they had a lot in common and an instant rapport was struck. Fenton bent down and asked the boy about the toy fire engine that he was carrying.

Grant looked at his watch and announced that he and Jamie would have to be off. He thanked Jenny and shook Fenton's hand before ushering Jamie out the door.

Jenny closed the door and looked at Fenton. "You should still be in hospital," she accused.

Fenton smiled and said, "It's good to be home."

Jenny kissed him. "It's good having you home."

By the following Wednesday Fenton was climbing the wall with boredom. Still confined to the flat he made endless cups of tea, pacing up and down between times with occasional pauses to look out at the rain. He telephoned Charles Tyson at the lab to be told that he was out at a meeting. He did speak to Ian Ferguson for a while but ran out of things to say after being assured that the lab was coping well despite his absence.

In mid- afternoon Fenton answered a ring of the door-bell to find Nigel Saxon standing there.

"How's the invalid?" asked Saxon.

The conversation, as most conversations involving Saxon usually did, degenerated into talk of women, cars and booze but it did cheer Fenton up and made him smile for the first time in days. In addition Saxon announced that he was giving a dinner party for everyone in the lab to celebrate the successful conclusion to trials on the Saxon Analyser.

"When?" asked Fenton.

"Saturday evening."

"Where?"

"The Grange Hotel. It's not too far from the lab so the duty staff will be within bleeper range and can flit back and forth if necessary.

Jenny arrived home with the news that she would be going on night duty after the week end. "But I'm off all this week end," she added in response to Fenton's expression.

"Good, then we can go to the party." said Fenton. He told her about Saxon's invitation.

On Friday morning Fenton visited his general practitioner to be declared fit to return to work. Having had no need of a doctor in the past year he had neglected to re-register with a practitioner nearer his home and so had to cross town to the doctor he had originally been listed with when he had first arrived in the city.

Was this really the system envied by the world? he wondered as he sat in a crowded room surrounded by peeling wall paper and coughing people. The windows hadn't been cleaned for decades by the look of them and there was a strong smell of cats' urine about the place. Three back copies of Punch, a two minute consultation and he was free of the system but not the despondency it inspired.

The return bus took an age to cross town and Fenton had to keep clearing the window with his sleeve to see where he was for the atmosphere on the top deck was heavy and damp and reeked of stale cigarette smoke. A fat woman, weighed down with shopping bags plumped herself down beside him, her face glowing with the exertion of having climbed the stairs. The smell of sweat mingling with the tobacco proved to be the last straw for Fenton. He got off at the next stop and walked through the rain; he was soaked to the skin by the time he reached the flat.

CHAPTER FIVE

The party at the Grange Hotel was a disaster. But then, as Fenton reasoned afterwards, it was always going to be in the circumstances. Their host, Nigel Saxon, tried his best to foster a spirit of light-heartedness and jollity and the generosity of the company in terms of food and drink could not be faulted but Neil Munro and Susan Daniels were just too conspicuous by their absence. In addition the knowledge that the killer had not yet been identified was still uppermost in most peoples' minds. Pulling together and presenting a common front in times of adversity was all very well when you were certain of your neighbours but when it was possible that the murderer might be sitting at the same table introversion and circumspection became the order of the day.

Alex Ross was the exception to the rule. He drank too much whisky and, to his wife's obvious embarrassment, had quite a lot to say for himself. Jenny, whom Ross was very fond of, did her best to humour him and tried to prevent him becoming too loud in his opinions by diverting his attention to other matters. Ross' wife Morag, a woman of large physical presence and wearing for the occasion a purple dress smothered in sequins and a matching hat which she kept on throughout the dinner, tried to minimise the damage to her pride by smiling broadly at everyone in turn and asking where they planned to spend their summer holidays.

Ross eventually grew wise to Jenny's intervention and decided to bait Nigel Saxon about the speed with which Saxon Medical had obtained official approval for their product. For the first time since he had met him Fenton saw Nigel Saxon lose his good humour. Ross, despite his inebriation sensed it too and was inspired to greater efforts. He said loudly, "If you ask me the funny handshake brigade were involved!"

There was uneasy laughter and Jenny leaned across to Fenton to ask what he meant.

"Free masonry," whispered Fenton in reply.

Saxon managed a smile too but Ross was still intent on goading him. "Or maybe it wasn't," he said conspiratorially, "They're too busy running the police force!"

There was more laughter but then Ross suddenly added. "I think it was more like the Tree Mob."

Fenton had no idea what Ross meant and gathered that many other people were in the same boat but it certainly meant something to Saxon for the colour drained from his face and his hands shook slightly as they rested on the table. "I think you have said enough Mr Ross!" he whispered through gritted teeth.

Jenny and Fenton were mesmerised by the change that had come over Saxon and a complete silence came over the table before Ross who like many drunks seemed absolutely amazed that he had managed to offend anyone said loudly, "What's the matter? It was only a wee joke man."

Ian Ferguson quickly stepped in to defuse the situation by getting to his feet and saying, I've no idea what this is all about but I'm going to have some more wine. Anyone else?"

Glasses were proffered and the moment passed.

"A fun evening," whispered Jenny in Fenton's ear.

"We'll go soon," Fenton promised.

As the table was cleared Jenny was engaged in conversation by Liz Scott the lab secretary and Fenton found himself standing beside Ian Ferguson.

"Have you had any more thoughts about the stuff we found in Neil's cupboard?" asked Ferguson quietly.

Fenton shook his head and said, "No. You?"

"No, but it's worrying me," said Ferguson.

"In what way?" asked Fenton

"I think we should have told someone."

"Who?"

"You know, someone in authority, the police."

"Why?" asked Fenton, knowing full well that he was being obtuse but perversely wanting to hear his own fears expressed by somebody else.

"We know that the killer is using anticoagulants and we know that Neil Munro had a whole cupboard full of them hidden away in his lab."

"Neil couldn't have been the killer."

"I know that but it's an uncomfortable coincidence don't you think?"

Fenton didn't get a chance to reply for they were joined by Charles Tyson and Nigel Saxon who asked them if they were having a good time. He held up a bottle of whisky in front of them. Fenton declined but Ferguson offered his glass to have it topped up.

"Dr Tyson tells me you are on duty on Sunday morning Ian is that right?" asked Saxon.

"All too true I'm afraid. Why do you ask?"

"I have to dismantle the Saxon analyser some time in the afternoon. I wondered if you might be willing to stay on to give me a hand?"

Ferguson made an apologetic gesture. "If only you'd said sooner," he said. "But I've arranged to meet my girlfriend in the afternoon. Maybe I could put her off if I..."

"I'll do it," interrupted Fenton.

"You're sure?" asked Saxon.

"Of course. I've been idle for so long it'll be a pleasure."

"Well, if you're quite certain..."

Fenton arranged to be at the lab by two o'clock on Sunday afternoon.

On the way home Jenny asked Fenton, "What did Alex Ross mean by the 'Tree Mob'?"

"I've no idea," replied Fenton.

"Charles Tyson knew," said Jenny. "I read it in his face."

Nigel Saxon was waiting outside the lab when Fenton arrived on Sunday afternoon. He was stamping his feet and throwing his arms across his chest to keep warm as he patrolled the kerb near his parked car.

"Not late am I?" asked Fenton, checking his watch to find out it had just gone two.

"Not at all," smiled Saxon. "I'm grateful to you for helping out. The company is a bit short of demo models and this one has to be shown at Glasgow Royal tomorrow. You can have it back afterwards for a few more days."

The two men set about dismantling the Saxon Analyser with Saxon concentrating on the hardware and Fenton disassembling the supply lines and removing the reagent reservoirs. Fenton came to a blue plastic container among the tubing and asked Saxon what it was.

"Be careful with that," warned Saxon. "It's the acid sump."

"I'll get rid of it down the drain in the fume cupboard," said Fenton disconnecting the blue cylinder from its manifold and removing it carefully.

Saxon said, "I'm just going to nip out to the car for a moment to get my socket set."

The door banged behind Saxon and Fenton carried the blue container slowly across the lab to the fume cupboard to place it inside the chamber. He turned on the fan motor and heard the extractor whine into life. The fan would suck any toxic fumes up through a flu and vent them to the outside through an aluminium stack on the roof of the building.

Fenton had unscrewed the cap of the acid bottle and was about to start pouring the contents down the drain when suddenly he froze. There was a bottle of benzene sitting inside the cupboard and he realised that he could smell it! He could smell benzene!

How could that be? he asked himself. The bottle was on the other side of the glass screen and the fan was running. How could the fumes escape? He put the cap back on the acid container and took a few steps backward. Everything looked and sounded normal but there was something very wrong. He lit a piece of scrap paper in a Bunsen burner and held it to the mouth of the fume cupboard. The flame did not flicker. The extractor fan was running but there was absolutely no air movement through the flu. As a safety device it was totally useless.

Puzzled as to what the fault could be Fenton brought some step ladders across to the fume cupboard and climbed up to inspect the motor housing. It seemed in good condition. He then moved on to the filter block in the chimney stack and found the source of the problem. The fire damper had closed. Fire dampers were fitted as a safety measure to fume cupboards. In the event of a fire in the lab they isolated the chamber and prevented flames from reaching highly volatile chemicals via the flu. In this case the damper had apparently closed of its own accord and rendered the fan ineffectual.

The satisfaction that Fenton felt at discovering the cause of the problem was immediately replaced by distinct unease when he saw why the damper had closed. The retaining clips were missing. He searched the area at the base of the filter block but failed to find them. There was a chance that they had snapped and fallen down inside the flu but there was also a possibility that they had been removed deliberately.

Fenton came down the ladders and rested his foot on the bottom rung for a moment while his mind raced to find a motive for sabotaging the fume cupboard. After all nothing drastic would have happened if he had gone ahead and poured the acid down the drain - an unpleasant whiff of acid fumes perhaps but nothing too serious unless . . .

Fenton's gaze fell on the drain he been about to pour the acid down and a dark thought crossed his mind like a cloud across the moon. Wondering if paranoia were getting the better of him. He squatted down and examined the pipe leading down from the drain. He was looking for signs of recent dismantling. He failed to find any but remained uneasy. He had to know for sure. He fetched a spanner from the lab tool box and undid the coupling at the head of the bend. Gently he slid out the curved section of pipe and looked inside. His fingers were shaking slightly as he saw signs of a chemical lying in the trap. Cautiously he sniffed the end of the pipe and recognised the smell. It was potassium cyanide!

If he had poured acid down the drain on top of cyanide crystals when the extractor was non-functional the whole lab would have been filled with hydrocyanic gas within seconds and everyone in it would have died.

Everyone in it? thought Fenton. He was the only one in it and where was Saxon? He had been gone for ages.

Nigel Saxon came in to the lab carrying a tool box. "Couldn't find the damn thing. It was under the back seat."

"Really?" said Fenton looking Saxon straight in the eye.

"Good God. What's happened?" asked Saxon as he caught sight of Fenton's face. "You look as if you've seen a ghost."

"There's something wrong with the fume cupboard," said Fenton.

"Is that all?" asked a puzzled Saxon.

"There are cyanide crystals in the drain."

"You mean the drain is blocked?"

Fenton stared at Saxon for a full thirty seconds before saying, "If I had poured acid down it..."

Saxon shook his head and said apologetically, "I'm sorry. I'm not a chemist. What are you trying to say?"

Fenton was desperately trying to appraise Saxon's behaviour. He seemed genuine enough. But did he really not know what the consequences would have been? Had it really been coincidence that Saxon had chosen that particular moment to be out of the room?

Fenton's head was reeling. Had someone really tried to kill him? He searched desperately for another explanation but all he found was a new suspicion. He faced the possibility that the incident in the pub had been no accident either, no act of mindless violence as the police had called it. It appeared that someone wanted him out of the way and whether it was temporary or more permanent did not much seem to matter. But why? Whoever it was must think that he knew more than he did. How ironic if he were to end up being killed for something he never knew in the first place.

The flat was empty when Fenton got in for Jenny had gone to visit some of her old flat mates. But Fenton was glad of the time it gave him to calm down. His hands still shook a little and his insides still felt hollow but a stiff whisky helped fight the symptoms and prepared him to confide in Jenny when she did come in.

"But why?" exclaimed Jenny when Fenton told her.

"I keep telling you I don't know," maintained Fenton.

"Who knew you would be in the lab today?" Jenny asked.

"Lots of people. We discussed it at the dinner party the other night."

"So it has to be one of the lab staff?"

"Or Saxon," said Fenton. "He picked that very moment to disappear."

"What about when he came back?" asked Jenny. "Did he look guilty?"

"No," conceded Fenton.

"What other possibilities are there?"

"I suppose it is just possible that the damper failed for some technical reason.

"And the cyanide crystals?"

"Coincidence? We use cyanide a lot."

"I think I prefer that notion," said Jenny.

Fenton preferred it too. He just did not believe it.

Jenny was still sleeping when he left for work next morning. She had not stirred when he kissed her so Fenton tip-toed out of the room, taking great pains to close the door quietly behind him.

It felt good to be back on the bike again although his ribs still hurt when anything more than light pressure was required on the handlebars. He gunned it up the outside of a long queue of cars in Lothian Road and joined the leading one at the traffic lights. They changed and Fenton was just a memory to its driver before the man had had time to engage first gear.

Charles Tyson arrived in the car park at the rear of the lab as Fenton was heaving the Honda on to its stand. They exchanged pleasantries and walked into the lab together. There were two engineers from the hospital works department working on the fume cupboard and Tyson paused to ask what was wrong. He asked Ian Ferguson but it was Fenton who answered. "It broke down yesterday," he said.

By ten o'clock Fenton felt as if he had never been away for, within minutes of sitting down at his desk he had picked up the threads and was back in the old routine. Hospital biochemistry kept him fully occupied until Wednesday when he found some time to chase up those who had volunteered to give blood for the Analyser tests. Charles Tyson was the last on the list. Fenton withdrew the blood, ejected the sample into two plastic tubes and took them along to his lab. He brought out the relevant rack from the fridge and placed Tyson's samples in the last two holes. He now had the required number of samples to begin the tests.

As he made to put the rack back in the fridge he noticed something odd about Tyson's specimen in the second tube. It hadn't clotted. He withdrew both tubes and shook them gently, one should have remained quite fluid for the test tube had anti-coagulant in it but the other contained nothing save for the blood. It should have clotted. Fenton looked at his watch and saw that ten minutes had passed since he had taken the sample. Far too long! He raced along the corridor and burst into Tyson's room, getting a startled look from both Tyson and Liz Scott who was taking dictation. "Your blood isn't clotting," he blurted out.

Tyson looked at the inside of his arm and said, "It isn't bleeding. It stopped normally." Fenton still looked doubtful. Tyson said, "Probably a dirty tube...but just to make sure, pass me a scalpel blade will you."

Fenton opened a glass fronted cabinet and removed a small packet wrapped in silver foil. He handed it to Tyson. Liz Scott screwed up her face and said, "What on earth..." as Tyson slit through the skin of his index finger and watched the blood well up. He dabbed it away with the clean swab that Fenton handed to him and checked his watch. Fenton and Liz Scott watched in silence as Tyson continued to dab blood away. At length he said, "There, it's stopping. See? Quite normal."

Fenton let out a sigh of relief and said, "Thank God, I thought for a moment that you were number five." Now able to think of more mundane matters he realised that he was short of one blood sample and said so.

"Perhaps Liz?" Tyson suggested, turning to look at the secretary who screwed up her face before agreeing with more than a little reluctance. "I hate needles," she said as she rolled up the sleeve of her blouse.

"Look up," said Fenton, before inserting the needle smoothly into the vein and drawing back the plunger. "There now, that didn't hurt did it?" Liz Scott agreed that it hadn't. "Just hold the swab there for a minute or so," said Fenton placing the gauze over the puncture mark, "then you can roll down your sleeve."

Fenton brought the tubes back to his lab and held them up to the window. One of them remained fluid while the other was clotting normally. He put them in the fridge to wait with the others until later. He would run them through the Analyser in the evening when everyone had gone and Jenny had started her shift on night duty.

Fenton came downstairs to the main lab to see what lay in store for him and read through the request forms from the wards. "I don't believe it," he said out loud as yet another request for a lead count appeared in the lists. "Twelve...fourteen...sixteen bloods for lead! What's going on?"

Alex Ross gave a thin smile and said, "You've got Councillor Vanney to thank for that."

"Vanney?"

"He's been opposing an extension to the ring road; his latest tack is to scaremonger about lead pollution from car exhausts if the new road goes ahead. You know the sort of thing; IQ will drop by fifty points if you walk too near a Volkswagen Polo. He's been calling for the screening of all children living near the first stage of the road."

"What's his real reason?"

"The more cynical among us might suggest that the new road would screw up a development of luxury flats that Vanney and Sons are building on the south side."

"Turd."

"He's a powerful turd." said Ross.

"Who are the 'Tree Mob' Alex?"

Ross was taken by surprise at the suddenness of Fenton's question. What was more, he seemed to Fenton to visibly stiffen. "What made you ask that?" he stammered.

"The other night at the party you suggested that Saxon Medical had got special treatment because of the 'Tree Mob.' Who are they?"

Ross put his hands to his forehead and said quietly, "One day my big mouth will be the death of me."

"I don't understand," said Fenton.

"I've said too much already," said Ross.

"You can't leave me hanging," Fenton protested.

Ross looked doubtful then took a deep breath and said, "There's an organisation called the Cavalier Club which is currently trendy with the establishment. Their emblem is an oak tree. It's supposed to represent the tree that King Charles hid up when he was hiding from the roundheads.

"But what has that got to do with Saxon getting preferential treatment from the Department of Health?"

"There are a lot of powerful people in the club. They scratch each others' backs and what's more, they consider themselves to be above the law. Rumour has it their influence is growing all the time."

"But a club?" protested Fenton.

"More a society really."

"If you say so," said Fenton. "How come I haven't heard of it?"

"You were in Africa for a long while."

Fenton found it hard to believe what Ross had told him but one thing stopped him from saying so. He had remembered that the medallion that had fallen from Nigel Saxon's pocket in the car park had had a tree motif on it. He said nothing to Ross.

Fenton nursed his dislike for politicians all through the procedure for lead estimation for it was the least popular test in the lab. True to form his hands got covered in blood; they always did with lead tests. He was washing them for the umpteenth time when the phone rang and Ian Ferguson said, "Tom, it's Jenny."

Fenton finished drying his hands and took the receiver. "Don't tell me," he joked, "You just called to say you loved me?" The smile died on his face when he heard Jenny sobbing. "What's wrong? What's the matter?"

"I'm at the police station..." said Jenny before she broke down again."They're holding me..."

Fenton couldn't believe his ears. "Holding you? What are you talking about? You're not making sense."

"The murders, the police think I did them."

Fenton was reduced to spluttering incredulity. "Is this some kind of joke? What are you talking about? How can they possibly think you did them?" He heard Jenny take a few deep breaths in an attempt to calm herself, then she said, "My brother Grant's boy, Jamie, you remember, the one who was down in Edinburgh? He's dead. He bled to death! Oh Tom, I'm scared. Please come."

The phone went dead before Fenton could reply; he clattered the receiver down on its rest then snatched it up again and called Jamieson.

"Nurse Buchan is at present helping us with our inquiries Mr Fenton," said the gruff voice at the other end of the phone.

"Come on man! I'm not the bloody press. What's going on?"

"I am afraid I have nothing to add sir," said Jamieson.

"Well, can I see her?"

"No you can't."

"Is brain death a prerequisite for the Police Force?" snarled Fenton.

"I must warn you sir that..."

Fenton slammed down the receiver. His immediate thought was to rush round to the police station and demand to see Jenny but the fact that he was in the middle of the lead tests prevented him from doing something, which he realised after a few minutes thought, would have been pointless. The police would not be impressed by histrionics. What Jenny needed was expert help, the help a lawyer could give. He went to speak to Tyson.

Charles Tyson was as shocked as Fenton had been when he heard the news.

"Jenny needs a lawyer," said Fenton "I wondered if perhaps you could recommend anyone?"

"Of course," said Tyson, opening his address book. "Phone this firm." He copied down a name and a telephone number on to a piece of scrap paper and handed it to Fenton. Fenton thanked him and said that he would keep him informed of developments. He returned to his own lab and dialled the number. They would send someone round to the police station.

Fenton found that lack of information was the main obstacle to his coming to terms with the situation. Jenny had said that Jamie was dead but he had to know more, he had to find out when, where and how and that might be difficult in the circumstances. The circumstances were that Fenton's contacts with Jenny's family were few and far between...and not that cordial. Her sisters-in-law regarded Jenny as something of a scarlet woman for living in sin, as they saw it. Her brothers, although a little more tolerant of the situation than their wives, did not have much time for a man who did not work with his hands and, therefore, did not conform to their notion of what a real man should be. He had detected a certain coolness in Grant Buchan when he had met him briefly the week before. But there was no alternative, Fenton decided. He would have to phone the Buchans; the number would be in Jenny's address book in the flat.

Fenton grounded the near-side foot rest as he swung the Honda out of the hospital grounds and on to the main road. The lurch from the machine served as a timely warning to him that he would be no good to Jenny dead. He forcible restrained himself and bit the bullet at every set of traffic lights.

The phone seemed to ring for ages before a woman with a strong north-east accent answered and Fenton said who he was. There was a silence then the receiver was put down, but not on its rest, on a wooden table by the sound of it, thought Fenton. A few moment later a man said, "Yes, what is it?"

Fenton recognised the voice as that of Grant Buchan. "Grant? I'm phoning to say how desperately sorry I am about Jamie. But something awful has now happened down here. They're holding Jenny in connection with Jamie's death!"

The expected outburst did not happen. Instead, Buchan said, "I see."

"What do you mean, you see?" Fenton exploded. "Did you hear what I said? The police are holding Jenny! They think she had something to do with Jamie's death!"

Buchan was unmoved by Fenton's outburst. He sounded as if he was under some kind of sedation as he said, "My boy cut himself playing down by the harbour. By the time he had covered fifty yards he was dead, every drop of his blood was on the stones, I can still see it in the cracks, it won't wash away.

Fenton felt the man's agony, he rubbed his hand on his forehead and said softly, "I'm sorry, believe me, I know what it's like to lose a child, but you must see that some awful mistake has been made. No one in their right mind could think that Jenny was a murderer."

After a long pause Buchan said, "No but my son died because his blood wouldn't clot. He had been poisoned with anti...anti..."

"Anti-coagulants."

"Anti-coagulants. The method used by the Princess Mary Slayer."

Fenton winced at the tabloid jargon.

Buchan continued, "My laddie was never anywhere near the Princess Mary Hospital but Jenny works there and we stayed with Jenny when we were in Edinburgh."

"You can't seriously believe that Jenny had anything to do..." Fenton broke off in mid-sentence. "It's crazy!" he protested. "The thought of Jenny being involved is just too ridiculous for words!"

"People get sick some time...sick in their heads."

"No way," said Fenton decisively. "Jenny is not sick. Jenny is the sweetest, nicest, sanest person who ever lived. She did not kill Jamie; she did not kill anyone else. Let's get that straight!"

There was silence from Buchan.

Fenton was filled with the frustration. "Look Grant," he said, "We can't talk properly over the phone, I'm coming up there."

"I don't think that's a very good idea..." began Buchan.

"I'm coming," said Fenton and put the phone down. He thought for a moment before picking it up again and dialling the lawyer's office. Yes, their Mr Bainbridge was still at the police station and no, they did not have any further information.

Fenton paced up and down the flat like a caged tiger, he opened the drinks cupboard then closed it again without taking anything out.That wasn't what he needed. He opened another cupboard and took out his running shoes.

The pavements were wet but the wind had dropped as Fenton pounded out the first mile at a pace designed to replace tension with physical pain. Every time he found his mind straying to thoughts of the police or Grant Buchan he would lengthen his stride till the surge of anger was quelled inside him. By the end of the third mile his mind was calm and he had become more relaxed. He slowed to an easy jog and thought about what he was going to do.

He had told Grant Buchan that he was coming up to Morayshire but was that really the right thing to do? he wondered. What good could come of it? What could he hope to find out? A sudden gust of wind caught the bare branches of the trees above him and made giant raindrops fall like diamonds under the street lights. Several hit him on the face making him wipe them away with the back of his hand. He moved off the pavement to avoid running directly beneath them. The answer! That was what he could hope to find out. Jamie Buchan's death must hold the key to the whole affair. There must be a link between Jamie and the Princess Mary. The police thought that Jenny was that link but he knew that she was not. Find it and he would have the answer to the whole nightmare. The sweat was trickling freely down his neck as he turned for home.

Fenton lay awake in the darkness watching the reflection of raindrops on the ceiling of the bedroom. The run had pleasantly stretched his muscles and the bath had relaxed him but the flat was so empty and lonely without Jenny. Where was she now? What were they doing to her? The police would not give out anything other than the clockwork statement that they were still holding her. Sleep was out of the question and he still had a long night ahead of him before travelling north... But did he? Fenton saw the alternative. He could leave right away! If he rode through the night he could be there by morning. That would be better than lying brooding in the darkness. He dressed quickly, donned his leathers, and collected a few odds and ends and tip-toed downstairs to rock the Honda off its stand.

Fenton kept the revs to a minimum as he turned in and out of the streets of Comely Bank at two in the morning for he had no wish to disturb the sleeping citizenry. He pulled out on to the main Queensferry road and headed for the Forth Bridge and the motorway.

Fenton closed the throttle for the first time to negotiate the toll barrier at the South end of the bridge. The man in the booth raised the boom without comment while high up on top of the main towers red lights flashed at intervals to warn aircraft of their presence. Far below lay the dark waters of the Forth.

Fenton could feel the temperature dropping as reached the north shore and entered Fife. The wind sought out every weakness in his clothing as he pointed the Honda towards Perthshire.

An alarming numbness in his hands brought him to a halt at a service station at the head of the M9 motorway which spilled out inviting yellow light on to the wet tarmac. He went directly to the men's room and filled up a basin with warm water, resting his hands in it as it filled. He cupped them and bathed his face slowly, gasping involuntarily as the warm water soothed his raw skin.

"It's no' much o' a night fur the bike," said a lorry driver behind him, noting Fenton's leathers.

"You're right," said Fenton, continuing his love affair with the basin.

"They're a'right in summer they things," said the man.

Fenton grunted in reply and began to dab his face dry with a succession of coarse paper towels. He caught a glimpse in the mirror of his companion, short, round and dressed in green bib overalls with a company logo which he failed to read backwards.

A largely one sided conversation continued over tea and bacon sandwiches, the driver having followed Fenton to the table and sat down beside him. In the circumstances it had seemed the natural thing for him to do for they were the only two customers in the place.

They both turned to look out of the window as an articulated lorry lumbered into the car park outside. The arrival of new custom prompted the man behind the counter to turn on the juke box and fill the place with electric noise. The bass notes made the salt cellar vibrate on the red Formica table.

CHAPTER SIX

The grey morning light was highlighting the white tops of the waves as Fenton reached Buchan Ness and stopped to rest his aching limbs. He coaxed the Honda off the winding road and paddled it with his feet over a stretch of shingle to lean it against the petrified stump of some long dead tree. It made contracting metal sounds as he walked stiffly over the scree to reach the water's edge and stretch his arms up to the colourless sky. He picked up a handful of pebbles and threw them aimlessly into the rough water as seagulls screamed overhead in protest against the intruder. It was a cold, grey world, he decided and thoughts about the day ahead held nothing at all to colour that view.

The road traced the edge of the shore and wound between trees that were naked after a winter of rape by winds howling in off the North Sea. Fenton was relieved when the barren monotony of the landscape was broken by a neon sign advertising a transport cafe, open to service the early morning fish trade. He swung off the road and followed the arrows.

The tea was hot and sweet and Fenton felt it travel all the way down to his stomach, making him think of sword swallowers. He rubbed the back of his neck where the leather had been chafing and kneaded the backs of his thighs which were threatening cramp.

The road turned inland to cut across a stretch of barren headland and Fenton had to stop and check his map as he came to a junction with no sign posting. He made his decision and turned right to find himself, after a few minutes, heading towards the sea again. He stopped as he came to the top of a hill and looked down on the village where the Buchans lived. Pulling off a glove, he took a card from his top pocket and checked the address on it, 8, Harbour Wynd.

He let the bike free wheel silently down the hill and brought it to a halt on the cobblestones in front of the harbour. He let his foot rest on a pile of fish boxes while he looked down at the smooth oily surface of the water as it rose and fell against the slimy green stonework.

Three lanes radiated out from the hub of the harbour; one of them was Harbour Wynd. Fenton put the Honda up on its stand and walked slowly up over the cobbles to find number eight. He found the heavy brass knocker surprisingly muted by the thickness of the door.

"Oh it's you," said Grant Buchan with no trace of pleasure in his voice, "I suppose you had better come in." Fenton had expected no better.

"Who is it?" cried a woman's voice.

"It's Jenny's..." Buchan's voice trailed off as he sought a suitable description.

"Fancy man," said the frosty faced woman who emerged from the kitchen to dry her hands on her apron.

Fenton's heart sank. He had only met Grant's wife once before and that had been when the whole family had been together. He remembered that she had maintained an air of prim disapproval throughout the entire meeting. Mona Buchan stood in the doorway like an angel of the Lord, hair tied back severely in a bun, the shapeless cardigan buttoned up to the neck, eyes shining with self righteousness from a fair skinned face that had never known make-up.

"I'm very sorry about your son Mrs Buchan," said Fenton ignoring the jibe.

"What do you want here?" hissed Mona Buchan. "Haven't you and that...that..."

Grant Buchan stopped the situation getting out of hand. He put his arm around his wife's shoulders and said, "Easy woman, make us all some tea eh?"

Mona Buchan disappeared into the kitchen. "I'm sorry," said Buchan, "She's very upset."

"I understand," said Fenton, sitting down where Buchan indicated.

"But she's right. I can't see why you came here either," said Buchan.

"Because the answer is here! It must be. Jenny did not kill your boy. You must know that? The idea is just too ridiculous for words." Fenton looked hard at Buchan who held his gaze for a moment then he sighed and looked away. "I just can't think straight any more..."

Mona Buchan brought in the tea. She clattered the tray down with bad grace and turned on her heel. "I'm afraid I have work to be getting on with," she announced. The kitchen door closed again and Buchan continued, "But why should the killer pick on Jamie? It just doesn't make any sense."

"I know," said Fenton softly, "I think Jenny must have been the unwitting link between the killer and your boy. That's what we have to find out."

"What do you want me to do?" asked Grant.

"Tell me everything you did in Edinburgh, everyone you met, everywhere you went."

Fenton took notes as Buchan spoke, not that there was much to record, a fact which made him more and more depressed as time went by. The Buchans had gone from the train to the flat, from the flat to the clinic and from the clinic to the train. They appeared to have met no one save for the staff at the clinic but the fact remained that at sometime during these twenty-four hours Jamie Buchan had been poisoned so that a week later the blood would drain from his body to leave him a pale corpse on the cobblestones of his own village. If the answer did lie in the brief notes in front of him Fenton could not see it. "Did anyone give him sweets?" he asked.

"Only Jenny," Buchan answered, making Fenton wish that he had not asked. "Do you think I could see Jamie's room?"

"He is in it."

The answer shook Fenton rigid. He had not considered that the boy's body might be in the house.

"We got him back yesterday," said Buchan quietly. "Mona wanted to have him home once more before he goes away...tomorrow."

Fenton nodded silently, a lump coming to his throat at Buchan's distress. "I'm sorry," he said softly, "I just thought that if I saw his things I might notice something that you may have overlooked. But in the circumstances..."

Buchan stood up. Without saying anything he motioned to Fenton to follow him.

Fenton had to duck his head to accommodate the slope of the roof at the head of the narrow stairs before they entered Jamie's bedroom. The room was cold and smelled of dampness, old dampness, dampness that had been seeping through the thick stone walls for years. It had invaded the furniture and fabric, leaving the same musty odour that Fenton associated with the seaside boarding houses of his youth. The little white coffin was bathed in pale grey light from the tiny dormer window that faced north to the sea; Jamie looked like a marble cherub. Fenton bowed his head and stood still for a moment in sadness.

"We haven't moved anything," said Buchan.

Fenton looked about him. It was a boy's room, trains, boats, planes, an unfinished Lego model. The Millenium Falcon stood on its window-sill launching pad, ready to transport the plastic figures beside it to some far off galaxy. Jamie's Jedi sword lay on his pillow. "He was Luke Skywalker," said Buchan.

An anguished cry came from the stairs. The rumble of footsteps stopped with Mona Buchan framed in the doorway, her eyes burning with anger. Fenton was transfixed by the look of hatred on her face, white flecks of spittle pocked her lips as she turned on her husband. "What in God's holy name possessed you?" she demanded, "To let this...this animal near our son?" Buchan looked shaken. "And you," she hissed at Fenton, her voice a coarse rasp, "How dare you...how dare you."

Mona Buchan's anger soared beyond the bounds of all reason and, unable to contain herself any longer, she flung herself across the room, fingernails bared, blind to everything except Fenton, the object of her hatred. As she lunged forward her foot caught the edge of the trestle bearing Jamie's coffin and sent it crashing to the floor to spill him out. Clad in his white shroud he lay there like a sleeping china doll among the toys.

Mona Buchan's rage evaporated. She collapsed to her knees and broke into uncontrollable sobbing as she rested her cheek against her dead son. Fenton knew that he would never be able to forget the sight. "Go!" said Grant Buchan, "Just go."

The Honda was the centre of attraction for a group of small boys when Fenton returned to the harbour and their Star Wars gear suggested that they might have been contemporaries of Jamie. There was something familiar about one of the boys, thought Fenton, but he could not think what. Perhaps he was a relation of Jamie's. A brother? He could not recall if the Buchans had more than the one child. "Your name isn't Buchan is it son?" he asked.

"No Mister. He's deid."

"Yes," said Fenton reliving the awful scene in the bedroom.

Fenton got on the bike and fastened the chin strap of his helmet.

"Can I have a hurl on the back Mister?" asked the boy, resting his hand on the handlebars.

"Another time," said Fenton.

Fenton did not look back as he reached the top of the hill above the village; he gave a cursory glance to the left for traffic then joined the main road to head for Fraserburgh at an easy pace for concentrating was difficult. He stopped at a harbour cafe in Fraserburgh hoping that eating would help alleviate the awful emptiness he felt inside but it did not. He gazed out of the window at the boats nuzzling the quayside but all he saw was Jamie's lifeless body.

As he headed east on the coast road Fenton reflected on what his visit had achieved. Nothing, he decided, not a damned thing. Grant Buchan had not told him anything that could possibly be of help in solving anything. Jenny was in as much trouble as she ever had been. He drew to a halt as he reached as far east as he would travel and took a last look at the grey northern water before turning to head south. It was cold but it was dry and the wind would be behind him.

Jenny was in the flat when Fenton got back. They held each other for a long time before either spoke. "I found your note," said Jenny. "Did you find out anything?"

"Nothing," admitted Fenton. "What's been happening here?"

"The police released me this afternoon but I have been told not to leave the city and the hospital have suspended me."

Fenton could see that Jenny had been crying a lot, her eyes were puffy and red. "Morons," he said. "Absolute morons." He drew her even closer.

"The funny thing is," began Jenny, half laughing half sobbing, "I can see their point of view. How could the hospital killer come into contact with Jamie . . . unless it was me?"

"That's what we must figure out," said Fenton with all the reassurance he could muster.

"We're not terribly good at figuring things out. Remember?" said Jenny.

"We'll do it," said Fenton.

They lay still in the darkness taking pleasure in their closeness. Fenton's fingers intertwined with Jenny's, his thumb gently tracing an ellipse on the back of her hand. Her shallow breathing was like music.

In the small hours of the morning Fenton lay awake while Jenny lay beside him fast asleep. She had been mentally exhausted but reassured enough by his presence to fall into a sound sleep, her head still against his shoulder. For the first time in many hours she had felt safe, safe from the strange and the unknown, the overweight men in crumpled suits who smelled of sweat and down market after shave. The men who sneered at everything she said, the red faces who shouted at her, mocked her, accused her. Surely these men could not have been policemen? Policemen were quiet, well mannered, helpful; they told you the time and gave you directions, patted children and inspired confidence, not fear. How she had been afraid, she had never known such fear.

The disorientation caused by being taken to a strange place full of hostile men had destroyed her self confidence in one fell swoop. Her initial stance as an outraged citizen demanding her rights in a free country had collapsed within minutes leaving her confused and afraid. A pleading note had crept into her voice as the ordeal had continued and she had been filled with a desperate desire to please her inquisitors, to say yes to anything that would breach the seemingly impenetrable wall of hostility. Only an innate strength of character stopped her from travelling along that road, but she had seen it and seen it clearly.

Fenton sighed in the still darkness of the room as once again his thoughts came to nothing. What was the connection? Just what was it? Only one fact stared him in the face like an ugly mongrel, there had been no opportunity at all for the hospital killer to reach Jamie directly. He squeezed Jenny's hand involuntarily as the unthinkable crossed his mind. Something was wrong with his train of thought, he decided, something basic.

An hour later, and after much mental wrestling, Fenton came up with a new hypothesis. It was forced on him by the facts. There was no killer, no lunatic, no psychopath. It was a disease! A bacterium or a virus! A virus had destroyed the clotting mechanism in the blood of all the people who had died. Why not? New diseases were being discovered all the time. Legionnaires' disease, Lassa fever, AIDS. The more he thought about it the more obvious and possible it seemed. The virus must be endemic in the hospital, lurking in unseen corners, just as the Legionnaires bug had hidden in the showers of an American hotel. Jenny must have carried it home and infected Jamie. The fact that not everyone was susceptible to it would be typical of viral infection. Everything pointed to it being a virus...except Neil Munro.

The Kraken of Neil Munro, burnt flesh peeling from his face, rose up from Fenton's subconscious to slow him down. No virus had pushed Munro into the sterilizer. A compromise was demanded. Neil had been murdered, of that there was no doubt, but the others? No, it had to be some kind of infective agent. All he had to do now was prove it.

Jenny turned in her sleep and Fenton kissed her lightly on the shoulder. The question now was how he should go about substantiating his theory. Elementary. It was first year student stuff. You isolate the thing and show it does what it does by sticking it in to laboratory animals. But how to get his hands on infected material . . . that was the real question and that was going to be quite a different matter.

He would need material from the people who had died, tissue, serum, and for that he would need help, top brass help and that meant Tyson...or did it? He was still smarting from the way he had made a fool of himself over the Doctor David Malcolm affair. He did not want it to happen again. Could he possibly do it alone?

It occurred to Fenton that maybe it had been done already! Perhaps the Pathology Department had already screened tissue from the victims for infective agents? If that were so then his suggestion would be about as popular with Pathology as his last one had been with the Police. That would be the last straw. He could just see MacDougal, the consultant pathologist and not the most patient of men, sneering at him and saying, "Do you imagine that we are all stupid down here Fenton?"

He glanced at the digital clock on the bedside table. Ten past four, four hours before he would get up and go to the hospital, four hours in which to decide. Outside the wind began to rise and moan through wires on the roof. The bedroom window rattled as it denied entry to the night. Thoughts of a commando style raid on the Pathology Lab conjured up visions of being caught and the implausible explanation that he would have to offer to the police. Inspector Jamieson's superior little smile appeared in the glow from the clock. There had to be another way.

The other way presented itself as an obvious little idea that made Fenton feel stupid for not having thought of it sooner. The Medical Records Department! He could simply go along and request the file on one of the victims. There might not be one for Susan Daniels or the Wilson woman but there would certainly be one for the Watson boy for he had been a patient at the time. His file would contain a full post mortem report and details of all the lab tests requested.

Fenton got up at seven and was in the lab by eight. He had left Jenny sleeping, partly because she needed the rest but partly to avoid any discussion about what he was going to do. He got straight to work on his excuse for the medical records people and thumbed through the day book until he found the last entry for Timothy Watson, a blood glucose estimation. He copied down details of the result and took a virgin report form from Liz Scott's desk. Using two fingers and a great deal of concentration he tapped out a stuttering copy of the original report before getting ink over his hands as he altered the date stamp to match the date of the request in the day book. He now had his excuse, a biochemistry report to insert into the Watson Boy's file.

The Medical Records Department was situated in the Administration Block and smelled of dust and old cardboard. It had a blue carpeted floor that deadened the footsteps of two young girls as they moved up and down narrow gangways between towering rows of patients' files. Cecil McClay looked over his glasses as Fenton entered through the swing doors and approached his desk. He continued writing and finished the sentence before saying, "Yes?"

McClay managed to endow the single word with the suggestion that Fenton was intruding but Fenton had been prepared for it for he knew McClay of old. The man had been Medical Records Officer at the Princess Mary for over twenty years and, like many time servers, had assumed proprietorial rights over his department. To him medical records were an end in themselves. Outsiders wanting to see them were a nuisance to be discouraged wherever possible.

Had Fenton been on a legitimate errand McClay's attitude might have been as a red rag to a bull but, as it was, he was sweetness and light. He apologised for the inconvenience and asked if he 'might possibly' take a look at the file on Timothy Watson.

"Your authority?"

"My own, I'm Fenton, Biochemistry. I have a report to add to the file. It must have been overlooked."

"Leave it there. I'll see that it's entered." The eyes dropped down behind the glasses.

"Actually...I really would like to make sure that this is the only one we overlooked..." Fenton hoped his smile looked more genuine than it felt.

McClay considered for a moment then swung round in his chair and said to one of the girls, "Hilary! Watson, Tee, March three, Ward four."

The girl handed the file to Fenton with a look that promised more than a cardboard file should he choose to follow it up. He smiled and took it to a vacant desk.

The post mortem findings were brief; Timothy Watson had died from loss of blood. Cross reference was made to the haematology report which described high anti-coagulant activity in the sample and complete failure of the clotting mechanisms in the boy's blood. No mention was made anywhere of specimens having been taken and sent for bacterial or viral investigation. His idea was still valid. Everything was yet to play for.

Fenton looked at the short hand on the back of the pathology report and found what specimens had been taken at autopsy and how they had been stored. Four ticks under 'F' were dismissed as being useless because samples fixed in formalin would have lost all biological activity. There were two ticks under 'FR' for freezer, one was serum and the other heart tissue, either of these would do for his purpose. He made a mental note of the reference numbers, closed the file and laid it gently on McClay's desk. "Thank you," he said. McClay grunted in response and did not look up.

The question of how to get his hands on the post mortem samples occupied Fenton's mind for the remainder of the morning. He knew a few people in Pathology but not well enough for what he wanted. He would have to 'borrow' them on his own but how? Forced entry was out of the question. He was prepared to manipulate matters, use a little deception, generate 'misunderstandings', flirt around the edges of illegality but not to brazenly cross the line.

The idea came to him as he washed up before going to lunch. The Pathology Department had a washroom too. If he could find some reason to go to Pathology at around five- thirty he could sneak in there and hide until everyone had left. Then he could find the specimens at his leisure and let himself out. The idea became the plan.

At twenty minutes past five Fenton left the biochemistry department with his pulse rate rising for there now seemed to be a dozen reasons for not going ahead with the plan and more occurred to him with every step he took towards the pathology lab. He came to the double green doors and paused for a moment to steady himself. His mouth was as dry as the desert. Only a brief thought of Jenny made him push open the doors and walk through.

The sickly sweet smell of formaldehyde engulfed him as he approached the reception desk and smiled at the girl technician who stood there. The girl smiled back and read his coat badge. "What can I do for you Mr Fenton?"

Fenton held up the empty brown bottle that he had brought with him from biochemistry and said, "I've run out of this stuff and the stores closed at five. Could you possibly let me have some until the morning?"

The girl took the reagent bottle from him and read the label. "Of course," she said and left him alone for a moment. Fenton looked anxiously over his shoulder to see the entrance to the male cloakroom. It would be immediately to his right as he left the reception area. The sound of a door opening made him spin round in time to see the consultant MacDougal leave his office and walk across the front of Reception. Fenton smiled, MacDougal ignored him.

The technician returned with a full bottle of reagent and handed it to him with a smile. "There you go," she said.

Fenton thanked her and promised that he would return a full one in the morning. He left the reception area and side-stepped smartly into the gents' cloakroom to find it empty. He breathed a sigh of relief, so far so good. He chose the end cubicle and sat down to wait with a glance at his watch; he did not lock the door, just pushed it almost shut, reasoning that anyone in doubt as to whether or not a cubicle was occupied would automatically use one of the other two. A locked door would be a sure sign of occupancy and might attract attention. If he was discovered he would simply flush the toilet and leave.

For Fenton the next thirty minutes passed like years. The initial symphony of slamming locker doors and 'Good nights' gave way to increasingly intermittent footsteps and distant door closing. Just as he thought he might be alone at last the cubicle next to his became occupied for a full five minutes forcing him into raw-nerved silence with every intake of breath a challenge to self control. The occupant terminated his relief by pulling, what sounded to Fenton, like reams of paper from the holder. 'Ye gods!' he thought ...'he's building a kite.'

The toilet flushed and the door banged open. There was the sound of running taps then the outer door bounced on its brake. Fenton was alone again. He had prepared himself for a thirty minute wait after the last noise had died away. He checked his watch and re-read the writing on the wall.

Fenton tip-toed out of the cloakroom and into the reception area to find it dark and silent. No light escaped from under any door; he was alone...Please God he was alone. The blood pounding in his ears told him that his nerves were already at fever pitch and he had not yet begun his search. He took a few deep breaths in a deliberate attempt to compose himself before following the signs to the post mortem suite. There was enough light coming from the street lights outside to show him the way, which was just as well for he had not thought to bring a torch.

He pushed open the blue door and found it pitch black inside. The post mortem suite had no windows. He stepped inside and closed the door behind him before running the flat of his hand up and down the cold tiling until he had found the light switch. Three strip lights groaned into life.

Fenton looked about him, his nose wrinkling at the heavy scented air freshener used to mask the lingering smells of death. The room was large, high and round. In the middle two stainless steel tables stood on their pedestals like traffic islands. They were free standing, all services, plumbing and hydraulic lines for the tilt mechanisms, having been run under the floor. Everything in the room was hard and smooth, predominantly stainless steel and tiling, nothing that would be harmed by constant sluicing.

The room might have been mistaken for an operating theatre at first glance but the instruments on the wall gave it away, saws, hammers, drills, chisels, things more associated with carpentry or butchery. The spring balances and meat scales swung the analogy in favour of butchery. The precision of the paper thin scalpel blade took a back seat in this environment. Here the long, black, bone-handled knives on the wall plied their surrealist art on the cold tables.

Three heavily insulated doors furnished with metal clamps advertised the body vaults. Fenton opened one, recoiling slightly as a waft of cold, damp air caressed his cheek. There were two occupants inside, hooded, shrouded and identified by luggage labels round their toes. The small size of the bundles said that they were children. Fenton took one of the limp labels between thumb and forefinger and read it...Amanda Wright...age twelve. He closed the door.

The large chest freezer looked as if might contain what he was looking for but he found the lid reluctant to rise. He had to thump the heels of his hands against the clasp before the ice around the rim cracked and allowed the lid to lift with a groan. The large eye sockets of an aborted foetus stared up at him through a plastic bag causing him to take in breath sharply. Half afraid of what he would find next he began brushing away ice from the tops of plastic containers, a hand, an ear...the misty outline of a child's leg presented itself through the plastic of its box. Fenton slammed the lid down on the hellish Meccano and rested his hands on it for a moment, breathing erratically. His impulse was to run, to get out of the place, out into the night where he could walk in the rain, smell the grass, let the wind free him from the cloying warmth of the path lab.

His anxiety subsided. He could think again. Where would they keep small specimens? His attention came to rest on a double bank of steel handles on the wall; they were lettered in alphabetical order. He went over and pulled out 'A'. They were freezer files! Row upon row of little glass vials stored in numbered racks. He had found what he was looking for.

Using the reference number from the medical records file on Timothy Watson he found the correct serum sample and removed the vial. He took it to the sink and held it under the tap until it had melted. Now then...a clean vial. Fenton searched through a series of drawers and was lucky at the fourth attempt, clean sterile vials. Now a pipette...again he found one quickly and transferred a small quantity of the serum from the original vial into a fresh one. He replaced the original and closed the file with a click. It was over. He had got it. The compressor on the freezer shuddered into life and his heart missed a beat.

The thought that, should he drop dead from fright, he might well end up on one of the steel tables with his rib cage wrenched open and a hose sluicing out his chest cavity, put wings on Fenton's heels. He switched off the lights in the post mortem room and listened for a few moments before opening the door. The smell of the air freshener seemed stronger in the darkness. It threatened to choke him. The sounds were friendly enough, clicks from thermostats, hums from fridges, inanimate neutral sounds. He sidled out into the main lab.

The short wait in darkness had accustomed his eyes to the gloom. Again he waited and listened before stepping out smartly into the corridor and containing his urge to run. He could not lock the door behind him for he had no key so some poor soul was going to get a rocket in the morning for having left it unlocked... C'est la vie.

The old villa was in darkness when he reached it. He unlocked the front door and switched on the light in the hall, taking comfort from the friendly, familiar smells of the solvents used in biochemistry. He checked the duty roster to find out who was on call. It was Mary Tyler, no problem, no explanations would be necessary should she come in while he was still there. He took the serum sample from his pocket and fixed a self adhesive label to it adding a fictitious name, Mark Brown. He put it safely away in his own freezer and with that done he donned his leathers and left for home

CHAPTER SEVEN

When Fenton arrived home he found that a good night's sleep and a day on her own had done little to restore Jenny's spirits. Her smile of greeting lacked conviction and her lank hair and lack-lustre eyes spoke of the strain that she was under. He sensed that something else was wrong but did not enquire, feeling that she would tell him in her own time. Half way through their meal she said, "I phoned Grant today."

Fenton went cold; he put down his knife and fork and said, "Oh."

"He told me what happened."

"Jenny, I'm sorry. I should never have gone there."

Jenny was close to tears. She said softly, "It's all right. I know you were only trying to help. Grant knows that too, in fact, I think you managed to convince my own brother that I did not kill his son." There was bitterness in her voice before she covered her mouth with her handkerchief. Fenton got up and put his arms round her from behind. He put his cheek against her hair and rocked her gently from side to side.

When Jenny had calmed down Fenton told her of his virus idea. It was a candle in her darkness. "Do you really think so?" she asked with more animation in her voice than had been present for some time. Something persuaded her to have second thoughts. She added hesitantly, "You're not just saying that are you?"

Fenton was adamant that he was not and went on to give his reasons. Jenny found his enthusiasm infectious and, with very little prompting, was able to add substance to the foundations of his argument. Despite this, and although desperate to believe it, she still felt compelled to play Devil's advocate. "But there are no viruses that cause uncontrolled bleeding are there?" she asked.

Fenton countered the doubt by saying, "There was no Legionnaires' disease either until a whole bunch of Americans dropped dead of it. Then people all over the world started recognising similarities to cases that they had been seeing for years and dismissing as 'viral infections' or pyrexias of unknown origin."

Jenny accepted the argument and Fenton pressed home his case. "What we are seeing is very acute haemophilia. Before you say it, I know that haemophilia is a genetic disorder but I can see no reason why, given the right set of circumstances, a virus should not be able to simulate the condition if it attacks the right cells."

Jenny was sold on the idea. She asked Fenton what he planned to do.

"Get some material from one of the victims and find the virus," said Fenton.

"But how?"

"I've already got it." Fenton told Jenny his tale of derring-do and saw her mouth drop open. "But what if you had been caught?" she said.

"I wasn't and I've got the sample."

Fenton said what he planned to do next. He would send the sample off for analysis under cover of a fictitious patient's name. He would make a special request for animal inoculation and ask for blood samples from the test animals. When he had evidence of the infective agent he would present it to Tyson.

"How long?" asked Jenny.

"Five days."

With hope restored to her Jenny's morale began to improve. She began to think of her return to work, of hearing the apologies, the assurances that, 'not for one moment had anyone really believed...'

Fenton was pleased at the change in her, it was so good to see her smile again, but he also felt a burden grow on his shoulders. What if the tests should prove negative? How could he bring himself to tell her? He knew very well that the repair to Jenny's psyche was only in the nature of a temporary patch. If the patch were to fail the wound might well split open and that could be disastrous as he knew from experience. Life could so easily become a desert of depression, a limbo where time stood still. That must not happen to Jenny.

Tired with talk of the weather. She said, "You will get the report today."

"Should do," said Fenton in what he hoped was a matter of fact voice. In truth he had thought about little else all night. His stomach was tied in knots at the very thought of it. Unwilling to look at Jenny in case she read his mind, he went to the window and drew the curtains back. "I have had it with 'Bonnie Scotland'," he announced, spitting out the words as he looked at the rain lashed roofs. "You have got to be a bit soft in the head to live here. Why don't we get married, pack up and get the hell out?" He turned to look at Jenny.

"You will phone and tell me?" said Jenny, ignoring everything that he had said.

"I'll phone. But whatever it says, nothing changes. I love you and you love me and, sooner or later, this will all be sorted out. OK?" Fenton's voice hardened on the 'OK' as he saw Jenny's eyes begin to drift away.

"All right," she said softly.

Fenton was sitting at his desk when Liz Scott brought in the package. The yellow envelope on the outside said that it was the microbiology report; the box would contain the blood samples. He sat and stared at it for several minutes, anxious to know but afraid of what he might find. He brought out a paper knife and turned it over in his hand before committing it to the flap of the envelope and slitting it slowly and perfectly open.

SPECIMEN REPORT:MARK BROWN
BACTERIAL SCREEN: NEGATIVE
VIRAL SCREEN: NEGATIVE
BLOOD SAMPLES ENCLOSED AS REQUESTED

The report threatened the same effect on Fenton as the yob's fist had when it had swung in to his stomach. The microbiology labs had found no evidence of any infecting agent. He felt completely drained.

After a few minutes of deep depression Fenton saw an argument. The report was not conclusive. If there was a new bacterium or virus in the specimen then it might well require special culture conditions, in fact, it almost certainly would otherwise it would have been isolated and described before. The real answer would lie in the blood samples of animals inoculated with serum from Timothy Watson.He opened the box and his agony was complete. Both samples had clotted perfectly. There had been nothing in Timothy Watson's blood to infect the animals. He had been wrong...again.

Fenton pondered the consequences. He had built up Jenny's hopes and now this. He could not have done a better job of pushing her towards a nervous breakdown if he had meant to. What a stupid...He crunched up the report in his fist and flung it across the room. Jenny would be waiting at home for his call, she would be pretending that she was reading or dusting or cleaning or listening to the radio but really she would just be waiting, waiting for the phone to ring.

Fenton dialled the number. It was answered at the first tone.

"Jenny? The report hasn't come yet. Maybe this afternoon."

Fenton felt worse than ever but he could not tell her, not like that, not over the phone. He needed time to think.

So there was no virus involved, no convenient infective agent to take the blame and clear up the mystery. So what did that leave? A poison? That seemed unlikely for too many people seemed to be immune, besides, you did not carry a poison on your person and pass it on inadvertently...

Fenton suddenly saw a crack in an otherwise smooth-walled enigma. Jenny must have passed on the agent to Jamie but if it wasn't a bacterium or virus she must have known about it! She must have given Jamie Buchan something that she believed to be completely harmless but it had not been. It had killed him.

Anger, superseding disappointment, erupted in Jenny. "No damn it! I did not give him anything. How many times do I have to say it! You are on the wrong track!"

Fenton felt the unspoken 'as usual' hang heavily in the air. He stopped badgering to create a silence in the room that threatened to be louder than the argument. Reining his voice, he said softly, "Jenny, you must see that it is the only logical explanation. You must have given the boy something, something you would not give a second thought to, something you have forgotten about, please...think?"

"No! No! No!" Jenny's eyes blazed as she refused to have any more to do with the notion. Fenton made to put his arm round her but she turned away and stared intently at the fire. Fenton got up and went to the kitchen to make some coffee. The kettle was empty so he had to re-fill it and wait until it boiled. He did not return to the living room in the interim, choosing instead to stare distantly out of the kitchen window at the blackness with his hands in his pockets. Jenny had never turned away from him before. He felt angry, sad, sorry, ineffectual, stupid and, after standing still in the kitchen for some time, cold. He poured the coffee and took it through.

Jenny did not look up when he put the mug down beside her; she continued to stare at the fire. He sat down on the other chair and looked steadily at her left profile until she did relent and turn towards him then he broke into a half apologetic, half self-conscious grin. "I'm sorry," he whispered.

"Oh Tom..."

They held each other tight while the tears, the whispered apologies, the cheek nuzzling tenderness, combined to soothe the wounds that they had inflicted on each other. A new silence ensued but this time it was a comfortable pool of serenity with both of them reluctant to speak lest they ripple the surface.

Fenton woke at three, his body damp with cold sweat. He sat bolt upright to free himself of the images of a nightmare, Neil Munro's face, a fountain of blood from Timothy Watson's mouth and, through a red mist, the spectre of Jamie Buchan's dead face. A forest of arms had reached out towards him in the dream, Mona Buchan's arm had pointed and accused, Timothy Watson had held out both arms in pitiful appeal and anonymous arms had reached out from a deep freeze to wave like pond weeds. Luke Skywalker had wielded a sword; this image remained with him as he reeled into consciousness. In the darkness of the room he saw again the boy at the harbour, the strangely familiar boy with his hands on the handlebars of the Honda. "Can I have a hurl Mister? Can I have a hurl please?"

The image of the boy's face exploded into nothingness as Fenton realised something. It was not the boy himself who was familiar it was what he was wearing! He had been wearing coloured plastic bands round both wrists...hospital name tags!

Fenton shook Jenny hard in his excitement and coaxed her into wakefulness. She covered her eyes from the glare of the bedside lamp.

"Think Jenny think! Did you give any hospital name tags to Jamie Buchan?"

An overture of confused sleepy noises gave way to silence as Jenny considered the question. "Yes, yes I did." Her eyes cleared with the recollection. "I had a bunch in my uniform pocket. I gave them to Jamie to play with."

Fenton stared at her without saying anything.

"All right, so you were right, I did give him something, I gave him a few name tags but surely you are not going to suggest that he ate them and poisoned himself are you?"

Fenton conceded that he was not but he was not going to be ridiculed either. He took both Jenny's hands in his and said, "It's a start and what's more it's a connection, a connection between Jamie and the Princess Mary. What else did you give him?"

Fenton's surge of confidence overwhelmed any argument that Jenny might have considered. She thought deeply before answering. "No, I'm quite sure this time, nothing else."

"Good, make some coffee will you."

Jenny's eyebrows arched but Fenton was deep in thought and didn't notice. He sat on the edge of the bed staring into space, his right thumbnail tapping rapidly against gritted teeth. Jenny made coffee and brought it through. "Your coffee oh wise one."

Fenton ignored the sarcasm or, more correctly, it did not register. He took the cup and said, "Well if all you gave him was a plastic name tag...that's what must have killed him."

Jenny, with less reason than anyone to scoff at suggestions which diverted suspicions from herself, was forced to do so at this one and said so in no uncertain manner.

Fenton remained adamant. "If the name tags are the only connection between the hospital and Jamie then they are the reason. It's logical, however unlikely it may seem."

"How?" said Jenny accusingly.

"I've no idea," said Fenton.

Jenny shook her head. She said, "You said that you saw Jamie's friend wearing the arm bands. He was quite healthy wasn't he?"

"Yes."

"Well?"

"I don't know, but I repeat, if the arm bands were the only thing you gave to Jamie then they are responsible. Do you still say you gave him nothing else?"

"Nothing," said Jenny.

"I'm going to talk to Tyson in the morning but meanwhile..."

"Meanwhile what?"

"How long is it since we made love?"

"Quite a while," said Jenny.

"That situation is about to end."

"Do I have some say in the matter?"

"Not really," said Fenton.

"Shouldn't we discuss this first..." murmured Jenny, her body beginning to respond to his touch.

"No," whispered Fenton, "I've already decided."

Tyson listened patiently while Fenton told his tale and did not interrupt but Fenton could tell that he was failing to convince. Tyson's eloquent silence diluted his enthusiasm until the implausibility of what he was saying loomed up at him like guilt for some long past sin. Tyson cleared his throat and began to speak. Fenton could tell that he was editing what he had to say in the cause of politeness. "What you are really saying is that Saxon plastic kills people. Frankly, that is ridiculous."

The words, coming from Tyson, carried the weight of a punch. Fenton tried to defend himself. He began, "I know it sounds a bit..."

"Not a bit, a lot. It is just plain ridiculous. Saxon plastic has been through every test in the book and passed with flying colours. Do you know what tests any new health product must pass before it ever gets near a hospital?" Fenton did not but he could guess.

"Saxon plastic is safe. It is non toxic, non poisonous, non inflammable. It is safe when you heat it; it is safe when you freeze it and safe if you are stupid enough to want to eat it! Now I know that you have been under great strain but this kind of nonsense is dangerous. We have enough trouble in this hospital without a law suit from Saxon Medical. Understood?"

Fenton sat in his lab silently licking his wounds. Nothing Tyson had said had made him change his mind; he clung to his belief like a bull dog gripping a rag. The only thing now was he would have to prove it all on his own.

Fenton's lonely war was waged on a battlefield of paper as he read and re-read every scrap of information he could find on Saxon Medical and their new product. He examined all the graphs and tables from the original trials and re-plotted the data in what turned out to be a fruitless search for flaws. Quite simply, there were none, a fact that he had to come to terms with after a week of silently preoccupied evenings during which Jenny had plied him with coffee and kept, what politicians liked to call, a low profile. As he conceded defeat and put down his pen to rub his eyes on Friday evening he heard the sound outside of an ambulance siren floating above the wind and rain. It made him wonder if its occupant was bound for the Princess Mary. She was.

The week had been special for Rachel Morrison because it had been her eighth birthday on Wednesday, a day she had been looking forward to for weeks because of an anticipated bicycle. As her father had promised it had been waiting for her at the foot of her bed when she had woken on Wednesday morning, all red, white and shiny chrome. Her happiness had been complete, well almost complete for the weather had been so bad that she had been unable to take it outside to ride it, but it was there and she could touch it and that was the main thing.

After school several of her friends had come to the house for a special birthday tea and they had laughed and played and eaten ice cream and meringues till they were exhausted. Rachel ate so much that she got a pain in her stomach, at least that was what her mother had said, but the pain had become worse as the evening had progressed until, finally, her tears had convinced her mother and father that the doctor should be called.

By the time the doctor arrived the pain had moved down and to the right so that he had had no difficulty in diagnosing acute appendicitis and summoning an ambulance. There was nothing to worry about; appendicectomy was probably the simplest and most routine operation in the book. On the following day Rachel Morrison died in the Princess Mary following a massive haemorrhage.

The fact that Rachel Morrison and Jenny Buchan had never met and that Rachel had been admitted to the Princess Mary during Jenny's suspension ended that suspension and freed Jenny from suspicion. Although it had not been discussed, both Fenton and Jenny had been aware that the deaths had appeared to cease after Jenny's suspension. Now they spoke openly about it. Jenny was prepared to construe the pause as an unfortunate quirk of fate, just her luck, but Fenton read more into it.

It now seemed obvious to him that there would be a pause in the deaths for a pause would be bound to occur when all the susceptible people had died leaving a stable immune population. No one else would die until a susceptible person appeared on the scene again, a new member of staff perhaps or, much more likely in the case of a hospital, a new patient. He blamed himself for not having predicted this earlier.

Jenny put a stop to his self recrimination by pointing out that it would not have made the slightest difference, a fact he eventually had to agree with. But should he tell Tyson? Predictions made after the event, he decided, were about as useful as three pound notes. He would say nothing, besides, with Jenny in the clear he felt so much better, more able to concentrate, much sharper. He would find the link.

Jenny looked up from the newspaper she had been buried in and said, "Listen to this, someone...a James Lindsay, aged forty three, committed suicide after being dismissed from Saxon Medical for alleged theft. He threw himself under a train."

"Poor devil."

"Where is Saxon Medical?"

"On one of these industrial estates in Glasgow."

"That would fit, it's a Glasgow address." said Jenny.

Fenton took the paper and read the story for himself. He finished by saying, "He wasn't an executive with that address."

"You know it?"

"It's near where I was born."

"Is that the mist of nostalgia I see in your eyes?"

"No it isn't. They should have pulled that place down years ago."

"Then what were you thinking?" asked Jenny.

"I was thinking that I might go to see Mrs Lindsay."

Jenny was aghast. "Whatever for?" she gasped.

"Anything to do with Saxon Medical...I am interested."

Fenton went to Glasgow on the following Tuesday. The Honda ate up the forty odd miles or so between the Capital and Glasgow in as many minutes and Fenton weaved his way expertly through the derelict buildings and cratered sites that defaced the east side of the city until he found the street that he was looking for. He pulled the bike up on to its stand and walked towards the tenement block pulling his gloves off.

There was garbage everywhere, fish and chip wrappers, potato crisp bags, rotting fruit and the inevitable red McEwan's Export beer can. He flicked it aside with his toe, thinking that one of these cans should be in any time capsule as a universal artefact of Scottish life. There seemed to be one lying on the foot of every river and on the top of every hill.

The entrance to the close was stained with dried vomit, the protest of a belly too full of beer being asked to accommodate take-away food. Fenton thought of his father and his nights 'on the bevy.' As always when he thought of his father, he experienced mixed feelings of guilt and regret for he had never really known him at all, had never understood what had gone on in his head.

To all intents Joe Fenton had appeared to have been a simple, rather uncommunicative man who had spent all his adult life labouring in the shipyards of the Clyde. He would work Monday to Friday, drink himself into oblivion on Saturday and lie in bed all day Sunday. His routine had never varied.

Although by no means untypical of the lifestyle of the area Tom Fenton had always believed that there had been more to his father's behaviour than the blinkered following of macho tradition. There had been something missing in his father's make up, something he had often tried to define in the past but always without success. He had never known his father to display any kind of enthusiasm for anything in all the years he could remember. It was as if he had lived his entire life on a pilot flame fuelled with enigmatic sadness.

Even when drunk Joe Fenton's thoughts, if any, had been concealed behind a moist eyed smile. The burning political issues of 'red Clydeside' had left him unmoved as had the titanic struggles between Rangers and Celtic football clubs. It was as if, at some early stage in his life, he had discovered some deep, dark secret, some awful truth, so terrible that it had straightened out the parallax of optimism and forced him to view his existence as one long inconsequential tunnel from birth to grave.

Tom had never discovered what his father's secret had been, whether he had found out the meaning of life or that there was no heaven or hell or whether there was just no point. The last possibility seemed the most likely. Joe Fenton had lived his entire life as if there had been no point, no point at all. He had died in the year that Fenton had graduated, never having said much more to him than an occasional, 'Aye son,' in passing, a 'guid fur you,' when he had done well or, 'We'll hae nae mair o' that,' when he had done wrong.

To Fenton's mother Rose, a simple, kind hearted woman, Joe had been a 'good man,' but, within the parameters of marital behaviour in the area, this had simply meant that he had not physically abused her and had handed over his wage packet unopened on a Friday night. Conversation and companionship had been alien notions from another world.

For some reason, not totally clear to him even now, Fenton hoped that his father had been proud of him when he had graduated, perhaps because he feared in his heart of hearts that it had really not mattered a damn, it probably hadn't rated a mention in the pub. Maybe it had even been an embarrassment.

Fenton edged deeper into the mouth of the close to be assailed by the competing smells of fried onions and cats' urine. As his eyes adjusted to the gloom he saw the iron gate that barred the way to the back passage and drying greens and was forced to smile at the nostalgia it evoked for it had been down one of these dark passages that he had received a great deal of his street education.

Levoy had been a popular game among teenagers in the area, a variation on hide and seek that had involved a great deal of hiding in dark closes with members of the opposite sex and not too much seeking. One girl, some two years older than himself, and whose name he now desperately tried to remember, had taken it upon herself to see that he had not wearied during the long dark vigils. He recalled with fondness his early sorties into Betty McAlpine's underwear, his discomfort at being unable to unhook her bra, his ecstasy as for the first time a female hand had unzipped his fly and ventured inside. He remembered his bewilderment at being stopped when he had moved his own hand under her skirt to explore a magical maze of underskirts and suspenders. "Sorry," she had said, "The flags are up." Failing to understand and construing this as obligatory feminine modesty – part of the etiquette of back-close loving, he had pressed on to find his hand taken in a vice like grip. "Are you bloody daft or somethin'?" the girl had hissed. The harsh admonishment had dampened his ardour to the point where his proud member had begun to wilt but then the girl, realising his complete ignorance of female menstrual matters, had launched into a kindly explanation as to why he could not go 'all the way.'

With both his confidence and his erection restored he had rewarded her by having an orgasm all over her dress.

Fenton climbed the dark stone spiral stairs, stooping down as he came to each door to examine the name plates. He was half way along the landing of the second flat before he reached 'Lindsay'. He paused for a moment to listen to the sounds of the close, harsh laughter from female throats conditioned by cigarette smoke and endless bawling at errant children, that self same bawling as yet another woman screamed her frustration and inadequacy at her offspring. He pulled the door bell and found it unconnected to anything. He replaced the handle and knocked instead. The door opened a few inches to reveal the haggard eyes of a woman about five feet tall and those of a child some three feet below. "I've told you, "she began, "I'll pay you when I can; I just haven't got it right now."

Fenton assured her that he was not there to collect money. "Then what?" she asked.

"I would like to talk to you about your husband."

"What about him?" asked the woman suspiciously.

"Nothing bad I promise. I just want you to tell me about him. Can I come in?"

"You're another reporter," said the woman.

Fenton was about to deny it when he noticed that the woman seemed pleased at the prospect of his being a reporter so he smiled instead and she opened the door.

They sat down to talk in a small, sparsely furnished kitchen cum living room which impressed Fenton with its tidiness and neatness. It seemed almost an act of defiance against an ever encroaching desert of filth and squalor.

"My Jimmy never stole a thing in his life," insisted the woman, "Someone planted that drill in his locker."

"Why would they do that Mrs Lindsay?" probed Fenton gently.

"Because they wanted him out that's why," said the woman.

Fenton's throat tightened as he saw the possibility of a management intrigue against James Lindsay because he knew too much about something.

"Who are 'they'" he asked.

"The men he worked beside."

Fenton's heart fell. "Why did his work mates want him out Mrs Lindsay?"

"They were jealous because he was such a good worker. Jimmy said that when the company expanded to make the new plastic they would probably make him a foreman and we could move away from here." The woman looked around with disgust at her surroundings, her eyes settled on a damp patch on the wall paper. "We were going to buy a bungalow in Bearsden," she said mistily, "And Jimmy was going to buy a Sierra. He said that he would get me a Mini for the shopping and taking the weans to school..."

Fenton thought he recognised the story. Jimmy had been either a dreamer or a drunk. He continued to probe gently for the woman desperately wanted to believe that her husband had been innocent...but he had not, a fact that became more and more apparent with every answer. A familiar tale unfolded. Drink, gambling, money lenders charging enormous rates of interest, threats, fear, desperation and, in James Lindsay's case, suicide.

The woman started to sob quietly while the child who had never let go of her skirt for an instant since he had come in, continued to stare at him and pick his nose unconcernedly. Fenton supposed that he must have seen a lot of crying over the past week or so. He looked for some way of changing the subject and his eyes fell on a photograph of a man in uniform on the mantelpiece. "Was that your husband Mrs Lindsay?" he asked.

The woman nodded, then blowing her nose and tucking the handkerchief into her skirt, she added, "He was an Argyll. He looked so lovely in his uniform..."

Fenton sensed that the tears were about to start again and stood up. "He was a fine looking man," he said softly, "And a daddy you can be proud of," he added, bending down to press a five pound note into the child's hand.

Fenton restrained himself from taking an almighty kick at the beer can lying in the entrance to the close and compromised by flicking it aside once more with his toe. As he did so he suddenly became aware of two men who had been pressed up against the doorway. He spun round in surprise.

"Is this the wan Bella?" asked one of the men, half over his shoulder to the darkness of the close.

'Bella' emerged from the shadows, a shambling mass of flab in stained apron and carpet slippers. She scuffled towards Fenton and chewed gum while she examined him. "Aye," she announced, "That's the bastard."

The questioner, a full head shorter than Fenton but squat and powerful with a scarred face and a noseline that altered direction more than once, looked at Fenton with granite eyes. His companion, an emaciated figure suspended inside a dirty black suit several sizes too large stood one pace behind. His skin, a sickly yellow colour, looked as if it had been stretched over his cheek bones like the wing fabric of a model aircraft. He puffed nervously on a cigarette, holding it between the bunched finger-nails of his right hand while his eyes darted nervously from side to side.

"I hear you were botherin' Mary Lindsay, pal," said granite eyes with quiet menace. Fenton felt fear climb his spine like a glacier on the move. The memory of the last time filled his head making the thought of so much pain again just too awful to contemplate. "I've been to see Mrs Lindsay, yes," he said in carefully measured tones that had been filtered to remove any inflection that could possibly be construed as antagonistic.

"Oh hiv ye," said granite eyes moving towards him slowly, "Do you hear that Ally? He's been to see Mrs Lindsay, yes." He exaggerated a sing-song posh accent as he said it. The yellow skinned corpse withdrew his left hand quickly from the drapes of his jacket pocket and flicked his wrist to reveal an open razor.

"What in Christ's name is this all about?" asked Fenton, his mouth dry with fear.

Granite eyes smiled with no trace of humour. "When will you bastards ever learn?" he hissed through gritted teeth. "You canny get blood frae a stone. Mary Lindsay hisnae got any money pal, savvy? Nae money!" His finger stabbed at Fenton's chest as his voice rose. "So why dae youse bastards keep comin' round here? Are ye tryin' tae kill her like ye did Jimmy?"

Fenton could sense that granite eyes was working himself up into a frenzy and bringing the yellow skinned corpse with the razor with him. This was not going to be any kind of warning. He only had seconds left. The fat woman stood idly by, chewing her gum as if she were watching television. In a moment she would change channels.

"There's some mistake," said Fenton hoarsely.

"An' you made it pal," hissed granite eyes moving on to the balls of his feet.

Fenton bunched his stomach muscles and prepared himself for what he now saw as inevitable. Granite eyes was the big problem. The other one had the razor but granite eyes was the real hard man and it would take more than one blow to take him out. He dismissed the notion of kneeing him in the crotch, it was too obvious and granite eyes would expect it for amateurs always tried that. He would go for a punch to the throat. If it connected the man would go down. If he could then get in with a couple of kicks quickly he might stay down long enough for him to deal with yellow skin. Razor or no razor, with granite eyes out of the way, Fenton knew that he could take him, in fact, the man looked so ill that one blow might splinter his consumptive frame like a matchwood doll.

Fenton looked into his opponents eyes and was gratified to find a flicker of doubt there as if he had suddenly realised that Fenton might not be the complete amateur he had taken him for and, if that were the case...he was big. Fenton knew what granite eyes was thinking and took comfort from it. Correct, he thought, I've been away a long time but I know the game too. You don't realise it but I know you...I've known you all my life..."

"Stop it! Stop it!" cried a woman's voice from above but Fenton did not look up, neither did granite eyes. They held each other's gaze, afraid to give the other any advantage.

"Leave him alone Scobie! And you too Ally! He's not one of them, he's a reporter!"

Fenton gave thanks to any god that happened to be listening at the time as he saw granite eyes turn and look up. He turned back again and said, "Is that right pal? A reporter eh?" He said it as if nothing at all had gone before and they had just been introduced. His smile revealed rows of rotten teeth. "Doin' a wee story on Jimmy are you? Exposing these money lendin' bastards? Good fur you, pal."

"I'm doing my best," Fenton lied.

"Well, ma name's Scobie McGraw and this here's Ally Clegg - two gees by the way." The yellow corpse grinned. "If there's anythin' we can do tae help ye only hiv tae ask."

I don't believe this, thought Fenton. They want their names in the paper. He smiled wanly and said, "Thanks, I'll remember that."

"Right then," said granite eyes, "Is that your bike ower there?"

Fenton said that it was.

"Well ye better get oan it then!" Granite eyes broke into bronchitic laughter at his own joke and turned to yellow skin and the fat woman for support. Fenton smiled weakly and started to walk towards the Honda.

"Just a minute pal!"

The words hit the back of Fenton's neck like bullets; he turned slowly.

"Whit paper did ye say ye worked fur?"

"The Guardian," said Fenton, saying the first name that came into his head.

"Jesus," said granite eyes as if that were sufficient.

Fenton continued towards the bike feeling as if he was walking on thin ice with a thaw in the air. He heaved it off its stand and mounted it as casually as he could in the circumstances then pressed the starter as if it were the ejector button in a burning aircraft. The Honda growled into life and sounded like a Beethoven sonata. He was moving, motion beautiful motion, spinning wheels, faster, faster, up, up and away.

CHAPTER EIGHT

To Fenton's annoyance Jenny found the story funny when he told her what had happened in Glasgow. She rocked with laughter when he told her of the feeling in his gut when he had first seen the open razor. "It serves you right for prying," she said.

"It was no joke," Fenton protested, "These things can cut you to the bone before you even realise it and you'll end up carrying the scar for the rest of your life, assuming there is a rest to your life."

"I'm sorry," said Jenny, "It was just the way that you told it. You know I couldn't bear it if anything happened to you."

They sat down and Fenton told Jenny of his conversation with the Lindsay woman.

"So you are no further forward?" said Jenny.

"I suppose not," agreed Fenton. He leaned back on the couch and Jenny snuggled up close to him to play with the hairs on his chest through a space between his shirt buttons.

"What did you hope to find out?" she asked.

Fenton sighed and said, "I suppose...I hoped to discover that Lindsay had not committed suicide at all, that he had discovered something awful about Saxon plastic and had been murdered to keep his mouth shut."

Jenny rolled her eyes and said, "That was a bit strong."

"It was also wrong," said Fenton.

"Then he did commit suicide?"

"There's not much doubt about that. He was up to his neck in debt to back street money lenders and not the kind who were content to send him rude letters."

"Poor man."

"I think he must have seen stealing tools from the factory as a way out of his troubles but when he was caught his position became absolutely hopeless, no money, no job, no nothing."

"How will his wife manage?"

"The way women do," said Fenton quietly.

Saxon Medical again featured in the newspapers on the following day, this time in the financial section. It was not a part of the newspaper that Fenton would normally read but the word 'Saxon' had caught his eye as he flicked through the pages and had registered in much the same way as hearing one's name mentioned in a crowded room. He read that rumours of a take-over involving International Plastics were rife in the city and a deal, said to be worth millions and founded on Saxon having obtained a license for their new plastic, was in the offing. The new material, it was predicted, would revolutionise equipment in science and medicine. Saxon Medical, a small family based concern, was deemed too small to exploit the enormous potential of the new discovery and was now up for grabs to the highest bidder.

"Have you seen Saxon since the Sunday you helped him with the analyser?" asked Jenny.

Fenton said that he had not.

"Then he doesn't know you think that there's something wrong with the plastic?"

"No. Tyson told me to keep my mouth shut about it in no uncertain manner. You don't walk up to a manufacturer and suggest that his product is a killer without the slightest shred of evidence. You could get very poor that way."

"Or worse," said Jenny thoughtfully as she considered the affair with the fume cupboard.

"Or worse," agreed Fenton.

"Did you tell Tyson about the fume cupboard?"

"No."

"Why not?"

"The engineers who came to re-set the fire damper found the retaining clips in the flu. They said they were in bad condition. They could have failed of their own accord causing the damper to close."

"But the cyanide in the drain?"

"We use cyanide quite a lot in the lab. I couldn't prove anything. It could have been coincidence."

"But you don't believe that?" asked Jenny.

"No," replied Fenton.

Jenny's sigh was full of frustration.

Fenton said, "I'm going to take a good look at the people who have died so far. Perhaps they have something in common, something that would point to why they were susceptible and others were not. You could help if you could lay hands on the ward files on the dead children?"

"I'll try," said Jenny. "Have you considered talking to Inspector Jamieson again?" she asked.

"No I haven't," snapped Fenton.

"That sounded a bit personal," said Jenny.

"It is entirely personal," said Fenton, recalling his conversation with the policeman just after Jenny had been taken into custody.

"But they are the professionals."

Fenton remained adamant.

Fenton found a message lying on his desk when he got in to the lab. It was from the Blood Transfusion Service and said simply, Phone Steven Kelly. He did so and had to wait for what seemed an eternity while someone on the other end went to look for him. He was on the point of putting down the receiver when Kelly finally answered. "It's about the blood that Neil Munro asked for...Can I take it that you don't need it any more?"

Fenton had forgotten all about the request that Munro had made. He said so to Kelly and apologised, adding truthfully that he had not as yet come across any reason for Neil having asked for it in the first place.

Kelly accepted Fenton's apology with his usual good humour and then said, "So I can take the donors off stand-by then?"

Fenton was puzzled. He said, "I thought Neil ordered blood from the bank?"

"No, he needed fresh blood; we had to send out postcards to suitable donors."

"Was this the first time Neil had asked for blood?" asked Fenton.

"The second," said Kelly. "We had to call in a donor about a week or so before. The blood was taken off in your lab as I remember."

Fenton had a vague recollection of having seen Munro in the lab with a stranger about seven or eight days before he was murdered. He said so to Kelly.

"It's just that we sent out postcards to three people warning them that they might be called at short notice. Two of them have phoned to ask if that is still the case."

"You can tell them no," said Fenton, trying to think at the same time as talking. "Are you absolutely sure that Neil never mentioned what he wanted the blood for?" he asked.

"Absolutely," said Kelly.

Fenton had an idea. He said, "Do you think you could give me the name of the donor who gave blood the first time? It's just possible that Neil might have said what he was using it for, especially if the donor came here to the lab and he had to make conversation."

"Hang on."

Fenton put down the phone and read back what he had scribbled down on the pad. Miss Sandra Murray, 'Fairview', Braidbank Avenue, Edinburgh.

It was a quarter past seven before Fenton had finished the day's blood lead estimations. As a consequence he had to alter his original plan to go back to the flat before going up to Braidbank Avenue. Instead he would have to shower at the lab, grab something to eat at the pub...no, better not, he did not want to smell of beer. He would eat in the hospital restaurant and go straight from there. He called Jenny to say that he would not be home before she left for the hospital. She assumed that he would be working late at the lab and, while not actually saying that this was the case, Fenton said nothing to disillusion her.

As the shower head cleared its throat and spluttered into life Fenton shivered in its margins until the temperature had settled down. The controller was faulty, making the water either too hot or too cold until adjusted with micrometer accuracy. Fenton made do with tepid rather than play around any more.

He soaped himself and tried to remember what the stranger he had seen in the lab with Neil Munro had looked like, the woman he now knew to be Sandra Murray. About five foot three seemed to be the limit of his recollection. Marvellous, he thought...Fenton of the Yard.

He turned the water off and stepped out to towel himself down, pausing briefly to listen if the rain had stopped outside. There was no sound coming from the dark skylight above the washroom although he could see water running down it. Condensation from the shower, he decided. No rain would be an unaccustomed bonus but the fact that the wind seemed to have dropped as well made it all seem to be too good to be true. It was. He stepped out of the lab into thick fog.

The Honda's headlight beam bounced off the swirling mist creating a translucent corona that slowed him down to a crawl as he edged out on to the main road and wiped his visor more in frustration than of necessity. Bloody weather, he grumbled inwardly for, to Fenton, Edinburgh's weather was part of a vendetta being waged against him personally. His meteorological paranoia now suggested that the fog was a gambit to prevent him finding Braidbank Avenue.

He knew vaguely that Braidbank would be part of a well heeled, comfortable sprawl of leafy avenues that fringed the lower slopes of the Braid Hills in Edinburgh so he headed off in that direction, slowly at first because of the fog, but then gathering speed as the fog thinned with his climb out of the city. He slowed to turn off Comiston Road and began to work his way through the quiet back-roads.

The contrast between the Braids area of Edinburgh and the Glasgow streets where he had found Mrs Lindsay could hardly have been more marked. Braidbank Avenue, when he found it was absolutely silent and exuded an aura of solidity and order. Twin rows of Victorian mansions stood like rocks of the establishment amidst mature and cultivated greenery. They stretched out like troops guarding a royal route for two hundred metres or more up to an intersection where they separated into echelons left and right.

There would be no Scobie or Ally to worry about here, no ineffectual bawling and screaming. This was where life's winners lived; these were the homes of the successful, either by profession or birth, where cheque books and pens substituted for fists and razors, where quiet telephone calls removed troublesome intruders without obliging the caller to do so much as lay down his gin and tonic or lift his eyes from the pages of 'Scottish Field.' It was an open-plan fortress with no walls or gates and its garrison recognised each other by accent and attitude.

'Fairview' boasted a black, wrought iron gate that squealed on its hinges when Fenton pushed it open. He closed it slowly to avoid any further histrionics but the latch still fell with a loud metallic clang when he turned his back. His feet crunched on the gravel making him sure that everyone within a two mile radius must be aware of his presence but there was no sign of stirring from within the house. He pressed the polished brass bell push, an action that had no audible effect, but he waited just in case something had happened deep inside the dark temple. He was about to try again when the area in which he stood was suddenly bathed in light and a series of rattles came from behind the front door.

"Yes?" said the silhouette of a large ungainly man who now filled the doorway.

"I wonder if I might have a few words with Miss Sandra Murray?" said Fenton.

A silence which probed the edge of embarrassment followed before the man said, "Come in."

Fenton had to wait in the hallway while both outer and inner doors were secured with double locks and, in the case of the outer one, a chain. At his host's bidding he followed him into a subtly lit room and accepted an invitation to sit.

Now that he could see him more clearly, Fenton saw that the man was even more ungainly than he had taken him to be. He was very large, well over six feet, with narrow, sloping shoulders that hung above the fat of his middle. His general untidiness was accentuated by the fact that his double breasted jacket had been buttoned on the wrong hole and his squint tie bore distinct signs of egg as did the front of his jacket along with contributions from other past meals. Hair jutted out from his head at odd angles almost nullifying the attempts that had been made to comb it. He peered at Fenton through metal framed glasses, perched on his nose like a see-saw at rest.

"What did you want to see my sister about?" he inquired.

Fenton thought he detected an effeminate nuance in Murray's voice. His suspicion was reinforced by the way Murray held eye contact a little too long.

"I would prefer to speak to Miss Murray personally if that's possible?" replied Fenton.

"You can't." said Murray.

Fenton waited for an explanation but none was forthcoming and he got the impression that Murray was enjoying his discomfort. "Is she indisposed?" he asked. The word had been forced on him by the sheer elegance and quality of the room and its furnishings. No one could be merely 'sick' in such surroundings; they would have to be indisposed.

"No," said Murray. "She's dead."

Fenton was shaken. He had been expecting some trivial explanation like flu or an evening class but dead? Once again he noticed that his host was observing his reaction like an owl. Murray appeared to have deliberately engineered the shock for his own ends. Fenton's discomfort grew."I'm sorry," he said, wondering whether or not he should inquire further.

In the event the Murray took the initiative. "She was knocked down by a car," he said, "The bastard didn't stop."

"How awful," said Fenton.

"Were you a friend of Sandra's?"

Fenton confessed that he had not known her at all. He responded to Murray's exaggerated frown with the reason for his visit.

"Another one!" exclaimed Murray, fixing Fenton with an unwavering stare.

Murray was making Fenton feel distinctly uncomfortable but the significance of what Murray had just said now superseded everything else."Another one? I don't understand," he said.

"You are the second person to come here from the Blood Transfusion service." said Murray. "Don't you people ever talk to each other?"

Fenton was annoyed. Why had Steve Kelly not told him that he himself intended visiting Murray? He apologised for the intrusion, explaining that he himself had no direct connection with the Transfusion Service but was a biochemist from the lab where his sister had kindly donated blood to help with a research project.

"Ah yes, with Dr Munro. Sandra told me about it."

Fenton felt a sudden excitement creep over him. "What did she tell you Mr Murray?" he asked.

Murray's fingers scratched at his unruly hair and he screwed up his eyes as he tried to recall what his sister had told him. "Something about a new plastic, I think. Dr Munro wanted to do some tests."

Fenton had to make a conscious effort to control his excitement. He asked, "Did she happen to say what kind of tests Mr Murray?"

Murray replied, "I'm sure she did but it wouldn't have meant much to me. Sandra was the scientist in this family. I'm an artist. Science is a complete mystery to me."

"I understand," said Fenton, swallowing his frustration and trying to keep calm. "But is there nothing you can remember Mr Murray?" he prompted.

Murray lapsed into dramatic silence as if he were in a trance. Fenton, although outwardly remaining calm, felt as if his head were full of broken glass. The seconds ticked by.

Murray eventually looked at Fenton out of the corner of one eye and let out an enormous sigh."I'm afraid not," he said. "But I do remember he wasn't happy with it ..."

Fenton hid his disappointment and said, "No matter. Don't worry about it."

Fenton had fallen at the last hurdle but he could see that he had learned a lot. If nothing else he now knew that he was on the right track. He said, "I mustn't take up any more of your time Mr Murray, particularly as my colleague has already bothered you."

"He didn't bother me," said Murray. "He spoke to my sister."

Fenton was confused. He said, "I thought he had been here today."

"No, this was three weeks ago," said Murray.

Fenton realised that he had been jumping to conclusions. He had assumed that Steve Kelly had called to see Murray after their telephone conversation. Kelly could not have been the caller three weeks ago or he would have said so. Someone else from the Blood Transfusion Service must have visited the house but why? "Was something wrong?" he asked Murray

"I don't think so," said Murray, scratching his head again and looking more puzzled than ever. "As far as I remember the gentleman wanted to know the same sort of things as you..."

Fenton noticed the hint of an accusation in Murray's voice and set up a defensive screen. He said, "I'm afraid things have been in a bit of a muddle since Dr Munro's death." He apologised to Murray again for the intrusion and got up to leave.

"May I offer you a drink before you go?"

Fenton declined politely, saying that he had to drive and if the fog were still around he would need all his wits about him. As the front door opened Fenton saw that the fog was worse than ever.

Fenton opted for a warm bath as being the quickest way of heating up after becoming chilled to the marrow by the painfully slow journey home. He lay back and sipped whisky from a glass that he had placed on the soap shelf. There was a lot to think about before morning. For a start why had Blood Transfusion run a check on a donor? Was this normal practice or had they some particular reason in Sandra Murray's case? And why had Steve Kelly not told him? Surely he must have known? But this question paled into insignificance when he considered what he had learned from Murray about Neil Munro's interest in the plastic.

In finding out that Neil had suspected that there was something wrong with it he had, not only uncovered the reason for Neil's preoccupation in the weeks leading up to his death, he had found a possible motive for his murder. Someone had wanted to stop him probing too deeply into Saxon plastic, someone who must have known that he was beginning to have doubts about it, someone who had been close to Neil at the time and, of course, someone who had something to gain by covering it up.

There was only one candidate. The bloated face of Nigel Saxon swam into the steamy air of the bathroom. That would also confirm his suspicions over the incident with the fume cupboard. Saxon must have feared that he too would eventually discover whatever Neil had found out about the plastic. Saxon must have set him up with the acid-cyanide trap and then made an excuse to leave the room. True, he had covered it up well when he had come back but that just served to show the devious cunning of the man.

"The bastard," whispered Fenton as more began to make sense. Saxon and Neil had been working closely over the new Blood Sampler. If Neil had said anything to anyone about his fears it would probably have been to Saxon. Perhaps they had agreed to keep it between themselves if Neil had not been sure what the problem was. But when Neil had become certain Saxon had killed him to keep it quiet. Millions, the newspaper had said, Saxon Medical was worth millions with a license for the plastic.

Fenton's grip on his glass tightened as he came to terms with reality. He could not prove it. He still did not know what was wrong with the plastic and, when viewed coldly, the only additional evidence he had obtained lay in the word of an eccentric up in Braidbank who had told him that a dead man had told his sister, also dead, that he thought there was something wrong with the plastic too. Jamieson would just love that.

Perhaps he could get some kind of corroboration from the Blood Transfusion Service, thought Fenton. If he could speak to the person who had visited Sandra Murray he could get a first hand account of what Sandra Murray had told him and that might be good enough to convince Jamieson.

The bathroom had grown too full of maybes. The water had grown cold and his glass empty. Fenton dried himself and rectified the problem with the glass. The flat still seemed cold.

Jenny got home just before eight in the morning and stifled a big yawn with the back of her hand, keys still held in it. "Now I know what a whore feels like in the morning," she sighed. "What a night."

Fenton listened patiently while Jenny told him all that had happened in a busy shift. When she had finished he said, "I went out somewhere last night."

"Really? Where?"

Fenton put down a cup of coffee in front of her and told her of his visit to Murray and what he had learned. Jenny looked shocked. Fenton had to prompt her, "Don't you see?" Neil thought there was something wrong with Saxon plastic too!"

"But what?" asked Jenny.

Fenton admitted that he still did not know but pointed out that just to have his suspicions confirmed by what Neil had believed was a step forward. "And it provides a motive for his murder," he added. "This is what connects Neil's death to the others."

"Saxon!" said Jenny.

"Saxon," agreed Fenton. "He was working closely with Neil and he had everything to gain from the plastic getting a license. It had to be him." said Fenton.

Jenny could find no real argument. "If you are right this is absolutely incredible," she said. "But...you could still be wrong."

"I know, I know." said Fenton getting up to refill their coffee cups.

"Why did Neil use this Sandra Murray woman as a donor?" asked Jenny.

"I don't know" confessed Fenton.

"You people usually use each other when you want volunteers don't you?" said Jenny.

"I suppose he wanted a different blood group," said Fenton almost automatically then both he and Jenny saw the importance of what he had said at the same time. "Could that be it?" he said softly. "Different blood groups? People in one group are susceptible while others are not?"

Jenny broke the spell of the moment by beginning to rummage through the black leather bag that rested on her knees. She pulled out a cardboard folder and handed it to Fenton saying, "These are the details you asked me to get on the child victims. I only managed to get the one; this is the ward file on the Watson boy."

Fenton flicked open the cover and traced his finger down the page till he found what he was looking for...'AB', the boy had been group, AB, a pretty rare group. Now if Sandra Murray had been in the same blood group...he was in business.

Fenton nearly bowled Ian Ferguson over as he entered the lab and rushed up the stairs, assisting his rate of climb by strong pulls on the banister. The young biochemist half turned to receive an apology but was disappointed when Fenton pressed on regardless and shut his lab door behind him.

With his white coat only half on Fenton dialled the Blood Transfusion Service and asked to speak to Steve Kelly. Kelly answered as he was holding the receiver between shoulder and cheek in order to get his left arm into his coat.

"Good morning. How did you get on?"

"Just tell me one thing. What group was Sandra Murray?"

"Is that my starter for ten?"

"It's important."

"All right, hang on."

Fenton drummed his fingers on the desk while he waited impatiently for Kelly to return.

"She was B positive."

Fenton swore.

"Are you always this sweet in the morning?" asked Kelly.

Fenton apologised for his rudeness explaining that a pet theory had just died.

"Want to tell me?"

"Some other time. You didn't tell me that someone from BTS had interviewed Sandra Murray?"

"What are you talking about?"

Fenton repeated what Murray had told him.

"No way," said Kelly.

"I don't understand," said Fenton.

"He must have been mistaken," said Kelly. "No one from this department would have gone there because we have no interest in what the blood is used for. As far as we are concerned we received a request from Biochemistry for fresh group B blood. We did the paperwork and complied with the request. That was the end of the matter.

Fenton's spirits hit the floor. He started to say something but dejection destroyed any motivation to go on. He managed to summon up enough energy to thank Kelly for his help then put the phone down.

It had started to rain again outside. Fenton idly tapped his pencil end over end as he gazed idly at the drops on the window and faced up to the latest question. If no one from Blood Transfusion had gone to see Sandra Murray, who had? After a moment's thought Fenton found the answer obvious. Neil Munro's killer, that's who. The killer must have gone there to find out how much Sandra Murray knew and when it had turned out to be too much he...had arranged for her death as well...the hit and run accident was no accident at all.

Fenton, almost afraid to face up to this latest possibility, played with the information in his head. It was a piece in a puzzle; he turned it round and round and tried to make it fit. A mistake! The killer had made a mistake he decided. From the way Murray had spoken he might have seen the man who had visited his sister pretending to be from Blood Transfusion and, if that were so, Murray could identify the killer. What was more, if Murray described Nigel Saxon, then he would have enough to go to the police with. They could nail Saxon without actually knowing what was wrong with the plastic.

Jenny telephoned at eleven saying that she couldn't sleep; she had to know about the blood group idea.

"Wrong again, confessed Fenton."Sandra Murray was group B not AB."

Jenny made disappointed sounds. "It might still be worth checking further," she said.

"Maybe," said Fenton without any real conviction, "But there's something else."

"Oh yes?"

"I think that Sandra Murray was murdered. I think that Neil told her something was wrong with Saxon plastic and the killer found out. Her death wasn't accidental at all. She was murdered just like Neil."

There was a short silence before Jenny said quietly, "Tonight Tom, tell me tonight," then she put the phone down.

Fenton was irked at Jenny's failure to share his excitement but tried to rationalise it. She had been working all night and hadn't had any sleep but . . . she had a point. He was not short of ideas. The trouble was that none of them seemed to be proving right in the long term.

Ian Ferguson came into the room while Fenton was still deep in thought. Thanks to that and the fact that the rain was hammering on the window Fenton did not hear him come in and was startled when he spoke. Ferguson apologised and said, "Is everything all right? The way you rushed past me on the stairs I thought maybe something dreadful had happened?"

"Just the death of another theory," said Fenton glumly.

"Want to tell me?" smiled Ferguson.

"There's not much to tell. I thought I had discovered a fatal flaw in Saxon plastic, something to do with patients' blood groups but apparently I was wrong."

"What made you suspect that?" asked Ferguson.

"A number of things. Neil Munro thought there was something wrong with the stuff too."

"But this is serious. Have you spoken to Dr Tyson about it?"

"He assured me there was nothing wrong with the plastic."

"How about Saxon themselves?"

"I have no evidence to back up my suspicions. I can't say anything."

"I see," said Ferguson. "But surely there is something you could do if you think there's a problem?"

"I have to find out what's wrong with the stuff before I can do anything."

"Is there anything I can do to help?"

Fenton thanked Ferguson and said that he would let him know if he thought of something. He requested that Ferguson say nothing to anyone else for the time being.

"Mum's the word," replied Ferguson.

When Ian Ferguson had gone Fenton considered his own reluctance to confide in anyone. The truth was that he did need help for he was getting hopelessly out of his depth. The question was who should he talk to? Who could he trust? He had been tempted to tell Ian Ferguson everything but the fact that Ferguson had considered resigning from the lab when the going had got tough had prevented him from doing so. He needed an ally without a question-mark over his character. The matter was to resolve itself at lunch time when Steve Kelly came into the lab and planked himself down heavily. "Fancy a beer?"

Fenton sipped his beer, aware that Kelly was appraising him but unable to relax and talk freely.

"You're a man with a problem," said Kelly.

"What do you mean?"

"I mean that you are so up tight about something that you are going to explode if you go on bottling it up. I thought you might want to talk about it?"

"I don't know what you m..."

"All right, forget I spoke," said Kelly turning to concentrate on his beer.

Fenton considered his own obstinacy in the silence that ensued. Steve Kelly was as good as they came, solid, blunt, unpretentious. He had a bit of a weakness for the women but, in hard times he could do a lot worse than have Kelly on his side. "All right," he confessed. "There is something."

They sat down to talk in one of the alcoves; the pub was still quiet before the lunch time rush. Fenton told Kelly the whole story as the first sunlight for many weeks, albeit weak and watery, rainbowed through the frosted glass and played among the dimples of the beaten copper table tops.

"And there you have it," said Fenton, finishing and taking a sip of his beer while Kelly digested what he had heard.

"That is some story," said Kelly, shaking his head, "I didn't bargain on anything like this. To be frank I had thought that you and Jenny might not be hitting it off or some such thing, but this...Jesus."

"Now you know."

"When are you going back to see Murray?"

"Tonight," said Fenton.

"Want some company?"

Fenton accepted.

CHAPTER NINE

The intermittent screen wipe on Kelly's Ford Capri flicked away the drizzle like a cow's tail dealing with summer flies.

"I hope you gentlemen have a productive evening," said Jenny as she got out of the car at the hospital gates to go on duty.

"We'll try," said Kelly.

"Good night Jenny," said Fenton softly, answering the look that was meant for him.

"Take care."

The Ford turned off the main road and Fenton gave Kelly directions as he nosed it along the wet side streets.

"You don't live up here if you work for the Health Service," said Kelly noting the size of the houses."

The headlights caught an elegant lady, swathed in furs, out walking her dog.

"I suppose it just had to be a poodle," said Fenton as they passed.

"Very nice too," murmured Kelly, looking sideways and not referring to the dog.

"Forget it," said Fenton. "You couldn't keep her in dog food. Take the next on the left."

Kelly turned slowly into Braidbank Avenue and Fenton directed him to Fairview where he stopped and turned off the engine to restore satin silence to the night.

"How do we play it?" asked Kelly.

"By ear," said Fenton. "Let's go."

Kelly pushed open the gate. Fenton anticipated the squeal.

"Did it ring?" asked Kelly as he pushed the bell.

"Yes," replied Fenton.

Murray appeared in the doorway. "Yes?"

"It's me again Mr Murray, Tom Fenton. I was here last night."

"Yes?" repeated Murray without any acknowledgement of Fenton's last visit.

"I wonder if we might have another word with you?"

Murray's contorted his face as he strained to see Kelly in the shadows. Fenton introduced them and Kelly held out his hand. Murray ignored it and turned round. "Come," he said and led the way inside.

Kelly shot Fenton a glance as they followed Murray indoors but Fenton pretended not to notice. Murray sat down in the chair he had been sitting in, judging by the book and the half empty glass beside it, and gestured to the two men to sit like candidates for interview.

Fenton noticed that the 'formal' double breasted jacket of the last occasion had been replaced by a more casual Fair Isle pullover whose already intricate pattern had been augmented by dried tomato seeds, custard, the ubiquitous egg and some green stuff that defied visual analysis. Murray seemed to be in a constant state of agitation, continually searching through his pockets without ever seeming to find what he was looking for.

Fenton waited for a few moments then coughed to attract Murray's attention. The pocket searching stopped and Murray stared at Fenton without blinking until Fenton spoke.

"We are puzzled about the man who came to see your sister Mr Murray. Are you absolutely certain he said that he was from the Blood Transfusion Service?"

"Yes," said Murray without hesitation.

"Then you saw him?" asked Fenton.

"Yes."

"Can you describe him?"

Murray produced one of his dramatic pauses before saying, "Why?"

"I know this is going to sound strange but the BTS say that no one called to see your sister Mr Murray."

Another long pause then Murray decided that the easiest course of action was to answer the question. "He was of medium height and build, slim, fair and somewhere in his middle twenties."

Fenton felt a crushing sense of disappointment for there was no way that Nigel Saxon could be described in these terms, not even by a loving mother. With unerring accuracy the slings and arrows of his particularly outrageous fortune had homed in on him again.

Fenton let Kelly continue the conversation with Murray while he wondered how to fit this latest piece of information to the puzzle. He became aware of Kelly asking about the fair haired man. "Is there anything more you can tell us about him Mr Murray?"

"Well...there was his ring."

"Ring?"

"He was wearing a ring...I recognised it." Fenton could sense the reluctance in Murray's voice as Kelly continued to probe.

"Go on."

"He was wearing a Cavalier Club ring," said Murray finally.

Kelly and Fenton both looked at Murray's hands and he saw them do it. "No, I'm not a member," he said.

Fenton felt the tension in the room. He detected in Murray the same reluctance to speak of the club as he had in Ross in the lab. He noted that Kelly seemed not to share his own ignorance.

Murray got up from his chair and crossed the room to a silver drinks tray. Without asking he poured out three whiskies from a crystal decanter and handed them round. He sat down again with slow deliberation, adjusted the glasses on his nose and said, "Now, you will tell me what this is all about." It was not a request, it was a directive.

Fenton could see that the eyes behind the glasses had gone cold and hard, the first indication of the inner man, he thought. It had come as no great surprise for he had already deduced that there must be more to Murray than the bumbling eccentric he had seen so far. You did not end up living in Braidbank by being a complete clown.

Kelly's look suggested that Fenton should answer so he did, saying that they themselves were not at all sure what was going on but it did seem likely that the man who had come to see his sister was in some way mixed up in the deaths at the Princess Mary Hospital.

Murray looked at him like an owl contemplating his dinner. He asked slowly and quietly, "Are you suggesting that my sister's death might not have been an accident."

Fenton moved uncomfortably in his seat. "It's possible," he said.

"Do police know of this?"

"All we have at the moment Mr Murray are suspicions," replied Fenton. "The minute we have anything more we will inform the police immediately."

"You mean that you haven't told them," said Murray, construing correctly what Fenton had said.

"Not yet," Fenton agreed.

"Murder is not a game for amateurs, Mister Fenton," said Murray.

"We realise that Mr Murray but, in this case, I think the professionals need all the help that they can get...judging by their success so far..."

Murray conceded the point with a slight nod of the head. He said, "I want to be kept informed of any progress you make, particularly if it concerns my sister."

"Of course," said Fenton.

"Spooky bloke," said Kelly as they walked down the path to the gate.

"Spooky is the word," agreed Fenton. He was glad to be out of the place. "Tell me about the Cavalier Club," he said "Or are you a member too?"

"I wasn't even a Boy Scout," said Kelly, looking over his shoulder before pulling away from the kerb. "I don't know that much myself but what I do know I don't like." He paused to look both ways at the intersection before turning right then took the Capri up through the gears. "As I understand it, it started out as a club for homosexuals in the city."

"There's nothing too unusual in that these days," said Fenton.

"But this one grew into something else, something much bigger."

"What do you mean?"

Kelly slowed for the traffic lights. "It's difficult to define but in every society there are a group of people who consider themselves above society in every way, I don't just mean that in the legal sense, I mean in terms of morality and social convention."

"You mean like the Marquis de Sade or the Hellfire Club?"

"That sort of thing," agreed Kelly.

"In Edinburgh? Are you serious?"

"I'm afraid I am," said Kelly with a seriousness that Fenton found uncharacteristic. "So they're a group of weirdos. It's a sign of the times."

"No, there's more to it than that," said Kelly. "This lot have power."

The traffic lights changed and Kelly moved off.

"How can they have power?" asked a disbelieving Fenton.

"The size and status of their membership decides that," said Kelly.

"So there are a lot of kinky people around, that doesn't make them powerful."

"Depends on who and what they are," said Kelly.

Fenton was still reluctant to believe what Kelly was suggesting. He said, "All right so you find the occasional judge that likes spanking schoolgirls' bottoms, that makes him vulnerable not powerful."

"Only while he remains in a tiny minority. As soon as you get a lot of judges with the same frame of mind it can get uncomfortable for schoolgirls."

"You're serious about this aren't you?" said Fenton.

Kelly stopped at another set of lights. He turned to Fenton and said, "Let me tell you a story. When the club first started some local yobs thought they would go in for a spot of poof bashing but they miscalculated. Most gays are ordinary law abiding citizens, bank clerks, office workers and the like, people who know nothing of violence and fair game for the yobs but the Cavaliers were different. They were experts in pain and violence. The yobs came second, a poor second as it happens. One of them finished up in a mental home and hasn't come out. The others refused to say what had happened to them they were so afraid so no charges were ever brought."

"Jesus."

"He is definitely not a member."

They drew to a halt outside Fenton's place. "What now?" said Kelly.

"A drink," replied Fenton, avoiding the real question and indicating with his head that Kelly should come up to the flat.

'A drink' became several and Kelly's wife phoned to ask if he was there. Fenton said that he was and asked if she wanted to speak to him. "No, no," said Mary Kelly. "As long as he's there with you Tom," she added with plain meaning.

Fenton came in from the hall somewhat unsteadily. "That was Mary checking that you weren't screwing some nurse," he said, diplomacy having been all but obliterated by the alcohol.

"She has a point," admitted Kelly.

"Damn right," said Fenton, refilling their glasses.

"Hell Tom, it's hard with all that pussy around."

"The trouble with you old son," said Fenton leaning forward in his seat, "is that it's hard all the time." The drink made the joke seem hilarious.

Jenny came in at eight in the morning."Is Steve still here?" she asked, "I saw his car outside."

"No, he walked home last night," replied Fenton sheepishly.

"I see," said Jenny.

Fenton pretended that he did not have a hangover and Jenny pretended that she did not know he had. She made coffee as Fenton told her of the latest visit to the Murray house.

"But if it wasn't Nigel Saxon, who could it have been?" Jenny asked.

Fenton shrugged his shoulders and admitted that he had no idea. but he told Jenny of the membership ring that Murray had recognised.

"So there still might be a connection with Saxon."

"Through this damned club. It's strange. Saxon doesn't seem to fit in somehow."

"I disagree," said Jenny.

"I don't understand," said Fenton.

"Oh I know all about the beer drinking, rugby playing, macho image he tries so hard to create but that's the trouble, he tries too hard. Women get a feeling about these things. But this isn't helping; it wasn't Saxon who went to the Murrays' house."

"True," said Fenton, still surprised at what Jenny had said. "But maybe...he sent a friend?"

Jenny opened her mouth to ask something but Fenton stopped her. He said, "Don't ask me what I'm going to do next, I don't know." He kissed her lightly on the cheek. "Have a good sleep."

By eleven in the morning Fenton saw that the day was shaping up to be a bad one. Mary Tyler had gone off sick and, in addition to the routine work that was coming in and the lead estimations that were extra, the surgeons at the hospital were performing a heart by-pass operation and required constant biochemical monitoring of their patient. Fenton, being the senior member of staff on duty, carried responsibility for the lab's part.

After six hours without a break Ian Ferguson came into Fenton's lab and said that he would take over for thirty minutes.

"But you're busy too," said Fenton.

"Just routine stuff. I'll stay behind this evening and clear it up."

Fenton was grateful. He went to eat in the hospital canteen and was back within twenty minutes. "I'm obliged to you Ian," he said to Ferguson.

"Think nothing of it."

Fenton said that he was ready to take over the monitoring again. Ferguson got up to go and said, "I meant to ask you yesterday. Did you ever find out what Neil Munro wanted the donor blood for?" he asked.

"Not yet but I'm getting warm," replied Fenton.

"Really?"

"He needed the blood for some kind of test connected with Saxon plastic"."

"If Neil was carrying out secret blood tests maybe that's what he needed the anticoagulants for?" suggested Ferguson.

"More than likely," agreed Fenton.

"Do you think this is why Neil was murdered?" asked Ferguson.

"Yes."

"I really think you should tell the police."

"Not just yet," said Fenton. "I need a bit more proof."

"If you say so." said Ferguson doubtfully.

As she waited for her bus, Jenny huddled in the doorway of a small shop that had closed for the night. The angle of the doorway was such that she had to keep peering out to make sure that she would see it coming but each time that she did so she got the full force of the wind and rain in her face. She avoided the brunt of it by burying her chin between hunched shoulders and narrowing her eyes till they were little more than slits. She counted and re-counted the change in her pocket as normal waiting time expired and seeds of impatience germinated in the icy rain.

The comforting hulk of a double deck bus loomed up out of the rain spewing light and throwing up spray. Jenny held out her arm and then stepped back smartly to avoid being splashed by the wheels as they approached the overflowing gutter. The driver noted her uniform and said, "Once again eh?"

"I'm afraid so," said Jenny.

"What hospital are you at?"

"Princess Mary."

"Better you than me."

Jenny took her ticket and moved to the back of the bus, thinking about what the driver had said. It annoyed her. The Princess Mary was a good hospital, one of the best in the world despite all the antiquated equipment and lack of money but all that had changed in the public's view. Now it was the hospital that harboured the killer, a place to be feared. True, he had not been as active lately but then again, the police had never caught him had they?

As she looked out of the window, trying to see through the reflections, she thought about Fenton's explanation for the deaths and realised how much faith she had been putting in it. Tom was right wasn't he? There couldn't really be a psychopath stalking the hospital corridors could there? She felt a pang of guilt at the thought but God...it was dark out there.

The bus deposited Jenny on the 'quayside' outside the hospital and set up a bow wave as it pushed off from the kerb. Her attempts to tip toe through the dark puddles were soon abandoned as pointless and her feet put the wet suit principle to the test as she squelched up the driveway with shoes awash. Her entry to the nurses' changing room brought squeals of laughter as she stood, framed in the doorway, hair plastered to her face, creating her own small but ambitious lake.

Dehydrated and with her circulation restored to something resembling normal, Jenny walked along the main corridor to her ward while, outside, the rain lashed and battered against the tall windows which were now full of night time reflections. Subconsciously she began to hum, 'For Those in Peril on the Sea.'

"Good evening Nurse Buchan," said a tall, rather severe looking woman as she entered the duty room.

"Good evening, Sister," said Jenny.

"Twenty three, including three new ones," said the woman, handing Jenny the patient list. "You might keep an eye on them?"

"Of course," said Jenny taking the list and scanning the names. She picked out the new ones, two were new admissions one was a transfer from surgery. She flicked over the page for details of the transfer and read, Callum Moir, investigation of severe stomach pain, exploratory laparotomy, pyloric obstruction found and repaired.

"He is asleep," said the day sister.

"And the new ones?" asked Jenny.

"One is asleep but the other has first night nerves, you know the form."

Jenny nodded and signed the take over form.

"Good night Nurse."

"Good night Sister."

Jenny began her rounds as the ward door closed, acknowledging the presence of the junior night nurse at the far end of the ward with a raise of the hand. Many of the children were already sleeping but she paused here and there to tuck in occasional arms and legs freed by their restless owners.

A pair of frightened blue eyes peered up at her from the mouth of their blanket cave. Jenny recognised the signs of first night nerves, one sign of sympathy from her and these full eyes would overflow. "Ah, good, you're awake," she began. "I could do with some help. Would you mind?"

Surprise replaced fear on the child's face for this was unexpected. Reassurance had been the odds-on favourite, possibly encouragement, even gentle chiding, but a request for help? The surprised look still had not faded as his feet, now slippered, hit the floor.

"Good, now follow me."

The slippers padded along behind Jenny until she stopped and pointed to the clip board hanging at the foot of a bed. She said, "I want you to read off these names to me as we come to them. All right?"

A nod.

"Well then?"

"A.n.g.u.s...Cam.e.ron."

"Check," said Jenny officiously and moved on. Three more names and all thoughts of home and family left the boy as he warmed to his new role as assistant to Night Nurse Buchan.

The child recovering from surgery was in a side ward sleeping peacefully. Jenny placed her hand gently against his forehead and felt it to be quite normal. She checked the boy's notes; no medication was indicated, no special instructions. All that was needed was a good night's sleep. She tip toed out of the room and closed the door behind her, a trifle more noisily than she had intended. She looked back through the glass panel. The boy had not stirred.

Midnight came and Jenny began to feel optimistic about the chances of a quiet night. She even said so to the junior nurse as they sipped illicit coffee in the duty room while the rain outside continued to pour.

"Brrr, I'm glad I'm not out in that," said the girl, trying to draw the curtains even closer together to shut a persistent gap in the middle.

"Pity the poor sailors," said Jenny.

"That's what my mother used to say," said the girl.

"Mine too," said Jenny.

"Do you think he's out there?" said the girl.

"Who?" asked Jenny.

"The killer of course."

"Let's not talk about that."

"Oh, I'm sorry, I forgot, I mean, I didn't..."

"Forget it."

At one o'clock the phone rang and Jenny raised her eyes before picking it up.

"I thought it was too good to last," said the junior."

"Ward 10, Nurse Buchan speaking...Yes...Yes...Understood." Jenny put down the phone and said, "Admission in ten minutes, seven year old girl, burns to both legs, hot water bottle burst."

"Poor mite," said the junior.

"Prepare number three will you?" said Jenny. "I'll get the trays ready.

As she went to get sterile dressings Jenny paused in the corridor to look through the glass panel at the surgical case. He was still sleeping peacefully, right arm outside the covers, fingers hooked over the side of the bed.

A distant siren gave early warning of the imminent arrival of their patient and the duty house officer came to the ward shortly afterwards. She had heard the same sound from her room in the doctors' residency. "Sounds like a bad one," she said.

"Burns are always bad," said Jenny.

The junior held open the ward door to allow the trolley to enter with its entourage of ambulance men, parents and a policeman. Jenny signalled to the junior with her eyes and the girl ushered the parents away from the procession and into a side room where they would be plied with tea and sympathy.

Jenny stood by as the temporary dry dressings were removed from the child's legs to reveal a mass of livid, raw flesh.

"Her mother used boiling water in the bottle," said one of the ambulance men quietly.

"She's going to need extensive grafting," said the house officer. "We'll transfer her when she' stable but in the meantime she's going to be in a lot of pain when she comes out of shock. I'll write her up for something." The house officer looked at Jenny and said, "She'll need specialling as well."

An hour later calm had returned to the ward. The girl had been sedated and installed in a side room under the care of an extra nurse who had been sent up to special nurse her, the policeman had completed his note book entry on the treble nine call and the ambulance men had returned to their stand-by quarters. The parents, stricken by remorse, and now to be haunted by conscience, had gone off to spend what was left of the night at home.

At 3am Jenny walked round the ward again, gliding quietly between the cots and beds in the soft dimness of the night lights. All was quiet. She opened the door of the side ward to check on the surgery boy and found him still asleep and lying in the same position as before. As she closed the door it suddenly struck her as strange that he was lying in exactly the same position. He was sleeping not unconscious and everyone moves when they sleep.

Jenny had a sense of foreboding as she went back in again and approached the boy to put her hand on his forehead. He was cold, icy cold. There was a sound at her feet like the contents of a glass being spilled but she knew that that could not be. She looked down to see a stream of blood pour from beneath the blankets and spatter over her shoes. She felt faint but pulled back the top covers slowly to reveal a sea of scarlet.

Jenny buried her face in Fenton's shoulder and tried to find comfort in his arms. "It was awful," she murmured. "He bled to death in his sleep. Oh God, if only I had looked in sooner..."

"Don't blame yourself," whispered Fenton. "There was nothing you could have done.

"You did say it would be another patient," said Jenny.

Fenton nodded.

"There's something else," said Jenny. "The boy had group AB blood like the Watson boy."

Fenton held Jenny away from him in disbelief. "But that is just too much of a coincidence," he said. "AB is a rare group."

"Did you check up on the others?" Jenny asked.

Fenton shook his head slowly and confessed that he had not, "I thought when Sandra Murray turned out to have group B blood that we were on the wrong track."

"Maybe not?"

"But if this is all to do with blood groups," said Fenton with a sudden thought. "That's what Neil Munro's book is all about!"

Fenton felt excitement mount inside him as the letters and numbers in Munro's book began to make sense. CT did not stand for Charles Tyson because it stood for 'clotting time!' The figures in the columns were the times taken for samples of fresh blood to clot in the presence of Saxon plastic!

Against the letter 'O' were figures equivalent to the normal clotting time for human blood. The separate columns were simply repeat tests on the same samples of group O blood. Fenton found a similar set of entries against the letter 'A' and concluded, as Neil Munro must have done, that there was no problem with either group A or group O blood and that would cover the majority of the population.

There was only one entry against the letter, 'B' and the initials, S.M. were appended. Sandra Murray! thought Fenton. Neil had used Sandra Murray's blood to test the behaviour of group B blood in the presence of Saxon plastic. He could have obtained blood of group O and A from people in the lab but for group B he had had to ask the blood transfusion service. The figures for Sandra Murray's blood, although slightly on the long side, were within the normal clotting time range. Underneath Neil had written down three dots followed by the letters, 'AB'...therefore AB. Neil Munro had known!

Munro had deduced that the plastic affected people with group AB blood and that meant something in the order of three percent of the population. That was why he had requested another donor from the Blood Transfusion Service; he had wanted to verify his conclusion.

Fenton picked up the phone and called Steve Kelly to get details of Munro's last request. Kelly told him what he was now already sure of; Munro had requested a supply of group AB blood.

Fenton had interpreted everything in Munro's book except the numbers on the first page. As a last resort he considered that they might conceivably refer to a routine lab specimen number. He went downstairs to the office to check through the files and found that there was indeed a blood sample bearing the five figured number in Munro's book. It had come from a patient named Moran and appeared to have been quite normal for all the tests requested.

Failing to see the significance of a normal blood analysis Fenton returned upstairs but stopped when he got to the first landing as the name, 'Moran' rang a bell. Of course! That was the name of the patient whose sample had been a failure on the Saxon Analyser during the trials. The failure had been put down to the specimen arriving in the wrong sort of container but when it had been checked on the routine analyser it had given perfectly normal readings. It had been the Saxon Analyser at fault not the specimen and Neil Munro must have realised that! That's what had started his investigation off in the first place!

Fenton checked with Medical Records and ascertained that the patient Moran had had group AB blood. More checking revealed that Susan Daniels had also had AB blood. A call to the records department at the Eye Pavilion told him that the same had been true for Jamie Buchan.

The conclusion was perfectly simple. Saxon plastic killed people with group AB blood. It totally destroyed the clotting mechanism. Susan Daniels had constantly been in contact with it through the samplers for the Saxon Blood Analyser she had been testing, the patients had had Saxon plastic name tags permanently against their skin, as had Jamie Buchan after Jenny had given him some to play with and the ward maid would have handled Saxon products every day in the ward. It made sense.

On the day that Neil Munro had worked out the problem with AB blood he must have told Saxon and gone down to the Sterile Supply Department immediately to have all Saxon plastic products withdrawn. Saxon must have followed him and pushed him into the sterilizer before he had had a chance to tell anyone.

It must have been Saxon personally, decided Fenton, for Neil had told no one else in the lab and he would have gone down to see Sister Kincaid as soon as he had realised what was going on. There would not have been time for Saxon to arrange for someone else to have done his dirty work. Saxon must have done it himself and for that, given half a chance, there would be a reckoning before society had its say.

CHAPTER TEN

Tyson was out of the lab at a meeting so Fenton called the hospital secretary, James Dodds, on his own authority. He was asked to wait while a lady with an affected accent checked to see 'if Mr Dodds was available.'

"Dodds here."

"Fenton, Biochemistry, I think you may find this a little difficult to believe..."

Fenton was right, Dodds found it hard to swallow. He indicated his difficulty by making spluttering noises into the phone and other sounds of incredulity.

"You must withdraw all Saxon plastic products at once," concluded Fenton.

"But are you absolutely sure?" protested Dodds.

"Absolutely. There is no madman on the loose in the hospital, it's the plastic."

"But Dr Munro's death?"

"I'll be speaking to the police about that," said Fenton. "But the main thing is to stop the staff using anything made of Saxon plastic."

"Of course, of course," murmured Dodds. "Right away."

Saxon products were withdrawn from circulation, a task accomplished without much difficulty due to the fact that stocks in the hospital were generally low as the initial gift from Saxon Medical had dwindled down to a few weeks supply. More was on order for when they became commercially available but now, thankfully, that would never happen.

Fenton wished that Tyson would return from his meeting for he felt the need of moral support. For the past two hours, ever since his conversation with Dodds, he had done little else but answer the telephone and deal with personal callers who wanted more details. He felt like the Caliph of Baghdad on a bad day but without the power to cut the heads from those who pleaded their case too strongly. If just one more person were to ask him if he was 'absolutely sure'...

"But are you absolutely sure?" asked Inspector Jamieson, making Fenton's foot itch. "Yes, I am," replied Fenton through gritted teeth. "But for conclusive proof I have asked the Blood Transfusion Service to provide some group AB blood for us to test."

"Who's bringing it?" asked Jamieson.

"Its owner. It has to be fresh blood. The donor will be coming here."

Jamieson suggested that a police car should be sent to collect the donor so Fenton gave him Kelly's number. He passed it to his sergeant. "See to it will you." He walked over to the lab window and looked out at the greyness. "So we have a plastic murderer," he said, still with his back to Fenton.

"So it seems," said Fenton. He could sense Jamieson's discomfort and could understand it. The man had been hunting a non-existent killer and there would be no glory in this for him, no self effacing media interviews, just another bumbling copper story. But there was still the Munro death. Fenton thought that he could read Jamieson's mind.

"I understand you have some ideas about the Munro death?" said Jamieson.

Fenton said, "I think I know why he was murdered and I think I know who did it." He brought out Neil Munro's notebook and said, "I didn't understand this at first but I do now. It proves that Neil Munro knew that there was a problem with Saxon plastic and, what's more, he had worked out exactly what."

"And you think this is why he was killed?"

"The license for Saxon plastic was worth millions."

"To the Saxon Company," said Jamieson.

"Saxon the company, Saxon the man." said Fenton.

"Point taken."

Charles Tyson came in to the room and broke the spell. He came straight over to Fenton. "I think I owe you an apology," he said.

"Let's just be glad it's over," said Fenton.

"I should have listened to you earlier. I could kick myself."

Fenton said, "You took the only line possible. Besides I was out of my head with worry over Jenny at the time."

Fenton's reference to Jenny had been for Jamieson's benefit. The policeman shifted his weight to the other foot but showed no signs of embarrassment. He said, "Perhaps you will let me know when you have completed the blood tests?"

"Will do," said Fenton.

Tyson asked, "What blood tests?"

Fenton told him about the donor who was on his way.

For Maxwell Kirkpatrick, senior clerk with the Scotia Insurance Company (est. 1864) this was the kind of call he had been waiting for all his life. His previous pinnacle of achievement in becoming secretary of the Grants Hill Church of Scotland Badminton Club (Monday Group) was now dwarfed thanks to a blood group that set him apart from mere mortals.

As the white police Rover with the fluorescent orange stripe squealed through the gates of the hospital and genuflected to the front door Maxwell got out and looked up at the Latin inscription above the stone arch. A missionary zeal shone from his eyes. He didn't understand it but somehow it seemed right. The policemen fired off a two door salute and drove off leaving Maxwell to enter reception. "Good day," he announced in tones that suggested he might also collect cigarette cards and go train spotting, "I understand that...you need me."

Tyson took the blood from Kirkpatrick and handed the full syringe to Fenton who ejected half the contents into a regular test tube and the rest into a Saxon plastic one. The click of the stop watches sounded unnaturally loud in the quiet of the room.

As time passed Kirkpatrick found it increasingly difficult to maintain his expression of expectant interest. His smile began to pucker like a beauty queen held too long on camera and his eyes moved backwards and forwards between Fenton and Tyson as he searched for clues from the pre-occupied men.

"This one has gone," said Tyson quietly. He tapped the side of the tube with his pen to make sure.

"This one hasn't," said Fenton who was monitoring the Saxon tube.

"Completely clotted," said Tyson.

"Quite, quite fluid," said Fenton.

"Game, set and match." said Tyson. He turned to Kirkpatrick and apologised for his rudeness. He explained what they had been looking for.

"Do you mean...there is no patient?" asked Kirkpatrick with an air of disappointment.

Tyson, sizing up the man, assured him that what he had just done would be instrumental in the saving of many lives. Fenton added his agreement and Kirkpatrick beamed. "Just doing what little I could," he said with a downward cast of his eyes.

"We are very grateful," said Tyson. "I'll ask the police to see to it that you are taken where you want to go."

"Really?" said Kirkpatrick, his eyes opening wide. He had not reckoned on being returned to the office in a police car. This was an added bonus. Would they use the flashing light on the return journey? And would a constable hold the door open for him when he got out? By God, this would show that bitch in accounts that Maxwell Kirkpatrick was not a man to be trifled with.

Tyson pulled on a pair of surgical gloves with traditional difficulty and took the test tubes to the sink as Inspector Jamieson arrived. He gently tipped the Saxon tube on to its side and let the blood stream out in a thin, even flow. "You know," he said, "It's quite ironic really, this stuff is probably going to turn out to be the most efficient anticoagulant known to man."

"I think Neil had plans to investigate that," said Fenton.

"How so?"

"He had a range of standard anticoagulants and a bottle of solvent in a locked cupboard in his lab. I think he must have been planning on trying to solubilise the plastic in order to test its anticoagulant capacity before he realised the significance of the blood groups."

Fenton was intrigued by the amount of care that Tyson seemed to be exercising in dealing with the plastic test tubes. As he checked his gloves yet again for signs of damage he became aware that Fenton was watching him. He said quietly, "Worked it out yet?"

The truth dawned on Fenton. "The dirty tube...it wasn't a dirty tube at all. It was your blood! You have group AB blood."

"Correct. I was lucky, I haven't had any reason to come into contact with the damned stuff for any length of time but I don't relish coming that close again."

"Any news about Mr Saxon, Inspector?" Tyson asked.

"Mr Saxon will be shortly helping us with our inquiries sir," said Jamieson getting up to leave Fenton screwed up his face at the official jargon but he had his back to the policeman.

"I take it you and Inspector Jamieson don't get on too well?" asked Tyson when the door had closed.

"Something like that," agreed Fenton.

"The business over Jenny?"

"I suppose so."

"You may not like it but Jamieson was right to do what he did. On the face of it he had every reason to suspect Jenny and what's more, the very fact that he saw the link between the deaths in the hospital and the boy's death up north makes him good at his job!"

"If you say so."

"I do. Now that we have established that, let's drink to the end of this damned business." Tyson opened a desk drawer and took out a half full bottle of malt whisky. "Fetch a couple of beakers will you? Glass ones."

Fenton lay along the sofa with his head on Jenny's lap and closed his eyes while she played with the curls of his hair.

"That's nice," he murmured.

"Nothing is too nice for the hero of Princess Mary."

"I just hope the police picked up Saxon," said Fenton.

"You know, I still find it hard to believe that Nigel Saxon was the cause of all this," said Jenny distantly.

Fenton opened his eyes. "What do you mean?" he asked.

"Well, he was brash and loud but basically I always thought of him as weak, just like a big Labrador dog. I just can't picture him killing someone in cold blood. Can you?"

Fenton thought for a moment then said quietly, "I agree but he must have done unless you have a better idea?"

Jenny shook her head. "No, but there's something not quite right about it..."

"What do you say we concentrate on something else?"

"And just what could that something be?" asked Jenny with a smile.

Fenton drew her to him and left her in no doubt.

The atmosphere in the flat might have been considerably different had Fenton known that, while he had been making love to Jenny, Nigel Saxon had not been safely in police custody. In fact, he was not even in the country for he had taken an afternoon British Airways shuttle flight from Glasgow to London Heathrow and had subsequently boarded an Olympic Airways flight to Greece.

Fenton was furious when he heard the news from Charles Tyson and immediately blamed Jamieson. "All he had to do was pick him up. I suppose he gave him a lift to the airport and carried his bags into the terminal!"

"It wasn't the Inspector's fault," said Tyson calmly.

Fenton looked sceptical.

"James Dodds phoned Saxon Medical after you called him yesterday. He saw no reason not to and thought that they should be aware of the problem with their product. He called them before he called the police so Nigel Saxon knew the game was up even before Inspector Jamieson had been informed."

"I'm sorry," said Fenton.

Fenton left Tyson's room and closed the door quietly. His thoughts returned to Saxon and his anger was reborn. He swallowed it for the moment but, for the rest of the week, it lay in his stomach like a lead weight.

Press and television coverage of the end of the 'Princess Mary Affair' was extensive and raised a number of questions and issues for ambitious politicians to exploit. Was the screening procedure for National Health Service products adequate? they asked. Perfectly so, said the government of the day. Clearly not, hollered Her Majesty's Opposition. Once again the government had been found lacking. The air vibrated with the sound of stable doors being slammed. The thalidomide tragedy was resurrected. Why had we not learned our lesson? The American Food and Drug Authority had banned thalidomide in the United States; the odds were that they would have spotted the problem with Saxon plastic as well. Nonsense, retorted the Health Department. Cover-up! cried the Opposition. Heads must roll! bayed the press and cast-on their knitting.

"Ye Gods, it's all so predictable," complained Jenny as she put down the evening paper. "If one says black the other says white."

The financial press had a different set of priorities. They paid lip service to the 'awful human cost' but it was the financial mess that Saxon Medical had created that really captured their imagination. Had the money involved in the take-over actually changed hands? they wanted to know and, if the license had been sold by Saxon, had the responsibility been transferred with it? Would International Plastics be liable to lose millions, not only in the loss of the product, but in law suits brought against them for compensation by the relatives of the victims?

Speculation along these lines had already done damage to International's share prices but the company remained silent, saying nothing in public, although it was not too hard to guess what they were saying in private. Fenton supposed that cohorts of their lawyers would be working round the clock in an attempt to shed blame.

Saxon Medical took a different approach. They simply shut up shop and went to ground. John Saxon, founder of the company and Nigel's father, walled himself up in his Georgian mansion in a Glasgow suburb and refused to see anyone. The workforce had been paid off and Nigel, of course, had fled to Greece.

No public mention had been made of any police interest in Nigel Saxon and, as yet, no enterprising journalist had sought to forge a link between Neil Munro's death and the Saxon plastic tragedy. This gave Fenton an idea for it occurred to him that a conviction against Nigel Saxon would be of monumental importance to International Plastics. If the company could establish that Saxon had known about the defect in the plastic before the license had changed hands surely the deal would be deemed to have been fraudulent? It was very much in International's interest that Nigel Saxon be brought to justice. The thing was, International knew nothing of any criminal involvement in the Saxon Plastic affair. What would happen if he were to tell them?

Fenton thought about it for the rest of the afternoon and began to like the idea. Surely in the circumstances International Plastics would mount their own investigation, employ the best agents in the country to track down Saxon, ferret him out, bring him back?

There was, of course, Interpol. Fenton had been brought up on films where Interpol were brought in but, on reflection, he could not recall a single real life incident where Interpol had played a major successful part. Once across the channel it seemed like it was home and dry for the villains. Even the occasional international arrest seemed to flounder in a welter of legal wrangles and territorial jealousies. The more he thought about it the more convinced he became that a private operation, based on sound mercenary principles stood the best chance of making Saxon pay for what he had done.

To Fenton, International Plastics was a name from the newspapers. He had no idea where the company was located and no notion of how to go about approaching them. The trouble with large companies, he was that so few people of importance seemed to be accessible within them. Such fish always surrounded themselves with smaller fish who, in turn, surrounded themselves with even smaller fry. Fenton could see himself splashing around in the water margins for some time, being shunted from one two metre square office to the next and having to explain to frayed collars and cuffs that what he had to say was not for their ears.

That in itself would be a problem, for suggesting, even obliquely, to a minion that what he had to say was not for his ears would be tantamount to an Israelite expressing agnostic tendencies while crossing the Red Sea. The resulting maelstrom of obstruction and red tape could be fatal to the spirit.

Fenton told Jenny what he had in mind and she exploded. Fenton had never seen her so angry. He reeled as her temper ignited like a stick of dynamite. "How dare you?" she blazed. "Is there no end to your arrogance?

Fenton sat, wide eyed and speechless on the couch. He could not believe what was happening. "Arrogance?"

"Yes arrogance! You always know better. The police are stupid. Interpol are useless. Everyone is incompetent where you are concerned. Well, understand this! Nigel Saxon's arrest is a matter for the police, not you. Leave it alone! I have had enough. Do you understand? Just forget it or...or I'll leave you." Jenny burst into tears and Fenton got up to gather her in his arms. "All right," he promised quietly. "I didn't realise."

Jenny banged her fist on his shoulder. "I know damn it," she said. "I know."

Jenny's outburst had shaken Fenton, but it had been what he needed for he now recognised that the hunt for Nigel Saxon had become an obsession. It irked him so much that Saxon appeared to have gotten clean away with his crime that he had thought about little else for many days to the detriment of everything else in life. He promised Jenny that there would be no approach to International Plastics, no more talk of Nigel Saxon. They would go back to being Tom and Jenny, the folks who lived on the hill.

Jenny drew the curtains and turned up the gas fire as the wind got up outside. She switched on a small table lamp and put an album on the stereo before lying along the couch with her head on Fenton's lap. For once, the wind contributed to the feeling of cosiness inside the room. Fenton's fingers played the opening bars of Beethoven's Moonlight Sonata on the back of her neck.

"Tom, I'm sorry," said Jenny softly.

"Don't be. You were right."

The music, the warmth, the soft lighting and the hiss of the fire lulled them into a comfortable drowsiness. It was shattered when the telephone rang. Jenny got up to answer it and padded out into the hall in stockinged feet. She came quickly back and stopped in the doorway looking ashen. "It's for you," she said. "I think it's Nigel Saxon!"

Fenton rose like an automaton. He felt cold all over as he sidled past Jenny into the hall and picked up the receiver. Slowly he said, "Tom Fenton."

The dialling tone filled his ear and brought instant relief. He let out the breath he had been holding and put the phone down. "No one there," he said, knowing that Jenny was standing behind him.

"It was him, I know it was," said Jenny evenly.

"Maybe a wrong number, someone who sounded like him."

"He asked for you by name. Saxon has a distinctive voice and he phoned here several times to ask how you were when you were in hospital. It was him," said Jenny in an unwavering monotone.

"But why? Why phone me? He knows Neil was a friend of mine. I would be the last person in the world to help him." said Fenton.

"I don't know why. I only know it was him."

Fenton rubbed the back of his neck.

"What are you going to do?" asked Jenny.

"Nothing I can do," replied Fenton.

In spite of their efforts to re-create the earlier peace of the evening the phone call had ruined it. The warmth, the music, the cosiness were still there but the mute telephone rang in their ears until bedtime. They had gone to bed and were just on the point of falling asleep when it rang for real.

"I'll get it," said Fenton getting out of bed and hoping against hope that it would be anyone in the world rather than Saxon.

It was Nigel Saxon.

"You've got a nerve," hissed Fenton.

"Just hear me out, that's all I ask.

"Well?" snarled Fenton, continuing to listen against his better judgement.

"I know what you all think but I didn't kill Neil Munro. Believe me. I didn't do it."

"Is that the best you can do Saxon?"

"All right, all right, I know it looks bad, that's why I made a run for it but I didn't do it!"

"Then give yourself up."

"My feet wouldn't touch and you know it. All the police want is a nice quick conviction to regain some credibility and I fit the bill to a tee. No, there's only one way I can prove my innocence."

"Go on."

"I have to give the police the real killer."

Fenton paused before saying, "Assuming that it isn't you, and I don't say for one moment that I believe you, how do you propose doing that?"

"I think I know who the real killer is."

"Who, dammit?"

"I don't want to say just yet, but when I'm sure I may need your help. What do you say?"

Fenton was in a quandary. What did he say? What would Jenny say? Was Saxon lying and, if so, what was his angle? What did he have to gain? Could he be telling the truth? "How long before you're sure?" he asked.

"A day, maybe two."

"Two days, then I tell the police."

"Thanks."

"Where are you?"

The phone went dead.

Fenton returned to the bedroom, half afraid to meet Jenny's eyes. She said, "It was him, wasn't it?"

"It was him."

"Why? What in God's name did he want?" asked Jenny in exasperation.

Fenton told her.

Jenny held her head in her hands and said, "Oh my God, what next?" She slapped down her palms on the bedcovers and looked up at him. "Promise me one thing," she said. "If Saxon suggests any kind of meeting, you won't go alone. Take Ian Ferguson or Steve Kelly, or better still tell the police, but don't go alone."

"I promise."

Fenton fell asleep but woke at two and was unable to drop off again. He lay in the darkness listening to the sound of the wind but felt so restless that he was obliged to get up before he woke Jenny with his constant changing of position. He pulled on a dressing gown and went to the kitchen to make coffee.

When he came through to the living room it was icy cold so he relit the gas fire and huddled over it while he faced up to the old questions. A stream of doubts turned up again like unwelcome relations on the doorstep. Why could real life not be like the films with a beginning, a middle and an end? Goodies and baddies and never any doubt which was which. Things had just appeared to have resolved themselves nicely when this had to happen. The arch villain turns up pretending to be innocent and the big question now was, was he pretending?

"Are you all right?" came Jenny's voice from the bedroom.

"Sorry, did I wake you?" said Fenton.

"No, it's always the same when I get a night off. I waken up anyway."

For two days the question had to wait like a garden gnome with a fishing rod. Fenton had almost decided to phone the police when Saxon called at seven in the evening and said, "I know who killed Munro and tonight we can prove it."

The word 'we' rang out loud and clear in Fenton's head. He asked what Saxon meant.

"I want you to be here in the flat when he admits it," said Saxon.

"Who's he? What flat?" asked Fenton.

"I am back in Edinburgh. I have a flat here that nobody knows about. Will you come?"

Fenton felt distinctly uneasy. "What's the plan?" he asked.

"I want someone here, quietly concealed in the flat, to witness what is said when my visitor comes."

"All right," said Fenton, feeling that he was jumping in with both feet. "Where are you?"

"Do you promise? No police?" asked Saxon.

"I promise," said Fenton.

Saxon gave an address in the New Town. It had the suffix 'a'.

"Is it a basement?" asked Fenton

"Yes."

Fenton was scribbling down the address on the phone pad when he sensed Jenny at his shoulder. "You haven't forgotten what you agreed?" she asked.

"I said that I would not contact the police but I did not say I would be alone," said Fenton. He picked up the phone again and called Steve Kelly. They arranged to meet in a bar near the west end of Princes Street.

"Whisky?" asked Kelly when Fenton arrived.

Fenton nodded and looked around to see if there were any seats free. There were not so they stayed standing at the bar. "What's going on?" asked Kelly, handing Fenton his glass and sliding the water jug towards him. "I thought this thing was all over."

Fenton added meat to the skeleton of the story that he had given Kelly over the phone and ended by saying, "That's as much as I know."

Kelly let his breath out through his teeth and whispered, "Good God, how do I let myself in for these things?"

"In this case, you didn't. I let you in for it and I'm grateful," said Fenton.

"Where is this place exactly?"

Fenton told him.

"At what time?"

Fenton told him.

"Then we've got time for another one?"

Fenton ordered two more whiskies.

As they left the pub Kelly pulled up the collar of his overcoat and thumped his fist into the palm of his hand."God, it's cold."

He was right. Frost hung in the night air and painted haloes round the street lights as they walked east along Rose Street, once the haunt of the city's whores but now appropriated by the bars and boutiques of the trendy.

They had to step off the pavement as a crowd of young men spilled out of one of the bars full of liquored bravado. By their clothes and accents they were from well to do families. One of them bumped into Kelly who ignored him but the drunk put his hand on Kelly's shoulder and said aggressively, "Who do you think you are shoving?"

"Go play with your train set Alistair," said Kelly with a look that made the drunk back off.

"How did you know my name was...Alistair," asked the drunk, looking more confused than dangerous.

"It always is," said Kelly.

They walked on.

The streets quietened suddenly as they took a left turn and walked down into the New Town. Solid Georgian frontages guarded by black iron railings lined their way, presenting their credentials on brass plaques as they passed. Architect followed solicitor followed surveyor. An occasional interloper from North Sea Oil, an occasional dentist for the private mouth.

"They say," said Kelly, "That on dark nights...you can hear the dry rot sing."

"Here it is," said Fenton, looking up at the street sign. "Lymon Place." They were standing at the top of a steep hill that curved elegantly down to the left in quiet darkness, the pavement slabs glistened with frost as he checked a few numbers. "It's on the right," he said.

24a was half way down and it was in complete darkness. Fenton opened the iron railed gate at pavement level and descended the stone steps to the basement area. Kelly followed and they skirted round a blue painted barrel which, in season, would contain bedding plants.

The brass knocker sounded loud and hollow but there was no reply. Fenton tried again and they waited in silence while their breath rose visibly in the freezing air.

"I don't think there's anyone there," said Kelly, sounding less than disappointed.

"He said nine o'clock," said Fenton.

Kelly checked his watch but said nothing. Fenton tried turning the handle of the door. It swung open with surprising ease and quietness and the street lights were reflected in an inner, glass door. Fenton tried that too.

"Isn't this burglary?" whispered Kelly as it opened.

Fenton ignored the question and stepped quietly inside. "Saxon?" he called out softly, repeating it as he moved along the passage. There was still no reply.

"I smell burning," said Kelly.

Fenton sniffed and agreed. "As if someone had singed their hair," he said.

The flat appeared to be completely empty. "I don't get it," complained Fenton after he had tried the last room. "Why the hell did he ask us here?"

"What's this?" asked Kelly tugging at a door in the hallway.

"Cupboard?" suggested Fenton.

Kelly pulled it open and a yellow light shone up from the floor. "Stairs!"

"A sub-basement," whispered Fenton.

They descended the spiral stone steps, steadying themselves with their hands on the white washed walls.

"God, what a stink," said Kelly as the burning smell got stronger and threatened to overpower them.

"Look at this," said Kelly. He was standing in front of a large door that had been tooled in leather and inset with heavy brass studs.

"Try it," said Fenton.

"I feel like Jack and the Beanstalk," said Kelly as he turned the heavy ringed handle. The door swung slowly back to reveal a stone floored dungeon lit exclusively by wall torches set in wrought iron holders. In the middle of the floor lay the black smouldering remains of something they both recognised barely as the body of a man.

Fenton covered his face with a handkerchief and approached slowly. He knelt down beside the bundle as smoke rose from charred flesh like the pall from burning leaves on an autumn day. He recoiled in revulsion as he suddenly realised something. Kelly looked at him and then the corpse and saw the same thing.

"He's...not dead," said Fenton, unwilling to believe what he himself was saying.

Kelly saw the smoke come from the man's blackened mouth in short regular breaths. "He must be," he whispered. "Is it Saxon?"

"Yes," murmured Fenton, steeling himself to kneel down again. "Saxon?" he whispered. He looked for some part of the man that he could touch without hitting raw nerves, some way he could make contact but it was useless. A groan came from Saxon's throat and threatened Fenton's own nerves. "Die man, for God's sake...die." he murmured. As if in response a convulsion quivered through the burned flesh and a hoarse gurgle came from Saxon's throat. It culminated in a brief sigh and his head moved to one side.

"He's gone," said Fenton.

"Thank God," said Kelly.

Kelly looked round the room and said, "Will you look at this?"

Fenton could see what he meant for the dungeon theme had been pursued in meticulous detail. The bare stone walls were decked with manacles and other articles of bondage. Whips of varied size and material stood erect in a long chain link rack next to some kind of table equipped with stirrups and iron wrist clamps. The whole place was the manifestation in wood and iron of some medieval nightmare.

Kelly found a leather bound book and opened it. It was a photograph album. "Jenny was right," said Fenton as he saw the photos. "She thought that Saxon was bent, sounded too macho, tried too hard, she said."

"Bent is not the word," said Kelly, looking through the pages of the album.

"Takes all sorts as my grandmother used to say," said Fenton.

"So what happened here?" said Kelly, putting down the book and looking at Saxon's body. "Some trick go wrong?"

"No," said Fenton. "His hands are still bound. He couldn't have set light to himself." He looked at the blackened corpse for a moment before starting to search round the room. He found a green jerry can and sniffed the contents. "Paraffin," he said to Kelly. "Some bastard shackled him, doused him in paraffin and started throwing matches."

"Where does that leave us?" asked Kelly quietly.

"Up to our necks in something I'd rather you didn't make waves in," said Fenton ruefully.

Fenton could see that he was in trouble no matter which way he turned. If he phoned the police it would be tantamount to admitting that he had known the whereabouts of Nigel Saxon and had failed to inform them. If he kept quiet and Jamieson found out later then that might even be worse. Jamieson might even suspect that he had been Saxon's killer with revenge for Neil Munro as the motive.

"You are sure it's Saxon aren't you?" Kelly asked.

Fenton nodded. "I'm sure," he said. "Even like that, I knew him well enough to recognise him."

"So what do we do?"

"Get out of here and pray that no one saw us come in," said Fenton.

CHAPTER ELEVEN

Fenton and Kelly stood still for a moment in the quiet of the basement area and courted the shadow of the wall while they listened for sounds coming from above. When they were sure that all was quiet they climbed the steps quickly to the pavement and started walking.

Like Christians cast into some Georgian Coliseum they looked furtively out of the corners of their eyes for signs of lions. They saw nothing, but Fenton was far from convinced. He imagined hidden faces behind every tall rectangular window. Their description was already being noted and telephones were being lifted. They suppressed the urge to run but doing so filled them with the nervous tension of thorough-bred horses held under rein.

"Up here," said Fenton, seeking the earliest opportunity of returning to noise and bustle. The lights of a white painted pub attracted them like harbour buoys and the crowd inside absorbed them into welcome anonymity.

"God, I needed that," said Kelly after downing his whisky in one gulp. Fenton ordered two more and they began to take stock of their surroundings. The clientele were mainly young, fashion conscious and noisy. The bar list boasted sixteen different cocktails. It said a lot about the customers.

"Why! Steven Kelly!" said a loud female voice behind them. Fenton froze but he felt Kelly's eyes on him before he turned round.

"Fiona Duncan, how nice," said Kelly, failing his audition for RADA.

"Whatever brings you here?" continued Fiona at the top of her voice. Kelly was struggling but Fenton realised that it did not matter for Fiona was not listening to the answers. She was only interested in her own performance. Fenton knew the type. Conversations were opportunities for self projection, chances to display an ever changing slide show of facial expression to whoever might be watching. The loudness of the voice was designed to swell that number.

"Tom, meet Fiona Duncan," said Kelly looking like a wet spaniel. "She used to be a nurse at the Princess Mary."

Fenton nailed Kelly with a glance before shaking hands with the loud girl. "And where are you now Fiona?" he asked politely.

"The Western General!" said Fiona. She announced it like the winning number in a raffle and her right hand gave a little cheer.

Fenton smiled, passing her back to Kelly.

"So what are you doing with yourself these days Steve? Behaving?" asked Fiona.

Fenton saw the look that passed between Kelly and the girl and knew what had gone on in the past. He marked time with a fixed smile on his face until Fiona decided that she had to 'dash'. Her friends were waiting for their drinks. He almost felt the spotlight go out as she moved her cabaret to the bar.

"Sorry about that," whispered Kelly, looking sheepish.

"They should have cut them off at birth," muttered Fenton.

Jenny welcomed them with a sigh of relief and a barrage of questions that made Fenton hold up his hands. "You had better sit down," he said. He told her what they had found, trying to leave out as many of the gory bits as possible. Jenny kept probing. He added the gory bits.

"But supposing he lies there for weeks before anyone finds him?" Jenny pointed out. "Could our nerves stand it?"

The consensus was no. "How should we do it?"

"Anonymous call," said Kelly. "I'll do it on my way home. Go to 24a Lymon Place. There's a dead man there."

The story was too late for the morning papers but local radio carried it in their morning bulletins. Nigel Saxon, son of the owner of Saxon Medical, the company at the centre of the lethal plastic affair, had been found dead in a city flat and the police were treating the death as murder. There was no more. Fenton thought that it seemed so clinically clean and tidy, nothing at all like the hellish reality of what had lain in that basement. Nothing to convey the sight, the smell. Only the police would know that. It made him wonder how many other stories were deodorized every day, cellophane wrapped, sanitised for public protection. Did it matter?

The evening paper seemed to think that it did.' New Town Funeral Pyre for Plastics Boss' concentrated on the charring and disfigurement of Saxon's body, managing to use the phrase 'barely recognizable' three times in the story. For the first time the police admitted publicly that they had been looking for Saxon in connection with their enquiries into the death of Neil Munro. The simple statement invited the public to draw their own conclusions, the very reason they made it, thought Fenton. No mention was made of the sex angle however, something that made Jenny suggest cynically that the police were going to sell it to the Sundays. She was wrong. The tabloids got it on the following morning and made a meal of it with, 'Sex Secrets of New Town Basement.'

No 'secrets' were actually revealed but the suggestion of homosexuality and the persistent use of the word 'apparatus' was enough to alter the nature of the crime for the law abiding citizens of Edinburgh. Outrage at the murder became muted. The unspoken view that this was an affair that God-fearing folk were better off not knowing about became the prevalent one. Some perverted creature from a strange twilight world had got his just deserts. I'll make the cocoa Agnes, you put out the cat.

Fenton could not help but feel that the police had orchestrated the whole thing and it had worked. The pressure was off them for, to all public intents and purposes, they had tracked down Neil Munro's killer and he was dead, better than a conviction for the rate payers. As for Saxon's killer? They would go through the motions, follow routine but there was very little pressure on them this time. No one cared about Saxon or his seedy society. At least this was what Fenton had concluded but he had to change his mind when the police issued a description of two men that they wanted to interview in connection with the New Town murder.

Fenton held his breath as he listened to the descriptions. Two men aged between twenty and thirty, one six feet tall and dark, the other slightly shorter with fair hair and broad shoulders. Both had been seen leaving the area of the basement flat on the night in question

Fenton's first instinct was to phone Steve Kelly but he talked himself out of it, deciding that it was a panic reaction. Kelly phoned him. There was nothing really to say.

Kelly phoned again in the evening just after eight when Jenny was leaving for the hospital. "We've got trouble," he said and Fenton's heart sank. Jenny, who had been in the act of leaving, paused in the doorway and said, "Should I wait?"

"No," said Fenton. "Just go, see you in the morning."

Jenny threw him a kiss and closed the door behind her.

"What trouble?" asked Fenton.

"Fiona Duncan called me. She pointed out that 'The White Horse' is very near Lymon Place and I've got fair hair and broad shoulders."

"Just what we needed," muttered Fenton, trying to think at the same time.

"I'm sorry about this," said Kelly.

"I think we had better go to the police before they come to us." said Fenton.

"Do you think if I strangled Fiona I could ask for one other case to be taken into consideration?"

"I'll come round to your place," said Fenton.

Fenton apologised to Mary Kelly for having got her husband into his present predicament but she was in a less than forgiving mood and her look came straight from the freezer. As they left Kelly gave his wife a peck on the cheek and said, "See you later."

Don't bet on it, thought Fenton.

"Good evening sir," said the desk sergeant, expecting a lost dog story.

"I think you are looking for us," said Fenton, feeling as if he were throwing away a key.

The sergeant stared at them until he saw a six foot tall dark man accompanied by a shorter man with fair hair. "Good God," he said and lifted the telephone. Jamieson was summoned from home.

Fenton and Kelly were held separately during the wait, each accompanied by a silent constable. Fenton found his room oppressively quiet and free from distraction, furnished only with a table and four chairs and painted in institutional pastel green. At least the table creaked when he put his elbows on it and, in this respect, it was more communicative than the constable. There was a vaguely unpleasant smell of disinfectant about the place, something that made Fenton wonder why it had been necessary to use it in the first place. It conjured up visions of lice and filth and vomit and generally added to his feelings of unease.

"Any chance of a cup of tea?" he asked.

The constable shook his head mutely.

An awful thought struck Fenton. As yet, no one had asked for his name or any other details. Everything was being saved for Jamieson. It would be a surprise for him when he walked through the door. He wondered what he would say.

"Oh Christ! This is all I needed," said Jamieson. "Mr smart-arse Fenton.

Fenton struggled to adopt the right facial expression but couldn't find it. Aggression was out, definitely out in the circumstances, but contriteness went against the grain, especially with Jamieson. He settled for something along the lines of a British tourist being harangued by a foreign official in a language that he did not understand.

Jamieson finished his opening salvo and settled down to enjoying his work. He was going to play this particular fish for a while.

"Why did you do it Fenton? Revenge? Was that it? He cooked your mate, you cooked him?"

Fenton spluttered out a denial but the truth was that he had not seen the poetic justice angle. Things were even worse than he thought.

"How long have you been a practising homosexual Fenton?"

Fenton clenched his fists.

"Is that why you got beaten up in that pub Fenton...in the toilets wasn't it?"

Fenton made for him. The constable dived in to restrain him while Jamieson just smiled.

Jamieson was in his element, he had not had so much fun for ages. He ran rings round Fenton, laughing away denials, playing him out, reeling him in, digging the hook in deeper until, at last, he saw the fight in Fenton begin to subside. It was always the moment he enjoyed most. He brought his face close to Fenton's and said threateningly, "Let me tell you this, laddie, it gets very boring being taken for a mug by every half-arse who's seen The Pink Panther. You might just ponder on the fact that Nigel Saxon would be alive today if you had contacted us as soon as he called you.'

Fenton pondered the fact.

Fenton and Kelly were released at a quarter past midnight, a sober and wiser pair. They exchanged stories of their questioning as they walked down the High Street to collect Kelly's car. "Do you know, he suggested I was queer," complained Kelly. Fenton managed to summon up a smile in the darkness while a distant clap of thunder echoed over the roof tops. "Bloody rain," he said.

Fenton went back to the Kellys' flat where Mary Kelly was waiting up. She seemed much happier to see Fenton this time and apologised for her earlier frostiness. Fenton said that it had been understandable.

"So what happened?" asked Mary Kelly.

"We got our bottoms smacked," replied Kelly.

"About sums it up," agreed Fenton.

Mary Kelly went to bed leaving Fenton and Kelly drinking whisky and mulling over the past two days.

"Did Saxon kill Neil Munro or didn't he?" asked Kelly.

Fenton tilted his glass slowly from side to side, keeping the fluid level horizontal. "It pains me to say it but I think he might have been innocent. I think he was about to shop the real murderer when he got killed for his trouble. The killer must have got wind of what he planned to do and turned up early."

"The same man who called on Sandra Murray?" suggested Kelly.

"He could have killed Saxon but not Neil. The killer must have been in the lab when Neil discovered the truth about Saxon plastic. It couldn't have been a stranger.

"You do realise what you are saying?" said Kelly softly.

Fenton nodded. "If the killer wasn't Saxon it must be someone in the lab. Someone who primed the fair haired man to ask the right questions. Someone who knew what would happen when you added hydrochloric acid to potassium cyanide..."

The thought put both men to silence.

"But why?" asked Kelly.

Fenton shook his head.

"Did you tell the police about Sandra Murray's visitor?" asked Kelly.

"No, did you?"

"No."

"Here we go again," said Fenton.

Fenton got up and went over to the window. "The rain's stopped." he said. He drained the contents of his glass.

It was very late and the streets were practically deserted as Fenton walked home. The temperature had fallen with the clearing of the skies but the air was still and the stars twinkled brightly above him as he rounded a corner and saw the source of the eerie white light that lit up chimneys on tenement roofs. A full moon hung in the sky like a communion wafer. A cat fled from a dustbin and dissolved in shadow.

Fenton fell into a troubled sleep but kept waking at almost hourly intervals until at four o'clock he got up and made coffee. He had gone through each member of lab staff in turn at least three times and had still failed to find any motive for killing Neil. It was safe to eliminate all the females for Neil's murder had demanded physical strength but that left all the men. The motive had to be linked to the Cavalier organisation Fenton decided. That was the link between Saxon and the fair haired man. It was reasonable to propose that that was the connection between Saxon and the killer in the lab.

Charles Tyson? He had defended Saxon plastic throughout and had done everything possible to dissuade him from pursuing the faulty plastic angle. What was more Jenny had noticed that he had known what Ross had been talking about when he mentioned the 'Tree Mob.' He was also unmarried and never spoke of his personal life. But what about Ross himself? Ross had told him about the club in the first place but that might have been cleverness on his part, a ploy to make himself the least likely suspect...Fenton gave up. There was no way he was going to guess who the killer was. The fair haired man was the key to the puzzle. He must know who Neil's killer was. Fenton resolved to contact Jamieson in the morning.

Fenton phoned Kelly when he got into the lab and Kelly agreed to come too. They arranged to meet at noon and adopted Fenton's suggestion that they should use the Honda to avoid lunch time traffic and parking problems.

At a quarter to twelve Kelly phoned to point out that, as it was blowing a gale and the rain was almost horizontal, the Honda might not be such a good idea. He would come round for Fenton in the car.

Kelly cursed as he tried to reverse the Capri into a small gap that they had found after crawling up and down side streets near the police station and found it particularly difficult because of the rain and condensation on the windows. "Hell, that'll do," he decided, abandoning the effort for neatness and leaving the car with its nose jutting out.

They ran up the hill, keeping close to the wall in an effort to avoid most of the weather but took it full in the face as they rounded the corner at the top with fifty metres or so still to cover before reaching the shelter of the police station.

"Do you think God has something personal against Scotland?" asked Fenton, shaking the water from his hair in the doorway.

"I think it's a character building agreement he has with John Knox," said Kelly. "Let's face it, if you were having a good time you'd only feel guilty."

Jamieson looked up from his desk as Fenton and Kelly were shown in by a constable who seemed strangely reluctant to let go of the door handle after opening the door for them. Both had to enter sideways.

Jamieson clasped his hands together under his chin and said, "Don't tell me. Let me guess. You have a suspicion that the Queen Mother did the Brighton Trunk Murders?"

Fenton grinned painfully and conceded Jamieson's right to some come back over his behaviour in the past. He told the policeman of their visit to the Murray house and what Sandra Murray's brother had told them about what a man pretending to be from the Blood Transfusion Service had asked at the house.

Jamieson knew the name Sandra Murray well enough. "Hit and run death, up the Braids way?"

Fenton nodded.

"And you are saying that she knew about the Saxon Plastic problem?"

"Maybe not the details, but she knew that Neil Munro thought that there was something wrong with it."

"And that's what this fair haired man wanted to find out?"

"It seems like it."

Jamieson sucked the end of his pen in silence for a moment then said, "Did Murray tell you any more about this man?"

Fenton told him about the ring and watched Jamieson's expression change. The policeman put down his pen and rubbed his eyes with the heels of his hands before saying quietly, "That lot."

"You know them?" asked Fenton.

"Oh yes, I know them all right," sighed Jamieson. "We all know them. The force is now full of senior officers who have tangled with that bunch and ended up giving road safety lectures to five year olds."

"You are serious?" asked Fenton in disbelief.

"I'm serious," said Jamieson quietly.

Fenton looked at Kelly who shrugged as if to say, I told you so.

"But you are the police. I thought..."

"I know what you thought," interrupted Jamieson. "You thought I could nip up to Braidbank, pick up Sandra Murray's brother, and get him to identify the man?"

"Well, yes."

Jamieson shook his head and said, "Let me tell you what would really happen. Assuming Sandra Murray's brother was willing to co-operate, and if he knows anything at all about this mob he wouldn't be, we would start making enquiries. A few days later I would be directing traffic in Princes Street and Murray would be running for his life."

"You can't be serious," Fenton protested.

"I am," said Jamieson. "These buggers have so much power it scares me shitless."

Fenton was shaken by the admission. "So where does that leave us?" he asked.

Jamieson ran his finger round the inside of his collar and said, "Now that you have told me this I am obliged to go see Murray and ask him formally if he thinks he could identify the man. Frankly, I hope he says no or there could be another hit and run accident in Braidbank within the week."

Fenton was having difficulty in coming to terms with the frankness of Jamieson's admissions but he did have an idea and said so. Jamieson grimaced and Kelly smiled. Fenton said, "Murray told me that his sister was the scientist in the family and that he was an artist. If he really is an artist, a brush and paint artist that is, he might be able to sketch the man for you and no one would ever know how you got on to him?"

"Sounds a good idea to me," said Kelly.

Jamieson took his time but finally conceded that he too thought it was worth considering. He said, "If we could find out who the man was without his knowing it would give us time to build up a case against him. We could go in strong."

Kelly suggested that he and Fenton should approach Murray and keep the police out of it in Murray's own interest. Jamieson agreed but Fenton sensed that he was uncomfortable. He wanted to say something else but it was having a difficult birth. "Gentlemen," he began, tapping his finger tips together, "With your agreement..." The words struggled over invisible barriers. "I would like to keep this on...an unofficial basis for the time being.

Fenton and Kelly waited for an explanation and it was even more laboured when it came."Frankly, once a report is written...I can't be sure who is going to see it."

"I see," said Fenton. He said it calmly but felt anything but. "Perhaps it would be better if we met on neutral ground next time?" Jamieson nodded, relieved to see that Fenton had taken the right implication from what had been said without any further explanation being necessary.

It was still raining heavily when they got outside so they made a dash for the car although it was all to no avail when Kelly dropped the keys into the overflowing gutter in his haste to unlock the door. His curse was lost on the wind as Fenton turned his back and held up his collar while he waited.

"Did I dream that?" asked Fenton when they were safely out of the rain.

"If you did I had the same one," said Kelly.

Jenny looked aghast. "But they are the police!" she protested. "They don't say things like that!"

"That's what I thought too," said Fenton. "But I'm telling you exactly what Jamieson said."

"Oh Tom," said Jenny in exasperation. Fenton put his arm round her and tried to assure her by saying, "It's still a police matter. It's just that Jamieson wants to conduct it a little unconventionally."

"When are you going to see Murray?"

"Tonight," said Fenton.

The object of the exercise, decided Fenton, was to get the sketch from Murray with as little explanation as possible. They should say nothing about any possible connection with the Saxon murder and should not mention the police at all. This was just a little afterthought from their previous visit. But was Murray the right kind of artist?

"Actually I am a sculptor," said Murray. "But I think I can manage a rough outline."

It had turned out to be easier than Fenton had thought it might be. He had the sketch in his hands and Murray had hardly asked a thing, in fact, the man seemed positively subdued. He wondered whether the whisky beside Murray's chair was to blame but abandoned that notion in favour of a box of pills that he saw lying open on the table. He sneaked a look at the label when Murray had his back turned for a moment and saw that they were tranquillisers. They were a relatively mild brand but the alcohol was enhancing their effect.

Fenton looked at the sketch and admired Murray's competence.

"Thank you for your help Mr Murray," said Fenton, getting up to go.

"A drink before you go?" said Murray.

Fenton looked at his watch as a prelude to an excuse but the pathetically baleful look in Murray's eyes made him change his mind. "Thank you," he said. "Whisky for me."

"Do you still think my sister was murdered?" Murray asked as he handed Fenton and Kelly their glasses.

"I think it's possible," replied Fenton.

"I miss her you know," said Murray distantly. "I never liked her much while she was alive but now that she's gone...I miss her."

Fenton and Kelly exchanged embarrassed glances while Murray's eyes were fixed on the middle distance. He appeared not to notice and continued, "You see, she was the only person in my life who ever really liked me and now she's gone..."

Kelly shrugged his shoulders in discomfort and Fenton moved uneasily in his chair. Murray brought his eyes back and apologised for his rudeness. "Another drink?" Fenton declined the offer and thanked Murray again for his help.

As they walked down the path to the gate Kelly turned and looked at the house. "Poor bastard," he said.

The clock on the dash said eight forty-five and Kelly suggested that they call Jamieson on the number that he had given them. Fenton did so by using a phone box on the edge of Braidbank. He looked down at the lights of the city while he waited for Jamieson to answer. The rain had stopped but water was still running down the gutters from the hill. Jamieson answered and Fenton told him that they had the sketch.

"Do you know 'The Gravediggers' pub?" Jamieson asked.

"Corner of Angle Park?" said Fenton.

"That's the one, opposite Ardmillan Cemetery."

"When?"

"Thirty minutes?"

"We'll be there."

"I know it," said Kelly when Fenton told him. "Where can we park down there?"

"There's a railway footbridge near there, park in the street on the other side and we can walk over it."

Kelly followed Fenton's suggestion and they found a parking place with no difficulty. A diesel express thundered under the bridge as they crossed it, illuminating the banking with flickering light for a few brief moments before it was suddenly plunged back into darkness.

Jamieson was already there. He got up as they came in and ordered a round. "Any problems?" he asked as they sat down.

"None," replied Fenton, reaching into his inside pocket to take out Murray's sketch and hand it over.

Jamieson pursed his lips and made tutting noises. "Well, well, well," he said slowly.

"You know him?" asked Fenton.

"I do, indeed I do," replied Jamieson, still mesmerised by the sketch. "That's Gordon Vanney, Councillor Vanney's son."

Fenton thought that Jamieson looked as if he was being forced to remember something that he would rather have forgotten and did not intrude. He and Kelly remained silent until the policeman began to speak in his own time.

"Four years ago," said Jamieson, "A girl named Madeline Gray took her dog for a walk on Corstorphine Hill; she was fourteen at the time. Four youths set about her. They stripped her, tied her up and raped her in turn. When they had finished they stuffed stinging nettles...into every opening in her body and left her, still staked to the ground."

Fenton and Kelly listened in horror as Jamieson continued.

"When she could speak she named one of the youths as Vanney. She had recognised him because he lived in the same neighbourhood. We arrested Vanney but his old man got him out on bail." Jamieson paused and sipped his drink as if the words were paining him. "The very next night, while Madeline's father was out walking her dog, the dog ran off into the trees. It ran off with four legs and came back with three. Wire cutters, the vet said. Two days later the leg arrived by post addressed to Madeline. It was in a flower box so her mother let her open it by herself. A note suggested that it might be her leg next time if she didn't keep her mouth shut. She did and Vanney went free. The girl still isn't right, takes four baths a day."

"What a story," murmured Fenton.

"And you never traced the others?" asked Kelly.

"We never did," agreed Jamieson. "A pity because, before she stopped talking altogether, the girl told us that Vanney wasn't the ringleader, he was just the one she recognised. That singular honour went to a six foot tall dark haired youth, wearing some kind of college or university scarf. He had a piece missing from his right ear lobe, she was very sure of that; she had concentrated on it while he was raping her."

"Four years ago Inspector? You have some memory." said Kelly.

"So would you if you had seen that wee lassie," replied Jamieson.

Fenton asked what Jamieson was going to do about the sketch.

"Watch and wait. Find out who his associates are. See who's an organ grinder and who's a monkey."

"You don't think Vanney could have killed Sandra Murray and Saxon?" asked Fenton.

"Vanney's a shit but he's small fry. Someone else always pulls the strings."

"Any ideas."

Jamieson shook his head and said, "No, I haven't. We kept tabs on the bastard for a while after the Madeline Gray affair, you know the sort of thing, anyone farts in a built-up area and we pull in Vanney. But his old man pulls a lot of weight in this city. He started shouting harassment and we had to back off."

"The same thing might happen this time," suggested Fenton.

"No." said Jamieson, "This time it's unofficial, and personal."

"You mean you are going to do it by yourself?" asked Kelly.
Jamieson nodded.

"Can we help?" asked Fenton.

Jamieson smiled faintly. "Aye," he said, "Aye, you can."

Fenton grew to know Vanney well over the next couple of weeks.
The fact that Jenny was still working nights let him share night time
surveillance with Jamieson and back- leave that he was due took
care of some day time work. Steve Kelly took over on the nights that
Jenny had off.

Vanney lived in his parents' house on Corstorphine Hill, a
sprawling modern bungalow with large gardens and a gravelled
frontage that accommodated three cars. The Lotus belonged to
Vanney junior. Each week day morning he drove it to work in the
city, leaving at eight thirty and arriving at a merchant bank in the
New Town at five minutes to nine. Lunch was one till two and he ate
it in a pub in Rose Street called, 'The Two Shoemakers.' He always
ate with the same people, a tall, ginger haired man with buck teeth
and a loud voice and a short, squat, olive skinned man who looked
Italian, maybe Spanish. Both worked in the same bank and it seemed
just to be a lunch time friendship for neither featured in Vanney's
evening social life.

Vanney had a girl friend and it surprised Fenton for he had
assumed that a connection with the Cavalier Club inferred
homosexuality although Kelly had said in the past that the club had
broadened its horizons. The girl seemed nice and came from a
similarly well heeled background to Vanney himself. She was tall,
nearly as tall as Vanney, and good looking in a country girl sort of
way. Fenton liked her on sight and wondered what she saw in
someone like Vanney, and vice versa if Vanney really was
homosexual.

Jamieson provided an answer to the second question. The girl's
father was a director of the bank where Vanney worked. "Vanney to
a tee," he snarled, "Brown nosing the boss's daughter."

"What do you suppose her father thinks about it?" asked Fenton.

"Probably encourages it," said Jamieson wryly, "Son of a
prominent councillor, heir to a concrete shit empire, an excellent
choice for their wee Denise. That's her name by the way, Denise
Hargreaves.

Vanney and Denise Hargreaves saw each other twice during the week and again on Saturdays. One disco, one trip to the cinema and dinner out at the week-end. He played golf with his father on Sundays and stayed in on Thursdays. That left Mondays and Wednesdays.

CHAPTER TWELVE

On Monday Jamieson lost Vanney in town traffic and it was accepted as just one of those things, but when the same thing happened to Kelly on the Wednesday, the three men met to discuss tactics.

"Do you think he realised that he was being followed?" asked Fenton. Jamieson replied that he did not, adding that Vanney had shown no sign of 'awareness' on any of the other nights. Fenton had to agree with that, saying that he himself had had no trouble following Vanney on the previous Friday and the wrestling match that he had had with Denise Hargreaves in the car outside her house had not suggested the actions of a man who thought that he was being watched.

"How did he get on?" asked Kelly.

"She slapped his face," said Fenton.

"Good for her," said Jamieson.

Jamieson and Kelly compared notes and found that they had lost Vanney at the same place in town. He had made a left turn out of Leith Street and had apparently disappeared into thin air. "He must have turned into a lane or something," said Kelly and no one disagreed. Jamieson suggested that they should all attempt to follow Vanney on Monday. One of them should pick him up as he left his house just, in case he should do something different, the other two would wait in Leith Street, around the area where they had lost him on the previous occasions. Fenton said that he would follow Vanney from home. Jamieson and Kelly agreed where they would position themselves for the wait.

On Monday evening Vanney left home at seven thirty and Fenton followed on the Honda, keeping some two hundred metres behind and with at least two vehicles between himself and the Lotus at all times. Traffic was light enough at first and the only problem was the persistent drizzle which caused problems with his face visor.

Vanney appeared to be taking his usual road to town and Fenton automatically assumed his route, an assumption that nearly caused him to lose the Lotus when he found himself trapped in the inside lane when Vanney decided to turn right. By the time he had recovered the Lotus had disappeared. He had to make a guess. Did he go down to the Grassmarket or up to the High Street?

Fenton bet on the High Street and gunned the Honda up Castle Terrace which wound round and up the side of the floodlit castle rock. The needle was touching sixty-five when he braked at the top of the Royal Mile in time to see the tail lights of the Lotus as it sat at traffic lights. He free-wheeled the bike down the steep cobbles, allowing a taxi and a Ford Escort to reach the Lotus first.

The lights changed and Vanney turned left. He was heading back towards Princes Street after having gone out of his way by nearly two miles. It didn't make sense, thought Fenton, unless of course, he was taking routine precautions to avoid being followed on Mondays and Wednesdays. The idea excited Fenton.

As the traffic high above Princes Street began to flow down the Mound, a steep hill connecting the Old Town to the New Town, Fenton's pulse began to quicken. It looked as if Vanney was now heading for Leith Street. He hoped Kelly and Jamieson were alert.

Traffic at the east end of Princes Street was heavy as night time commercial vehicles headed towards the main road south. Vanney was third in the queue at the lights and Fenton was seventh with an articulated lorry lying in fourth place.

The Lotus was three hundred metres ahead before the lorry had swung its tail clear of Fenton and he had a clear road in front. He fought the impulse to twist the throttle. There was no point in arriving in Vanney's rear-view mirror like a bullet. He passed the artic but held back as he saw the Lotus slow for a roundabout. There were now four vehicles between him and the Lotus, an ideal number.

Fenton took his turn at infiltrating into traffic coming from the right and saw the Lotus turn left. Same as last time, he thought and leaned into the corner. He straightened up to find that the Lotus had completely disappeared. There was a long straight road ahead but no Vanney. Fenton pulled into the side and cut the engine. He was relieved to see Jamieson come out of a shop doorway and walk towards him.

"All right, I give up," said Fenton.

"Basement garage," said Jamieson, "Twenty metres along on your left. The door was already open. He just swung into it and the door closed behind him. The whole thing took less than five seconds."

Kelly joined them from the other corner and said, "It all looks pretty dead to me." All three looked at the building. It was deserted and dark, no lights, no sounds.

"What now?" Fenton asked.

"We try to find out where Vanney entered the building. There must be an internal stair from the garage because he hasn't appeared on the street."

Fenton volunteered to have a look and Jamieson agreed. "Enter by the front door nearest the area of the garage."

Fenton climbed the short flight of steps to the main entrance of the dark building and entered the common stairway. The cold and damp was accentuated by the blackness. It felt like a tomb. He examined the ground floor doors as best he could, relying largely on light from the headlights of cars passing outside. They were filthy and the grime on the locks and handles said that they had not been used for a very long time. The smell of wood rot was everywhere.

He searched for stairs that might lead down to the garage and found some though he half wished that he had not for they were in complete darkness. He stretched out his hands and touched both walls as he felt his way gingerly down them with the toe of his boot. He came to the bottom and found himself in a passage that ran through the building. There was a scurrying sound nearby which made him lash out with his foot. The sound stopped but Fenton's imagination made his pulse rate soar.

Feeling his way along the wall he came to a door and groped for the lock. He found a bolt but had difficulty in trying to free it. He could not see the rust but felt it with his fingers as he tried to budge it. The tongue of the bolt began to move and Fenton worked it backwards and forwards until, at last it gave and clattered back against its stop, only slightly cushioned by a finger that got in the road. He put his finger to his lips, simultaneously stemming the blood and the curse. He pulled the door open with his other hand and stepped out into a dark lane which ran along the back of the building.

There was a garage door to his right. Fenton looked at it and mentally plotted its relationship to the opening at the front where Vanney had entered. His heart sank as he realised the truth. The garage ran straight through the building. It had a front and a back door. Vanney was not in the building at all!

Fenton ran along the lane and round to the front of the building to tell Jamieson and Kelly.

"Did you check to see if the Lotus was still there?" Jamieson asked.

"I assumed that he had driven straight through," confessed Fenton.

"We had better check. He may have changed cars too," said Jamieson.

Fenton and Kelly walked round to the garage door at the back where, unlike the modern metal door at the front, it was made of wood and was rotting badly. Kelly knelt down to peer through at the bottom where the wood had decayed to leave the base like a row of rotting teeth. "It's still there," he announced. "He changed cars."

They agreed to keep watch in shifts until Vanney returned. One of them would stay near to the entrance of the lane while the other two could stretch their legs, get coffee at a cafe nearby or whatever.

Vanney did not get back till one in the morning. Jamieson was on watch when a green Mini slowed and turned into the lane. He got a good view of Vanney at the wheel and noted down the number. The Lotus left shortly afterwards and ten minutes later Fenton and Kelly returned.

The three men agreed to meet again on Monday near the entrance to the lane and follow the green Mini when it left. In the meantime they decided to abandon routine surveillance on Vanney, a move that proved equally popular with Jenny and Mary Kelly. Fenton wondered later about Jamieson. Was he married? The subject had never come up. It was not the sort of thing you asked him, it was the sort of thing he asked you.

Spring came suddenly to Edinburgh. It flooded the city with a yellow sunshine that highlighted the rash of buds that had broken out on the trees in Princes Street Gardens. It made drops of rain water, which had persisted from the previous night's rain, sparkle like precious stones on railings as Fenton rode to the lab through the morning traffic.

Faces were held high as heads that had spent most of the winter bent forward against wind and rain were lifted to receive the kiss of spring sunshine. Feet slowed as the lure of office central heating lost its grip on the imagination and people stopped to speak to each other in the streets. They were smiling; the annual war was over and the survivors were glad to see each other.

The sunshine had even invaded Fenton's lab. It sought out the dust that coated reagent bottles and illuminated the intricacies of a large cobweb. Now that he had seen it the dirt began to annoy him. He fetched a wet cloth and started to wipe each bottle individually. He was doing this when Charles Tyson came in. He said, "I'd like to see you in my room in ten minutes if that's convenient?"

Fenton nodded.

Fenton joined Tyson and Liz Scott brought in coffee. Tyson stirred his and said, "I'm considering recommending to the Health Board that you be made official deputy head of department, Neil's position."

"Thanks," said Fenton.

"Don't thank me just yet. I said I was considering it."

Fenton waited for Tyson to elaborate.

Tyson looked hard at Fenton and said, "A senior position like this demands something more than just scientific ability. It requires a certain degree of diplomacy. It requires discretion, a willingness to operate within accepted guidelines. A willingness to drift with the prevailing current rather than a tendency to...rock the boat. Do I make myself clear?"

"Perfectly," said Fenton controlling his temper. He was being warned off and offered an incentive. The question was what was he being warned off? Was it just his natural tendency to go to war with the hospital authorities that Tyson was concerned about or was it something more sinister? He couldn't tell anything from Tyson's expression.

"Well?" said Tyson.

"I don't think I'm your man," said Fenton. "I reserve the right to play the game as I see it."

"I see," said Tyson tapping the end of his pen on the blotting pad in front of him. "Don't be too hasty. Sleep on it."

Fenton got up to go.

"There is one more thing," said Tyson.

"Yes?"

"I'm going to recommend to the board that Ian Ferguson be upgraded to senior biochemist. Do you have any views?"

"That's fine by me," said Fenton.

"Good," said Tyson. "I hoped you'd say that. He put down his pen and rubbed his eyes. "I'll be glad when everyone can concentrate solely on their work again."

Was that another warning? Fenton wondered. He looked for signs of an accusation but Tyson's was concentrating on his papers again.

Fenton was checking the day book in the main lab when Liz Scott came in and told Ian Ferguson that Tyson wanted to see him. Ferguson made a face at Fenton and said, "When the trumpet calls..."

Fenton smiled but did not say anything.

The good weather lasted over the week-end and Fenton and Jenny took the opportunity of taking their first real walk of the year. They went out to Colinton Village and climbed up into the Pentland Hills, a gently rolling range that lay to the south of the city. As they reached the top of Bonaly Hill they stopped to catch their breath and look at the view. Jenny was standing slightly lower down than Fenton so, as she looked north over the houses to the Forth Estuary, he looked at her. Her hair was like spun gold in the sun and her fresh complexion seemed to embody the spirit of the season. He stooped to kiss her lightly on the back of the neck and she raised her hand to touch his cheek. She did not speak.

"I love you Jenny," whispered Fenton.

Jenny still did not speak.

"All right, I don't love you."

Jenny smiled and turned. She said, "Tom, you will be careful tomorrow?"

Fenton reassured her and hugged her tightly from behind.

They walked through a pine forest on the way to Caerketton Hill and their feet were silent on a thick carpet of needles. Sunlight sneaked through the branches to create little pools of light on the floor of the woods.

On Monday morning Jamieson rang Fenton at the lab to finalise details about following Vanney. He and Kelly would tail the Mini in his car, an unmarked Ford. Fenton was to follow on the Honda. If Vanney should tumble to the Granada Jamieson would turn off leaving Fenton to pick up the tail.

Fenton was glad that Jenny had already left for the hospital when he got home because he felt nervous and needed to be alone. Where would Vanney go? Would they be any closer to discovering the truth about Neil's death at the end of the evening?

The butterflies in his stomach did not subside until the Honda had started and he had set out for Leith Street. Jamieson was already there when he arrived, although he was not late. He handed him a two way radio and gave him a crash course in how to use it while they waited for Kelly to arrive.

Kelly arrived and, with ten minutes to go if Vanney were to be his usual punctual self, Fenton got back on the Honda and moved some two hundred metres away from Jamieson's car. He parked it again and waited in a doorway watching the street.

Two minutes late, the Lotus swung into the street and nose dived into its garage. Fenton felt the adrenalin begin to flow as he changed to watching the far end of the lane. The lights of the green Mini appeared at the junction; it paused then turned left on to the main road. Fenton saw the Granada start to move. He walked out from his doorway, as if he had just emerged from the building, and got on the bike. He took off from the kerb and settled at a comfortable distance behind Jamieson, feeling pleased at how smoothly it had all gone.

The Mini was making for the coast. Fenton hoped that it might take the main road south where there would be plenty of traffic to provide cover but it was not to be. Vanney made a left turn at the edge of town and joined the old, winding coast road which meticulously followed the southern shore of the Firth of Forth. The Granada's headlights would be in Vanney's mirror all the time, thought Fenton. The odds were that it would not alarm Vanney unduly but that he might feel obliged to take routine precautions to prove to himself that he was not really being followed.

The test came as they entered the small coastal village of Port Seton. The Mini's left indicator began to flash and Vanney pulled in to the side and stopped beside some shops. The move obliged Jamieson to drive straight past. Fenton was able to stop well behind the Mini. The street lighting was good. Vanney would have been able to get a good look at the Granada as it passed, maybe even taken its number. There was no way that Jamieson could take up the tail again.

Fenton got out his radio and called up Jamieson. He told him what he thought and suggested that he should pick up the tail on Vanney from now on.

"All yours," replied Jamieson.

It started to rain and the sound of the drops hitting his leathers sounded unnaturally loud to Fenton as he sat, motionless, waiting for the Mini to move off. It was a full five minutes before he heard the rattling drain sound of the Mini being started. Vanney moved off from the kerb and Fenton prepared to follow but held back until the Mini had left the edge of the village and disappeared round a right hand bend for he did not want Vanney to get a look at him under the street lights.

As soon as Vanney was out of sight Fenton gunned the bike to the edge of the village then took a risk. He throttled back and turned off his lights. He reckoned that if he could pick up the Mini quickly he could ride on its tail lights. The rain on its rear screen would also help to obscure his presence.

Fenton could see red lights some two hundred metres ahead. With his heart in his mouth he accelerated to close the distance between himself and the car, knowing that the road between him and Vanney was an unknown quantity. One unseen pothole could bring disaster. He closed to within fifty metres and felt more comfortable with the Mini's headlights now acting as pathfinders. The winding road did not allow the Mini to move fast. Just as well, thought Fenton.

They had travelled about three miles when Fenton thought that he had caught a glimpse of something metallic off to his left, something in the sand dunes among the maram grass. As he passed the spot he saw that it was Jamieson's Granada; it was sitting with its lights out. Fenton wondered if Vanney might have seen it too but concluded not for it was still raining heavily and the Mini's side windows would be speckled over. Vanney's view would be confined to the two hemispheres cleared by the wipers.

Another two miles and the Mini's brake lights lit up the night like Christmas candles, making halos of pink rain. Fenton's foot shot to the brake pedal but he stopped himself in time for his own rear brake light would give the game away. Instead he clawed at the front brake lever, full of apprehension as he concentrated on keeping the bike perfectly vertical. The slightest angle on the front wheel in the wet and it would be off like soap in the bath.

Fenton let out his breath as the Honda slowed to walking pace and conceded control to him. Up ahead the Mini was turning off to the right but not on to another road. It was entering what appeared to be the driveway of a big house. Fenton got off the bike and walked across the road to the entrance. 'Helmwood' said the letters etched in the stone pillars. He looked up the drive but there was nothing to be seen but darkness. He listened for a moment but there was just the sound of the sea and the rustle of the conifers over the wall.

Fenton radioed the news to Jamieson who said that he knew the place. "Move on a quarter of a mile. There's a beach track to your left. We'll meet you there."

Fenton got into the back of the Granada and felt the warmth for he had not realised how cold he had been getting standing around. He purred appreciatively.

"Monkton's place," said Jamieson.

Fenton needed more.

"Lord Monkton, ex-minister of state, pillar of the community, power, wealth, influence, just the job for the Cavalier mob.

"Shall we go take a look?" said Kelly.

Fenton detected a note of caution in Kelly's voice and recognised it as the reticence displayed by even the most law abiding in the company of policemen.

"Why not," replied Jamieson. "There's no law of trespass in Scotland."

They got out of the car into the salty night air and made their way up to the road. It had stopped raining but the grass and the trees were heavily pregnant with water and a conifer delivered on Kelly as he brushed against it.

"Ssh!" said Jamieson as Kelly cursed.

Fenton had an advantage over the other two in that he, at least, was dressed for the occasion, immune to the wetness inside his leathers and safe from sand and mud inside his boots. It was he who led the way back to the entrance to Helmwood, flattening a path through the long grass for the others to use.

The sound of an approaching car prompted Jamieson to say, "Down!"

The three men crouched in the grass as a sleek Jaguar saloon slowed and turned into the driveway. They had barely got to their feet when another car arrived. Fenton did not recognise the make but it looked Italian and expensive.

When all seemed quiet they stepped out of the grass and on the tar of Helmwood's drive. "I think we had better stick to the trees," said Jamieson.

"This side," said Fenton, picking the less dense pine woods and smelling the pine resin that made him think briefly of the previous day. But this forest was different, it was hostile. The tall trees waved their branches threateningly against the dark sky as they made their way towards the chinks of light that advertised Helmwood House.

"Must be having a party," whispered Jamieson as they crouched at the edge of the trees and counted the number of cars in the car park. "I'd like to collect some numbers." he said.

Fenton and Kelly waited while Jamieson sprinted across to the car park in a low crouch and disappeared among the gleaming machinery, notebook at the ready. It was ten minutes before he returned, slightly out of breath. "This should keep the computer happy for a bit," he panted.

"What now?" asked Kelly.

"A closer look?" suggested Fenton.

"All right, but let's take it easy," said Jamieson.

"Do you hear music?" Fenton asked the other two as the wind dropped momentarily.

"I keep thinking I do," said Kelly.

"There it is again."

"Must be coming from the other side of the house," said Jamieson. "There are very few lights on this side."

"We could circle round," Fenton suggested.

They sank back into the trees and moved laterally to hug the contour of the pinewood fringe as they made their way towards the back lawn of the house. They could now see that a bank of windows were brightly lit on the first floor and the music seemed to be coming from there.

"What kind of music is that anyway?" asked Kelly.

Fenton shook his head, "Some kind of string instruments maybe."

The size of the windows where the sound was coming from suggested that it was a very large room. "A ballroom?" suggested Kelly.

"A ballroom with a balcony..." added Fenton. He looked at Kelly and said, "I can't see them coming out on the balcony on a night like this can you?"

Kelly took his point and said, "There's a fire escape running up the side of it."

Jamieson pretended that he had not heard but Fenton and Kelly stared at him until he conceded that he had. "All right," he said. "Let's take a look."

Fenton climbed up the fire escape ladder first, Kelly followed and then Jamieson. Fenton got to the top and swung his legs over the stone balustrade. He nestled down in a corner, taking comfort in the fact that there was no danger of them being overheard because the music and laughter coming from within was far too loud. The only problem would be the possibility being seen in the light that flooded out from the tall windows.

The music stopped and the hubbub started to subside. Almost imperceptibly the lights began to dim. "Something's happening," whispered Kelly.

"I wish we could see what," answered Fenton. The lights continued to dim and Fenton decided to risk wriggling out along the base of the balcony to a point just below one of the windows. Kelly bit his lip as he watched him do it then signalled that it was safe for Fenton to raise himself up for there was no one standing near the window.

Fenton raised himself slowly till his eyes were above the level of the sill and his mouth fell open. He was looking at ancient Rome, a palace of the Caesars.

Men clad in togas and sandals reclined on couches to be waited on by slaves bearing wine jugs and trays laden with food. At one end of the room three musicians sat with lyres. At the other, centurions in full leather armour guarded tall double doors. Another was standing in the middle of the room and he carried an ornate standard. Fenton thought at first that it was a Roman eagle but then saw that it was not that at all. It was a golden tree, the symbol of the Cavalier Club.

Fenton saw Vanney inside; he was sitting near the musicians and threw back his head to drain his goblet as Fenton watched. It was refilled almost immediately. Fenton crawled back along the balcony to join the others.

"A theme party?" suggested Jamieson.

"It looks too real," Fenton replied. "Everything, the mosaics, the marbles, the clothes, the trappings. They all look real."

Before there was any more time for questions a fanfare sounded from inside and Fenton signalled that they should move out to the windows again. Jamieson joined Fenton at his window; Kelly took the next one along.

"My God," murmured Jamieson.

A large square of rush matting was being spread out on the floor by four men dressed as slaves. When they had finished, one of the Romans, a tall distinguished man wearing a purple trimmed toga, raised his arm for silence.

"That's Monkton," whispered Jamieson.

The double doors at the end of the room were opened to admit two gladiators, naked to the waist, their bare torsos glistening with oil. They marched down the centre of the room and saluted Monkton by crossing their forearms across their chests. Monkton nodded and the wrestlers began to circle each other on the mat. All lighting in the room had been extinguished save for wall torches and candles. Their spluttering flames were reflected in the sweat of the combatants as they struggled to gain advantage.

Fenton could not take his eyes away from Monkton's face for the man was in the grip of some terrible excitement. He was no longer the urbane man he had been at the beginning, his mouth quivered as he exhorted the wrestlers with silent words to greater efforts. His hand reached out almost absent-mindedly and gripped the thigh of the slave who stood by his couch. The boy, an extremely pretty youth, winced as Monkton's fingers dug into his flesh but he smiled as soon as Monkton looked up at him. Savagely Monkton pulled the boy's face down on top of his.

"Nice to see a return to Victorian values," whispered Jamieson.

A few minutes later, as the wrestlers finished their bout to loud applause, Monkton and the boy left the room. Several other pairs did the same. The lighting came up again and the music re-started Fenton and the other two crawled back along the balcony floor and into the safety of the corner.

Fenton asked Jamieson if he had recognised anyone else in the room.

"A few," replied the policeman. "Mind you it's hard without their normal clothes. It took me ages to figure out who one of them was, although I knew the face well enough. Then I thought of him in a dog collar..."

"Did anyone see who Vanney was with?" asked Fenton.

"Couldn't see for the pillar," said Kelly.

Jamieson nodded and said, "We'll have to wait until he stands up."

Once more the lights began to dim inside and they returned to their positions beneath the windows in readiness. Fenton could see that the absentees had come back and Monkton was smiling, his features restored to distinguished calm. He raised his arm and the music ceased.

Four slaves marched towards Monkton carrying silver trays with wine jugs and goblets and waited until Monkton personally had poured a little wine into each goblet. All the Romans in the room gathered in a large circle as the wine was handed out then they raised their goblets in some kind of toast and drank in unison.

One of the slaves dropped his jug and it threw up a plume of red wine over Monkton's pristine white toga. Even in the dim lighting Fenton could see the anger roll across Monkton's face. The slave dashed himself to the floor but Monkton ignored him and made some kind of signal to the man Vanney had been with, the man who had been hidden by the pillar all night. The man had his back to the windows. He was wearing an elaborate head-dress and carried some kind of silver baton in his right hand. A centurion approached him and took orders.

Fenton watched spellbound as a metal frame was brought in to the room and dragged up in front of the man with the baton. Another signal and the slave who had dropped the wine was tied to the frame. One of the guards from the door approached and removed his helmet and cape. In his hand he held a whip.

The man with the baton spread the fingers of his left hand twice to indicate the number ten and the punishment began. Through the glass Fenton and the others could hear the sound of leather hitting flesh. The slave's teeth were bared in anguish and his eyes rolled as the skin on his exposed was back was cut open to mingle blood with the sweat of his fear.

After five lashes his torturer paused to adjust his stance and cover new ground. As the man raised the whip again Fenton got a good look at him and felt weak. "He was the bastard who beat me up in the pub!" he whispered to Jamieson.

The slave appeared to have passed out. The Roman with the baton put his hand out to his neck to check but as he did so the slave suddenly sank his teeth into the back of his hand. The Roman wrenched his hand away and raised his baton in anger. Fenton waited for it to fall but it did not. The Roman regained his composure and spread his fingers to indicate another five lashes.

The unconscious slave was carried out and the floor cleaned of blood. The lights went up again, glasses were replenished and Monkton held up his hand for silence. "To business, gentlemen!

A murmur ran round the room and then it became quiet. Fenton noted that Jamieson had taken out his notebook. He smiled at Kelly.

"The figures please!" said Monkton.

Monkton stood to one side and another man, small and balding with several long strands of dark hair combed individually across his scalp got to his feet. He held a sheaf of papers in front of him.

"Hale-bloody-lujah," whispered Jamieson.

Fenton and Kelly looked at him and the policeman said, "That's Vanney senior."

Vanney cleared his throat and said, "Fifty thousand pounds from Theta Electronics for rating concessions on their new premises." There was applause in the room.

"Two hundred thousand pounds from Corton Brothers for assistance with planning permission for their new housing estate and re-defining of the green belt in that area.

More applause.

"Forty-two thousand pounds for motorway maintenance contracts, fifty thousand pounds for housing stock maintenance contracts in the central region and a total of one hundred and eight thousand pounds for various supply contracts in the country as a whole."

Loud applause.

"And now gentlemen, an extra item."Twenty thousand pounds from Saxon Medical for our assistance in obtaining a Department of Health license for their product. Despite subsequent 'problems' I am reliably informed that the sale of the license by Saxon to International Plastics will be deemed tomorrow by the courts to have been made in good faith."

Vanney held his hands up and shouted above the hubbub, "I think you all know who we have to thank for that!"

There was general laughter.

"This concludes my report."

Monkton got to his feet again and announced an end to business for the evening.

"Let's get out of here," whispered Jamieson.

Nobody spoke until they were back at the car then Fenton said, "I think I'm out of my depth."

"You are not alone," conceded Jamieson. "To do this right is going to take time but I'm going to get every last one of them."

Fenton said, "I wish I could have seen the face of the man with the baton. There was something familiar about him."

"I thought that too," confessed Kelly. "But I'm damned if I can think why."

CHAPTER THIRTEEN

Fenton deliberately chose to drive home fast on the winding coast road for he needed some distraction from thoughts of the evening. Controlling the Honda at speed demanded his total concentration. Bend after bend loomed up ensuring that the bike was seldom upright for more than a few seconds before being swung over yet again. The road surface had almost dried out, leaving only the occasional puddle to be thrown up into the waving grass caught in the headlight.

By the time he reached the outskirts of the city he was both physically and mentally drained. He slowed for the final roundabout and sat upright to proceed sedately along the well lit tarmac until he reached the flat.

The gas fire burst into life and Fenton switched on the kettle to make tea before sitting down to think. Jamieson was right. It would take time to put the case together against the Cavaliers if he were to break the organisation as a whole and that was certainly the way to do it. An isolated prosecution would only put the Cavaliers on their guard and give them time to re-group. But he was off to a flying start with the names and figures he had obtained from Vanney's report. He knew exactly where to look for evidence of corruption and that was half the battle.

Fenton still had difficulty in accepting how widespread and powerful the Cavalier organisation was. It was frightening but his resolve to see Neil Munro's killer brought to justice was undiminished. The kettle started to whistle and he returned to the kitchen to make tea.

There had been no mention of Nigel Saxon at Helmwood and this was both disappointing and puzzling. It meant that he could still not be sure where Saxon had fitted in to the scheme of things. If Saxon had been the originator of the plan to defraud International Plastics why hadn't he rated a mention at Helmwood? And if millions of pounds were involved in the fraud why was only the relatively paltry sum of twenty thousand pounds mentioned. Even if Saxon in the end had turned traitor under pressure surely something would have been said or was the elimination of a fellow member by murder too insignificant a matter to merit comment? Fenton found it a chilling thought.

A fitful night's sleep did not help improve matters. Fenton was still in bed when Jenny came home. She opened the curtains.

Fenton said, "Isn't it strange, you can't get to sleep all night yet the minute it gets light..." The words tailed off and Jenny said that she knew the feeling. She sat down on the edge of the bed and asked how things had gone.

Fenton told her everything and watched her face register shock as he told her about Helmwood and disgust when he told her about the slave.

"What's Jamieson going to do?" she asked.

"He's going to get to work on breaking them but it will take some time to gather all the evidence."

"And then what?"

"I don't know."

"What about Vanney junior?"

"That's up to Jamieson."

Jamieson phoned Fenton at around ten thirty to tell him that things were well under way with the investigation into the corrupt contracts and the police computer when fed with the registration numbers that Jamieson had collected at Helmwood had obliged with some very interesting names.

"What about Vanney?" asked Fenton.

"With Murray's help and a bit of luck over the car we think we will be able to nail him for Sandra Murray's death. With that facing him and being the little shit he is he might be spill the beans about the rest. Mind you, I still think that it was Saxon who killed your friend Munro. He was the only one with a motive."

"But if it really was Saxon how could he have hoped to blame it on someone else? Just coming up with a name would have been no good. The killer had to be someone in the lab at the time Neil discovered the truth about the plastic.

"Saxon was probably in a blue funk when he phoned you and prepared to blame it on anyone whether it made sense or not."

"Maybe," Fenton conceded.

"People do strange things when they're desperate." said Jamieson. "Believe me. I've seen it all."

Charles Tyson came into Fenton's lab just before noon and said, "I've got a staffing problem. Ian Ferguson has just phoned to say that he has injured himself working on his car. The point is he was due to be on call tonight and I have to go out this evening. Mary Tyler has a meeting at the school and..."

"No problem," said Fenton. "I'll do it. I wasn't doing anything."

"Thanks," said Tyson.

At eleven thirty that evening Fenton had cause to regret his generosity in agreeing to take over Ferguson's duty. He had been working almost non stop since seven in the evening and now the acetylene gas cylinder had run out. He would have to bring up a new one from the basement on his own and change over the reduction valve, a task best carried out by two people.

Cursing his luck, Fenton ran down the stairs and switched on the basement light. He wheeled the cylinder transporter over to a row of gas cylinders and rolled an acetylene one out on its heel. He manoeuvred it with some difficulty on to the transporter and secured it with the catch chains before pressing the button for the service lift and waiting while the painfully slow motor brought it down.

As he came up in the creaking lift he heard a car draw up outside the lab and this was followed by a key rattling in the lock. Fenton assumed that it would be Tyson coming in to check on things after his evening out and was surprised to see Ian Ferguson appear at the head of the stairs while he was manhandling the transporter out of the lift.

"I thought I would drop in and apologise for this," said Ferguson, holding up his bandaged hand.

"You picked the right night to be off," said Fenton. "I've been running around like a cat with its arse on fire since seven o'clock and now this!" He nodded to the cylinder.

"I'll get the spanners," said Ferguson.

"What happened anyway?" asked Fenton.

"I changed my car on the strength of my promotion. I was checking the oil in it and the bonnet fell on my hand."

"Nasty," said Fenton. "Anything broken?"

"No, just bruised."

Fenton brought over the empty cylinder to change over the head gear and looked to see if Ferguson had come up with a spanner.

"Will this one do?" asked Ferguson, holding up a spanner with his back still to Fenton as he continued to look in the drawer.

Fenton's blood ran cold. He was transfixed by the sight for, in his head, the spanner was transformed into a silver baton. The back view of Ferguson was the back view of the Roman with the baton!

Ferguson turned to see why Fenton had not answered. His smile faded when he saw the look on Fenton's face.

"You!" Fenton accused in a hoarse whisper. "The knowledge, the motive and the opportunity! Neil told you about the plastic! It was you at Helmwood! There was no accident with the car. The slave bit you!" The look on Ferguson's face told Fenton that he was right.

Surprise gave way to arrogant resignation. "Well, well, well," said Ferguson quietly.

"You bastard, it was you who killed Neil!"

The spanner hit Fenton just above the left eye. He had been totally unprepared for it when Ferguson suddenly threw it at him and now the room burst into a galaxy of stars as he slid to the floor.

When he came round Fenton found himself bound hand and foot with the chains from the transporter. Ferguson was looking down at him with a sneer on his face. "So you finally worked it out Fenton," he said.

"Bastard!"

"Tut tut. You always were a bit rough Fenton, bright but rough."

"Why? For Christ's sake why?" asked Fenton, struggling impotently with the chains.

Ferguson looked as if he was enjoying Fenton's discomfort. He looked down at him like a parent patronising a five year old. "Money. What else?" he said.

"But how? What did you have to gain?"

"Saxon was in love with me," said Ferguson. "I played him along and made out that I loved him. It was too good a chance to miss. Everyone wants to fall in love with a millionaire" Ferguson laughed at the thought. I arranged for him to become a member of the club and we helped him get his license for a fee. He was pathetically grateful. The fat clown promised that when the deal went through with International Plastics, he would sign over half his share to me and afterwards make me the sole beneficiary in his will, just as if I were his wife."

"And you had to kill Neil to make sure that the deal went through?"

"When Munro told me about the flaw he had found in the plastic that morning I saw all that money disappearing. I couldn't have that now could I? I took a short cut down to the Sterile Supply Department and waited till he arrived. You know the rest."

"Was Saxon in on it too?"

Ferguson seemed amused at the suggestion. "Don't be ridiculous," he sneered. "That idiot knew nothing at all about it. He didn't have the nerve to play for high stakes."

"But you did," said Fenton quietly.

"That's what being a Cavalier is all about Fenton."

"Did you kill Saxon too?"

"The slow witted clod finally twigged to what had been going on. I think he wanted to break off our engagement." Ferguson laughed at his own joke.

Fenton felt sick but he had to know it all. "Sandra Murray too?" he asked.

"She knew too much."

"Don't you feel anything?" Fenton asked, horrified at Ferguson's lack of emotion. He was angry with himself for not having suspected Ferguson sooner. Now when he thought about it, it had been Ferguson who had been on duty in the lab immediately before the incident with the fume cupboard and Ferguson had been present to hear him volunteer to come in that Sunday to help Saxon.

"All that nonsense about wanting to change your job because you were scared..." said Fenton.

"I thought that was rather a nice touch," said Ferguson.

Fenton saw his own death warrant in Ferguson's eyes and was desperately afraid. The thought that he would never see Jenny again was unbearable.

Ferguson looked around him and thought aloud. "An accident with the cylinder I think." He said it as if he were thinking about the seating arrangements for a dinner party. "Yes, that's it. You were changing the heavy cylinder all on your own when it fell on you and knocked you out. The lab filled up with gas from the leaking valve on the cylinder and there was...a fire...an explosion."

Through his fear Fenton saw that he had one chance. Ferguson would have to bend down to release the empty cylinder. If he could hit the transporter at just the right angle and at just the right moment..."

Ferguson bent down and Fenton's feet shot out to send the heavy metal transporter crashing into him. One of the bars caught Ferguson behind the ear and he went out like a light. But for how long? That was the question that bred new panic in Fenton. He was still tied up. What could he do? Could he risk trying to roll across the floor and down the stairs? What was the point? He couldn't open the front door even if he succeeded. The phone! If he could just get the receiver off the hook surely he could dial three nines even with his hands behind his back.

Getting across the floor was more difficult than Fenton had anticipated, his frustration and fear growing with every second that passed. His mouth was drier than a desert when he finally succeeded in raising himself to his knees beside the table where the phone was but a sudden groan from Ferguson almost panicked him into losing balance. It took four attempts to get the phone off the hook, then, clatter, it was done.

Ferguson groaned again and Fenton turned to see him move slightly on the floor. He managed to dial one nine then slipped and cursed. Ferguson moved again and Fenton knew that it was hopeless. Even if he did manage to make the call Ferguson was going to come round long before the police would arrive. Despair threatened as he searched for a way of injuring Ferguson more permanently.

Outside, a police siren started to wail. "Please God, make them come here," said Fenton out loud as he failed to see any way he could keep Ferguson out of action. To Fenton's amazement the siren grew louder and louder until it stopped outside the door of the lab and he heard car doors being slammed. Fenton heard the front door being broken in and the sound of heavy footsteps on the stairs. "I'm in here," he yelled as Ferguson struggled on to his hands and knees.

Jamieson entered the room first. He was followed by two uniformed constables. He looked at Ferguson and then at Fenton's chains as Fenton fought to regain the power of speech.

"How?" stammered Fenton. "Just how the hell did you know?"

Jamieson said, "I didn't really. The truth is we didn't get a computer report for one of the cars at Helmwood until twenty minutes ago because of a recent change in ownership. When I found out that the car belonged to one, Ian Ferguson and bearing in mind what you said about Saxon not being Munro's killer and how the murderer would have to be someone in the lab I put two and two together. Ferguson wasn't at his flat so I put out an APB for the car. It was reported outside the lab...so here I am."

Ferguson was now fully conscious. Jamieson bent down to caution him and place him under formal arrest. Fenton told him all that Ferguson had confessed to.

"Is that a fact?" said Jamieson quietly.

"I'm saying nothing," said Ferguson.

"Of course not sir," said Jamieson with a sneer.

Ferguson put his hand up to his head to feel the place where the transporter had hit him and, in doing so, lifted the hair away from his ear. It had a piece missing from it. Fenton froze when he saw it and knew that Jamieson had seen it too.

Jamieson turned to the two constables and said, "Wait downstairs." The men looked puzzled but trooped out obediently and closed the door behind them. Suddenly and without any warning Jamieson spun on his heel and swung his right foot into Ferguson's face. Fenton winced but Jamieson remained expressionless. "That," he said looking down at the gasping Ferguson, "was a wee something for Madeline Gray."

When he could speak again through a mess of blood and teeth Ferguson spluttered, "You won't get away with this you bastard!" He turned to Fenton and said, "You saw that Fenton! You saw what he did to me!"

"Saw what?" said Fenton.

The winter was finally over.

THE END

Reviews for Ken McClure

'His medical thrillers out-chill both Michael Crichton and Robin Cook.'
Daily Telegraph.

'McClure writes the sort of medical thrillers which are just too close to plausibility for comfort.'
(Eye of the Raven)Birmingham Post.

'Well wrought, plausible and unnerving.'
(Tangled Web)The Times

'A plausible scientific thriller . . . McClure is a rival for Michael Crichton.'
(The Gulf Conspiracy)Peterborough Evening Telegraph.

'Contemporary and controversial, this is a white knuckle ride of a thriller.'
(Past Lives)Scottish Field.

'Ken McClure looks set to join the A list at the top of the medical thriller field.'
The Glasgow Herald.

'McClure's intelligence and familiarity with microbiology enable him to make accurate predictions. Using his knowledge, he is deciding what could happen, then showing how it might happen . . . It is McClure's creative interpretation of the material that makes his books so interesting.'
The Guardian.

'Ken McClure explains contagious illness in everyday language that makes you hold your breath in case you catch them. His forte is to take an outside chance possibility, decide on the worst possible outcome . . . and write a book.'
The Scotsman

'Original in conception . . . its execution is brilliantly done . . . plot and sub plot are structured with skill . . . the whole thing grabs the attention as it hurtles to its terrifying climax.'
(Requiem)Independent Newspapers (Ireland).

'Absolutely enthralling.'
(Crisis)Medical Journal

'Pacey thrillers from Scotland's own Michael Crichton.'
Aberdeen Evening Express

'Fear courses through the narrative, unhinging the characters. It leaks through the government, corrupts the body politic and infects the nation. It is fear, too, tinged with curiosity, that keeps the reader turning the pages.'
(White Death)The Independent

Printed in Great Britain
by Amazon

FACING
THE WIND

FACING
THE WIND
MIRACLES FROM GOD. BASED ON A TRUE STORY

By
Twaambo Mwiinga Mudenda

Book Title: Facing the Wind
Copyright © 2022 by:
Twaambo Mwiinga Mudenda
Contact: twaambomd@gmail.com

Edited by: Rev Femi Imevbore (femiimevbore@gmail.com)

Dedication

This book is dedicated to my mum Mrs. Edith Malumbe Mwiinga and my first daughter Vianah Lushomo Mudenda (May their souls rest in peace); my beloved husband and life partner, Maclane M Mudenda; my family and friends for their inestimable support to me throughout my life's ordeals.

I also dedicate this book to all who are going through various

issues in life and those who are about to give up and to say to them, stay strong because God has not finished with you!

May God bless all of you abundantly in Jesus' name, Amen!

Table of Contents

INTRODUCTION

One of the reasons why many people, especially atheists do not believe in God, is that they are unable to find answers to why a good God would allow his children to encounter evil. This is a question that many of us cannot readily find answers to, but in hindsight, I have come to realise that God is good to his children even in the face of trials and tribulations.

I have decided in this book to share with you my experience through all my pains and how God has shown me that he is good and has my best interest at heart. This book is meant to be a source of encouragement to those who are facing various trials and who cannot find any answers as well as for those who will face trials later in life. One thing that is for sure is that no man is immune to temptations (trials) and the challenges of life.

This work is not primarily meant to answer any theological question as to why Christians suffer or go through hard times, and if because of coincidence it does, then it will be an added plus. However, my primary aim is to let the reader know that the Bible is not fiction nor is it an abstract work of art. The Bible is real and if we do what they did, we will get the same result they got.

From my childhood which was unruffled to an adult life of serious trials, I can say with confidence, that whatever you are going through just hold on because that too shall pass away.

I was praying one night, and I felt a strong urge in my spirit to share what I have gone through so that someone out there will be saved through this testimony and be encouraged not to give up. If God saw me through all my troubles, he will see you through if you will only hold on.

I am praying that my testimony will be an inspiration to someone and help to expand the kingdom of God.

Shalom

Chapter One

THE WAGER

The answer to the question of evil is a complex one and something that we may not be able to find all the answers to on the side of reality. This is because the Bible tells us that the hidden things belong to God and that the things that are revealed belong to us and our children. In other words, some things may remain hidden from us unless God in his infinite mercies reveals them to us.

I remember the issue of the Prophet Elisha and the Shunammite woman in 2 Kings 4, whose only son had died even though she had been generous to the man of God, providing accommodation for him and taking care of him. The interesting thing is that she had not asked God for a child; it was the prophet that saw the need in her life and prophesied that she was going to have a son. The son came but alas the boy suddenly died, and Prophet Elisha didn't know that the boy was going to die because as he said, "God had hidden it from me" 2 Kings 4:27 (KJV).

If a Prophet in the mould of Elisha, the man who made a piece of iron to float and did double the miracles his master (Elijah) did then who are we to question God when unexplainable things happen to us? When things are not very clear to us; when we don't understand what's going on, what do we do? I have found that the answer is to turn to the word of God.

"All scripture is given by inspiration of God and is profitable for doctrine, for reproof, for correction, for instruction in righteousness." 2 Timothy 3:16 (KJV).

Let us for a moment explore an incident that happened in the Bible and see if we can find comfort in God's word.

"There was a man in the land of Uz, whose name was Job; and that man was blameless and upright, and one who feared God and shunned evil. And seven sons and three daughters were born to him. Also, his possessions were seven thousand sheep, three thousand camels, five hundred yokes of oxen, five hundred female donkeys, and a very large household, so that this man was the greatest of all the people of the East. And his sons would go and feast in their houses, each on his appointed day, and would send and invite their three sisters to eat and drink with them. So it was, when the days of feasting had run their course that Job would send and sanctify them, and he would rise early in the morning and offer burnt offerings according to the number of them all. For Job said, "It may be that my sons have sinned and cursed God in their hearts." Thus, Job did regularly." Job 1:1-5 (ESV)

Job was a godly man who had the reputation of being the greatest man in the east at that time not necessarily because he had much possession but because the Bible says he was blameless and upright, one who feared God and ran away from evil. Therefore, God blessed him. In a bid to ensure that all was well with his family he ensured that regular sacrifices were offered to ward off any evil befalling his family. All these events were happening here on earth but something else seems to be going on in heaven.

"Now there was a day when the sons of God came to present themselves before the LORD, and Satan also came among them. And the LORD said to Satan, "From where do you come?" So, Satan answered the LORD and said, "From going to and fro on the earth, and from walking back and forth on it." Then the LORD said to Satan, "Have you considered my servant Job, that there is none like him on the earth, a blameless and upright man, one who fears God and shuns evil?" So, Satan answered the LORD and said, "Does Job fear God for nothing? Have you not made a hedge around him, around his household, and around all that he has on every side? You have blessed the work of his hands, and his possessions have increased in the land. But now, stretch out your hand and touch all that he has, and he will surely curse you to your face!" And the LORD said to Satan, "Behold, all that he has is in your power; only do not lay a hand on his person." So, Satan went out from the presence of the LORD." Job 1:6-12.

Unbeknown to Job, there was a discussion going on in heaven about him; God seemed to have entered a wager with the devil over Job and he was to face untold evil and hardship for being an upright man who feared God and shunned evil.

Why would God decide to wager Job's children, Health, fortune, and family? Did God not know that Job will be mocked, ridiculed, frustrated and forsaken; abandoned by his wife? What was Job's offence except that he shared his wealth with the needy?

> "For I assisted the poor in their need and the orphans who required help. I helped those without hope, and they blessed me. And I caused the widow's heart to sing for joy." Job 29:12-13.

Such a man with sterling credentials ought not to face troubles in life but the reality is that troubles come to all. While Job was living a successful life and doing his thing on earth, there was a debate in heaven that saw things turn around for the worse for him. I have come to realise that trials and temptations are allowed by God to test our commitment and allegiance to him. It is easy for many to serve God and shout "hallelujah" when things are going well but not so easy when it appears the whole world and even God has turned against you.

The inevitable truth is that you and I will have our own Job experience in various degrees, but the question is whether we can stand like Job when our trials come, or we buckle under the pressures of life?

Chapter Two

THE ENCOUNTER

"Before I formed thee in the belly of thy mother, I knew thee and before thou camest forth out of the womb, I sanctified thee and ordained thee a prophet to the nations. Jeremiah 1:5 (KJV)

Predestination is a concept that is sometimes difficult to understand, but when we realise that God is intentional about all that he does, we start to realise that life is more than what we perceive it to be. We are not just an occurrence, but we are part of his grand design because it is about what he wants to do with our lives more than our desires and ambitions.

My name is Twaambo Mwiinga Mudenda and I was born in Macha Mission Hospital, Choma located in the Southern Province of Zambia. Macha Mission Hospital was started in 1906 as a Christian Mission Station, aimed at converting the local population to Christianity. Founded by Hannah Frances Davison, an American

Missionary from the Brethren in Christ Church (BIC), this initiative with humble beginnings, has grown into a community center with a church, Hospital, Malaria Research Centre, a Nursing School, Secondary Schools, and Primary Schools in Macha.

Choma is a town of approximately 250,000 people and serves as the capital of the Southern Province of Zambia. It also serves as the commercial hub of the central part of the province, with extensive market-related industry. Rural farming and kinship family networks are the major occupation of the people.

It is in this environment that I was nurtured as a child and started my school education. My father was a radiographer and my mum a Pharmacy Assistant working in Macha Mission Hospital. From an early age, I was introduced to the worship of God. Although my parents were deeply religious, I experienced what many PKs (Pastors Kids) go through as I did not come to know Jesus for myself until I got into secondary school. At home, one was compelled to follow all the religious laws as a matter of obligation rather than conviction. So many times, you just flow with the motions without any sense of commitment.

Fortunately for me in secondary school, I was in the boarding house, and it was here that I knew more about God and came to realise that it was not only about religion, but that i needed to know and accept Jesus as my personal savior. I got born again in the year 1994, started baptism classes, and eventually got baptised. However, the basic tenets of Christianity, values, and discipline were inculcated into me as a young child.

In secondary school, I became a science student, but I always had a heart of service to the people, and this led to my calling. So, after completing secondary school, I signed up for nursing training. It was while going through my nursing training that I met my husband Maclane, who is also in the medical profession.

Ours started as a friendship and after 6 months he asked me to be in a serious relationship with him. Since both of us were committed Christians, we laid down rules for our relationship, based on the Bible's requirement for such a relationship. It was not long after the relationship started that he relocated to Botswana but promised that he would come back for me.

I completed my nursing course in July 2002, and he came for my graduation. It was a joyful moment because I had not seen him for two whole years but more importantly, it was the same time he proposed to marry him. After all the engagement celebration, he, now my fiancée, had to travel a few days later back to Botswana.

On his way to Botswana, a terrible accident happened but we thank God he survived. It was really a hard time for me as I heard the news of what had happened in Botswana. However, the word of God reminds me that HE IS THE ALPHA AND OMEGA. Only God was my comforter and it made me draw closer to Him.

He returned to Zambia and on the 21st of December 2002, we had our wedding which we celebrated with families and relatives. A few weeks later we had to leave Zambia and start our married life in Botswana. At this stage of my life, things were simple going on fine and my entire days were filled with joy. As a child of God, I expected that this would last forever and that I would never encounter any troubles but how wrong was I?

Chapter Three

THE BEGINNING
OF TROUBLE

"My thoughts are not your thoughts and ways are not your ways says the Lord" Isaiah 55:8

"I have told you these things, so that in Me you may have (perfect) peace and confidence, in the world, you have tribulation and trials and distress and frustration: but be of good cheer (take courage; be confident, certain, undaunted)! For I have overcome the world (I have deprived it of the power to harm you and have conquered it for you.) John 16:33 (AMP).

After my husband and I moved to Botswana, we had plans of what we wanted as a couple, but our plans were not God's plans. Like most couples, we couldn't have a child in the first year of our marriage as we prayed and waited for the fruit of the womb, and it was not happening. After two years of our marriage, people started talking; asking questions about why after two years of marriage we had no child? My husband

and I stood together and believed that at the right time God will surely bless us. It was not an easy thing to go through, because in Africa childlessness is seen as a curse and a taboo. We were reckoned by many to be barren and for those who had the courage to ask us directly, all we could answer was that "when it is time surely you will all see".

In our 6th year in Botswana, my husband wanted to go back to school and specialise as a Sonographer at Cape Town University in South Africa. This meant that he will be relocating from Botswana, a different country, South Africa and so agreed that once his contract ends in the year 2007, he will not be renewing it. Thank God the plan worked, as he was offered a place at Cape Town University and was expected to start in 2008. I had to go back to Zambia and get a job so I could start working while I waited for him to finish school.

In the year 2007, God answered our prayers as I started feeling a bit sick and when we checked what was wrong, we found out I was pregnant. God had answered our prayers, and five (six) years of waiting finally came to an end. Though excited about the news, my husband and I decided to stick with the plan of him going to school with me moving back to Zambia.

I was five months pregnant when I moved back to Zambia and stayed with my elder sister in the capital city of Lusaka, while I waited to be given a job in the ministry of health. To settle down, we started looking for a house we could rent. One day it happened that we saw this house which we liked and decided to contact the number on the advert. The person we spoke with agreed, and we made arrangements that the next day we could meet so we could inspect the house. My husband by then was still in Botswana finalising things.

The next day I had to go alone for the inspection because my sister was working so she was unable to come with me. I met the person at the agreed place, and he said we would have to get into his car to pick up the person with the keys, as he wasn't in possession of the keys to the house at the moment. We got into the car, and he started driving. Because I am not familiar with Lusaka, I did not know where we were going. However, I observed that he made a couple of turns and said we had reached the place where we could find the person with the house keys.

To my surprise on stopping the car, two men entered the car, one sat in front and the other joined me in the back. I immediately knew something was wrong and I started to pray in my heart. They started talking about diamonds and the man driving demanded I give them all the money I had with me. It was at that moment I came to fully realise what I had gotten into and was scared for my life and that of my unborn baby. I did as they said and removed all the money I had in my bag. They wanted more but I told them I had no more money and the driver said he could drive me back home to get more. All this time he was driving around, and I had no idea where I was. As he kept driving, I looked through the window, then I saw a place which had many people around and after that, I noticed a previous place where we had just passed. My instinct just kicked in and, in my spirit, I heard "open door", immediately I opened the door of the moving car and found myself on the ground. They did not stop the car, so I got up and started running towards where people were situated, shaking not knowing if my unborn baby was fine.

Thank God my phone was in my bag, so I started walking and was also looking around to see if the car would come back. When I felt safe enough, I then picked up my phone and called my sister telling her about my narrow escape from death. She immediately said I should remain where there were many people, that even if the car comes back that they will not be able to do anything. I didn't know where I was, but I was able to describe what was around me to her and thank God because she knew the city quite well, she was able to discern where I was and came to get me.

After the incident, I was a mess, confused, shaking, just about every emotion ran through me. My sister took me home and checked if I was injured in any way but thankfully, I just had some bruises on my leg when I fell from the moving car. My sister, being a Midwife checked to see if the baby was fine, "the baby seems fine" she said, but we still had to go to the hospital and get checked properly. After the hospital checked that everything was fine, I had to tell my husband what happened. The following day, he started off from Botswana to come and see me as he was really worried as well.

When he arrived, we discussed what the next plan will be and agreed that I move to another town, Livingstone, and stay with his parents, to get a job nearby considering the condition I was in and after escaping being kidnapped in Lusaka.

My narrow escape from the jaws of death was a miracle and one would have thought that my trials were over but alas there was still more trouble ahead.

Chapter Four

THE VALLEY AND
THE SHADOW

"Yea, though I walk through the valley of the shadow of death, I will fear no evil, for thou art with me, thy rod and thy staff, they comfort me" Psalms 23:4

As a young kid growing up Psalms 23 was one common Psalm we could recite by heart because we were taught this Psalm in school. However, the import of this Psalm never meant anything to me until things began to seem like all hell was let loose against me.

Before moving to Livingstone, the Ministry of Health gave me a job and the posting was at a Mission Hospital not far from Livingstone. All this was God's doing as the Bible says "all things work for good to those that love the Lord (Romans 8:28).

I was able to move to a new place and accommodation was provided for me. I settled well at the new hospital and the pregnancy proceeded without incident. When I was almost due to give birth to our first fruit of the womb, as per tradition, I had to go to my parent's house and wait for the day the baby would be born. This is so because mothers usually help their daughters to nurse their first babies due to inexperience on the part of the new mother.

My husband was doing well at school, and we kept in touch every day. It was on the 27th of April 2008, in the early hours of the morning that I began to feel some abdominal pains. I told my mother how I was feeling, and she said it could be the baby that was about to come. We prepared to go to the hospital, which was not far away, and we stayed at my younger sister's house who lived very close to the hospital.

On getting to the hospital, I was checked by the Midwife who confirmed that I was already in labour with dilation of about 3cm. I was immediately admitted but the progress of the labour was slow, and I spent the whole night in the hospital with severe pains. The following morning being 28th April 2008, I got so concerned that my baby could be tired or in distress as the movement had drastically reduced. I asked the Midwife if I could speak with the doctor, and she said she will inform the doctor because, at that moment, he was very busy. After waiting a few hours, the doctor came, and I expressed my concerns about the delay and the slow progress of labour being a nurse myself and understood the apparent risks involved if something was not done quickly. He asked if he could check how far I had dilated. He checked and confirmed that it was just 4cm after over 24 hours.

Straight away, the doctor said there is no way the baby can be born vaginally, as she was a big baby, and the passage was small. So, he discussed with me that a Caesarean Section (C-Section) needed to be done immediately. I was prepared for the operation and taken into the theatre. Thankfully my mum and sister were there with me. The C-Section was done, and my beautiful baby girl was born weighing 3.8 kg.

While still on the operating table the anesthesia had started to wear off and I could feel the doctor still stitching. I told them I was in pain but was reassured that they were almost done, that it was only one stitch remaining. Meanwhile, I kept praying that God will give me strength and take away the pain. What a C-Section it was but finally all was done, and I was moved to the ward and was given some pain relief which made me sleep.

I woke up later to find my mum and sister there and I was able to hold my baby girl for the first time; what a blessing. My husband was informed of the good news, and he couldn't wait to come and see his daughter. He named her "Vianah" which in my local dialect means graceful. After two days I was discharged from the hospital and went to my sister's place so I could recover before we could go to my parent's house, as it was in the same town.

The baby was healthy and sucking well but the issue was with me because mostly at night my body temperature could go high, and I would be feeling so hot. I was discharged from the hospital on antibiotics, and after one week I had to go back for the regular check-up. I told the doctor how unwell I was feeling, mostly at night and how I was having some abdominal pains. The doctor suggested we do an ultrasound which turned out not to be a good report. He suggested I start another round of antibiotics for a week and thereafter he will review me.

Unfortunately, the pain continued, and I was feeling so sick that I couldn't even walk properly due to the pains. I had to go back to see the doctor before the appointed time. On getting to see him, he said he wasn't sure why I was having such pains and repeated the ultrasound scan but nothing significant was showing. I was advised to keep on taking antibiotics.

At this juncture, my mum had informed her pastor at church, and they decided to come to my sister's home to pray with me. We believed God for healing as it was now three weeks after the operation and there was no improvement in my case. The day before my doctor's appointment my brother and other members of the church joined us in prayer, and then I went to see him.

When the doctor saw me, he asked me how I was feeling, and I told him I wasn't getting better but worse. He became concerned and didn't know what to do next since we had already done two scans. I then suggested to the doctor that we do an x-ray to which he agreed. After the x-ray I was told by the Radiographer to go back to the doctor that they will send him the report.

To our consternation the x-ray showed that they had left a swab in my body when they did the C-Section. The doctor panicked, and didn't know what to do, especially because I was a Nurse who also worked at the same hospital before. He had to discuss with the doctor who had done my C-Section, and immediately they said they will have to admit me and prepare me for an emergency operation to remove the swab.

By then I was not sure what to feel whether to be annoyed, to cry or to scream blue murder! I just asked to go home and tell my mom and my sister about the development and breastfeed my baby. Upon hearing this news everyone was so confused, but at the same time it was an answer to our prayer because God helped us to detect the source of the illness. Had we been blind-sighted, I would probably not be alive today. My sister had to inform my husband and parents- in-law about what happened.

The next day, I was then taken to the theatre by 10am, and was told that they will do a laparotomy, so I needed general anesthesia. The next time I woke up was in the ward around 8pm. I was told that the surgery was very complicated because they found that the swab was rotten and so had to do proper cleaning, and that it took time for me to wake up from the anesthesia as I was not responding to it. My mother was at the bedside with my baby and started telling me how the baby had been crying due to hunger, and that they had to give my baby bottled milk. I had a lot of tubes in me making it difficult for me to hold or breastfeed my baby. My mother in-law (May Her Soul Rest in Peace) travelled that same day of the operation to come see me while my husband was updated by phone as he was unable to travel immediately.

After a week I was discharged from hospital, and went back to my sister's place, recovering well. I was feeling stronger, and we went to my parent's house as I was still on maternity leave. My husband was able to come and see me as well as meet his baby girl for the first time. What a joy, we thanked God for what he had done for us.

After a few weeks with my parents, it was time for me to go back to my house as my maternity leave was coming to an end. My husband and I left as he still had a few days left before he would go back to school. We bonded with our baby girl, enjoying each other's company. My husband was looking forward to finishing his school so we could stay together as a family. Even though I could still feel some abdominal pains, it was manageable. As the days went by the pain kept getting worse, I had to see the doctor at my workplace, tests were done, and I was told that I had developed some Ulcers. I was put on medications which did not help at all even after taking them for many months.

At this point, we needed a second opinion so I had to travel to Lusaka to do some more tests, because by this time I could not eat much and started losing a lot of weight. I was in so much pain that I could barely get anything done for myself. Tests were done and I was told that I got gall bladder stones which needed to be removed. That meant another operation and the news didn't settle down well with me. I was confused and started asking why this was happening to me. Many thoughts were flashing through my mind but amid my predicament I could hear a small voice telling me "Though you pass through the fires I will be with you".

The operation was scheduled, and it was 10 months from the other laparotomy I had, and I was told they will need to do another laparotomy. Two operations within the space of 10 months were something difficult to fathom. How was I going to cope with taking care of my baby and going to work amid all of these? In any case I was consoled by the fact that God gives strength to his own children, so I had to trust him more. One prayer I was constantly praying was asking God to give me a chance to see my child grow.

Chapter Five

THE TEST OF FAITH

"Consider it all joy, my brethren, when you encounter various trials." James 1:2 (NAS)

Back at the operating theatre, it was agreed that general anesthesia will be needed, thank God my brother-in-law was the anesthetist. He reassured me that he will take photos of what will be happening, and he will keep in touch with my husband, so he knows what is going on. During the procedure my brother-in-law realised that the anesthesia they had used on my first laparotomy which affected me negatively, was the same one administered and I was reacting to it. We thank God that he was able to notice it on time and was able to correct it in good time. The operation took about five hours and after I recovered from the medication, my brother-in-law came to tell me what had happened.

It was shocking to discover when they opened me up that there were a lot of adhesions. My intestines were stacked together like glue, no wonder I was unable to eat. He showed me all the pictures of my gallbladder being removed and my intestines were separated. Shockingly, it was discovered that my appendix was removed during the first laparotomy. I had no idea this had transpired as the doctor who did the first laparotomy to remove the swab did not mention anything about removing my appendix.

After a few days, I was discharged from the hospital and was recovering well as I could eat with no pain. I was regaining my strength, getting better and enjoying parenthood as I was not sick anymore.

We left Lusaka back to our house in Zimba; I went back to work, and all seemed well. Happy baby and mother just counting that my husband will be coming to visit us and soon he will finish school. It was short-lived happiness as my baby suddenly got unwell one night at the age of 1-year 3months. Since I was staying in the hospital compound, I took her to the hospital where they did some tests on her. I felt she had malaria, but the doctor said she didn't have malaria but decided to admit us, since it was late in the night and said we could go home in the morning. All this time I was communicating with my husband, and we prayed together for the healing of our baby girl. Relatives were informed, and my mum said she will start coming early the next morning since it was late in the night.

When it was morning the next day, we were preparing to go home around 8am when one of my husband's relatives who stayed in the same compound with us came to see us in the ward. We chatted and told her that I was just waiting for the doctor to discharge us. At that point the baby seemed fine. But just in the twinkling of an eye my baby started having difficulty breathing. By this time, I panicked and got on the phone with my husband, telling him what was happening. The doctor was called by the time he reached the room, my baby girl had passed away in my arms.

I could not cry as I was confused as to what was happening. My husband's relative was there with me, and many other colleagues came to me. The doctor certified that my baby was dead and after what seemed like a century, I asked to see the baby before she was taken to the mortuary. What happened in there I cannot say, but I was told that when I entered, I held my baby and knelt down with her in my arms? I started to pray for almost 30mins then I stood and handed my dead baby to the nurse.

After that, I was taken to my house and my mum arrived. The funeral was held and that's how my baby girl was put to rest on the 14th of July 2009.

At this point, I was lost and didn't know what to do anymore as all hope was gone to continue living. My faith was shaken, tested, battered, you name it. I was trying to make sense of what was going on in my life. I tried to find the answer to why as a child of God the only thing I have ever asked God for was gone. I was at the lowest point of my life as the incident really got me down.

However, I had support from family, friends, and colleagues many of whom were Christians who tried to encourage me, but still, nothing was making sense at all. As far as I was concerned all hope was lost, I stayed at my parent's place and never wanted to go back to my house or work anymore. My mother was my shoulder to lean on. My husband was almost finishing his studies and was coming back to Zambia.

Four months later my husband was finally back but we had no home of our own for I completely refused to go back to Zimba where I had a house.

Chapter Six

THE BOUNCE BACK

"Instead of your (former) shame you shall have a two-fold recompense; instead of dishonor and reproach (your people) shall rejoice in their portion. Therefore, in their land they shall possess double (what they had forfeited); everlasting joy shall be theirs." Isaiah 61:7 (AMP)

My husband came to my parent's place, since I refused to return to our home with all the memories of my departed baby and discussed what our next plan will be. While I was grieving little did, I know that God was working behind the scenes to change my shame to fame and my trials to triumph! The Bible says God works in mysterious ways and I manifested right before our eyes because the same month we lost our child which was July, we received good news that my husband was given employment in the United Kingdom. This was the beginning of our restoration.

However, there was one condition required to be able to access the appointment and that he will have to present the degree of his studies as a sonographer which was given to everyone whom they considered. My husband and I agreed that we move to Livingstone to his parent's place as he waits for his degree to be out and see how things will go.

Sometime in December 2009, the results were released, and my husband passed. Therefore, the hospital upon receiving the results started processing his visa. At this point, we had a lot of financial challenges because he was not working, and income was low. We were dependent on my nursing income which was not even enough to meet all the required fees for the visa. Thankfully to God, our families came in to help and all papers were done.

My husband was set to leave for London to his new job in a few months' time precisely in April of 2010. Meanwhile, I finally got a transfer to move from Zimba Mission Hospital having been given a job in Livingstone. We decided that we will stay at my husband's parents place for now, since he was to leave soon, and I was recovering from the loss of our baby girl.

In December 2009, I started working at one of the clinics in Livingstone, and things started looking good. Having my husband around also helped a lot in the healing process.

This however was short lived because one evening January 2010, I received a phone call from my sister telling me that mum had passed away in a road accident. I was devastated because my comforter was gone just seven months after losing my baby girl; the first fruit of my womb. How do I survive all these things, that kept ringing in my head? I just had no answers to that question.

That same night we prepared and my husband, his sister, mum, dad, and I drove from Livingstone to Choma where my parents lived. It was an unbelievable situation since 4 people had died in the accident and all were close friends. My mother was put to rest and when the funeral ended, those who came to mourn her started going back to their homes.

Reality started to kick in now that mum was gone and no more. My husband had to go back to prepare his documents, as he was to leave for his new Job in London, United Kingdom. In my parent`s house, gloom and dejection were rife in the air as my siblings and dad were trying to process what had happened. During my mum's funeral, a lot of things happened that shocked us; there were many stories making the rounds and people started treating us differently but that's another testimony for some other time.

After a few months I had to go back to work. My husband had to leave for the United Kingdom, and he told me I needed to be strong, and not listen to what people were saying about my mum's death. He went on to say, "I will leave you here at my parent's for now, be strong it shall be well".

It was such a difficult time for me when my husband left, I felt so defeated and had no will to live but just to go and join my daughter and mother on the other side. Things got worse as the devil was fighting from every corner. My husband was getting emails from people in Zambia that he should not plan for me to join him. Short of calling my father and one of my younger sister as involved in Satanism, there were a lot of accusations, but God is Faithful, and I was encouraged that HE WILL NEVER LEAVE ME NOR FORSAKE ME.

In the United Kingdom, my husband was settling down well, and immediately he got there, he applied for a family apartment so I could join him. We kept in touch, and I thank God for my Husband and his wisdom. As a God-fearing man, he did not listen to what people were saying, but kept his marriage vows.

After 6 months, he was given the family apartment while waiting for the time when the apartment will fully be ready, we started the process of getting my visa. My husband cautioned me not to tell anyone that we were processing my visa so I could join him. Eventually, all paperwork was submitted, and I was given a spouse' visa to join him. It was such exciting news that finally we will be together again.

Since a lot had happened my husband decided not to buy me a plane ticket saying, "If you come, stories will change that you followed me here by force; instead, I will come and get you, so that they will be saying he came for her." We agreed on that strategy to silence the mockers and finally my husband came in for a few weeks.

All the while, we kept the processing of my visa a secret so when we said our goodbyes to my family, they were surprised that I already had my visa. On our last night at my parents-in-law home, he had a meeting with his parents, and it was at that time that he informed them that by the next morning, we will be leaving together for the United Kingdom. It was a shock to them as well, but we had good reason to keep our secret to ourselves until the appropriate time. One thing the whole saga taught me was the need for discretion and wisdom in taking sensitive decisions in life. Remember, Jesus told his disciples and anyone who cared to listen that a man's enemies shall be members of his own household. In any case, my husband and I left the next morning for the UK without any incident.

We landed at Heathrow on the 1st of January 2011 and our new life began. All thanks to God. With just me and my husband in the foreign land, we had each other exclusively to ourselves and we were able to make decisions without the influence of our families, so we agreed that we were going to establish ourselves here. It was not an easy journey, but we managed to adjust.

One day my husband asked if we could try for a child. Initially I was against it and never wanted to hear anything about kids, because I was still too traumatised about the death of my child. However, God works in mysterious ways and slowly the healing process began to take root and then we asked Him to bless us again as we knew that children are heritage from Him.

In the year 2013 I went for a checkup and received the good news that we were expecting a child. I was overwhelmed with joy, but it was short lived when I had a miscarriage at 4 weeks which was a painful and devastating news. We did encourage ourselves and believed God that with Him nothing was impossible. We looked at different stories in the Bible and just said our time will surely come. As the Bible says though it might tarry but surely it will come to pass.

Therefore in 2015 God blessed us with a son who was delivered through another C-section. His coming brought so much joy into our lives as finally God gave us tears of joy. The news was shared to our families, and everyone was so happy for us knowing what we had been through.

This time around I recovered so well from the C-section and our son was healthy; things were going on so well and I was able to go back to my calling working as a nurse. Then in 2018 God blessed us again with a baby girl delivered through yet another C-section. God does miracles and He is a story changer. It is not over until God says so.

While pregnant with my last girl it was discovered that I have diaphragmatic hernia, but nothing could have been done until the baby was born. After 6 months of having the baby, I went for a review and the doctor said if the hernia was not giving me any problems it was better to leave it. But two years later in 2020, I started feeling so much pain that I went to see the doctor who ordered that an ultrasound be done. It was discovered that I have 5 diaphragmatic hernia and he referred me to see the consultant.

In Early 2021 I was booked to see the consultant who suggested that I will need to have an operation, but before then he requested, we do some blood tests. When the results came out, my Hemoglobin level was so low that he said he cannot attempt any operation. Instead, he requested we do more tests to find the root cause of the low Hemoglobin. An Endoscopy, Colonoscopy and a CT scan where done. Unfortunately, the CT scan detected something that didn't appear so well, hence an MRI was requested. The results were not so good as it was found that I had adhesions and a lot of restrictions in my small bowels requiring another laparotomy to sort it out.

Upon hearing the news from the consultant, I was so deflated that I did not know what to think anymore. I asked myself how many operations I will need to have. Having had two laparotomies and three C-sections, I felt it was just too much for one person to go through. The consultant mentioned that he will have to talk with the other consultant who was to repair the diaphragmatic hernia so they can do just one operation instead of two. While waiting I was referred to the Hematologist to help with the issue of my low hemoglobin before they can decide when the surgery can take place.

I was seen by the hematology consultant on the 20th of April 2022, and it was decided that I will need to have iron infusion which will be done in two parts as it will be a high dose. I was told doing so will help my hemoglobin level go up in preparation for the surgery. The appointment for the first dose of iron infusion is booked for 11th of May 2022. For now, I am trusting God that the iron infusion will help increase the hemoglobin level for surgery to be done so these pains can be corrected. I believe all shall be well.

Epilogue

This is my life now! In 2022 I am a happy mother to two lovely children. In the year 2019 when I was about to go back to work after the delivery of my last child, I needed to find a way to be more present in their lives and not miss out on their growing up. Since our pattern of work as nurses is 12 hour shifts whereby you go to work while the kids are sleeping and come back late while they're already asleep, I prayed for God to make a way for me.

Thankfully I found something that I was able to do alongside my nursing career. It was a blessing because I was able to start my own digital business, which allows me time with my family as well as create another stream of income for my family. I developed a mindset of pure abundance which in turn has handed me more than enough of the things I never felt I had enough of. I have been able to do away with working full-time as a nurse to spend more time with the family and still supplement our income through the digital business. To me it was answered prayer because starting this digital business means I will leave a legacy for my children since I cannot pass my nursing career to them. The digital business is named after my son and daughter IMA DIGITAL MARKETING (IVAN MUDENDA ABIGAIL). www.imadigital.net

Am forever grateful for all these open doors that I now mentor people who are looking for change and want to learn how to start their own digital business. I believe true success is in helping others succeed. I feel so blessed to know that I have helped someone out there change their lives. I genuinely believe that no one should sacrifice special moments in life and choose between work and family. I believe that everybody deserves the best things in life as much as possible. I am always reminded about the importance of focusing time on family, passion and health as life is very unpredictable. Time is our biggest commodity because once it is gone you can never get it back. Hold on and never lose hope!

It's not over until God says so!

ABOUT THE AUTHOR

Twaambo Mwiinga Mudenda was born in Choma, the Provisional Capital of Southern Zambia. As a child she grew up in a very religious family but personally gave her life to Christ in Secondary School. She went on from Secondary School and to study Nursing from 2000 to 2002.

She got married to Maclane Mudenda a Sonographer but her early marital life was one of unparalleled disappointment, pains, and sorrow. She was unable to conceive for over 5 years, suffered numerous miscarriages, lost her first child and her mother within the space of seven months apart; went through three C-sections and two laparotomies with one more surgery to go. Once she was kidnapped but miraculously escaped falling from a moving car while 5 months pregnant.

Through all the pains and heartaches, she was able to find strength through the word of God and today she is still a practicing nurse. In addition to her nursing profession, she is also a life coach and digital marketing entrepreneur who through her life experiences is helping others to stand.

She and her beloved husband reside in the United Kingdom and are blessed with two kids.

Printed in Great Britain
by Amazon

Men of Violence

Issue 11

Published November 2018

Edited by Justin Marriott

Copy-edited by Jim O'Brien

Contributors
Paul Bishop
Jim O'Brien
Morgan Holmes
Richard Toogood

Cover illustration Rik Rawling

All illustrations used for the purposes of historical information and no copyright infringement intended

The illustrations on the frontispiece and editorial are by Charles Keeping

The original art by Richard Clifton-Dey was taken from the Worlds of Wonder web-site

Dedicated to Richard Toogood, for his vision for this issue and passion for historical fiction.

THE SWORDSMAN

Page 10

Morgan Holmes reviews the many historical novels - and pseudonyms - of Gardner Fox.

TALBOT MUNDY; MYSTIC ADVENTURER

Page 22

Paul Bishop on the greatest of adventure writers.

FAMILY OF FIGHTING EAGLES

Page 44

Richard Toogood on the Aquila stories of Rosemary Sutcliff.

THE VIKING PAPERBACK BLOKE

Page 60

Jim O'Brien on Henry Treece who was a bloke who wrote some viking paperbacks.

LOVE LIKE BLOOD

Page 70

A black spot for anyone not reading this look at Rafael Sabatini's pirate fiction classic *Captain Blood*.

GUEST EDITORIAL BY RICHARD TOOGOOD

"Historical fiction has never been more popular. Pop into any local bookshop and you will find shelves awash with Romans and redcoats, Vikings and Visigoths, Greeks and gladiators. A welter of diverse series running to innumerable volumes, each one as violent as the times they reflect. In such a climate a special issue of Men of Violence dedicated to all things historical seems amply justified."

Historical fiction, by its very nature, has always been a pretty broad church. But like every other church it has suffered its own doctrinal schism. Nowadays a border divides history fiction proper from adventure fiction with a historical setting, even though the former can be every bit as romping as the latter and the latter just as authentic as the former. The division tends to betray itself in the sort of dichotomy that can see the "literary" Hilary Mantel win the Booker Prize (twice) with rare excursions into historical fiction whilst the prolific "populist" Bernard Cornwell has yet to come within musket range of the long list even once.

It wasn't always like this. And the absurdity of the situation is brought home by the fact that when Sir Walter Scott pioneered the historical novel at the beginning of the 19th century he did so with romances and melodramas which only the generosity of hindsight has invested with literary gravitas. The same holds true for the writers who followed in his wake from Harrison Ainsworth to Charles Kingsley to Robert Louis Stevenson and beyond. It speaks volumes about the post war attitude towards history fiction that Ainsworth's influential *Rookwood* of 1834 – which invented the romantic image of the thuggish Dick Turpin – could be reprinted as an Everyman classic whilst Arthur Howden Smith's comparable *Swain's Saga* of 1931 still languishes in out of print obscurity. The irony of the situation would not have been lost on Conan Doyle who esteemed his own historical melodramas over all his other work and yet is chiefly remembered for detective trifles which the passing of time has elevated to the status of an art form.

It was the story papers and pulps of the early 20th century that really popularized historical fiction as a distinct literary form, making stellar names out of their best contributors such as Arthur Gilchrist Brodeur, Rafael Sabatini and Talbot Mundy. And in the post pulp world it was such men and their contemporaries who provided the raw material for the explosion in luridly packaged paper-

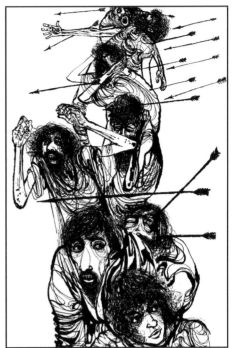

backs. At this point history fiction with literary pretensions attempted to distance itself by restricting publication to hardbacks. Even though the revenue brought in by the growth in paperback sales during the 1950s and 60s soon eroded that dynamic the basic attitude persists to this day.

Nowadays the gulf is such that it takes a rare sort of book to successfully bridge it. What Mantel's success has served to show is that it now seems easier for a literary work to strike an unexpectedly commercial chord than it is for the opposite to occur.

Here at **Men of Violence** we recognize no such contrived distinctions between what constitutes high brow and hack work. As long as it boasts something to interest our readers then it is assured of a warm welcome here.

But what we cannot ignore is the fact that, abundant as the stuff now is, it was the period between 1950 and 1980 that was the real high water mark for history fiction of whatever stripe. Not only did it see the publication of books of such enduring significance as Howard Fast's *Spartacus* - a novel which took its lead from Scott in using historical parallels to advance contemporary causes - but a mushrooming in paperback publishers coincided with the emergence of an extraordinary crop of writers as rich and varied as Alfred Duggan, Rosemary Sutcliff, Henry Treece, Robert Tapsell, George Shipway and Peter Green to name just a few.

Space considerations preclude us from doing any more than merely touching upon a small sample of the work of this extraordinary generation. But if the reception to this experiment is positive and the interest is there then maybe the opportunity will arise to revisit this fascinating subject at a later date.

FORGOTTEN ARTISTS ONE: JACK HAYES

I know very little about Jack Hayes. I became aware of him when another artist pointed out a series of biblical illustrations with the simple signature of - HAYES -. I then began to spot this signature on a growing number of illustrations on historical fiction, especially on Pan Books in the UK. They were often for romantic historical fiction which is why I imagine Hayes is not better known. At Pan he illustrated Rafael Sabatini's Captain Blood and the cult bodice-rippers of the Angelique series. At Fontana he provided a series of lush illustrations for Stuart Cloete.

 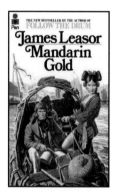  

 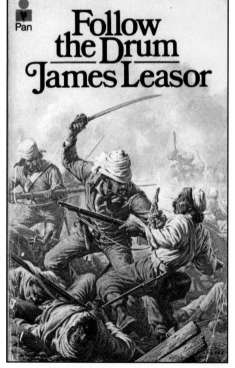

STUART CLOETE
TURNING WHEELS

STUART CLOETE
MAMBA

"A really powerful piece of work"
Daily Telegraph

Shaka Zulu
E. A. Ritter

Panther

CORGI
TOO FEW FOR DRUMS
R. F. DELDERFIELD
AUTHOR OF 'GOD IS AN ENGLISHMAN'

SONG OF AFRICA : STUART CLOETE

Stuart Cloete (1897 - 1976) is another one of those authors that were steady-sellers in their era but have since disappeared. Perhaps the political stand-point and subject matter of his works, very much steeped in African history from a white man's perspective, have rendered them culturally embarrassing.

Many of his 14 novels and most of his short stories are historically-based fictional adventures, set against the backdrop of major African, and, in particular, South African historical events although he was not adverse to exploring sleazier themes, such as white slavery.

His first published novel, *Turning Wheels* (1937), was about the 'Great Trek' of Dutch speaking settlers into uncontrolled areas of South Africa, while later title *Rags of Glory* (1962) was set in the Boer War. He is perhaps more comfortable with the short story, with 8 collections published, *The Mask* (1957) being a particularly evocative and earthy selection.

I haven't read his autobiographies, *A Victorian Son* (1972) and *The Gambler* (1973), but apparently Cloete was a larger-than-life character, wounded in the First World War and something of a carouser.

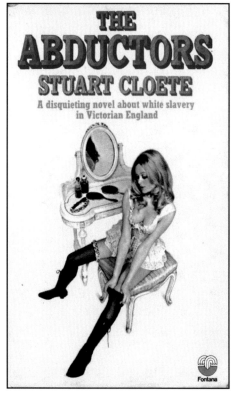

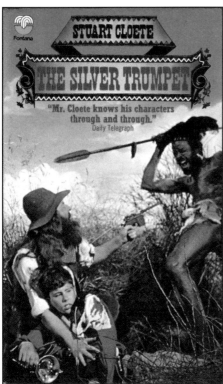

THE SWORDSMAN

Morgan Holmes studies the historical novels of Gardner F Fox.

Fox (1911-1986) is probably best remembered today for his comic book writing. He began comic book work in 1937. He wrote scripts for Batman very early in the character's existence. He created the Flash, Hawkman, and the Justice Society of America during the Golden Age of comic books.

He began writing fiction for pulp magazine starting in **Weird Tales** in 1944. He was a regular in **Planet Stories** in the late 1940s. He also wrote a fair number of stories for the sports pulps and the western pulps until 1957.

As the pulp magazines died out in the 1950s, historical fiction was on the rise. Mika Waltari and Thomas B. Costain were two popular writers of the genre in that period and the market was lucrative enough to attract science fiction writers L. Sprague de Camp and Poul Anderson into the field. Fox made the transition from pulps to original mass market paperback books and a large part of his paperback output in the 1950s and early 60s were historical adventures and dramatizations of historical figures.

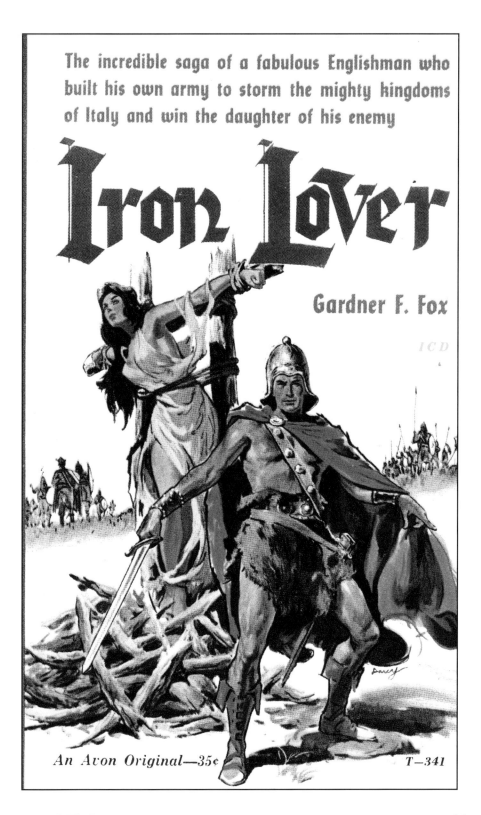

The incredible saga of a fabulous Englishman who built his own army to storm the mighty kingdoms of Italy and win the daughter of his enemy

Iron Lover

Gardner F. Fox

An Avon Original—35¢

T–341

From 1953 to 1976 Fox wrote forty-two historical novels; twenty-four as Gardner Fox, sixteen as 'Jefferson Cooper,' seven as 'Kevin Matthews', two as 'Jeffrey Gardner', one historical as 'John Medford Morgan,' and one as 'James Kendricks'.

Thirteen of the novels are based on historical and biblical figures– Cleopatra, Sheba, Delilah, Jezebel, Helen of Troy, Catherine the Great, Sappho, Ivan the Terrible, Casanova, Veronica, Baibars, Jack the Ripper etc. With later figures, he is constrained by documented history in some cases with what he can do with the story. His *Ivan the Terrible* attempts to make Ivan the victim of circumstance.

He wrote two novels with a Roman setting, *Slaves of Roman Swords* (Pa-perback Library, 1965 as Jefferson Cooper) and *The Roman and the Slave Girl* (Signet, 1959 as John Medford Morgan). *Slave Girl* is set interestingly in early 5th Century Roman Britain. Surprisingly, Fox never wrote a Viking novel. It is a shame as he probably could have produced a rousing tale of swords of the North.

Fox wrote some American revolution and early frontier novels, two being written for the American Bicentennial in 1976. He wrote a few pirate novels such as *Captain Seadog* (Pocket Books, 1959 as Jefferson Cooper).

The Swordsman (Cardinal/Pocket Books, 1957 as Jefferson Cooper) is Fox's stab at doing the big sprawling historical epic based on the life of

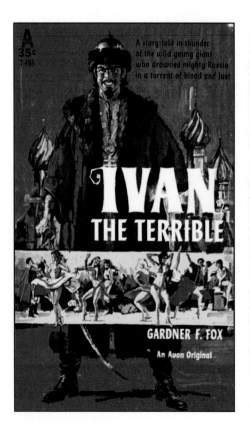

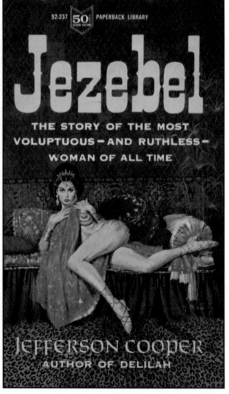

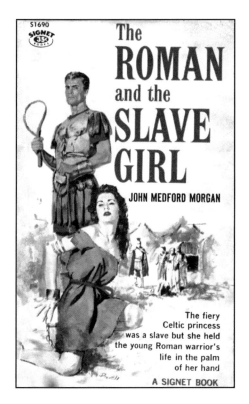

the Mamluk Sultan, Baibars. Fox is generally good with historical details and avoids anachronisms. His action scenes are exciting and well-choreographed. His novels always have a love interest to them as part of the plot.

Two of Fox's main outlets for his historical fiction were for Gold Medal and Avon. Fox was Gold Medal's main writer of historical novels with eight novels to his credit. Gold Medal was never a big publisher of historical novels, preferring hard-boiled crime and westerns. On the other hand, Avon published a steady number of historical adventures novels in the late 1950s and early 1960s.

This was the era of the Bantam and Ace "Giants", but Avon Books went for slim efficient novels instead of big, sprawling epics. Poul Anderson's *The Golden Slave* and *Rogue Sword* are prime examples of this sort of short novel.

The time that Gardner Fox made his own was the late Middle Ages and the Renaissance. He wrote nine novels set between the early 1300s and 1678. He returned to the Italian condottiere– mercenaries who fought for various Italian city state and principalities in the Renaissance.

In his introduction to *The Lion of Lucca*, Fox has this to say about the Condottiere:

"The professional war captain– or condottiere– was a direct outgrowth of the economic emergence and affluence of the city-states of Italy during the late medieval and early Renaissance periods. Citizens of Venice and Genoa, Florence and Mi-

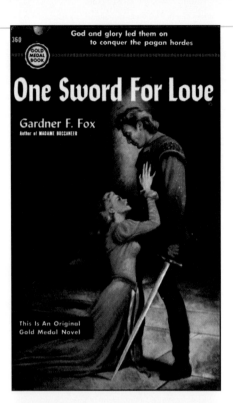

God and glory led them on
to conquer the pagan hordes

360

One Sword For Love

Gardner F. Fox

Author of MADAME BUCCANEER

This Is An Original
Gold Medal Novel

A stableboy with a magic sword
and the fame and love it won him

The Borgia Blade

Gardner F. Fox

ginal Gold Medal Novel—Not a Reprint

lan, would rather pay out ducats and florins than their lives to protect and strengthen their borders, or to acquire new territories and thus more riches. The mercenary soldier became a commonplace, and wealthy after a fashion if he was clever enough to win victories in the field for his patrons."

The book that started it all was *The Borgia Blade* (Gold Medal, 1953). Illarion the swordsman takes service with Cesare Borgia in the early 1500s. There are some large-scale battles in addition to one-on-one rapier play.

The Iron Lover (Avon, 1959) has Englishman, Sir John Hawkwood, who soldiered in northern Italy in the 1300s. *The Questing Sword* (Perma Books, 1958 as Jefferson Cooper) features Bartolommeo Colleoni in the Fifteenth Century. As a "Jefferson Cooper" novel from a Pocket Book imprint, it is longer and bigger in scope. You have Milanese halberdiers, Genoese crossbowmen, and Swiss pike men all adding to the color and splendour of the time.

As to influences on the Italian Renaissance novels, Rafael Sabatini is likely. Sabatini is remembered for pirate swashbucklers but he also wrote a fair amount of fiction of the time of Cesare Borgia. Fox also probably read Frederick Faust writing as "George Challis" in the pages of **Argosy** magazine in the 1930s with the Tizzo series set in this period. The Tizzo series in **Argosy** were also set in the time of 16th Century Italy. Tizzo is a master swordsman and fighter in general. One of the finest swashbuckling series ever written.

The Hundred Years War is another topic that Gardner Fox visited, with

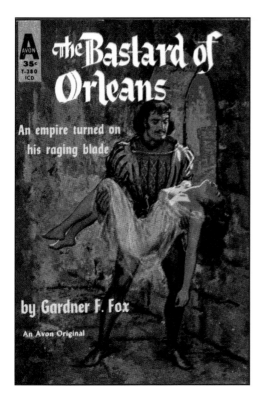

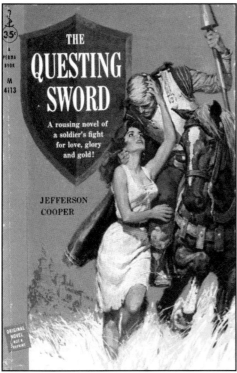

Edward the Black Prince as the main character of *The Conquering Prince* (Crest, 1957). There is action and romance.

The time of Joan of Arc is the setting for *The Bastard of Orleans* (Avon, 1960). Jean le Batard is the bastard cousin of the King of France. He is not only fighting the English but planning vengeance on his father's murders. This novel tells the story at 191 pages.

Fox channeled Dumas for *The Devil Sword* (Hillman, 1960 as Kevin Matthews). A masked woman attempts to murder King Louis IVX's best swordsman at the beginning, but they team up. Intrigue and violence ensue!

The historical novel boom ran down in the early 1960s. Fox's last Renaissance novel was *The Lion of Lucca* (Avon Books, 1966). Castruccio Castracane fights for the Donati in 14th Century Italy. Fox also throws in a love triangle that is not easy for Castracane.

While the historical novel wound down, Fox began writing science fiction again in the mid and late 1960s for Ace Books and Paperback Library. There was a sword & planet fiction boom in the wake of popular Edgar Rice Burroughs reprints. Fox wrote two sword and planet novels for Ace with plenty of swordplay.

A sword & sorcery boom followed in the wake of the success of Lancer Books packaging Robert E. Howard's Conan of Cimmeria in mass market paperbacks. Fox wrote five novels featuring Kothar, Barbarian Swordsman for Belmont Books in 1969-70. If you read Kothar, you will see touches here and there harkening back to his historical novels, such as Fox using his research on weapons and armour.

If you are looking for pulp flavoured, action oriented but well researched historical novels, look for Gardner Fox's novels. Some of his novels are available in electronic form and the plan is for all of them to be converted for e-readers.

Gardnerffox.com has a list of Fox's fiction and which novels have been transcribed. E-books can be purchased at Amazon.com

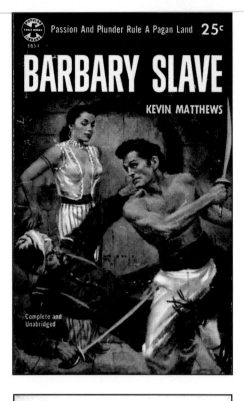

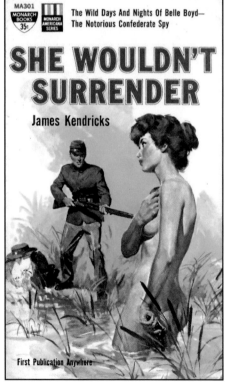

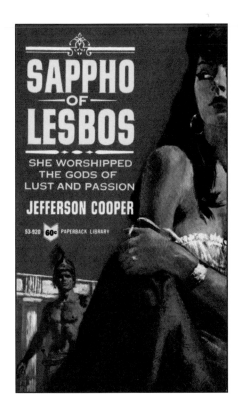

SAPPHO
OF
LESBOS

SHE WORSHIPPED
THE GODS OF
LUST AND PASSION

JEFFERSON COOPER

53-920 60¢ PAPERBACK LIBRARY

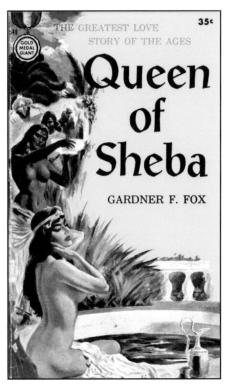

THE GREATEST LOVE
STORY OF THE AGES

35¢

GOLD
MEDAL
GIANT

Queen
of
Sheba

GARDNER F. FOX

With cutlass and pistol
she ruled the Spanish Main

328

GOLD
MEDAL
BOOK

MADAME
BUCCANEER

Gardner F. Fox
Author of THE BORGIA BLADE

An Original Gold Medal Novel—Not a Reprint

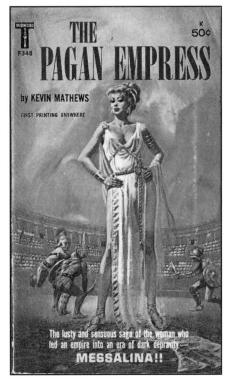

MIDWOOD

T
F348

THE
PAGAN EMPRESS

K
50¢

by KEVIN MATHEWS

FIRST PRINTING ANYWHERE

The lusty and sensuous saga of the woman who
led an empire into an era of dark depravity—
MESSALINA!!

FORGOTTEN ARTISTS TWO: BILL FRANCIS PHILLIPS

One of the unsung heroes of British paperback illustration is the relatively unknown and forgotten William Francis Phillips. His lush brush-work and looping signature were unmistakable on paperback covers at Pan in the 60s and New English Library (NEL) in the 70s. He worked across all genres, although less so on SF and horror, and more in historical fiction and thrillers, which is probably why he is not well-remembered today.

His series of portraits for Alfred Duggan novels for NEL are classic examples of his approach, a beautiful collision of romantic, expressive brush-strokes and gnarly, weathered execution. Faces are grimy and wind-burnt, clothes are worn by the elements and eyes speak of hardship. I can't imagine any images more representative of life in the Middle Ages or Ancient Rome. Both were the favoured settings of archaeologist Alfred Duggan for his series of historical novels (1903–1964) which used meticulous research, often through field work, to produce nuanced and sophisticated accounts of key periods of change for the British Isles.

The cover on the bottom left of page 20 looks more like the work of SF artist Bruce 'Dune' Pennington. I'm confident the other three are Bill Phillips.

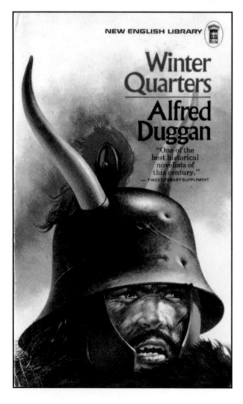

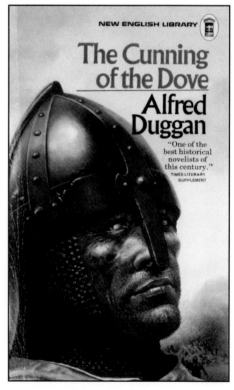

BARBA THE SLAVER
NO.1 IN THIS EXCITING SERIES
DAEL FOREST

HAESEL, THE SLAVE
NO. 2 IN THIS EXCITING SERIES
DAEL FOREST

BROTAN THE BREEDER
NO. 3 IN THIS EXCITING SERIES
DAEL FOREST

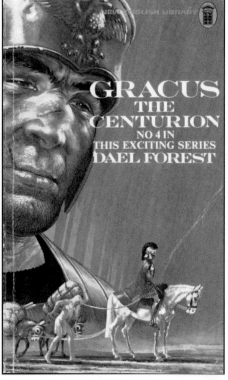

GRACUS THE CENTURION
NO 4 IN THIS EXCITING SERIES
DAEL FOREST

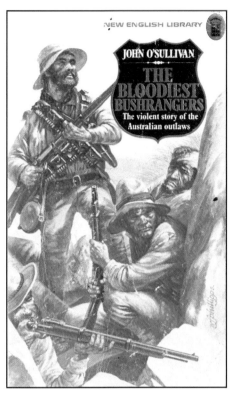

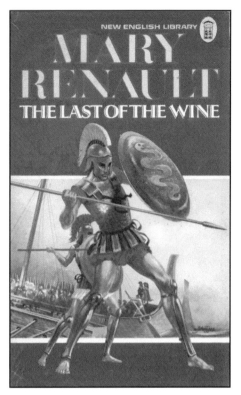

TALBOT MUNDY THE MYSTIC ADVENTURER

by Paul Bishop

Entering the world in London in 1879, Talbot Mundy (born William Lancaster Gribbon) was destine to become one of the greatest adventure writers of all time. Considered a rogue as a young man, he travelled the world—sometimes involving himself in less than reputable circumstances—before arriving in America in 1911. A con man and adventurer in India, he sought to reform his ways in his newly adopted country. However, his only stock in trade was the experience earned through his wanderlust and the esoteric knowledge it bestowed upon him.

At the suggestion of a friend, he began writing stories aimed at the pulp magazine market. His success was almost immediate, penning a number of classic adventures—such as *Rung Ho!*, *The Eye of Zeitoon*, and *Hira Singh*—appearing first as serials then later collected as novels. These tales grabbed the imagination of both editors and readers alike.

While he would publish in many of the top pulp magazine markets of the day, Mundy formed a close relationship with **Adventure** magazine, often considered the most intellectual of the pulps. After publishing a non-fiction article by Mundy, **Adventure** bought one of early pulp stories, *The Phantom Battery*, beginning a long and profitable association with the man who would arguably become their most popular author.

TIME-LOST SERIES
CENTAUR PRESS

$1.25

CAESAR DIES
Talbot Mundy

His early adventure stories mixed orthodox touchstones with exotic escapades in Africa and the Near East. He often sent his heroes on quests where loyalty, honor, and a willingness to explore strange spiritual concepts were needed to survive. Mundy's first-hand knowledge brought colorful life to his exotic locales. It also led him to add depth to his ethnic characters, displaying a respect ignored by his contemporaries—who preferred the established demeaning stereotypes. His plotting was complex, but always tight, never straying far from the main emphasis of a story.

His popularity as a writer brought comparisons to H. Rider Haggard and Rudyard Kipling. However, his stories often voiced anti-colonialist rhetoric and showed a progressive awareness of Asian religions and philosophies. This indelibly marked him as different from his worthy contemporaries.

In 1916, a nine part serial published in **Everybody's** magazine was collected as Mundy's third novel, *King of the Khyber Rifles: A Romance of Adventure.* Adopting the name Khyber Rifles from an actual regiment serving in India, this tale of high adventure sealed Mundy's reputation as a great adventure writer.

Drawing on his own sojourns in India and his penchant for Western esotericism (fascination with ancient Asian religions), Mundy tasked his protagonist, Captain Athelstan King of the British India Secret Service, with preventing a German prompted Moslem insurrection in British India during the early days of the First World War. King's quests takes him deep into the mysterious and exotic Muslim-held land of the Khyber pass. There, he faces death as he is forced to deal with the Turkish mullah Muhammed Anim without being distracted by the mystical woman adventuress, Princess Yasmini.

Asked about the creative spark behind *King of the Khyber Rifles*, Mundy stated, "I remember sitting in the dark and seeing the throat of the Khyber Pass at sunset—gloomy, ominous, mysterious, lonely, haunted by the ghosts of murdered men and by the prowling outlaws who live by the rifle and shun the daylight. As if the words were almost spoken in my ear, I heard, "Death roosts in the Khyber while he preens his wings." It seemed like a good line, so I made a note of it."

Mundy was also considered a master of the mystical adventure—breaking new literary ground with stories turning on quirks of superscience, fantastical archaeology, dimensional disappearances, dangerous ancient technologies, and religious occultism. James Schuyler Grim, an American operative recruited by British Intelligence due to his knowledge of Arabs—who was known far and wide as Jimgrim—became Mundy's vanguard character for these tales. Jimgrim had a colorful band of cohorts to battle these threats alongside him, including American engineer Jeff Ramsden,

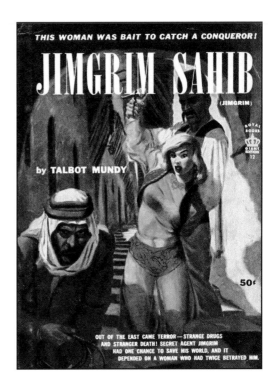

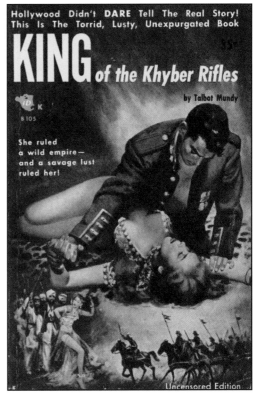

TALBOT MUNDY'S

CLASSIC ADVENTURE
OF IMAGINATION

OM:
THE SECRET OF
AHBOR VALLEY

A BOLD MAN DEVISES A FANTASTIC DISGUISE
TO PENETRATE THE FORBIDDEN.

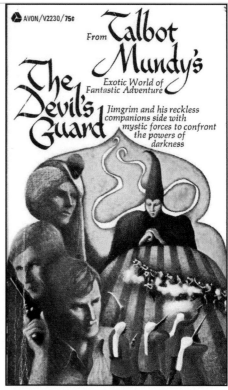

AVON/V2230/75¢

From Talbot Mundy's

The Devil's Guard

Exotic World of
Fantastic Adventure

Jimgrim and his reckless
companions side with
mystic forces to confront
the powers of
darkness

Sikh soldier Narayan Singh, an un-scrupulous Bengali *babu* (the equiv-alent of a con man) named Chullunder Ghose, and two charac-ters from Mundy's early India sto-ries— Athelstan King of the British India Secret Service, and Mundy's most memorable female protagonist, Princess Yasmini.

The best of the Jimgrim adventures include *The Mystery of Khufu's Tomb* (in which Jimgrim and his compan-ions are pitted against deadly an-cient Egyptian technologies), *Caves of Terror* (a vibratory superweapon possessed by a Hindu cult is in dan-ger of falling into the hands of Om— a villainous adventuress), *The Secret of Ahbor Valley* (a race for a powerful jade sphere from a great past civili-zation), *The Nine Unknown* (the pur-suit of missing gold from India leads

to a secret society, using the gold for atomic power), and *King of the World* (scientific secrets from Atlan-tis discovered in the Gobi desert threaten world domination).

Other elements created by Mundy for these types of stories include PSI powers, strange drugs, antigravity, mahatmas (super humans), trans-mutation of elements, and vibratory phenomena. Mundy imbued these outrageous concepts with rational and scientific explanations con-ceived from ancient wisdoms, which he explained were a body of knowl-edge once possessed by mankind, but since lost.

Mundy remains perhaps best known for his *Tros of Samothrace* tales. Ap-pearing irregularly in **Adventure Magazine** between 1925 and 1935,

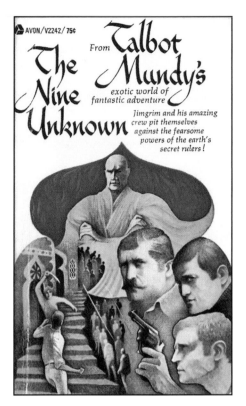

these stories were collected in book form as *Queen Cleopatra* (1929), *Tros of Samothrace* (1934) and *The Purple Pirate* (1935). Making minimal use of the fantastic, the Tros sequence is a succession of historical adventures set in Britain, Gaul, and the Mediterranean with Tros leading the early Britons as they fight the invading forces of Julius Caesar.

Popular with loyal readers of **Adventure**, the Tros tales aroused debate due to Mundy's depiction of Roman civilization, Julius Caesar, Cleopatra, and other historical figures as imperialistic and tyrannical. The debate raged to the point where **Adventure** editor Arthur Sullivant Hoffman stated the Tros stories were the most controversial the magazine had ever published.

In considering a much later reprint of the stories, **Kirkus Review** stated, *Tros of Samothrace, a worthy foe, a superman intellectually and physically, loving only his country and his ambition and his Druidical faith. The entire 900 pages are filled with deceit, treachery, killing, torture; a maze of battles and plots and counterplots, gladiatorial combats, tormenting of animals, slaves and prisoners; blood thirsty crowds of cheering men and women*—the problem is, **Kirkus** deliverers its conclusion as if it's a bad thing. It's not... *Tros of Samothrace* is Mundy at his finest.

In my opinion, however, there is one Talbot Mundy story which resonates like no other. Published by **Adventure** in 1912, *The Soul of a Regiment* centres around an Egyptian regi-

Talbot Mundy's
towering legendary warrior
Tros of Samothrace

HELENE

The fourth book of Tros of Samothrace

Talbot Mundy's
towering legendary warrior
Tros of Samothrace

HELMA

The second book of Tros of Samothrace

ment who are taught to play music by their English Sergeant-Instructor in the buildup to the Somaliland Campaign. Here Mundy's themes of loyalty and honour are expressed with chilling, heart rendering, clarity.

Mundy would go on to write better stories, but none would match the impact of *The Soul of a Regiment*. No other story in the history of **Adventure** magazine equalled its popularity with readers. **Adventure** republished it six times, and it was the first of Mundy's stories to be republished in England. Even though it was a short-story running approximately 5,000 words, it was

so revered it was published as a standalone book in 1925. I make a point of reading *The Soul of a Regiment* once a year. It never fails to tighten my chest and force me to check my emotions so as not to embarrass myself.

There are two excellent Mundy biographies published in the '80s—*Talbot Mundy: Messenger of Destiny* by Donald Grant, and *The Last Adventurer: The Life of Talbot Mundy* by Peter Berresford Ellis.

Mundy died in 1940, survived by his fifth wife. His literary impact today is minimal in a politically correct world, but read in the context of the times there is a thrill on every page.

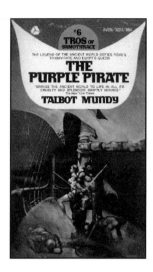

AVON/N251/80¢

'6
TROS OF
SAMOTHRACE

THE LEGEND OF THE ANCIENT WORLD DEFIES ROME'S
TRIUMVIRATE AND EGYPT'S QUEEN

THE
PURPLE PIRATE

"BRINGS THE ANCIENT WORLD TO LIFE IN ALL ITS
CRUELTY AND SPLENDOR: SWIFTLY MOVING"
The New York Times

TALBOT MUNDY

AVON/N247/95¢

'5
TROS OF
SAMOTHRACE

THE LEGENDARY WARRIOR CONFRONTS THE
MOST POWERFUL WOMAN OF THE ANCIENT WORLD

QUEEN
CLEOPATRA

"RICH AND STIRRING, FULL OF COLOR - SPLENDID!"
The New York Times

TALBOT MUNDY

AVON/S309/60¢

TALBOT MUNDY'S
towering legendary warrior
TROS OF SAMOTHRACE

HELMA

*Tros the Visionary faces
the Brother of Gods, Son of Dragons—
The Lord Taliesan, Master of Druids*

AVON/S303/60¢

TALBOT MUNDY'S
towering legendary warrior
TROS OF SAMOTHRACE

TROS

*Tros the Adventurer in fateful
confrontation with blue-stained Caswallon
and his queen, Fflur of the Second Sight.*

AVON/S316/60¢

TALBOT MUNDY'S
towering legendary warrior
TROS OF SAMOTHRACE

LIAFAIL

*Tros the Wanderer challenges the
powers of the Druids to build a ship
that staggers the ancient world.*

AVON/S318/60¢

TALBOT MUNDY'S
towering legendary warrior
TROS OF SAMOTHRACE

HELENE

*Tros the Marauder challenges the
mysterious Vestalis Maxima, in whose
gaze lies power over Caesar himself.*

THE ETERNAL CHAMPION

A review of the first
Casca book

Casca: The Eternal Mercenary opens in Vietnam 1970 with a mortally-wounded soldier dropped into a US army hospital. Treating medic Julius Goldman is amazed to see how the soldier's body regenerates and heals itself, and further intrigued by the discovery of a centuries-old arrow head lodged in the man's thigh. Rising from his death-bed, the soldier tells the stunned Goldman of the curse of eternal life he must carry as Casca Rufio Longninius.

Once a soldier of the legions of Imperial Rome, Casca's life was changed literally forever when he is detailed to watch over the death of Christ atop the hill of Golgotha. Looking to end suffering with a thrust of his spear, Casca only succeeds in further wounding the son of God. As the blood of Christ spills onto Casca's lips he is granted eternal life, "until once again they meet".

Casca is a world-weary and hard-bitten veteran with a speciality in cynicism - the distinctive scar on Casca's face is courtesy of a prostitute he attempted to short-change, which he's quite happy to let people assume was earned in battle - initially shaken by this encounter but soon shrugging it off, returning to his daily activities of sharpening his sword, gambling and womanising.

That is until a love-rival in a jealous rage administers a fatal sword-wound to Casca. Much to Casca's amazement he absorbs the blow and kills his assailant, possibly small comfort when he finds himself sentenced to life in hard-labour in a Greek mine for murder.   When his feet heal over-night following a punishment of fifty lashes on their soles, Casca realises the curse is more than the words of a dying-man, and spends his time in the tunnels of the mine plotting how to escape his shackles and fretting on the prospect of someone with eternal life being buried alive by a mine cave-in.

Casca's opportunity presents itself when there is such a cave-in and Casca saves the life of his overseer, Lucius Minitre, who shows his gratitude by switching his detail to being above-ground and promising to help him find freedom. Lucius' contrived attempt to earn Casca's freedom by setting up a local dignitary to be robbed by vagabonds and saved by Casca is only partially successful.   Although released from slave-labour at the mines, Casca's

"I read it non-stop, and would recommend it to anyone who likes a good story that tumbles out of the pages with the abandon of a jackpot on the dollar slots. It's a winner."
— Charles Durden, author of
No Bugles, No Drums

CASCA:

THE ETERNAL MERCENARY

#1

BARRY
SADLER

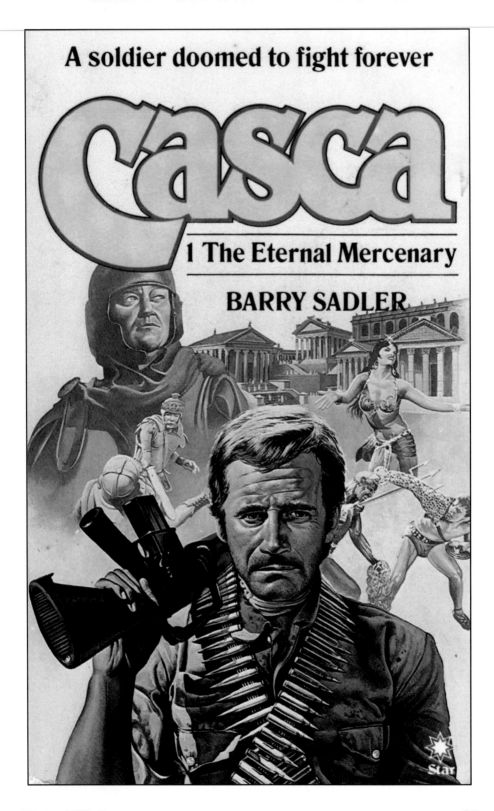

A soldier doomed to fight forever

Casca

1 The Eternal Mercenary

BARRY SADLER

Star

fighting skills have so impressed the dignitary he chooses to ship Casca back to Rome where he will be placed in gladiator school. During the voyage to Rome, Casca befriends a Chinese slave/Zen-master called Shiu Lao-Tze who provides Casca with a crash-course in martial arts.

Something of a star-pupil at gladiator school, Casca's success earns him much admiration. But also creates hatred from rival-pupil Jubala, a hugely muscled giant with filed teeth and a taste for human flesh. Finally pitched against one another in the arena, Casca wins the battle by discarding his weapons and killing Jubala with kung-fu! Earning the wooden sword of freedom in recognition of his bravery and showmanship, Casca promptly goes on an alcohol fuelled bender. Spotted drunkenly ranting at a statue of Emperor Nero and flinging a handful of faeces at it, Casca is punished by being stripped of his short-lived freedom and placed in the slave-galley of a ship.

Spending years on the ship, Casca's increasing strength and vitality when other slaves succumb to the strains of their back-breaking work begins to raise suspicions and fear amongst the crew. Before they can act on their suspicions, a storm destroys the vessel and Casca is washed up ashore in Greece. During an intense relationship with a local girl Neda, Casca begins to see how his eternal life is a curse, as he realises that his resistance to the ravages of time means he is always doomed to see the ageing and death of anyone he loves.

Casca returns to what he knows best by re-joining the legion in time to participate in the sacking of the Ctesiphon, the capital of Persia. Sickened at the slaughter and his part in it, Casca screams his anger to the darkening skies and drives his own sword deep into his chest. Much to his horror his heart forces the sword back out of his chest which immediately begins to heal.

Medic Goldman has been entranced by Casca's story, and by the time he snaps out of it, the eternal soldier has already disappeared....

Having torn through it in a few hours, I can totally understand why the Casca books enjoyed such popularity and can well imagine these books being incredibly popular with service-men. Sadler employs a no-nonsense narrative style, using contemporary slang and obscenities to grant the story-telling a real immediacy. Rather than exclaiming "Forsooth!" and proclaiming their intention to defend their ladies honour, Sadler's characters are more likely to be complaining about the blisters on their feet following a long-march or losing next month's salary in a game of dice or catching crabs from a whore. This ingenious stylistic tool provides the books with a contemporary feel which appeals to an audience that wouldn't ordinarily read historical fiction.

Sadler's perspective is earthy and brutal, telling the story from the foot-soldier's angle, with Casca excelling at his job of killing people yet struggling to fit in with the politics and customs of civilians. Historical details are accurate and communicated in a chatty style which provides authenticity without the reader from feeling as if they are being lectured, with the detail around military tactics and weaponry being particularly rich. It's with action scenes that Sadler excels, ultra-violent and un-forgiving: the

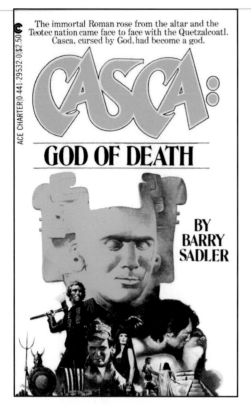

The immortal Roman rose from the altar and the Teotec nation came face to face with the Quetzalcoatl. Casca, cursed by God, had become a god.

ACE CHARTER 0-441-29532-0 $2.50

CASCA:

GOD OF DEATH

BY
BARRY
SADLER

Travelling toward the rising sun, to the land of the Great Wall, Casca encounters a new enemy and gains a new honor.

CHARTER 0-441-09221-7 $2.50

CASCA:

THE WAR LORD

BARRY SADLER   #3

following extract should tell you whether the Casca books are for you.

"Casca said softly, "Open your mouth and say, 'ah.' He kicked Jubala in the balls with enough force to completely smash the two testicles. Jubala opened his mouth to scream, and Casca placed the point of the sword in the gaping mouth, between the pointed teeth. "Die, you piece of shit, die!" He shoved, pushing the three-inch-wide blade out of the back of the black's skull just above where the neck bones connected to the head. Jubala's eyes widened in terror. The blade stuck, and Casca began to twist it slowly back and forth in the bone to break it loose.

The last sound Jubala heard was the terrible squeaking sound of the bones in the head being torn apart. The

bones themselves amplified the sound into a piercing crescendo. With a superhuman effort he stood up in his death spasms and tore the grip from Casca's hand and stumbled wildly around the arena, trying to scream, the blade of the sword in his mouth and about ten inches of it sticking out of the back of his head, the longer part of the sword waving up and down as if he were trying to signal for something. He fell to his knees."

There's no doubting Sadler's ability to produce a set-piece of power- I was absolutely agog during passages such as the above. Not so sure about Sadler's politics- one character is advised by Casca to go home and beat his wife with a stick for being so domineering. He later tells Casca his wife thanked him for it!

Also the villain dispatched above is a black African (Sadler never forgets to remind the reader he's black) with sharpened teeth and a taste for human flesh which strikes me as a rather dubious stereotype.

Another characteristic of the books is how Casca's immortality is tested, which gives rise to some fantastical and outrageous scenes. In *Warlord*, Casca falls prey to The Brotherhood of Lamb, a group of extreme Christians who wish to punish him for killing Jesus, which they do by chopping off his hand. Once crudely sown back on, the hand regenerates itself! In the same adventure, Casca's worst fear is realised when he is intentionally buried alive. In *The Persian*, Casca is burned at the stake until all that is left is an ash-covered skeleton. My personal favourite occurs in *God of Death*,

when Casca has his heart cut out as a sacrifice to the Aztec Gods.

"*Casca turned to the terrified masses below, his chest cavity agape and bleeding from the ragged, serrated edges of the golden knife. Holding his beating heart in his hand above his head, he cried out.*

"*I am the Quetza!" he screamed.*

He put his hands on either side of his open chest and pushed the edges together, sealing them. His heart back where it belonged, still beating, the terrible pain seemed to be a distant echo. Raising his arms to the sky, he cried out in Latin. The rain beat on his face and washed rivulets of blood down through the hairs of his chest and onto his legs, until the life essence of Casca ran red on the floor of the pyramid."

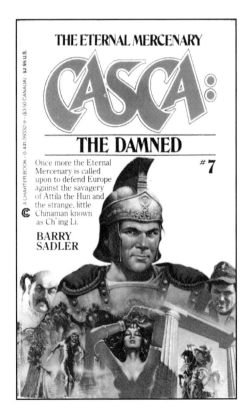

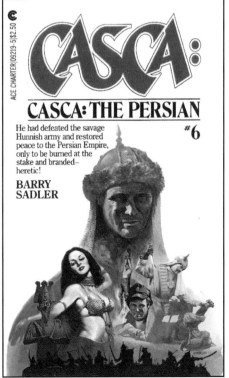

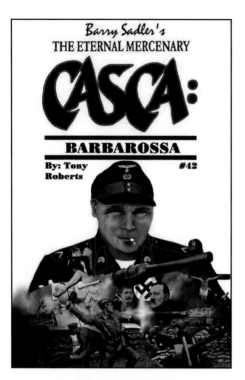

Barry Sadler's
THE ETERNAL MERCENARY

CASCA:

BARBAROSSA

By: Tony Roberts   #42

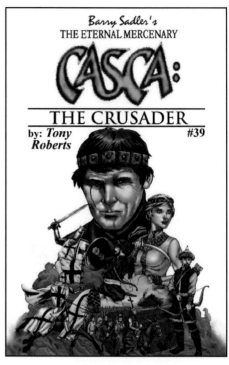

Barry Sadler's
THE ETERNAL MERCENARY

CASCA:

THE CRUSADER

by: Tony Roberts   #39

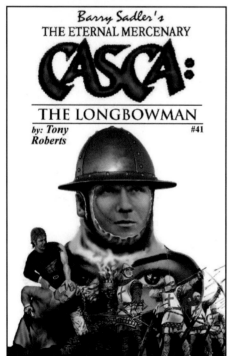

Barry Sadler's
THE ETERNAL MERCENARY

CASCA:

THE LONGBOWMAN

by: Tony Roberts   #41

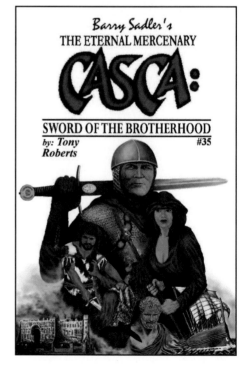

Barry Sadler's
THE ETERNAL MERCENARY

CASCA:

SWORD OF THE BROTHERHOOD

by: Tony Roberts   #35

CASCA THE IMMORTAL

Despite the death of their creator nearly thirty years ago, new entries to the Casca series are still being published. Bristol author Tony Roberts has written twenty-two from 2006 to date, with more in the pipeline. Men of Violence chatted to Tony about the series ongoing appeal and his involvement in continuing the cult character.

MoV: Tony, please tell the readers about your first encounter with Casca.

It began in 1986 when my late mother brought *Casca 3: The Warlord* back from a day trip to Bath. She knew of my liking for history and war and action books and often got me a little gift like that. I read the back cover blurb and was excited to get a book that ticked so many boxes for me. History, and a tale about an immortal. I'd just watched *Highlander* which remains one of my favourite films and getting this book was quite a co-incidence. Also, having been brought up as a Catholic I knew all about the crucifixion and this piqued my interest, too. Having read the book I was drawn into the easy writing style and historical setting. Also I felt the sadness of the character, never knowing a home or being able to rest. I so needed to find the first two that led up to the beginning of this story but it was a process that took me years to do so, having then discovered there were twenty-two to collect. It took me thirteen years.

MoV – So how did you go from fan to writer?

The Casca franchise was formerly owned by Barry Sadler, and on his death there was a ten-year legal battle over the estate and amongst it all, the series. When the dust cleared it fell to his widow, Lavona. She was unable to run the franchise so she did a deal with Barry's former manager and friend, Gary Sizemore, who would run the business side including finding a successor to Sadler. Lavona remained part owner in partnership with Gary.

Gary hired Paul Dengelegi to take over the writing in 1999 and Paul wrote two books, *The Liberator* and *The Defiant*, the second of which was published in 2001. By this time I was on the scene, having finished collecting the twenty-two Sadler books and looking on the internet for Casca websites. When I found there were none, I created one and it was launched in February 2000. I then got in contact with Paul and corresponded with him before the release of *Defiant*. I also got in touch with Gary Sizemore who authorised it as the 'official' website. As a result I began to get inside knowledge of what was going on. I was writing my own Casca stories by then, trying to do my own version of the storyline for my own pleasure. I was writing four separate Casca stories, *The Avenger, The Moor, Scourge of Asia* and *The Last Defender*. I got halfway through them all when in 2002 things started falling apart. Paul's contract was not extended, the publishers Jove (owned by New York company Berkeley Publishing) cancelled the contract with the franchise, and Gary Sizemore himself was diagnosed with cancer, and sadly died in 2003.

I was left watching the series wither and die before my eyes, so I then tried to find out who owned the series now Gary was no more. I sort of got the answer in a roundabout way. Paul Dengelegi, despite not having a contract, was writing a third story, *The Outcast*, and went to a different publisher, Americana Audio, with the intention of having it released as an audio book, and giving it the number 25. This of course was not authorised but until the official franchise got someone on the case, there was little prospect of any protest.

Anyway, I contacted the editor of this company, a man called Odin Westergaard, and asked whether he had the authority or if not, who did? He put me in contact with someone called Gail Rhine in Nashville, Tennessee who had spoken to him about Casca. I emailed Gail and got a quick reply saying he had been part of the franchise (having worked under Gary Sizemore) but had been released and was no longer connected. He told me, however that Lavona Sadler was now the sole owner of

the franchise and that if I wanted to get any information it would be from her, but he did warn me she would be unlikely to reply.

So at a dead end in 2004 I concentrated on finishing the four stories I was writing, and into 2005 I managed it. I then began a fifth story, *The Saracen*, and was halfway through it when, in September, Gail suddenly emailed me saying he was now the new CEO and partner of the franchise and was looking for a new writer. I promptly sent him *Scourge of Asia* which he was 'pleasantly surprised' at, and offered me the job, but not to publish that, but to work on the American Civil War. I also at that time informed him of the unauthorised *The Outcast* story and Gail promptly threatened to sue, but by then Americana Audio had gone bust, Odin had been released and *The Outcast* no longer had a publisher. It was never regarded as official.

I finished Saracen in November 2005 and instantly began my first planned Casca novel, *Halls of Montezuma* which was given the official number of twenty-five.

So there you go. A case of being in the right place at the right time.

MoV- Why do you think Casca still attracts a following?
The books have endured because they appeal to the military serving people. They identify with him and I have had so many emails and messages from serving or formerly serving military personnel over the years.

MoV - What are your favourites in the series?

I always have a fondness for Casca 3 for obvious reasons, but my other favourites of his are 1, 2, 5, 6, 9 and 22.

MoV - Why are the majority of your picks, the earlier books?
The early Sadlers were better and much of this was down to a number of reasons; Sadler's life took a turn for the worse in 1983 when he was sentenced to jail for killing someone (shooting him between the eyes) but got off with only thirty days because he pleaded self-defence, claiming the other guy was going for a gun (it was a set of car keys) after the deceased found Sadler with his girlfriend. Sadler was a terrible womaniser. He relocated to Guatemala and got involved with the Nicaraguan Contras, supplying them with guns etc. With all this and the fact he was writing other series, too, he didn't have time

to properly write Casca stories and the publishers got 'ghost writers' to write a lot of the stuff which shows in the varying styles from about Casca 10 onwards. Sadler sometimes wrote some of the books but he just didn't have the time or the drive to continue at the rate the publishers demanded. So I didn't find the later Sadlers as gripping, except 22 which he definitely wrote except for the last chapter.

MoV - What is it about 22?
Well, a long complex story, but my historical preference is the medieval period rather than the modern, and Casca 22 is about the Mongols under Genghis Khan. I love this period of history, and Casca 22 was mostly written by the time of Sadler's accident, and it was found in his Guatemala home after he was taken to Tennessee. It was brought back to

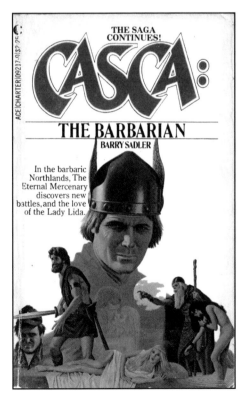

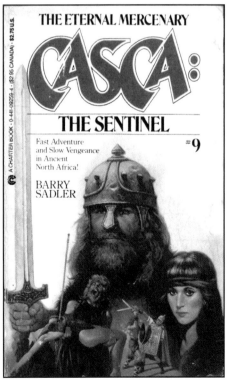

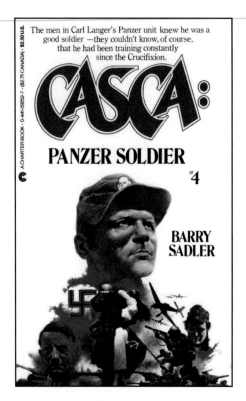

The men in Carl Langer's Panzer unit knew he was a good soldier —they couldn't know, of course, that he had been training constantly since the Crucifixion.

CASCA:

PANZER SOLDIER

#4

BARRY SADLER

BARRY SADLER

OVER TWO MILLION CASCA BOOKS IN PR

THE ETERNAL MERCENARY

CASCA:

THE MONGOL

#22

The Eternal Mercenary leads a conquering army across a bloodstained Asia!

Nashville and Gary Sizemore arranged for someone to complete the book (you can tell this as the last chapter reads differently to the rest).

MoV – Any views as to who Sadler's ghost-writers were? I know that a cover proof for a Casca book was found in the papers of the Ken Bulmer, the late SF writer who also wrote historical fiction under pseudonyms.
The rumours were that Bulmer wrote the majority of *Casca 4: Panzer Soldier*. Whether this was true or not remains a mystery, but if you do look at *Panzer Soldier*, oddly enough for the first half it runs in classic Sadler manner, with chapters etc etc. Then, suddenly, at page 149 we change. Up to then there are 15 chapters, but the last 69 pages are just one chapter. All very odd. And the prose becomes less

personal and a little more detached. Two writers? We shall never know. I do know that Cascas 20 and 21 were written by the same writer as they are identical in type and format and so different to the other Cascas and there's no way Sadler wrote those as they were historically so inaccurate it was embarrassing and there were so many fundamental Casca canon errors that Sadler could not possibly have written them

I doubt he wrote 13, 15, 17, 18 and 19 too, again as the style of these are so different, even from one another. But nothing that can be proven.

MoV – You mention historical accuracy. How much research do you undertake and how do you think it benefits the books?

I myself like to make any historical story as accurate as possible, both as a duty, as I see it, to retelling what is generally known about the past, and also to tell others. I have had so many people write to me and say they learnt their history by reading Casca books that it reinforces my intention to be as accurate as possible. I shake my head at the disservice Hollywood does to history with its pure fantasy insofar as some historically-set movies, and the trouble is so many people watch it and take it as fact. As to research, I tend to look up the main points of what happens in a storyline I am planning, set out Casca's role in the story, where he is and when he is and look up for particular things that happened at the same time and place. If there's a battle he takes part in, I get a book on that battle, if available, and read through it until I know it off by heart. For example, in 2019 I intend releasing *The Saracen*, and the 1187 Battle Of Hattin features in it, and what I wrote in it, actually occurred. Hattin is actually remarkable in that both sides who fought wrote about it and most of what they wrote correlates with the other side's version.

MoV- Filling Sadler's boots is quite a tall order. What's been the biggest challenge?
To satisfy the existing fans. I've listened to constructive criticism over the years and adapted my writing style slightly to fall into line with their expectation from the series and character. The reaction has mostly been positive, with many people thanking me. One or two have not been so enthusiastic but you can't please everyone.

MoV- There were issues with the new Cascas re-using plots from other books such as *Rambo 3*?
The plagiarism was the result of a second writer, Michael Goodwin, being hired alongside me to write in tandem. He wrote two books which both turned out to have been plagiarised and he was released from his contract by the then franchise owner. It did cause a fair bit of trouble but the decision by the owner to cancel both books and never resurrect them was a sound one.

MoV – What next for the Casca series?
Two more books in 2019. *The Commissar* (late WW1 and Russian Civil War) and *The Saracen* (Crusade period).

MoV- Anything else to add?
My website, by the way, is www.tonyrobertsauthor.com which not only gives links to my Casca website www.casca.net but also my other novels I have had published under my own steam here in the UK. I am writing two separate fantasy series, *Kastania* (an epic big-sweeping series that is a cross between **Game of Thrones** and *I Claudius*) and **Dark Blade**, a much lighter series and this one if only available in ebook format.

I also write the Siren series, about a fictitious rock band in the UK (based in Solihull) that covers the period 1979 to 2014 in five books (three of which have been published to date). I have also co-written three rock songs that go with the series, one of these songs has actually been played on BBC radio West Midlands and BBC Radio Worcester.

MoV- Thanks Tony.

THE CURSE OF CASCA

I don't typically read biographies, but Marc Leepson's *Ballad of the Green Beret, an account of the short life of Barry Sadler* (1940- 1989) was of interest to me because its subject was the author of the Casca men's adventure series, whose life was beset by mayhem and turmoil. As the book's sub-title puts it, "From the Vietnam War and pop stardom to murder and an unsolved, violent death."

Leepson is an experienced journalist and a Vietnam War veteran himself, which I'm sure accounts for his diligent research which is presented in a smooth accessible style, and also his ability to open up contacts in the military. For the most part Leepson maintains a neutral stance, which is refreshing considering previous coverage of Sadler had been in the likes of **Hustler** (ahem, I've been told) and **Soldier of Fortune**, although at times you can sense a certain laconic grin on his face as he reported some of Sadler's claims and exploits.

In summary, Sadler was raised in difficult circumstances, found his salvation in the Army, was discharged after being wounded with a punji stick in Vietnam, had a number one hit with the jingoistic *Ballad of the Green Beret* just as the anti-war movement began to gather pace, spent the early 70s unsuccessfully chasing a follow-up hit record, was accused of murder and moved to Guatemala where he received a gun-shot wound which would later end his life. Oh, and he produced the cult Casca series, about an eternal soldier doomed to travel across the centuries and from war to war.

Revelatory in its debunking in some of the myths surrounding Sadler, Leepson's crystal clear account of Sadler's role in the 1978 murder of a washed-up country singer was especially compelling. Accounts I had read suggested that Sadler mistook the glint of a van's keys in the cockpit of a van iluminated by road-side lights for a gun, and shot back in self-defence. But Leepson, with the input of the investigating homicide detective, presents a version of events in which Sadler clearly lied. Apparently after the cold-blooded shooting, Sadler climbed into the van to plant a gun and beat the mortally wounded-man with a night-stick, which he then left behind. It was personally engraved to Sadler from a local police force!

In this way the book is slyly subversive. Sadler was presented as the poster-boy for an Army desperate to stop the way public opinion was turning, an all-American Green Beret singing about his lost comrades. Page by page, Leepson peels back the layers to reveal that Sadler was violent, a womaniser and probably a racist. He may have been an amazing soldier, but he comes across as a lousy human being. You may have wanted Sadler knee-deep in a Vietnam paddy-field, but you didn't want to knock his elbow or spill his drink in your local bar.

A consistent theme running through Leepson's book is how the fame of *Ballad of the Green Beret* was probably the worst thing that could have happened to Sadler. Once the initial notoriety and money faded, it took him away from soldiering and set him on a path where he was chasing a stardom he could never achieve and fitting in with a society with which he shared little of the values.

Postscript

I wrote to Marc Leepson, the biography's author to say how much I enjoyed the book and to ask if he had made any discoveries as to author-ship of the series. Below is his reply.

"As for who wrote the Casca books, I believe that Barry did, indeed, write the first twenty-two of them."

"I base that on having read four or skimmed most of them, and finding that they all had the same author's voice. Plus in the fairly lengthy conversations I had with three of his editors, having a ghost writer never came up. Granted, I never asked them whether or not he wrote them, as I assumed he did. However, I did ask about what it was like working with him on the books, including the editing process, and all of them went into detail about it--and about him."

"None even hinted that he didn't write them. Nor that they say they did any kind of heavy editing. Mostly, they said they fixed grammatical errors and did line editing."

"Plus, I had several long conversations with Robbie Robison, his literary agent, a straight shooter if there ever was one. We talked a lot about Barry's writing process and, again, there was no hint that Barry had any help writing any of his books, including the Casca novels."

"There's one exception (sort of), which I talk about in the book, and that's *The Moi*. That book started as a screenplay that Barry tried to make into a movie when he was living in Tucson. His business partner then, Bob Barkwill, told me they hired a writer in Hollywood to put Barry's words in a screenplay format. Bob said his name was Rocky Graham. I put that in the book. So there was at least some input from a pro on that."

"I'm not ruling out the possibility that there was a ghost writer on some of the Casca books. But I didn't find anything to indicate that."

FAMILY OF FIGHTING EAGLES

The Aquila Stories of Rosemary Sutcliff
by Richard Toogood

I do not know what the sedate and sensitive Rosemary Sutcliff would have made of the idea of her work being discussed in a magazine called Men of Violence. I'd like to think that she would have been tickled pink at the recognition that there is a whole lot more to her work than simply being the foremost children's history fiction of its era. Sadly Sutcliff died in 1992 and so we will never know.

The acclaim afforded her as a children's writer has frustrated proper acknowledgement of her quality simply as a novelist of rare imagination and sublime skill. By her own admission she wrote for children aged between eight and eighty, thereby demonstrating her fundamental belief that the best stories succeed and prosper by their own merits and not by the allowances or whims of readership age. Sutcliff was renowned for never patronising her audience whether young or old. Roman place names, for example, were never Anglicized within the context of her narratives. The baffled or inquisitive reader would be politely directed to the glossary and maps she provided for the geography relating to Isca Dumnoniorum or Calleva Atrebatum.

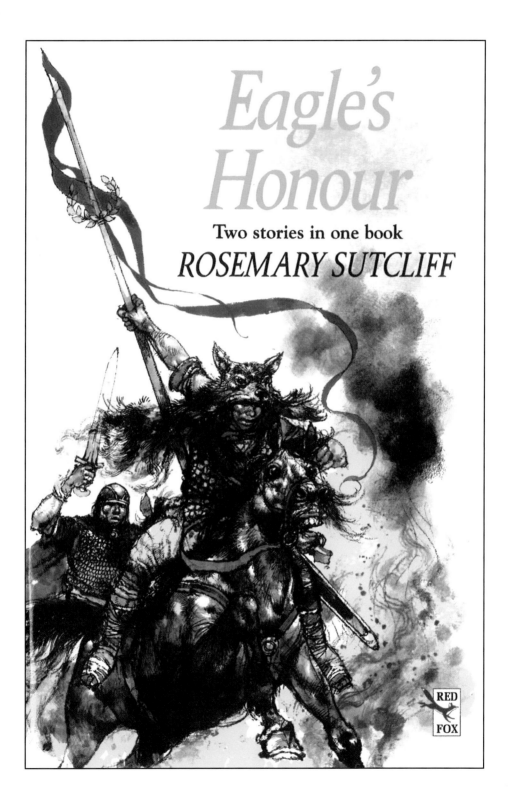

Eagle's
Honour

Two stories in one book

ROSEMARY SUTCLIFF

RED
FOX

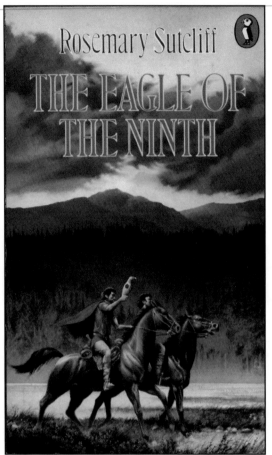

Rosemary Sutcliff

THE EAGLE OF THE NINTH

longed hospitalizations. Not that she owned up to having had any scholarly aptitude at that time to be affected by such, and in fact didn't even learn to read until she was past seven.

What she did have however was a dramatically affected mother who, in between her own bouts of depression, read to her tirelessly. But she would only be read such books as her mother could find to interest herself. As a consequence, in addition to a solid grounding in classical and north European myth cycles, Sutcliff found herself "reared on a fine mixed diet of Beatrix Potter, AA Milne, Dickens, Stevenson, Hans Anderson, Kenneth Grahame and Kipling."

Kipling was especially cherished and developed into something of a lifelong passion for Sutcliff, even to the extent of her adding her own monograph to the mountain of Kipling literature in later life. His importance to her as a child lay largely in his classic *Puck of Pook's Hill* whose "three magnificent stories of Roman Britain [Sutcliff acknowledged] were the beginning of [her] own passion for the subject, and resulted in the fullness of time in *The Eagle of the Ninth*."

Sutcliff's books are always scrupulous in their historical authenticity without wallowing in the squalor which lesser modern writers seem to believe is a prerequisite for conveying realism. She always went out of her way to research her settings diligently. Battles would be choreographed during field trips to the locations in which they had actually been fought.

What makes this effort all the more remarkable is the fact that Sutcliff was seriously disabled her entire life as a result of developing a form of juvenile arthritis called Stills Disease. Her education, which was already basic enough in itself, was interrupted by frequent and pro-

The Eagle of the Ninth remains Sutcliff's most famous and celebrated work; adapted for radio, television and, most recently, made into a pretty decent film. It tells the tale of a Roman centurion called Marcus Flavius Aquila who finds himself invalided out of the army after sustaining a leg wound in a battle during a native uprising in western Britain.

Twelve years earlier Marcus's father had been the standard bearer for the Ninth Legion, the Hispana, which had vanished after marching north to deal with a similar native insurrection beyond Hadrian's Wall. When rumours begin to circulate about a Roman eagle standard being worshipped by a Caledonian tribe, Marcus resolves to travel north and investigate in the hope of salvaging his father's blighted honour.

The Eagle of the Ninth was inspired by artefacts excavated at Roman Silchester during the nineteenth century which Sutcliff saw on permanent display at Reading museum. The book remains an adventure classic, as thrilling, fresh and original now as when it was first published in 1954.

Three years later Sutcliff produced a follow up which whilst less celebrated is, arguably, an even better book. *The Silver Branch* is set more than a hundred years later, towards the end of the third century AD. Two cousins, Justin and Flavius, descendants of the original Aquila, organise an underground resistance against the murdering usurper Allectus. It is a magnificent tale of salvaged honour which climaxes in a thrilling defensive battle fought in a blazing basilica.

Two years after that and Sutcliff culminated the original Aquila family trilogy with one of her very finest works. *The Lantern Bearers* is the story of a cavalry officer who deserts the army on the very last night of Roman rule in Britain, even as the transport ships are preparing to ferry away the last of the available troops to die beneath the walls of a totter-

ing Rome. Subsequently he is taken captive by a raiding party of Jutes and finds himself transported to a life of servitude in Denmark. But events conspire to return him to Britain where he escapes and joins up with the celebrated Ambrosius Aurelianus in his struggle to stem the barbarian tide and to preserve the lantern light of Roman civilization.

The Lantern Bearers is, quite simply, a masterpiece and deservedly won Sutcliff the Carnegie Medal. It is epic in scale and yet correspondingly deep in human drama. Its hero cuts the most tragic figure out of all the fighting Aquilas and yet survives to fill a subordinate role in *Sword at Sunset*, one of Sutcliff's relatively few intentionally adult novels. *Sword at Sunset* was one of the first attempts to tell the Arthur story stripped of the usual medieval trappings and re-

Song for a
Dark Queen

ROSEMARY SUTCLIFF

published in 1980. Boasting a plot which she cheerfully pilfered from *The Leopard and the Cliff*, Wallace Breem's worthy but terminally slow novel of the North-West Frontier, it is the story of one Alexios Flavius Aquila, a fourth century centurion who finds himself in disgrace after an error of judgement that results in the loss of a German fort and costs the lives of half his men.

Aquila's punishment is to be given command of a wild and undisciplined force of Attacotti frontier scouts stationed near the ruins of the Antonine Wall. Not only is he faced with the task of winning their respect, but when the tribes rise in revolt Alexios is confronted with the same stark choice as before: to withstand a siege or to evacuate his command to safety across a hundred miles of hostile country.

mains unsurpassed as an exercise in sustained imagination.

Reading Sutcliff's books what is abundantly clear is that she possessed a rare gift for capturing something of the mythic aspect of the past without compromising its historical authenticity. And it may be supposed that this signature quality is something she absorbed from her mother whose own taste for history, she reflected, was that of the minstrel rather than the historian's.

Sutcliff's last major work of Roman fiction was *Frontier Wolf* which was

Brief resumes of this nature cannot begin to do justice to books as rich in character, incident and historical atmosphere as Sutcliff's are. But what they can serve to show are the recurring themes of redemption and rediscovered purpose which all the Aquila stories have in common along with a good number of Sutcliff's other books. In this it may be argued that they mirror Sutcliff's own struggle to establish herself as a disabled woman in a time far less enlightened than our own.

Aquila is the Latin word for eagle and it does not seem unreasonable to conclude that her warrior dynasty personify Sutcliff's personal esteem of the Roman military machine. Cherish Roman history though she did she was certainly not blind to the reality that Roman imperialism was sustained on slavery and conquest. And she was not beyond writing of it from the opposing British perspective as in the brilliant *Song For A Dark Queen*.

There is undeniably an elegiac nostalgic quality to Sutcliff's work, a harkening back to a more vital and exciting period. But then the same holds true for all historical fiction. And as Sutcliff herself once put it "it would be an arid world without nostalgia". It might equally be said that the field of history fiction would be a far less fertile place without the books of Rosemary Sutcliff.

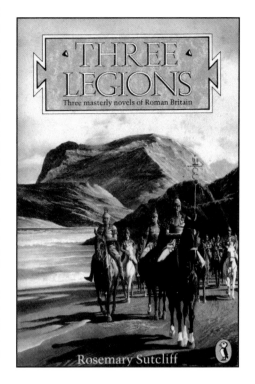

FORGOTTEN ARTISTS THREE: RICHARD CLIFTON-DEY

THE LAND OF MIST

If the job of the paperback cover artist is to sum up the book's themes, mood and plot in one defining image, to strike the casual browser right between the eyes in an instant, then there can only be one undisputed champion: Richard Clifton-Dey, or Dick as he preferred to be known.

Although best remembered for his exemplary work bringing to life the western character Edge, Dick's work for publishers New English Library and Mayflower in the 1970s bringing to life a number of slim and pulpy historical fiction titles was a high-point in the Golden Age of British paperback illustration.

Born in Yorkshire in 1930 but educated in Blackpool where he attended Art School, Dick graduated to the Royal Academy during the early 1950's. In 1958 he went to Paris for a planned two-week visit, fell in love with the city and stayed for eleven years, primarily working for the French publisher Hachette. Dick met his future wife Inge at that time, and they lived a Bohemian life together, splitting their time between a one room flat in the centre of the city and a small primitive house in Normandy.

Moving back to England at the end of the 60s, Dick found himself very welcome at the creative hot-house that was New English Library where he enjoyed a strong relationship with long-serving Art Director Cecil Smith. His mastery of anatomy and lighting, a by-product of his formal art training at the Royal Academy, resulted in Smith commissioning his brush for a number of genres. Although Dick would soon gain recognition for his western and science-fiction work, during these early days he also worked on horror, thrillers, gothic romance and period drama.

Several of Dick's initial paintings appeared on the covers of another NEL legend in the making, James Moffatt. Although NEL employed contemporary photography for Moffatt's infamous 'Skinhead' series, many of his early books were thrillers and Dick's dramatic and action orientated figure-work

Men of Violence

was a perfect match. For *The Last Hi-Jack* (1970) Dick shows a mastery for the female form in his depiction of a machine-gun toting Amazonian terrorist, and his image of a zombie nazi pointing his submarine towards the New York skyline for *The Sleeping Bomb* (1970) is a classic of its type.

Another highly prolific author at NEL whose covers Dick painted was Peter Leslie, whose output was predominantly war thrillers. For the likes of *The Bastard Brigade* (1970), *The Extremists* (1970) and *Storm Squad* (1971), Dick produced highly detailed panoramas of heroic and dynamic characters striding through bomb blasts and corpse littered rubble. Despite his natural flair for the gothic, NEL used Dick relatively sparingly on their many horror titles, which can be counted on the finger of one hand; *Night of the Vampire* and *Night of the Warlock* (1970 and 1971, Raymond Giles), *The Bloody Countess* (1971) and a Ray Bradbury anthology *The Small Assassin* (1970).

Instead, NEL invited him to join the team of artists responsible for updating the look of the perennially popular Edgar Rice Burroughs 'Mars' books, which had previously sported Josh Kirby covers. Although his first efforts were crude yet eye-catching, such as his cover for *Llana of Gathol* (1971) with a mad scientist wielding a phallic hypodermic as he looms over a prostrate naked blonde, the later covers showed an increasing assuredness. They no longer looked like updated versions of the US pulps the stories had originally appeared in forty years earlier, but now shone with sophistication as sultry goddesses with shimmering skin and lithe limbs emerged from gaseous mists,

with subtle hues of purples and greens forming other-worldly atmospheres.

1971 must have been a good year for Mars, as NEL also reprinted Michael Moorcock's 'Barbarian of Mars' trilogy, which had originally appeared at Compact Books in the early 60s under the pseudonym Edward P Bradbury. *City of the Beast*, *Lord of the Spiders* and *Masters of the Pit* all benefited from a Clifton-Dey makeover and reverted to Moorcock's name to capitalize on his deserved popularity.

In addition to looking to the future in their literature, NEL printed bucket-loads of historical fiction, which ran the gamut from well-researched and high-minded to the downright salacious. Dick contributed to both ends of NEL's output, but it's his covers for the politically incorrect 'slaver' novels which are amongst the most striking. Very much a product of their time, many of these books originally appeared with photo-covers, but as they went through a programme of repackaging it was Dick NEL looked to, to draw in the genre's target audience of frustrated housewives, with a series of visualizations of smouldering sexuality and forbidden desires.

NEL published dozens of these offensive yet popular books with Dick's artwork appearing on most, typically a combination of nudity, shackles, chains and a mind-boggling amount of phallic imagery; pistols, machetes, torches, swords and masts. Although it's difficult to ignore their racist themes, Dick's art is gorgeous, undeniably sultry and undoubtedly 'sold the sizzle'. Another highly controversial book Dick's art adorned was *Devil's Guard* (NEL, 1973), the supposed memoirs of George Robert Elford, an unregenerate Nazi who escaped the war crime trials in Europe after World War Two and joined the French Foreign Legion.

In 1972 NEL launched the Edge series; replete with cynical humour and brutal violence, they were NEL's literary interpretation of the increasingly popular Spaghetti Western films. Up until that point the art that adorned westerns was generic and clichéd at best, every western hero looked the same; blonde-haired, blue-eyed and brick-jawed. Rather than go to the cost of commissioning original art, thrifty publishers would often purchase work which had been used overseas and simply slapped it onto their unrelated westerns. That was until Dick delivered his cover for *The Loner*, the

first book in the Edge series, a portrait of an unshaven, craggy-faced anti-hero in black open necked shirt, neck scarf and Indian beads, haloed by a flock of scavenging vultures. Western covers would never be the same.

Building upon his mould-breaking debut, Dick worked in tandem with Cecil Smith to create a visual identity for the series that spawned a legion of lesser imitations. Element one was a fore-ground portrayal of the hard-eyed Edge in action pose, rendered in dusty ochres and muddy browns. Element two was the background which immediately summarised the book's plot, imagery such as a carnage strewn civil war battle or a naked woman tied to a burning wagon, always set against a pure white back-drop. Then

dropped in by Smith, element three; a circular badge informing the reader that *"Edge is a new kind of a western hero"* and the title and number of the book.

Ground-breaking and innovative, the covers defined a genre and became the template for a posse of rival cash-ins. With the books phenomenally popular and something of a cash-cow for NEL, Dick became increasingly frustrated at the publisher's refusal to acknowledge his crucial role in the series success and pay him an increased rate in the way a writer would benefit if his book enjoyed large sales. Already registered with John Spencer of the famous Young Artists agency Dick exercised his rights as a freelancer to seek more financially rewarding work and found a home at Mayflower in 1973, with his last

cover work for NEL –including the fourteenth book in the Edge series-seeing print in 1974

Although unashamedly populist, Mayflower wouldn't back down from publishing esoteric material and Dick illustrated a number of interesting books for them, including a pair of the three 'Cyborg' books by Martin Caidin, Philip Jose Farmer's re-imagining of Tarzan and his origins in *Lord Tyger* and *Tarzan Alive*, the bizarre 'Qhe!' series, featuring a mystical James Bond spy-type, and the excellent Robert Stallman werebeast trilogy 'The Beast'.

Inevitably Dick worked on Mayflower's western series, contributing all twenty-two covers to the 'Jubal Cade' series and all ten for 'The Gringos'. The Jubal Cade imagery very much followed the template set

Original art for The Eagles: Sea of Swords (1977)

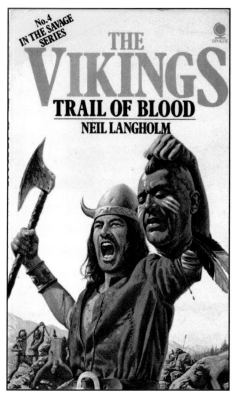

out by the Edge covers, although injected with a greater palette of rich, gorgeous colours. It was the action orientated covers for The Gringos that stood out, particularly to any fans of Sam Peckinpah's classic western *The Wild Bunch* who would have spotted many familiar faces. It wasn't unusual for Dick to look to film stills as source material, evidenced by the covers of *The Reunion* ("*a novel of violence*" by William Kuhns, 1973) and *The Treasure of the Sierra Madre* (B Traven 1974).

Dick's finest hour in terms of illustrating historical adventure was for a pair of series written by familiar names from his days at NEL; editor turned writer Laurence James and pulp veteran Ken Bulmer. Heavily inspired by Daniel P Mannix's non-fiction work *For Those About to Die,*

'The Eagles' was set in the brutal world of the Roman Amphitheater. Dick excelled with five blood-streaked and sweat drenched images of gladiators fighting for their lives and freedom in dusty arenas. Cinematic in their execution, Dick put the reader in the action, whether facing a warrior in mid-sword swing or being clutched in a tiger's jaws.

'The Vikings' was a reworking of a classic series of children's books by Henry Treece, and Dick continued with the rich vein of imagery he had struck with 'The Eagles' paintings, putting the reader behind the eyes of a polar bear being attacked by an axe-swinging berserker. Two of his most outrageous works adorned The Vikings; a decapitated head taking centre stage on the cover of *Trail of*

Blood (1976) and a fire-lit and shadow-rippled illustration of two naked female Vikings dueling with knives from *The Sun in the Night* (1975).

As the popularity of the fantasy and horror genres faded in the early 80s, Dick worked on Mayflower's repackaging of Edgar Mittelhozer's 'Kaywana' "plantation-passion" books, which must have felt like going back a decade to his earlier work for NEL, and many of Charles Whiting's (better known for is books as Leo Kessler, one his many pseudonyms) non-fiction World War Two books. Dick still managed to produce four beautiful new covers for the reprints of the Michael Moorcock's 'Runestaff' series, which although lacking the visceral gut impact of his 'Eagles' work, are technically superb and to me, the summation of his career in paperback illustration.

In the late 80s and early 90s Dick diversified into illustrating children's educational books on subjects such as horses and outer space, but became increasingly frustrated with the world of book covers as the publishers were changing hands frequently, old ties were broken, and the art direction was no longer handled by the art departments but whisked away into marketing and sales. It made the illustration for covers much less pleasing so Dick decided to move into the advertising world. He'd produced a lot of advertising work with Young Artists, particularly for film posters, but decided to move to an agency called Folio which specialized in ad work. Dick became ill in the late 1990's and died in 1997.

Dick's work is most closely associated with the Piccadilly Cowboys, the group of writers made up of Laurence James, Angus Wells and Terry Harknett, whose quintessentially British take on the western genre Dick so masterfully realized in his illustrations of Edge, Jubal Cade and The Gringos. Each year they would congregate for The Hack's Lunch, a lunch so liquid that, according to legend it once resulted in Inge having to coax a paralytic Dick out of the bows of a tall tree in their garden. It was a friendship which meant a lot to Dick who, like most artists, spent much of his time alone in his studio, where he would work throughout the day whilst smoking miniature cigars.

Undoubtedly the writers appreciated Dick as much as he did them. British pulp fiction legend Laurence James fondly dedicated one of his books to Dick with the words. *"This is for Dick. Like a lot of writers, I'm very conscious of how much I owe him for his magnificent covers."*

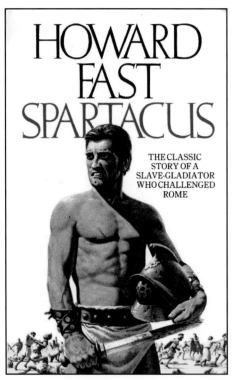

HOWARD FAST
SPARTACUS

THE CLASSIC STORY OF A SLAVE-GLADIATOR WHO CHALLENGED ROME

Men of Violence 59

THE VIKING PAPERBACK BLOKE

Jim O'Brien on Henry Treece

My first contact with Henry Treece was when I was doing my teacher training. We students were tasked with finding a historical novel that could be used in class to make the subject come alive for both boys and girls. In the College library I found a paperback copy of Treece's 1955 young adult novel, *Viking's Dawn*, with a great cover by Victor Ambrus. I took it out, reckoning it might do the job nicely.

Ultimately I had to think again, as the book had no female characters in it (an aspect of Treece's work I will come back to later), but the swirling colours of the Ambrus cover, the book's punchy title and several of the dramatic set pieces in it – a bloody Viking attack on a Pictish boat in which few prisoners are taken; the longship crew's nerve-wracking breakout from a prison cell in Ireland – all stuck in my mind.

To be honest I had very little idea then as to who Henry Treece himself actually was, and even as my knowledge grew in the years following I continued to muddle him with his near contemporary, Geoffrey Treace, who also wrote children's and young adult historical fiction in the 1950s and 60s.

Over the years since I have developed a sharper sense of the man. The writer I had had pegged simply as 'the Viking paperback bloke' actually first found fame not as a novelist but as a poet and poetry editor. A friend and biographer of Dylan Thomas, Treece was one of the moving forces behind the 1940s 'New Apocalyptic' movement in poetry, a war time backlash against those 1930s writers who privileged kitchen sink reportage over imaginative fiction. Treece and the other Apocalyptics were also eager to return to narrative poetry: given that Treece was to go on to write some 40-odd novels in his lifetime this should hardly come as a surprise.

Treece spent the war as an intelligence officer in RAF Bomber Command and then returned to a teaching career that lasted well into the 1950s, mainly as Senior English master at Barton upon Humber Grammar School in Lincolnshire. But the one-time poet soon turned to writing novels, finishing his first book, *The Dark Island,* in 1952. Set in Britain on the eve of the

Viking's
Dawn

Henry Treece

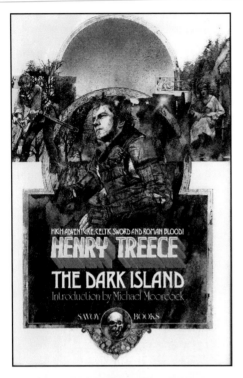

Roman invasion in 43 AD, the book weaves together the 'real' history of the Conquest with the adventures of two Celtic chieftains, Caradoc and Gwyndoc, as they battle to repel the invaders. Treece then went on to publish a further ten books for adults before his death (at age only 56) in 1966.

As a novelist for adults, Treece tackled historical subjects exclusively. He had studied History at University and by his own admission read pretty much only historical books as a child (I imagine plenty of Charles Kingsley and G A Henty). Treece's adult books are pretty broad in terms of period and location, with narratives that take in Neolithic Britain and Mycenaean Greece, Dark Ages Jutland and late Victorian Britain. Despite this last 19th century example (*The Rebels*, 1953), his titles were overwhelmingly about pre-modern historical periods – what my wife calls the 'swords and horses' bit of history.

Broadly, Treece's books for adults can be divided into three groups – those dealing with the 'Celtic' world (by his own acknowledgement, Treece's favourite historical period), those drawing on Classical antiquity for their subjects, and those about British history from the 18th century onwards.

The Celtic books comprised debut novel *The Dark Island*, along with *The Golden Strangers* (1953, about the clash of hunter-gathers, herdsmen and early farmers in Neolithic southern Britain), *The Great Captains* (1956, Treece's attempt to get at the origins of the King Arthur myth and the arrival in England of the Saxons) and *Red Queen, White Queen* (1958, and based around

Boudicca's rebellion against the Romans in 60 AD). These books are often described as Treece's 'Celtic Cycle' or 'tetralogy', although it is unclear whether Treece himself ever thought of them as a true sequence or set. Michael Moorcock, who provided sensitive introductions to several of the Celtic novels when Savoy Books reprinted them in the early 1980s, certainly treats them as a linked collection. But the Celtic books were not written chronologically in terms of the time periods they cover and there are no explicit character links between any of the books.

To this Celtic tetralogy is often added one later title, *The Green Man* (1966). Chiefly set in 6th century Jutland, the book draws upon Saxo Grammaticus's *Gesta Danorum* (the main source for Shakespeare's *Hamlet*) for its narrative. It also (like *The Great Captains*) features Duke (e.g. King) Arthur.

Treece's three Hellenic books – *Jason* (1961), *Electra* (1963) and *Oedipus* (1964) – saw the author retelling and reimagining key moments and figures from ancient Greek history and legend.

His later British history titles were the already-mentioned *The Rebels* (set in late 19th century Darlaston in the Black Country, and dealing with the struggles of wealthy local iron masters, the Fishers) and *A Fighting Man* (1960, set in London during the Regency).

It's probably fair to say though that Treece's profile today is chiefly as an author of books for children rather than for adults. I say 'children', but many of his titles were more precisely for what nowadays we'd call the

Young Adult market. Either way, Treece's first book for younger readers, *Legions of the Eagle* – an adventure set in Roman Britain – came out in 1954, two years after *The Dark Island* was published. Whilst Treece continued to pen both adult and children's books interchangeably thereafter, young readers' titles came to dominate his output, with some twenty-five books for children and young adults compared to just ten for adults.

Why the move sideways from adult novels? No doubt as a teacher Treece had a sense of the potential for children's historical novels, and could justifiably have felt himself well-placed to capitalise on this. At the time, children's historical novels were valued for their educational potential, and for their ability to 'improve' and edify young readers. In these ways they were often contrasted favourably with other forms of juvenile literature such as thrillers and school stories. The late 1950s witnessed a huge renaissance in children's historical writing, with Rosemary Sutcliff, Hester Burton and Ronald Welch (among many others) all selling well in the decades from 1950 to 1970. Mind you, it should be remembered that Treece himself actually wrote several thrillers for children alongside the esteemed historical books, including *Hunter Hunted* (1957), *Killer in Dark Glasses* (1965) and *Bang You're Dead* (1966).

As shorter books (many are just 100 or so pages on average, compared to the weightier 250 page + adult books) Treece may have seen his children's novels as more practical and thus potentially lucrative way to go about earning a living as a writer,

especially after he had given up teaching to write full time.

As with his books for adults, Treece's junior historical titles were set predominantly in pre-modern history, ranging period-wise all the way from the Mesolithic (in his last, near-experimental book *The Dream Time*, published posthumously in 1967) to Elizabethan England in *Wickham and the Armada* (1959), by way of a steady stream of books set in Roman and Saxon Britain. His Roman period books include *The Eagles Have Flown* (1954, a follow up to *Legions of the Eagle*), *War Dog* (1962) and *The Queen's Brooch* (1966 – like *Red Queen, White Queen* about Boudicca's revolt). 1962's *Man with a Sword* deals with Hereward the Wake's resistance to the Norman invasion of 1066. Treece roamed further afield too, with a novel set in the American West (*Red Settlement*, 1960) to his name, as well as *The Children's Crusade* (1958), which looks at the experiences of European children caught up in the Crusades in 1212.

Above all, however, Treece came to be known for his Viking stories, a theme not really tackled head-on in his adult fiction. Over the years, Treece was to pen a solid number of 'stand alone' Viking titles, including *Horned Helmet* (1963), *The Burning of Njal* (1964, and basically Treece's retelling of the 13th century *Njals Saga*), *Splintered Sword* (1965), *Swords from the North* (1967) and *Vinland the Good* (also 1967, and this time drawing heavily on the Norse *Vinland Saga*).

He also wrote two sustained Viking sequences, one for older readers and one for younger children. The trilogy

for young adults comprised *Viking's Dawn* (the book I had stumbled upon in the College library) and its follow-ups, *The Road to Miklagard* (1957) and *Viking's Sunset* (1960). All three books feature the adventures of Viking Harald Sigurdson who, at various stages in his life, sails to Scotland, to Constantinople and even to North America.

The sequence for younger readers is made up of *Hounds of the King* (1955), *Man with a Sword* (1962) and *The Last of the Vikings* (1964), and focuses on the life and times of real historical character, Harald Hardrada.

Whether writing for adults or for children, Treece's novels were, over the years, blessed with some outstanding illustrators both in terms of cover art and interior illustrations.

Early editions of his books included work by William Stobbs, Faith Jacques, Christine Price and Brian Wildsmith, while later reprints sport art by Victor Ambrus and John Raynes. The Savoy Books reprints of the Celtic tetralogy all featured moody interior illustrations by Jim Cawthorn and powerful covers by Mike Heslop.

Above all though, Treece was most often illustrated by the artist Charles Keeping. The two men's first collaboration was on *Horned Helmet* in 1963, after which Keeping provided illustrations for the first editions of *The Children's Crusade*, *The Last of the Vikings*, *Splintered Sword*, *Swords from the North* and *The Dream Time*. Treece acknowledged how much he liked Keeping's work for the books, and made a point of noting that reviewers tended to react particularly positively to books they had both worked on.

What can be said about Treece's books today, some sixty years after they were written, and just how good a fit are they for a journal called **Men of Violence**? First off, it has to be said that the books are historically detailed and – certainly as far as I can tell with only my layman's knowledge – authentic and accurate. (Mind you, that didn't stop Savoy branding the books as Historical/Fantasy fiction in 1980...). The impact of Treece's History degree and his boyhood reading are evident, and the books are a long way from any kind of simplistic 'wolf skin cloaks + a bit of woad = the ancient past' formula-writing.

Many of the books contain introductory historical essays or maps. (The map in *Vinland the Good* is by Treece's son, Richard – later the guitarist in early 70s rock band, Help Yourself – and Richard Treece also provided the title page decoration of the titular brooch for the Puffin paperback of *The Queen's Brooch*.) On other occasions Treece also provided footnotes (e.g. in *Viking's Dawn*), lists of suggested further reading (*The Great Captains*) or glossaries to help tutor readers in the ways of historical righteousness and accuracy.

But if all this sounds as dusty and dry as chalk, blackboards and school text books, the stories themselves remain what I am sure Treece intended them to be – exciting adventure tales. And this is as true for the adult books every bit as much as it is for the children's titles. The majority of Treece's novels take as

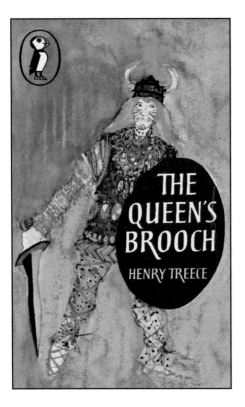

their starting point moments of crisis and conflict in (British, mainly) history and, as a result, battles and bloody, violent warfare are prominent in almost all of them. Although relatively coy by modern standards in the ways that sword-, axe- and spear-born bloodshed and death are described, Treece's delineation of men's actions *in extremis* is never unrealistic and certainly never dull.

This 'realism' extends to Treece's descriptions of religion and rituals. Without in any way descending into New Age mysticism, Treece treats the various pre-Christian religions he features (Druidry in Celtic Britain, his Viking warriors' Norse Gods, Mythras and other deities in the Roman period stories) seriously and without condescension.

Well away from the battlefield, Treece's worlds and the things that happen within them are often presented as being just as harsh and brutal. In *The Golden Strangers*, his novel of the clash of cultures in Neolithic Britain as new tribes migrate across the seas from the Continent, a visitor to the village is drugged before having his heart cut from his body as a blood sacrifice to the dark gods of the harvest; in *The Dark Island*, those held as prisoners by the tribe at the time of the old king, Cunobelin's, death, are staked out along the roadside to the village so that they can thirst to death in order to honour the chieftain's passing; in *Viking's Dawn*, black-hearted Ragnar calmly drowns a fellow Viking who has survived a shipwreck for no real reason other than that he and

his crew had clearly been unworthy of the name 'viking'.

Ragnar is cruel and merciless, and evidently not the charismatic focus of the book. In general however, Treece's heroes are just that – heroes, and not anti-heroes. In these more cynical times, his leading men's upright steadfastness and lack of moral ambiguity can seem anodyne. And they are very much leading <u>men.</u> While the adult books in particular do have important female characters in them, Treece's women generally lack agency compared to their male counterparts. The children's books have fewer female characters altogether, as if Treece knew very well he was in the main writing for boys who would want plenty of 'bloody axemen' burning down Saxon houses but not so much of the girlish domestic stuff actually going on inside those houses.

Certainly you won't find much sex in Treece, although there are moments of powerful eroticism – *Red Queen, White Queen* being a good case in point. The infamous beating of Boudicca and rape of her daughters by Roman tax collectors that is reputed to have sparked the great revolt against Roman occupation occurs off-page in the book and is never actually referred to as rape. Yet in the same book Treece paints vivid portraits of the sexually-voracious Lavinia, daughter of the Legion's commander, who contrives to have the book's main protagonist, Roman centurion Gemellus Ennius, sent on a suicide mission to assassinate Boudicca in part because he won't 'entertain' her one evening. In the same book Ennius finds himself bathing in a river with naked Celtic princess, Eithne, her body covered in the tattoo of a dragon. 'Where does the design finish, Princess? I can only see part of it from where you stand,' wonders our hero, all seeming innocence...

As it is for sex, so too it is for swearing and 'bad' language. Even in those books where the author was, by his own admission, reaching for dialogue that sounded rough and earthy, the results to modern ears are often almost comically polished and 'polite'. But if the dialogue can be awkward, Treece's writing is in general vivid, clear and full of resonant imagery. Although his earlier experience as a poet is often in evidence (particularly in his lyrical descriptions of landscape, nature and the weather) his writing is always accessible and direct.

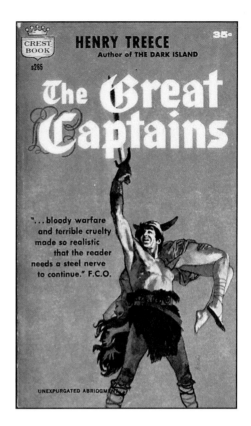

I think I can do no better than leave the last word to Michael Moorcock, enthusiastic cheerleader for Treece and a steady advocate of the writer's books. For Moorcock, Treece was above all a visionary Romantic – not a small r romantic with all that word's connotations of lovelorn dreaminess, but a capital R Romantic committed to imaginatively creating an entire world: "By making living men of his historical characters Treece joined the small group of novelists who used the historical romance for moral and literary purposes of their own...In my view Treece outshines them by virtue of a deeper understanding of the pre-Christian mind and a less self-conscious style which allowed him to express a greater intensity of emotion – and a greater range too. He was a committed Romantic, like Mervyn Peake (whom he knew) or Dylan Thomas (who was his friend) and refused to let any fashionable considerations distort his vision.'

LOVE LIKE BLOOD

Rafael Sabatini (1875-1950) was labelled by an American paperback house as "the master of swash-buckling adventure", a moniker to which many authors could put forward a claim, but even allowing for the over-zealous nature of paperback copy-writers, there is some mileage in championing Sabatini as the rightful heir to this particular throne.

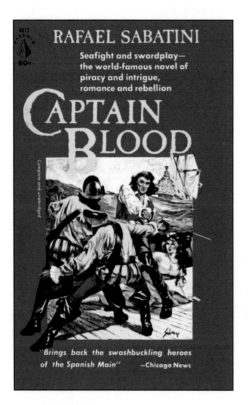

The Sea Hawk

A GIANT ARROW

RAFAEL SABATINI

3'6 NET

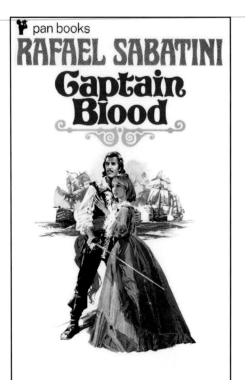

pan books
RAFAEL SABATINI
Captain Blood

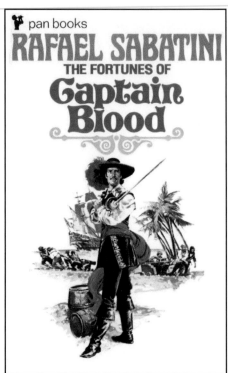

pan books
RAFAEL SABATINI
THE FORTUNES OF
Captain Blood

pan books
RAFAEL SABATINI
Scaramouche

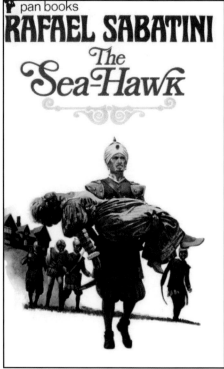

pan books
RAFAEL SABATINI
The Sea-Hawk

His books such as *Scaramouche* (1921), *Captain Blood* (1922) and *Sea Hawk* (1915), which used rich and detailed historical backgrounds over which he projected larger-than-life heroes battling the forces of injustice, were still in paperback on both sides of the Atlantic five decades after their original publication and twenty-five years after their creator's death. Pan issued the last UK edition around 1974 and Bantam in the US circa 1977.

From here, he sank without trace from a mass-market perspective. It seems that Sabatini was dragged down into the group of unfortunate authors who went from being constantly in print to off-the-shelves seemingly overnight. (Dennis Wheatley perhaps being the most famous example in my native UK.) It's worth noting that only five of his titles survived that long, a small part

of his prodigious output. And reading Sabatini now, there is no doubt that his books haven't aged as well as Robert E Howard for instance. But that is a high bench-mark to use for the purposes of comparison, and Sabatini's works carry a romanticism and warmth which are a welcome contrast to Howard's, and his books possess a wry sense of humour that to an extent protects the narrative from the ageing effects of time.

Sabatini had been pursuing a career as a writer in the early 1900s, transplanted from Italy to England by his travelling parents, with a handful of historical novels coming and going with little attention or notice. Fiction magazines were his training ground, earning his writing chops with short stories in magazines such as **Premier** in the 1920s. The tide turned in Sabatini's favour

CAPTAIN BLOOD *saves a* Woman *caught*

by Rafael Sabatini

The Expiation of MADAME

between the Devil *and the* Deep Sea

de COULEVAIN

Illustrations by Dean Cornwell

"When Knighthood Was In Flower" are the Thrilling Days the Modern Dumas Tells of in This, His New and Greatest Romance

Fortune's Fool

Part III

By Rafael Sabatini

Author of "Scaramouche" and "Captain Blood"

Illustrated by C. Patrick Nelson

when his 1921 novel *Scaramouche* was turned into a 1923 movie, bringing to life a quest to avenge an unpunished murder by a dastardly member of the nobility, set against the pyrotechnic background of the French Revolution.

Now the publishing houses, including the Americans who until this stage had steadfastly rejected his manuscripts, were beating a path to Sabatini's door to demand more of his brand of heroic romanticism and bold brush-strokes of derring-do. Caught out by his own "overnight" success, the newly in demand writer had nothing to offer, so in a move which became labelled as the "fix-up" in SF circles and mastered by A E Van Vogt, Sabatini began to weave together a number of previously published stories into larger novels. One result was *Captain Blood*, compiling stories which had been in **Premier**, with resultant sales that built on the success of *Scaramouche*.

Possibly the first portrayal of a heroic-pirate with a keen sense of justice, Captain Blood was a composite of two historical figures – Henry Pitman and Henry Morgan. Pitman was a surgeon who made the mistake of treating one of the Monmouth Rebels who were revolutionaries that failed in their 1685 plan to other-throw the King. This resulted in Pitman being sentenced as a traitor and sold into slavery on Barbados, where he made his escape by stealing a ship which was then boarded by pirates.

In reality, Pitman was released by the pirates and wrote up his adventures in *Relation of the Great Sufferings and Strange Adventures of Henry Pitman* (1689). Sabatini speculated that his wrongly-imprisoned doctor became a pirate leader with the name Captain Blood, basing this part of his creation on Henry Morgan who was a successful pirate in the West Indies granted mandate by

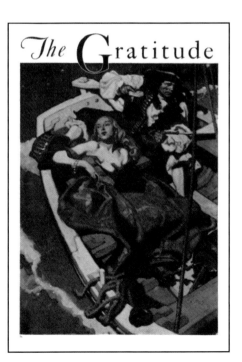

the British government to plunder Spanish vessels.

On top of this rich material, Sabatini added an arch-foe for Blood in the form of Colonel Bishop lord of the plantation from which Blood escaped, and a love-interest in the form of Bishop's niece Arabella. It all ends very neatly with vengeance served, albeit a mild version, and love's true course allowed to run.

Sabatini continued to produce more Blood shorts for magazines such as **Cosmoplitan** and **McCalls**, and these were then collected into *The Chronicles of Captain Blood* (1932) and *The Fortunes of Captain Blood* (1936). Both fitted into the existing chronology of Blood's origin, purporting to be the found journals of the cabin-boy.

Blood was reprinted around the world, with many paperback editions. In the UK, Arrow Books produced the first editions until Pan Books picked up the baton. In the US, Popular Library, Ballantine Books and latterly, Bantam Books would issue a steady stream of editions. It even received an Armed Services Edition in its peculiar landscape format. Apparently it was a hit in Russia, with several unofficial prequels produced to meet public demand.

Captain Blood stands along-side *Treasure Island* as the definitive portrayals of a pirate in fiction, and many of the subsequent historical novels of the next half-century owe much to its winning formula of a vivid historical background, energetic characters and skilful depiction of the classic theme of good-overcoming-evil.

Printed in Poland
by Amazon Fulfillment
Poland Sp. z o.o., Wrocław